Street

Life

Jihad

URBAN
BOOKS

Urban Books
6 Vanderbuilt Parkway
Dix Hills, NY 11746

ISBN 0-9743636-3-4

First Printing October 2004

10 9 8 7 6 5 4 3 2 1

Distributed by Kensington Publishing
850 Third Ave.
New York, NY 10022

Printed In Canada

This book is dedicated to my nephew, I-Keitz Garey, and all of the political revolutionary brothers being held captive behind the prison walls of America. I told y'all I wasn't going to forget and I wasn't ever going to quit. That is keeping it real.

ACKNOWLEDGEMENTS

All praise due to ALLAH, the creator for guidance, direction, and life. Street Life is the blood, sweat, tears, deaths, fears of everyone who walked with me at some time during my journey to now. All my love goes out to my father Elbert Lee Frazier Sr. (Smook), R.I.P; my mother, Arthine Frazier (my life support); my sister, La-ShI Marnease Frazier (always by my side); my other mom Clarissa Frazier (Momma Fluffy) (RIP); my brother Thomas Wiley; my brother Andre Frazier, my boy Corey Mitchell; my girl Pam Hunter; Michael Maddox R.I.P; Woody; Big Dave; Michael Johnson; Roland Johnson; Wille (the mechanic); Derrick Franklin; Latonia Graham; Ant Love; Martin Butler (Casanova); Garland Akins (UNO); Wayne (Woo); Pork Chop; Bam Bam; Shelly Robinson; Michelle Standifer; Rodney Daniel (Fat Boy); DJohn (Mad Dog) R.I.P; Dr. Albert Smith (Smitty) R.I.P; Cocaine R.I.P; Dollar Bill R.I.P; Big Pimpin' R.I.P; Barotto (Brot); Maurice Gant; Eddie Glover; and Sed Coleson.

Much love to all my revolutionary brothers living in hell behind the federal prison walls and fences. James Smith Bay, Eric Bozeman, Arthur Strong, Jihad Bell, Najee, Imam Saladeen, Vince, Imam Jabril, Otis, Big Stan Hall, Gene Davis, Sabir, Kyle, Hamzaa, Dawoo, Homicide, thank you brothers for giving me life.

Extra special appreciation goes out to two strong brothers I hope to one day emulate Dr. Na'im Akbar and Travis Hunter thanks for your support. Much props, and a very special thanks to my friend Ms. Victoria Christopher Murray, if it weren't for you no one would know me. Thanks for teachin me how to write. Thank you, Ms. Lolita Files, for everything, You are a doll. Eric Jerome Dickey, my publicist, Robilyn Heath, my publisher

Carl Weber, Thomas Long, Stephanie Johnson, Angel hunter, Dwayne Joseph, La Jill Hunt, Dwayne Joseph, the whole Urban Book family. Thanks. Special thanks to my brother, Thomas M. Wiley.

Special thanks goes out to Lynetta Mitchell for being my second set of eyes.

Thank you, Exodus INC., St. Luke Area III Learning Center for giving me a chance when no other high school would. Much love to Savannah State College, much love to Shephard Spinal Center and all the nurses and doctors who said I'd never walk again. By the way I'm not only walking I'm running. A very, very special thanks to my editor Chandra Sparks Taylor. Special thanks to all of the heroes and sheroes I failed to name, a space for you_____.

For all the brothas who did dirt and rolled with me from Motel 6's to Thomasville Heights to the Meadows to Wesley Chapel in the Dec, WAKE UP. To the brothas and sistas gettin' money slangin' and bangin' or gettin' high, WAKE UP. For more about Jihad go to www.jihadwrites.com

It's all Love
Jihad 4 Life
Go to www.jihadwrites.com

CHAPTER 1
Today

The leader squinted his eyes, trying to adjust to his surroundings. His heart rate must have done a tap dance. I was a helluva sight. I sat in my chair, rearing back, looking into the eyes of the fallen, squirming stick-up kid.

While my captives were taking an electrically charged nap, I had changed into my orange-and-black Savannah State sweatshirt, black jeans, black war boots, and a Huey Newton black tam cocked to one side of my head. This was a Kodak moment for the ages—me looking like a black revolutionary from the seventies, and the gang's fearless leader in shock, eyes like saucers. I just hoped he wouldn't pee on himself, or worse.

Groggily, he moaned, "What the—? Damn, man. What?" while rocking from side to side and struggling, while bumping one of the others.

"Junebug, get yo' ass off my shoulder. Mario, untie me, dog."

Now I had two names. The leader was Mario and Baby Huey was Junebug.

Junebug awoke first. "Man, what the hell goin' on?" He ranted to his not so fearless leader.

The driver blinked into consciousness as the leader and Junebug fought against the steel strap tape. The driver sat quietly, as if this was what he expected.

I calmly sat staring at the comedy act before me. I wanted to wait until some semblance of order had been restored, but I got tired of all the boo-hooing.

Finally, I yelled, "Shut up! When I want you to speak, I'll put words in your mouth." I reached down and retrieved my guns, using them to direct my speech.

"The only way you will come out of this alive is if you listen to what I have to say. You have a choice: you can live or you can die."

"But—"

"But nothin'. If you interrupt me again, I'll shoot you." I pointed my stun gun at the bunch of them, all tied up in duct tape, looking pitiful as hell. "If you have to pee, pee on each other. I taped you up loosely so you could be semi-comfortable, but if you're not, tough," I said as I paced the slate-tiled basement floor. "Y'all young bucks don't have an atom of an idea who you're messin' with. Hell, y'all so confused, you don't even know who you are. While you're here, you have one job, and that's to listen. If I catch you sleeping, I'll shoot you. Through what I'm about to say, if you dummies just halfway listen, I'll show you how your life has already been mapped out by others who have plotted your demise before you were even born."

CHAPTER 2
Yesterday

The only garden in the Garden Park Homes in rundown East Atlanta were the night-blossoming hustlers and the weedlike dope fiends who seemed to come out of the grassless dirt that separated the buildings. Each one of the 200 units crammed inside the red brick warehouse-like buildings should've been condemned. The walls were as thin as a house of cards, and the units were firetraps waiting for a spark. They were bug infested, rat infested, and too many of us infested. It was common to find pencil-sized peepholes in the walls leading to the next unit. Looking into other people's business was like watching a '70s version of *Jerry Springer*, at least until they blocked the holes with bubble gum or peanut butter.

Live electrical wires were exposed, units were boarded up, ghetto Picassos decorated the hallway walls, ceilings were falling in, and diapers and broken bottles littered the project grounds. The infamous GP were the projects of projects; danger was even too scared to come in at night. The rats only came to visit during the day. They didn't want to be caught alone after dark, probably from fear of getting robbed or crumb-jacked by a gang of possums.

Despite these conditions, there was still an 18-month waiting list to get in. The Garden Park Homes, as these tenements were ironically named, were overcrowded with derelicts, drunks, dope addicts, dealers, welfare mothers, and kids who were given little chance to survive, let alone succeed.

Beano's Junkyard, with hot parts for sale, was on one side, and a bustling highway was on the other. The Drunk Down liquor and check-cashing store was across the street. Loo Chi's 24-hour wash and dry laundry, One World Records, the pool hall, and Akbar's Market Basket were all in the same plaza.

And then there was me.

Born Lincoln Jackson on April 8, 1969, I started off in this dilapidated hood. I lived in a five-room deathtrap with my mother, younger brother, and older sister. As for rats, the only reason we didn't have any was because we couldn't afford them. They would have either starved or been somebody's Thanksgiving dinner. I had friends telling me all the time, "Rat tastes like chicken."

The roaches, however, were a whole other story. I think they just came over our house to party, and ate elsewhere. They knew better than to expect leftovers because we barely had enough for ourselves.

Still, we never went hungry. We didn't waste a thing. If something dropped on the floor, we would pick it up, wash it off, kiss it, and eat it.

Momma was Momma, Daddy, the warden and the police. Momma's word was law and strictly enforced. Word was that I was born with the gift of gab. Momma said I spoke better at two than I do now.

"Mommaaa. Hey, Momma!" I screamed.

"Little nappy-head nigga, shut up all that dang hollering," Bernice scolded.

Big, too many bon-bons booty, bugga-bear Bernice was one of Momma's closest friends. She didn't have kids, didn't like kids, and kids sure didn't like her.

"Can you please go get my momma?" I got all bug-eyed and dramatic as I asked it—oh, I mean her.

"Boy, you act like you ain't got no home training, screaming like you crazy," Bernice screamed.

Big, fat, dark brown, humpback, short, and sho' nuff oogly, she enjoyed doggin'and orderin' kids around. Even though she got on every one of my nerves, I still had to show her respect. Momma always told us to respect our elders and not to talk back, but she never said not to think back. If that big bugga-bear could read my mind, she'd have a whale.

"Boy, you know I'm doin' your sister's hair. Why'n the hell you screaming like a banshee instead of coming up these stairs? I ain't raised no alley rats. I taught you better," Momma shouted.

Bernice smiled and bobbed her big head, getting pleasure out of Momma's scolding.

"Girl, his butt is too big for his britches. I know what he needs. If'n he was mine, I'd beat the black off him," Bernice said in a loud voice for the benefit of me and everyone else within a five-mile range.

Thank God I ain't hers, and thank Him for not givin' her no kids, I thought.

"That's if he was yours. He's not, and I'll raise him like I see fit," Momma said.

Score one for Momma.

"Momma, I'm sorry, but I was trying to catch the next 115 so I could go to the boys club with Li'l Man. All I need is fifty cents for the bus. I already got the other half to get back."

"Boy, what you think, I'm made of money? Didn't I just give you money for the movies yesterday and some for ice cream the day before? I don't have money to give you every time you want something."

"Momma, that's okay. I probably done missed the dang bus anyway."

"Boy, you talking back? Do I need to get some soap for that mouth?"

"Naw, Momma."

"Boy, I'll knock your damn head off. Don't be shakin' your head at me like that. And you bet' not be rollin' your eight-year-old beady eyes at me."

"Momma, I'm just sayin'."

"That's your problem. You always 'just saying.'"

"I'll be over to Li'l Man's." I started walking off with Li'l Man.

Street Life

Corey "Li'l Man" Stevens was my ace number one dog. From beginning to end, we was in it to win it. We met when I was getting beat up by two boys and a girl when I was six. Out of nowhere, Li'l Man, then the size of a 4-year-old, beat the kids off me. They ran home crying. Me and Li'l Man were peanut butter and jelly from then on.

Li'l Man had been born addicted to heroin. The drugs may have affected his size, but his mind and his heart made up for that. His sister, whom we called Bay-Bay, was only seventeen when their moms passed from a heroin overdose. Bay-Bay had taken care of Li'l Man ever since.

"Damn, see what I'm sayin' man?" I said to Li'l Man as we left. "For fifty cents, all 'at."

We might have been broke, but we were never bored. There was always something to do in the projects. They never slept, never rested. Everybody hung out all dang day and half the dang night, mainly because if it was 90 degrees outside, then it was 110 inside the sweltering walls. Old folks sat outside drinking beer while mommas hung wet clothes on speaker wire and metal hanger clothes lines, and dope fiends zombied around day and night lookin' for a hit. Nappy-head kids ran around turning up dirt and getting in everybody's way. Families went across the street, to and from Goldstein's Plaza.

It was one thing to be hot, but to be hot and broke was unbearable. All Momma had to do was go in the pickle jar and get me two quarters. Shoot, she was probably upstairs gossipin' with her girlfriends while pulling my sister's hair out.

Ever since Momma caught me and Li'l Man eavesdroppin' on her woman talk last month, she put me out whenever her girlfriends came over. Shoot, she thought I was stupid. I knew what they was talkin' 'bout. It was the same every time. A couple of names changed, but it was always the same.

Last time they got together in the hot, noisy apartment, the aroma from fatback and collards cruised through the unit. An old metal straightening comb was heating on one of the burners across from the pot of food. While doing my sister, Marnease's hair, Momma, Fat Bernice, and Momma's bestest best friend, Ms. Tina, traded project gossip. These three made everybody's business theirs. Gossip, however, ran a distant second to their favorite subject—black men. They talked of being used and abused. These women had plenty of firsthand knowledge and loved to share their worldly wisdom. With such a profound grasp, the three called themselves "menologists" and held frequent conferences on the subject of "no-good black men." The hands-on research presented a constant love-hate struggle that was all about "I gotta get mine before he gets his." Ms. Tina was primarily the one out in the field doing most of the hands-on.

Ms. Tina was well proportioned, Amazoning at six feet. She had creamy, butter-brown skin, a dimpled, heart-shaped face, and big, hazel-brown eyes. She wore her hair in a short-cropped, reddish-brown Angela Davis natural. Instead of walking, she sashayed those jungle, cake mix hips of hers. She was a widgen-smidgen on the chunky side from giving birth to three high-yellow bad-behind Bebe kids. Nonetheless, she retained her movie star good looks. She loved kids, especially me. She was the prettiest woman in the world, next to Momma.

"You know George, that fine-ass man I been seeing?"

Every man was fine to Ms. Tina. She didn't care if he looked like Rin Tin Tin with a lone, faded, fake gold-plated tooth in his mouth. As long he had a job and a third leg, he was fine.

"Let me tell you what that lack mothafucka did. That nigga dropped me off last night at two in the got-dang morning. That black mothafucka had the nerve to put me out at the top of the mothafuckin' hill, talkin'

7

'bout he was scared of getting carjacked. Girl, I called that nigga everything but a child of God. And you wouldn't believe what else the black mothafucka did."

"What?" Bernice asked.

"The limp-dick, raggedy, yuck-mouthed mothafucka called his wife on one of those car telephones while I was in the car."

"Can you say mothafucka one more time to make sure my baby understands?" Momma said while greasing Marnease's hair.

"Baby, I'm sorry. Don't be like your aunt Tina," Tina apologized. "Why y'all heffas didn't tell me I was cussin' like a sailor? Y'all knows how I get."

"Ah, girl, don't pay her no mind." Bernice waved. "Go 'head. Finish your story."

"He told his wife, who was a secret to me, that he was working late."

"Just like a no-good nigga," Bernice exclaimed while puffing on a Newport, with one hand on her hip and the other slicing through the air.

"His scary behind let me out at the top of the apartments, two blocks away from my unit. Made me walk with my three-inch fuck—I mean 'do me' heels on. I couldn't believe the nerve of that black motha . . . What the hell I look like, my cute ass, walking down the dark street, a red summer dress two sizes too small hugging my fine behind? If he hadn't slammed the car door when he did, I would've cut his ass."

"Girl, goes to show you niggas ain't shit. They only want one thing. That's why you gotta make them pay, and I mean pay the bills with big bills. Let 'em know that cat might as well be a Cadillac, and to keep it purring you got to keep up the maintenance," Bernice said.

"At least my babies got school clothes and new shoes."

"Well, girl, at least you got an oil change and a full tank of gas out the deal," Momma teased. They spoke as if my sister wasn't even in the room.

Momma always let Marnease in on grown folks' stuff, told her how it was when she was a kid, and how she done everything we were doin' and thinkin' about doing. She felt like it was better coming from home than from the streets. She used to let me and my little brother D'Andre in too, until she caught me and Li'l Man eaves dropping instead of just having a seat and listening.

CHAPTER 3

Born Clarissa Jackson, Momma was named after her father Clarence, but everyone called her Rease. She grew up as an only child in Spartanburg, South Carolina, with her mother and functionally retarded uncle, Ray Junior, who we all called Ray-Ray. Her mother, Paulette, worked two jobs to support Ray Junior and Rease. The little spare time Paulette had she spent with countless boyfriends, but that was all right with Rease, because Uncle Ray-Ray lavished love, affection, and attention on her. Although Paulette loved her daughter, her brother was her number one priority, followed by the boyfriends, and finally Rease.

Momma walked three miles to and from school, rain, snow, or shine. As she came through the rickety screen door of their five-room duplex one Friday afternoon, Uncle Ray-Ray greeted her with a big hug.

"How wa' yo' day, baby gull?" he drawled. At twenty-five, Raymond Lamont Jr., had the mind of an 11-year-old. Standing six foot five and weighing 240 pounds, with a big, cheery face, he had been a gentle giant.

"Oh, it was fine. I had to beat this boy up at recess for calling me a yella white girl."

"Hope you whooped him good, 'cause if'n you didn't, he might go to messing with you again."

Paulette pulled a double at her part-time security guard job at the water company. Ray-Ray and his niece usually played cards and listened to the radio until they both fell asleep, but this Friday was different.

After arriving from school grungy and dirty from the fight, Rease went to the bathroom and drew a hot bubble bath. She returned from her bedroom wearing a long T-shirt, with fresh clothes and underwear in her hand. She placed them on the black vinyl toilet seat, removed her shirt, and drifted into the tub.

Soon after, Ray-Ray walked into the bathroom, sat on her clothes, and quietly stared at Rease's long, lithe, pecan tan frame. Overdeveloped for her age, Rease was a child trapped in a woman's body. It was as if Ray-Ray was seeing her for the first time. Rease asked her uncle if something was wrong.

"Nuttin', nuttin' wrong. Wha, wha, why? I was, I-I was just thinking."

"Thinkin' what?" Rease asked.

With catlike speed he dropped to his knees and splashed his meat hook arms and hands in the tub, touching, pinching, rubbing, lightly squeezing her body as if she were a plaything. She grabbed at his octopus arms. She fought, splashing water all over the bathroom. "You're hurting me," Rease cried.

The more she pleaded, the more excited he became. It was as if he were possessed.

"I won't tell, I won't tell. Please. Please. Oh God, please stop."

She removed her hands from his wrists and with all the strength she could manage, hauled off and slapped him.

As quickly as the assault began, it ended. He dropped to the floor.

"I sorry, I sorry. Didn't mean to. Didn't, didn't, mean to. I sorry." Between *sorry*s and *didn't mean to*s, he tried to crack the toilet bowl with his head.

Rease rolled out of the tub, splashing water over the white tile floor and onto Ray-Ray's back. She grabbed him by his 'fro and yanked. After rolling him to the cracked wooden door she grabbed his bloody head and cradled him in her arms. No longer crying, she took charge. Her unconditional love for him compelled her to his aid.

Whispering in his ear, she said, "It's okay. Don't worry. I'm all right, I won't tell."

Ray-Ray was uncle, brother, friend, and protector, and Rease did not understand the severity of what had happened. After all, it was Uncle Ray-Ray who had been raising Rease, yet it was he who traumatized and changed her life forever.

After seeing Ray-Ray in such a state of violent despair, Rease thought she could handle her uncle. Yet three Saturdays later, after Paulette left for work one morning, Ray-Ray tiptoed into Rease's bedroom where she was sound asleep and crawled under the white sheets. She awakened to him easing his index fingers inside her panties and yanking.

"Ahhhhh! Get off me, you crazy rapist! I hate you!" she managed to scream while scratching and kicking.

As if in a trance, after wishboning her stiff and trembling legs apart, he grabbed her wrists, pinned her down, and rammed himself inside of her. The hurt was so intense she fainted. Seconds later she awoke to a burning, searing pain. Ray-Ray continued rocketing himself into her, despite her pleas and weak cries of desperation. She fainted again.

Less than a 5-minute eternity had passed when he jumped up and ran out of the room, leaving Rease crying, bleeding, and begging for death. The person she loved and trusted the most had killed a part of her.

Confused and wondering what she had done to deserve such treatment, she lay knotted up on the crumpled, bloody sheets. After several attempts at getting up, she slid off her mattress and onto the floor.

Ray-Ray rushed back to her room when she let out a piercing scream at the sight of her own blood. She gave up. She went limp as Ray-Ray lifted her tired and hurt body. He carried her into the bathroom and placed her into a tub filled with warm water. He left, only to return a minute later with fresh underwear and a T-shirt that he placed on the toilet seat along with an envelope. The envelope had RESE printed on the outside. He left again without uttering a sound.

After soaking for an hour, Rease felt a little better physically, but emotionally she didn't know what to feel. She got out of the tub and opened the envelope with trembling hands. Two twenty-dollar bills fell to the floor as she removed a folded paper and read the note written on it.

I Nead U, I Am Soree, I Love U, Go By U Somethin Pritee.

Rease knew Ray-Ray got disability and a social security check every month, but she thought her momma took all his money.

Never had she had that much money.

After getting dressed, she went to her room and got her daddy's photo album from the closet. She placed the money behind his obituary, knowing neither her mother nor Ray-Ray would ever look inside the photo album, both too scared to bring up bad memories. Though she had never met her daddy, Rease often fantasized about him being a strong black man, taking her to the zoo and the fair, lavishing her with love and affection. He'd been killed by a hit-and-run driver three days before she was born.

Ray-Ray came to Rease once a month for the next five years, always during the first week of the month after his check had come. He handed over an envelope containing $40 each time he came to her. It became an easy $40 a month for five minutes of her time.

No longer did she care for Ray-Ray. She felt for him what she felt for a rock. The love she had faded after the first time. After the third time, she controlled when, where, and how their monthly escapades took place.

One night, when she was sixteen, she came home nervous, awaiting her mother's return from a date.

Paulette finally came in the house during the wee hours of the morning.

Rease, still wide awake, too scared to sleep, blurted out, "Momma, I need to talk to you."

"What do you want, girl? It's four in the morning and I am—"

Before she could finish, Rease blurted out, "Momma, I'm pregnant."

"You bitch. I knew you was whoring around. I just knew it," she shouted after slapping Rease to the floor. "Oh, you will have an abortion."

"No, I won't."

Ray-Ray came out of his room just in time to hear Rease announce she was not having an abortion. He watched the scene unfold. Rease stood, all six feet of her, towering over her mother. She stood there as a woman, crying, arms folded across her chest, glaring at her mother with fire in her eyes. "I'm having this baby, and there's nothing that you can do or say to stop me. It's too late for you to be a mother now."

With a girlish scream, Ray-Ray rushed to Paulette, grabbed her purse, and ran to the bathroom screaming, "It's all my fault!"

Paulette and Rease ran after him, but he had locked the door.

"Junior, open up this damned door now," Paulette demanded.

The ear-shattering blast of a gun filled the house.

Paulette slid to the floor as Rease screamed. Rease backed up then ran into the thin, wooden door, busting through. Ray-Ray lay in the tub, with what was left of his head resting on the rim. Blood and brain matter stained the entire bathroom.

Paulette regained consciousness as Rease vomited.

"My baby, my baby. Oh my God! What has she done to my baby?" Paulette cried as she cradled the remainder of Ray-Ray's head in her arms.

That was too much for Rease to handle, especially since the baby was not even Ray-Ray's.

After the funeral, Rease packed her clothes and the $1600 she had saved, and bought a one-way bus ticket to Atlanta. Three days after arriving in Atlanta, she rented a room advertised in the Atlanta Journal. Her landlady was the only one living in the house.

Ms. Margaret was a large, jolly woman in her mid-sixties. She and Rease became close friends. Seven months after leaving home, Rease gave birth to an 8-pound, 3-ounce baby girl she named Marnease. At that point, Rease was down to a little less than $100. Six weeks after Marnease was born, Ms. Margaret died in her sleep.

Back on the streets again, broke, alone, and the mother of a six-week-old baby, Rease was desperate. Staying temporarily at a seedy downtown motel, she went door to door through the city, applying for job after job only to face rejection after rejection. Dead tired from carrying the baby and walking all day, she rested on a bus stop bench. Directly across the street she saw a sign that read HIRING FEMALE DANCERS TODAY. Forgetting how tired she was, she jumped up with the baby in her arms and headed across the busy street. She walked into the club broke. Striding confidently to the bar, she smiled and asked to see the manager.

"Hey, Nimrod, someone here to see you," some guy sweeping the front of the club shouted.

A minute later, a short, slim, balding middle-aged brother limped out wearing a loud purple suit and brandishing a Goldie-Mack-daddy, pearl-handled cane. He gestured for Rease to follow him. Upon sitting, he introduced himself as Nimrod, the owner, and extended his arms, asking to hold the baby.

"Wha's yo' name, li'l gurl?"

"Miss Jackson."

"Okay, Miss Jackson, show me whatchu workin' with," he said before putting a triple fat half smoked cigar between his dark brown, crusty lips.

"Huh?"

"Look, gurl," he explained, shaking his head like a jack-in-the-box, "before I can give you a job, I gots to see hows you work it. Rick, put on something upbeat."

The club erupted with the Isley Brothers' ol' school hit "Pop That Thing." Knowing full well if she wanted to feed her baby she needed to be good, Rease walked onto the platform and turned it on. Provocatively gyrating to the bass beat, she twisted and turned, maintaining eye contact with Nimrod. All her life she'd been a performer. Alone in her bedroom, she'd danced and lip-synced to the Marvelettes and Supremes while watching herself in the mirror.

"Show some skin."

"Say what?"

"This is a strip club. Now, let's see some goodies," Nimrod leered while holding the baby.

Embarrassed, she jumped off the two-foot platform stage and grabbed her baby from Nimrod.

"Babygirl, I'll advance you five hundred dollars and guarantee you that with your body and the way you move, you will never make less than that a week dancing for President SDR. You heard of FDR? Well, I'm SDR, Sweet Daddy Rod, the poo-tang president."

She couldn't believe what she was hearing. "Five hundred dollars?"

"Dat's right." He smiled, nodding, flashing his diamond-studded gold tooth.

She took the job, and in no time was the headliner.

She was situated in an upscale high-rise a year later, with Marnease beanstalking.

Babygirl, the name Nimrod called her the first day she came into the club, had stuck. Babygirl was a star among the city's hustlers, movers, and shakers. She was six feet of sculpted beauty; long, curly, reddish-black hair cascading over her shoulders, dark brown eyes, smooth, pecan tan skin, a heart-shaped face accentuated with high cheekbones—all carried by a voluptuous hourglass figure. Looking down on the audience of men she captivated with her exotic dancing, she appreciated just how far she had come.

One night Rease decided to take off after arriving at the club. She returned home to find Marnease's babysitter and the babysitter's friend, two heroine-induced young girls, nodding in their oblivion. Rease found Marnease in the kitchen playing with two used needles. Usually calm and in control, Rease went off. She jerked her baby into her arms, ran upstairs and put her in bed. After checking her daughter for injuries, she headed back downstairs, pulling an already loose piece of wood about the size and width of a blackjack from the stair railing. She wielded the stick over her head and gave the drug-numbed girls a dose of reality. She swung wildly at the women, beating them while screaming every shade of profanity known to man or beast.

Somehow the women got out the door, but Rease continued to beat them until the stick broke. Neighbors ran out of their apartments to watch the scene, but were unwilling to restrain this wild woman from her savage attack. Babygirl never danced again.

The money dried up a year later, and working odd jobs just couldn't cut it. Pregnant again by another nobody, Rease was forced to apply for welfare and move into the projects.

CHAPTER 4

It was just another hot and humid day in the summer of '80. The overcrowded three-story housing project unit I lived in was void of air conditioning. The red brick exterior made the indoor heat index twice as smoldering. Flies swarmed in the day and vampire mosquitoes shot through the open windows to feast at night. Fans were only good for circulating the heat.

It was a typical Georgia summer day, temperatures ranging from hell-hot to nuclear hell.

Li'l Man and I walked through the hustle and bustle of the projects trying to find something to do and a place to keep cool.

"Dang, dog, what we gon' do now?" I asked Li'l Man.

"If you ain't chicken, I know how we can make some money."

"How?"

"Bay-Bay don't know I seened her in Akbar's while I was playing Space Invaders. You know we can't trick the machines at Akbar's no more. Unplugging and plugging it back up doesn't give us free games, so I went off to find her to get another quarter. How 'bout she was at the meat locker, and I seened her slide some meat under her dress. Then she strolled past the checkout counter calm as Kool-Aid. That night we got down on some New York strip steaks. Man, them things was good," Li'l man said, rubbing his stomach.

"Think she was scared?" I asked.

"Naw, dog. She was ice water. You know them big, funny-lookin' old lady flower dresses she be wearin'?"

"Yeah."

"That's what she wears so you can't see what she steals. And she probably wears some kind of stretch shorts to hold the meat so it won't flop to the floor.

"Nigga, is you crazy? I ain't no sissy, and I ain't 'bout to wear no dress," I said.

"Numb nuts, we ain't gotta wear no dang dress."

"Then how we gon' come up?"

"All we gots to do is wear sweatpants over biker shorts and a big shirt. Ain't nothin' to it but to do it," Li'l Man said.

"I'on't know. Momma gon' kill me twice if I get caught."

"Aw, man, you gonna be a scaredy cat all your life. Now who da sissy?"

"Yo' momma."

"Nigga, don't talk about my momma."

"Punk, you know I'm jus' playin'."

"You just watch out for anybody while I come up," Li'l Man said.

"Bet."

We went to his apartment. He dressed in black biker shorts, a pair of his sister's too-big sweatpants and a black T-shirt. He looked more and more like the incredible shrinking man wearing them big ol' clothes.

"We go into the store about a minute apart, and I'll walk to the meat section. You come in and walk around the long way and be looking around for Akbar and 'em. I'll get whatever meat got the biggest price on 'em. When I look your way, wave your hand if the coast ain't clear. If I don't see your hand, I'm gon' put 'em down my shorts. Let me leave first, and I'll meet you around the corner at the Drunk Down. Then we'll take 'em to you know who."

"Who you talkin' 'bout?" I asked.

"The candy lady, Big Momma, dummy. The only person that buy everything she can sell or eat," Li'l man said.

"Oh yeah, I forgot about Big Momma."

We entered Akbar's Alaskan winter-cool market two minutes apart. I didn't know about Li'l Man, but I was a tad bit scared, and I wasn't even doing the stealing.

The market was crowded as usual with early afternoon shoppers. Akbar's stayed busy because it was the only grocery store within two miles of the projects.

Li'l Man eased down the vegetable aisle toward the meat section. He stopped, grabbed a can of Campbell soup, and looked around for me.

Nervous but determined, I walked around to where Li'l Man was comparing cans. I looked to my left and my right. Neither Akbar nor his employees were around. Only the three-dimensional mirrors could see us, and I didn't see anybody in them.

Seeing nothing out of the ordinary, I nodded, giving Li'l Man the go 'head. Next thing I knew, Li'l Man was bee-lining to the door.

He must've chickened out. I didn't see an imprint of nothin' as he walked out. I decided to walk back around the way I came in.

Walking down the bread aisle, my mind was occupied with thoughts of finding somewhere to keep cool and have fun for free. I walked right into the short, hulking body of a serious-looking Saleem Akbar, the store's owner.

"Hey, hey, hey. Slow down. Where's the fire, li'l brother?" Akbar grasped my arms in his massive hands.

"Ah-ah-ain't none," I stammered.

"Little brother, is somebody after you? You in trouble?"

"No, sir, Mr. Akbar. I'm cool. I was looking for some pantyhose for my momma."

"In the bread and vegetable section?"

"How I'm s'pose to know where to look?"

"Follow me. I'll show you where to find them."

"Naw, it's okay. I just remembered she didn't tell me what size."

"What's your name?"

"Lincoln, sir. Lincoln Lee. Lincoln Lee Jackson."

Snapping his fingers, he said, "Clarissa's son, right?"

"Yes, sir."

"Boy, your mother is a fine woman."

My little chest puffed out. "Thank you, sir," I said.

"Drop the mister and the sir, li'l brother. Mister was my daddy, and Sir was my granddaddy. I'm plain ol' Saleem or Akbar."

"Okay, Akbar, I'll holler at you later."

"Asalaam aleikum," he said as I left the store.

I headed home, forgetting all about Li'l Man. As I walked in the direction of the Drunk Down liquor store, I heard a loud whistle. I turned toward the plaza and saw Maddog D-Con frantically waving his arms and kicking his feet in the air. Maddog was an ex-junkie turned drunkie. Heroin used to be his only reason for living. At first I didn't know what he was doing, then I remembered Li'l Man. That's when I knew this fool was trying to signal me.

Fifteen years ago, Maddog was the marvelous Marvin "Maddog" Green—six-two, 230 pounds of raw power. He had a boxing record of 29-0—twenty-eight wins by knockout and twenty of those before the third round. He was a mad dog, tearing his opponents to pieces with his fourteen-inch meat hook fists. As ferocious as he was in the ring, he was twice as gentle outside of it.

The day after Marvin Green signed on to fight for the World Heavyweight Championship, he was served his draft notice. Marvin was devastated. His management team hired lawyers and lined pockets to no avail. Next came the Ali fiasco, which really killed his case. Twenty thousand dollars and six months later, marvelous

Marvin "Maddog" Green turned himself in to the Tenth Street recruiting station in Atlanta to serve his time in the war.

Two and a half years later, thirty pounds smaller and four fingers less, Marvin Green returned home an injured, broken, 25-year-old war veteran. Vietnam killed the fire and transformed the one-time great, rock-solid, African warrior boxing phenom into a yellow-eyed dope fiend. He returned to Atlanta to live with his mother. His former mentor and manager tried rehabs and sabbaticals, but nothing worked. Maddog had given up.

He was content with his life.

On the morning of his twenty-ninth birthday, Maddog woke up with his jones coming down hard. He went over to his girlfriend Carmella's rodent-and-roach-infested apartment.

At six in the morning, Carmella was wide awake, having just gotten rid of a paying date for Marvin. He was worth more than all her customers combined; he got three steady veteran, social security and disability checks that he shared.

As Marvin arrived, she was spraying Lysol on her only piece of furniture—a beat-up, worn-out queen-size attress (the "m" was long gone) that sat in the middle of the dusty, funky, mildewed, trashy front room. The only reason the mattress hadn't been sold was because it provided a place for her business transactions.

He instantly thrust $50 into her hand as he entered her apartment. Marvin told her to go to the all-night dope man sitting in his squad car around the corner. No hug, no kiss, no "how do you feel." She left reeking of musk-funky sex with a twinge of lilac perfume.

Marvin paced. Finally, thirty-some-odd minutes later, Carmella returned with a glazed look on her once beautiful, now wrinkled and weathered face.

After preparing the cooker, used needle and cloth belt, they began to shoot up.

One of Carmella's get-high partners found Marvin and Carmella laid out across each other on the bed an hour later. Carmella's eyes were wide open and her face was frozen in a grotesque mask. Marvin was lying down, eyes closed. The paramedics didn't even attempt to revive her. She was dead with the needle still in her arm.

Marvin and Carmella had shot up a mixture of heroin, D-Con rat poison and milk sugar. Unfortunately, Marvin survived, but now he was really a mad dog. The poison left him half brain dead and spastic. Now Maddog had become Maddog D-Con.

He didn't stay sober for long. He soon found a new crutch, a new escape from the harsh world that threw an onslaught of curve balls his way—Wild Irish Rose, Maddog's new comforter.

Nowadays, Maddog stayed drunk; you just couldn't tell. He was normally crazy, but with alcohol in his system he seemed more lucid, normal, and relaxed. He religiously hung out on the side of the Drunk Down liquor store with the other wine heads. He could be counted on to be there, sitting on his milk crate, come hell or high water, even when the Drunk Down was closed.

I saw the crazy man walking back toward the Drunk Down. He was holding a dark blue milk crate like a lampshade in front of his face, looking like a walking lightpost. He whistled and made outrageous spastic arm and leg gestures. His antics got my attention and that of every other passerby.

Once I was close enough to smell his death-breath, he began to rave, "Niggas, niggas die. Niggas multiply and then more die. It ain't no mystery. They, them, look over there. Mr. Charlie writing us off another chapter in his story. Tricked me into fighting a war against other brown people. Holla if you hear me now as I preach from the steeple."

This doo-doo-breath joker was straight stupid.

"A people that had never raped my ancestors, a people that never forced me to change my name from Kunta to Chester. Stole our culture, stole our land. Mr. Charlie, the mu'fuckin' whip-crackin' white man. Shhh, I hear 'em."

"Aw, man, I ain't got time for this." I brushed his arm off my shoulder.

"Shhh, they're comin'."

"Shut the hell up," Li'l Man shouted while stepping from behind the liquor store dumpster. "Man, what took you so long? I had to put up with crazy-ass D-Con waiting on you," he said.

"I was on my way out the store when I ran into Akbar. Dude tried to act bad, but you know me; I ain't scared of nobody." I crossed my arms, nodding. "He asked me what I was doing, and I told him I was minding mine and leaving everybody else's alone. When I showed him I wasn't scared he acted like he wanted to grab me. You know me, dog. I ain't nothing to play with. I jerked back and told him I could become his worse nightmare if he put his hands on me. Guess what?"

"What?"

"I backed the fool down, and he apologized." As I told one lie, another was ready to follow. I loved a captive audience. "Finally, I just stepped. When I left, Akbar told me a-saamamma-laka or something."

"Liar, liar, big fat deep fryer," Maddog sang and danced.

"Man, you know you ain't talk to no Akbar like that. He woulda broked yo' back." Li'l Man laughed. "Akbar ain't afraid of the police. Come on. Let's roll out before the steaks thaw."

"Loose my money, lil' nnnniggaaaa," Maddog said.

"Get it like the Red Cross. I ain't got no dang quarter." Li'l Man laughed as we ran away. Maddog stood on his milk crate cursing us out, calling us every sort of SOB and MF and a few other choice names I'd never heard.

Walking in the early afternoon oppressive heat, I said, "So, show me what we got."

"We? What we?" Li'l Man joked.

"Aw, come on, dog. Wha's up?"

We stopped and leaned against an old beat-up pickup truck. Li'l Man pulled out a large package from his shorts. "Fill-let Mig-nons, fourteen oh five," Li'l Man read from the package.

"Filet mignon, fool. Not mig-non."

"Tomato, to-mothafuckin-motto. Whatever. It's the most expensive steaks in the store."

"You didn't get scared?"

"Naw, man." He Tarzanned his chest. "Dis me, dog."

"Let's head on up to Big Momma's before the sun starts cooking the meat."

We walked through the grassless apartment yard, past rusty swings, through the beer can and broken bottle strewn playground. Finally, we approached the steel cage burglarproof back door of the candy lady's place.

Before we knew what hit us, two of the candy lady's dirty, nappy-headed kids ambushed us with water guns. I grabbed one of the little brats by the neck. Just as I got my hands on him, a teenager bigger than me and Li'l Man together opened the door.

"Is Big Momma home?" I asked the can-opener-crooked-toothed, chubby girl with one fat hand on her hip and the other stubby one pointing at us.

"What you want with Big Momma? You know we's closed and Big Momma don't like no kids comin' round during her TV soap time. And another thing—ya know you ain't s'pose to be comin' to no back door lessin' it's business."

Speaking from my diaphragm in the most authoritative voice I could muster, I said, "Look, girl, this is business. My partner and I have something we know Big Momma want. Now please, if you'd be so kind to go get her."

"What you got?"

Not wanting to get into it any further with nosy-rosy fatty-watty, I said, "We got some Zsa-Zsa fresh filet mignon steaks."

Her big, fat silver-dollar eyes lit up like a police flashlight.

"Momma, one of them Jackson boys and Li'l Munchkin Man here to see you about selling some steaks," she hollered.

"I bet you couldn't pay that fat cow to call me no munchkin to my face," Li'l Man muttered.

Big Momma Ceely—or just plain ol' Big Momma—waddled to the door after making us wait for ten minutes until her soaps were over. She ran a candy store from her three-bedroom apartment in the projects. She also owned a small fencing operation. She bought anything she thought she could sell. Her apartment was full of enough stuff to start a pawnshop.

Everybody loved Big Momma. She was nice as all get out, but if you crossed her, you were in for an earthquake of trouble. Big Momma carried a thirty-two caliber two-shot Dillinger in her bosom, and she kept a small arsenal in her apartment. She'd been known to pop a cap in a nigga's ass.

She had eight adopted kids who ranged in age from five to fifteen. She would have adopted more if the state had allowed her. Everybody knew Big Momma only adopted them kids for the fat check she got every month from the state.

Big Momma was all of four foot ten and just about as wide, and she was one of those women who you couldn't tell if she was thirty-five or sixty-five. Her face was dark, round, and without wrinkles. She wore her black wig in a ponytail.

"Babies, you know Big Momma always busy. Now, what y'all want?"

Everybody and anybody was "baby" to Big Momma. She didn't care if you were eight or eighty and the president of Haiti, you would always be her baby.

While waiting for Li'l Man to make his pitch, I stood with a stupid smile on my face, wondering how Big Momma sat on the toilet.

"I'm waiting."

Seeing as Li'l Man wasn't about to say anything, I told Li'l Man to give me the meat. He pulled the thawed and bloody but still cold steaks from his soaked shorts.

"Me and Li'l Man helped unload a meat truck at Kroger's a little while ago. After we finished, the manager slipped us this package of fresh cut, top choice, USDA Grade A filet mignon. Seein' as we needed some money and we didn't want any meat, I thought, well, I know Big Momma would like some real good expensive steaks, so we came straight to you. I'm still thinkin' about last year's Christmas dinner leftovers you gave my momma."

The lies rolled off my tongue like running water. When Big Momma started grinning, I knew I had the steaks sold.

"Boy, I bet if you tilted your head sideways, shit would run out your ears." She laughed. "Big Momma know you babies done stole this meat, and you tryin' to hustle Big Momma."

"No, Big Momma," I insisted. "We just trying to make a little money so we can eat and go to the boys club," I said.

"You something else, boy. For a baby, you got a mouthpiece on you. I'll buy your meat. Not because I want it, but because you made Big Momma laugh. Boy, you better than Jake Pound on *The Young and the Hopeless*." She pulled out a maroon coin purse from her

27

triple-wide brassiere, opened it, and took out a small roll of sweaty bills.

After removing two dollars, Big Momma said, "I can't do nothing with one package of six steaks, but I'm a sucker for a smooth, sweet-tongued young man. Here, I'm gonna give each of you a dollar."

"Come on, Big Momma. You know how much this meat cost. I understand you don't need it, but we do need money, and I did lie to you. We didn't come straight here. If we did, the meat would still be frozen. We stopped up the street at Ms. Archer's. She offered us six dollars in food stamps. We didn't take it because I told Li'l Man that you would give us a fair price, and you would probably want some good food."

Big Momma removed a five-dollar bill from the roll and thrust her big, fleshy arms out toward me saying, "I got to get back to my soaps. Now, here's five dollars."

"Thank you, Big Momma," I said.

Before closing the door, she said, "You can come back and see me any time you help unload some meat trucks."

We left happily with money in our pockets and the whole day ahead of us.

"Man, you shoo' is slick. Who's Ms. Archer, anyway?" Li'l Man asked as he laughed while we walked toward the bus stop.

"Ah, man, you know the show *Starsky and Hutch*? You must didn't see that show where Ms. Amy Archer ran away from her boyfriend."

"Naw." Li'l Man shook his head.

"You know Huggie Bear knows everything that happens in the hood. So anyway, Starsky questioned Huggie about Ms. Archer's whereabouts. The cops wanted to use her to bait a trap to catch her boyfriend, Rico. Huggie already had everything figured out 'cause Ms. Archer already told him. Anyway, Huggie played stupid, like he didn't know nothin' until Hutch offered him twenty bucks for some info. Huggie told them that earlier he had been offered double that. That's when Starsky pulled out two twenties. Huggie told them Amy Archer was in the bar sitting on the last stool. Starsky and Hutch didn't even know she had begged Huggie to ask his cop friends for protection from Rico."

"What, they must've been looking for Rico?" Li'l Man questioned.

"Yeah," I said. "He robbed a jewelry store and shot the clerk. She didn't want to go down with Rico, so she decided to try and make a deal with the cops."

"I still don't see why you decided to use Ms. Archer's name," Li'l Man said, looking at me, bewildered.

"Dummy, it's the triple cross come-up. Huggie Bear used Ms. Archer to make money and even got a little extra by using some made-up characters to make the cops come off more bread."

We laughed until we reached the bus stop. We rode the 115 uptown to Atkins Boys Club.

"If it ain't mini-mouse and ass-fat," one of the kids joked as we approached the pool tables.

"I might be fat now, but I can lose weight. Li'l Man might be short now, but he can grow. What are you gon' do—no, better yet, what are you, your brothers and yo' ugly mammy gon' do about yo' horror movie, devil dog faces?"

"I ain't got nothing but sisters, so talk what you know," he shot back.

"Oh, I couldn't tell the difference," I said.

"Ooh," "Sizzlin' hot," and "Burned," chorused around us.

Hurt at not being the center of attention any longer, he got all up in my face. "I'mo kick yo' fat ass, you talk about my momma again."

"Welfare baby, whip me. I'll talk about that man you call yo' momma," Li'l Man said, jumping between us and glaring at him.

"Meet me in the ring, punk." The bigger kid pushed Li'l Man into a pool table on his way to the ring.

"Li'l Man oughta get paid for the surgery he 'bout to do wit' his fists on yo' face," I shouted.

"I'll go get Grasshopper," one of the other kids said, referring to the boys club director.

"After I beat your girlfriend down, I'm coming for you, fat boy."

"Promises, promises," I said, sighing.

The bigger kid looked to be two to three years older than us. He had Li'l Man by at least a half foot and thirty pounds. He was a stocky, hard-lookin' kid with fire in his eyes. True enough, his size and weight should have been considered a factor, but Li'l Man had defied the odds too many times in the past.

This kid had to be new around the boys club since he didn't know about Li'l Man's fight game. If he knew about Li'l Man's rep, he wouldn't have been running his big mouth. Li'l Man's small fists would chip away at his opponent's face and body like a jackhammer on speed. Li'l Man loved to fight, and he loved to fight older, bigger kids. He usually won because he was fast as lightning, agile, and Superman strong.

Grasshopper, the boys club director, loved to see Li'l Man at work. It was uncanny how this underdeveloped, much younger-looking kid would demolish his opponents. So, when Grasshopper was informed of the challenge, he dropped everything and got the glove box from the corner of his office.

Over the intercom, he announced, "Boxing exhibition, twenty minutes in the body room."

A colossal man at six-eight, Grasshopper strode to where the small crowd gathered around me, Li'l Man, and the new kid.

"Break it up. The only fighting outside the ring will be me whipping on one of you knuckleheads," Grasshopper said. "You again, Li'l Man? One day somebody is gon' knock your head off your shoulders," he said.

"Not as long as I'm around," I said.

"Son, you look familiar. Do I know you?" Grasshopper asked Li'l Man's opponent.

"Sir, I'm Tarik Jones. I just moved into this area. I came from Wheeler Boys Club."

Snapping his fingers, Grasshopper said, "Yeah, that's it. You the dude who placed second in the state Junior Golden Gloves Championship a couple months back."

That's when I knew the fix was in. Grasshopper set Li'l Man up. The exchange was too shady. Li'l Man had never gone up against a professional.

Tarik looked like Goliath to Li'l Man's David as the two stood in the center of the makeshift ring wearing oversized boxing gloves. The whole club gathered around the body room and outside the door in eager anticipation of watching Li'l Man face his most formidable opponent. I was the only kid allowed to remain ringside.

"How do you feel?" I asked.

"I'm ready to handle my business, baby," Li'l Man shouted.

Ding.

Grasshopper stood in the middle of the ring with his fisted hand outstretched. "Come out, hit the rock, and let's box," he said.

Li'l Man bobbed and weaved, danced and taunted. He looked like a miniature version of Sugar Ray, hitting Tarik, bing-bing-bing-bing, with a rapid-fire flurry of staccato punches.

Tarik, unable to land a flush blow, became frustrated, but with thirty seconds left in the round, he caught Li'l Man with a left that started out somewhere in Mississippi before it got to Georgia and to the ring, sending Li'l Man to the canvas.

"Stay down. Stay down, dog. I'll get a bat. We'll catch that fool when we leave the club," I said.

Stubborn and stupid with determination, Li'l Man yo-yoed to his feet.

The second round was uneventful. Li'l Man did less taunting and more bobbing, weaving, and running to frustrate the more experienced, bigger, stronger Tarik.

Li'l Man came out like Ali on speed in the last round. He was on Tarik, jabbing, and hooking. Tarik retreated, covering himself from the barrage. After two minutes of pummeling, Li'l Man slowed down. Tarik surged back and started throwing George Foreman haymakers.

The bell signaled the end of the fight. Both fighters collapsed onto the floor, full of respect for each other. Neither fighter cared that the fight was declared a draw.

With money from the steaks, we treated Tarik to double cheeseburgers and fries at White Castle.

CHAPTER 5

Li'l Man was a natural athlete. He loved fighting whether he won or lost. It was the one-on-one combat, the testing of individual will and skill that hooked him. Li'l Man rarely lost, and never lost to kids our age. The older kids staged fights between Li'l Man and bigger kids just for entertainment. Even the pushers waged bets as to the outcome of Li'l Man's fights. That's when I got the idea to start staging them myself.

Now with Tarik, I had two fighters. The fights were held in the back of the projects. The fence that separated the junkyard from the projects and the wooded area behind it served as the cover to shield the activity from five-O. I became the Don King of the projects. I wasn't worried about anybody trying to get over because I had two champs in my corner. Tarik and Li'l Man went 7-0 during the three moneymaking weeks. We managed to earn more than $200 each. A few years before, Momma had started going to church religiously. Whenever I did anything wrong or unethical she said, "God don't like ugly." When she heard about the fights, she added, "You won't be satisfied until you get one of them boys hurt." I gave her my word that I would quit setting up the fights when school started. She didn't know about the steaks.

Li'l Man and I expanded our grocery store operation throughout the year. After school we rode the bus from store to store, packing meat in our coats and taking it out the fire exit doors. We were rarely noticed, but when we were, we always got away. We both ran fast.

Li'l Man and I went into Akbar's market two weeks prior to grade school graduation. At the time, my 17-year-old sister, Marnease, was pregnant and ready to deliver at any moment. She needed baby stuff, and I needed some new gear to strut in when I marched to the podium to receive my grade school diploma. After all, Li'l Man and I had a baby cat-daddy hustler image to uphold.

The instant I walked out the store with two New York strips secured in the inside lining of my jacket, Akbar grabbed me and handcuffed me to a bicycle rack. He ran Li'l Man down shortly after he ran out the store. He took us to his office, sat us down, and showed us several pictures of us modeling his inventory.

"I bet you're wondering why I never called the cops," Akbar said as he paced the small office. "You're thinking if I knew you've been robbing me, why am I just now apprehending you?"

Li'l Man and I were silently trembling in fear.

"I'm the type of person who likes to watch people. I asked myself, hmm . . . " He paused. "Why would two eleven-year-olds be stealing from me?"

I dropped my head.

"Corey Stevens," he said as he pointed to Li'l Man, "Your sister dropped out of school to raise you. I'm sorry about your mother. I know where you live, go to school, and a whole lot more. I know life is hard, but that doesn't give you any reason to steal. Who will Bay-Bay have if you're locked up?" he asked, sighing and shaking his head.

"Lincoln Jackson." Akbar walked up to me and almost touched my nose with his forefinger, scaring me so bad that I peed on myself. "I know all about the sacrifices your mother has made for you, your brother, and sister." Akbar backed up off me and took a deep breath. "Your mother, Lincoln, and your sister, Corey, have enough problems, and I would only add to the list if I called them.

"The police are another matter. If I call them, they'll lock you up, and I'd still be out at least four hundred dollars. I'll give you a choice. You come work off what you owe me, baggin' groceries, or I pay a little visit to your folks. What'll it be?"

There was a brief silence, not because we had to think about it, but because we were waiting to see who would speak first.

As usual, I had to step up.

"Thanks, Akbar. We 'preciate you giving us a second chance."

"Corey, what about you?"

"Yeah—uh, uh, yes, sir; I want to work too," Li'l Man stammered with his head down.

Akbar unlocked the cuffs. "You two get out my store. I don't want to see you until Monday at 9:00 a.m. Don't be late."

"Akbar's cool. He had us dead to wrong, and he still gave us a pass," I said as Li'l Man and I walked toward the Second Avenue bus stop.

"Aw, man, he ain't any different than nobody else. He know he won't get no payback if he turn us in." Li'l Man spoke like he believed the nonsense he was talking. "I'm gonna split that scene as soon as I put in a week or two. I ain't gon' waste my summer baggin' eggs. Shoot, I gots to get paid."

As we got on the 117, we agreed that Akbar's was off limits. As if nothing ever happened, Li'l Man and I hit Winn Dixie, Krogers, and the A&P with a vengeance an hour later. We even doubled back to Winn Dixie and A&P. The day had turned out good, despite me smelling like pee.

I didn't even realize it was almost midnight when I got home.

"Where the hell you been?" Momma shouted, standing in the doorway, gown dancing, hands on hips.

"Momma, uh, me and Li'l Man, see, um, we was stuck across town at the boys club. See, after it closed we missed the bus, see, Li'l Man lost his fifty cents. We had to walk way down to the Waffle House on Sixteenth

Street and bum thirty-five cents off this waitress Li'l Man's sister knows. We only needed thirty-five cents because I had an extra fifteen," I lied, corpse faced.

"Boy, if you lying to me, I'm gonna beat you like you wrote like okra." I didn't know what "wrote like okra" meant, but the way Momma said it almost brought on the tears that were building up, waiting to explode from my eyes.

"I ain't lyin', Momma," I lied.

"Who you yelling at?"

"Nobody, Momma. I just—"

"You just what? Shut up and bring me the phone."

My stomach churned and my knees buckled. It was all I could do to keep myself from falling. I just knew I was dead now.

"Boy, I said bring me that damn phone now."

Wasn't no need in me getting Li'l Man in more trouble than he was in already. I hadn't rehearsed my story with him. Hell, I just made it up.

"Momma, I-I didn't go to the boys club. I was hanging out in the streets."

Momma giraffed forward and gorilla-slapped me so hard I did a cartoon three-sixty before falling on my behind.

"Momma, I'm sorry. I won't do it again. I'm sorry, Momma."

"Shut up all that lying and crying. I ain't gave you nothing to cry for yet."

That made me cry even louder, all the while crumpled on the kitchen floor. I tried to get up but my legs didn't want any part of Momma. Who could blame them?

My 9-year-old brother, D'Andre, was peeping around the corner.

"You must want some of this too."

"Nooo, no, Momma," D'Andre said, wiping sleep from his eyes.

"Then take your narrow behind back to bed."

Momma whipped out an extension cord from I don't know where. I scurried along the kitchen floor screaming bloody murder after every whap.

The next morning, after I'd had time to think, I decided the beating had been worth $120. Li'l Man and I had broken our all-time one-day record. For the rest of the week we hit 'em hard and Big Momma paid us soft. Of course, we didn't get close to the damage we'd done on the Tuesday I got beat like a runaway slave. After that, I made sure I was home every night before the streetlights came on.

On Saturday, we met Tarik at South DeKalb Mall to go to the movies. Two R-rated movies and one G-rated movie were playing. We chose the R-rated one that advertised sexual content and nudity. We all pitched in for one ticket, and Tarik paid to get in to see Lassie Comes Home. Once inside the theatre, he sneaked into the movie and opened the exit door so Li'l Man and I could sneak in. We *ooh*ed and *wow*ed through the movie. Li'l Man and I were knocking on puberty's door, and our hormones went wild whenever we saw any part of a woman's body. There was enough nudity to make us ogle through it twice.

We went to the arcade and played Pac Man afterward. I was a PacManologist. We left the mall after tricking a dollar out of two green white boys. We walked Tarik to the mall's bicycle rack where he showed off his new blue-jean Huffy ten-speed.

"Sweet," Li'l Man said.

"Yeah, my moms bought this as an eighth-grade graduation gift." Tarik beamed while fiddling around with the combination lock. "I can't remember this damned combination," he said, kicking the bike next to his.

Mall security pulled up right when he made all the bikes on the rack fall.

A Barney Fife-looking, beady-eyed white man yelled from a black-and-white Jeep, "Hey guys, what seems to be the problem?"

"Hey, dude, the problem seems to be that my pal here forgot his combination," I teased.

Tarik and Li'l Man's laughter only encouraged me.

"I need to talk to a parent who can verify ownership."

Tarik gave his mom's work number. Using his walkie-talkie, Barney called the main office, which verified that the bicycle belonged to Tarik. Then, using his pliers, the officer cut the lock as easily as cracking a peanut.

"What kind of pliers are those?" I asked.

"They're not. They're heavy-duty cable cutters," Barney replied.

I filed this info away for future use. A plan was forming in my head, but I didn't have time to think about it because it was time to head home. I enjoyed my life and didn't want to die young, which would be a distinct possibility if I let the streetlights catch me outside.

Li'l Man and I amassed $239 during that insane week. On Sunday, following my nap at church, Li'l Man and I purchased a pair of really slick outfits for graduation. We were straight-razor sharp. I sported some tight black Jordache jeans, a brown Jordache leather belt with a gold horse buckle, a doo-doo brown shiny silk shirt, and matching brown Stacey Adams covered my sockless feet. My gear set me back a hundred bucks. I gave the rest of my share to Marnease for her baby. Momma was suspicious of how I got the clothes, but I had her thinkin' that I was cleaning up at the boys club after school.

Li'l Man and I graduated from grade school to junior high, and to a higher level of cunning, gaming, and all-around hustling.

We started bagging groceries at Akbar's right after graduation. We assisted folks who needed help with their bags. Sometimes we got tipped, sometimes we didn't. Li'l Man complained every day; it was too early, the bags were too heavy.

Akbar called us into his office on that first Friday after work.

"There's hope for you two yet. I've received several compliments praising my new employees. I'm proud of you, and I believe in rewarding good work." Akbar smiled and handed us twenty dollars each. "Until Monday, little brothers. Asalaam aleikum." From then on, Akbar rhythmically said this each day. I finally asked him why, and what it meant.

"Little brother, I'm Muslim, and asalaam aleikum is Arabic, and Arabic is African for 'may peace be unto you.' Your reply in Arabic would be waleikum asalaam, meaning 'peace be unto you also'."

"Wa-layk-um-a-salaam?" I tried to repeat.

"Close." Akbar laughed.

"Why don't you just say hi, hello, or good-bye?"

Akbar sat on the corner of his desk, and with a philosophical look on his face, he started to explain. "When you leave here and go back to the projects, all around you, every day, twenty-four seven, you're surrounded by brothers and sisters of all ages who either are thinking about or actually are getting high on drugs or liquor. So when you tell someone hi, you're condoning his condition. Now, as for hello, black people in America have lived in hell on earth for 400 years. Hell is the lowest of the low-low. Hell-low. Again, saying is accepting, and accepting is condoning. Now, about good-bye; remember every bye is not good, and every good-bye ain't gone. See, good-bye has the hidden connotation of never seeing someone again."

A couple days later, double-steppin' through the projects, Li'l Man asked, "What you thinkin' dog?"

"Man, Akbar is cold-blooded deep. He say shit that makes you think. You know, what he was sayin' was on point. Look around us," I said.

"Yeah, maybe. Whatever."

"Dog, this shit is hell. We just tenants in the blood fire."

"So?"

"So, I'm gon' get paid and buy my young ass up out this piece."

"Nigga, you gon' do whatever the Man tell you, so kill dat noise," Li'l Man said.

CHAPTER 6

"Lee. Leeee. Linc. Wait up," my egghead little brother, D'Andre, shouted while he ran toward Li'l Man and me.

"Speed up. Here comes my little brother." Unfortunately, D'Andre ran faster than we could walk.

"What, man? What? What? What? Why you got to be screaming my name all loud and shit?"

"Oooh, you said a curse word. I'mo tell," he said as he pointed his stubby 10-year-old finger at me.

"You gotta prove it, punk. Now, whatchu want?"

"Big Momma. Big Momma."

"What about Big Momma?" I asked.

"She dead. She died yesterday night."

"How? What happened?" I grabbed D'Andre by his shoulders.

"I heard, they said a diet coma."

"A diabetic coma, fool," Li'l Man corrected.

"Yeah, dat's it," he said.

Li'l Man and I ran to my house, leaving D'Andre in our dust. I burst through the door all out of breath. My sister sat on the living room/kitchen couch breast feeding her baby.

"Marnease, where Momma at?"

"She down at Grady Hospital with Big Momma's kids, waiting on Big Momma's folks to show up. She said for you and Li'l Man to go and watch out for her apartment. You know how niggas is whenever they think there's an opportunity come up. Big Momma's crib is filled with some of everything worth something."

"Yeah, but Big Momma also got her place caged up like Fort Knox," I said.

"Just do what Momma said. Let something happen to that apartment and see when the next time you'll be able to sit yo' fat ass down."

41

Marnease was right. My ass was in danger—literally—if I didn't do what Momma said.

Li'l Man and I high-tailed it over to Big Momma's. When we got there, Maddog D-Con, bare-chested and skunk drunk, stood on Big Momma's front steps, a big rock in one hand and a half-empty bottle of Wild Irish Rose in the other.

"Yes, Lawd. I said yeees, Lawd. She-she was one of the good-uns. She ain't never, neeeeever-eeeeever ast no questions. The cheap bitch paid you for what you-you was a-sellin'." He threw his hands in the air, threatening the sky with rock and bottle. "Why, Lawdy? Big Momma, she call me M.D. She say to me, 'M.D., boy, you best quit doin' what you doin' and make peace with the Lawd. Now, iff'n you don't, He libel to take you away from that which you lovin' so much.' She say to me, 'M.D., stop lovin' on that bottle. Stand up. Be a man. Own up to yo' 'sponsibilities.' Then she'd give me twenty dollars for the TV or Betamax I done stole. I ain't gon' lie." He pointed his bottle at the few passersby. "She 'twas a cheap bitch." He sprayed a shower of spittle on me and Li'l Man. "But she was a good-un. Yes, Lawd."

Maddog went on and on, happy to have an audience on that cloudy, cool summer day.

Maddog had surprisingly attracted a small crowd; usually everyone simply ignored him. Li'l Man and I stood in the back of the crowd cracking up. Maddog took a drink like a preacher in the middle of a sermon, but instead of a cup of water, he drank from a wine bottle.

Big Momma's funeral was held on Saturday. Second Baptist Church was packed, standing room only. Me, Momma, D'Andre, and Marnease had to sit in the back. Wasn't nothin' like a good funeral. Everybody who was anybody in the projects showed up. The church was a fashion show, and the middle aisle was the runway.

Easter Sunday was never this packed or this well dressed.

I looked around for Li'l Man and his sister. They had a seat toward the front. Li'l Man was dozin' with his head tilted to the side, wearing his graduation outfit. I wore mine, too, with the exception of the jeans. Momma made me wear some ol'-timey hand-me-down gray bell-bottoms.

My eyes were on perpetual roam. Big Momma sure had a lot of relatives. There were eight limousines outside. Her relatives should've had their own comedy show. One big old buffalo-butt-lookin' Bookman lady with a beard fell over on Big Momma's big, double-wide brown coffin.

"Oh, Gooood, God. Oh my God, take me. Take me, God. Why my baby sister? Why? Tell me why, God."

She threw her arms in the air and looked up. The whole church followed, looking to see if God would answer. I cracked up when I thought about how fast the church would have cleared if God responded.

The ushers rushed to Big Momma's sister's side. She had a fit, feet stomping and head flailing, locking her hands around the coffin's brass railing.

"Ahh, fuck all you motherfuckers. Leave me alone." She evil-eyed the men trying to grab her. "Let me be. This is my damn sister," she said all proper-like.

"Estelle, stop acting a damn fool and sit yo' fat ass down. You ain't seen Ceely in ten years."

The castigation came from a skeleton-thin, short, bald, older man.

Dancing with the coffin's rail, she ignored him. She lifted up one of her humongous, hog-hamhock legs and swung it inside the coffin, landing a blow to Big Momma's chest. The church let out a gasp as the coffin starting to tilt. Before Big Momma tumbled out, half the front row was up, uprighting the coffin and the sister.

After righting the casket, Estelle was roughly escorted to the back of the church by several ushers. Finally, the good Reverend Samuel Parchman went on with the funeral.

"Ceely James, Big Momma, was a woman of heart, a woman of integrity, a woman of strength. A woman of spiritual girth."

"And as big as the planet Earth," an unknown voice shouted from somewhere in the congregation.

The reverend continued, ignoring the outburst. "Yes, she was. God knows she was a good, good woman. Always had a kind word. Yes, she did," he preached. "But you see, when God, hmph. I said when Gooood, hmph." He stomped and bowed his head. "Do you hear me now? I said when Gooood says it's time, it's time. Not when you ready, but when He's ready for you toooo rock steady. When he's ready for you to come hoooommmme, then he'll bring you home, to the dome, all alone. Scripture says 'from dust you come to dust you'll return.' Can I get an amurn?" he shouted as he James Browned down the pulpit. As he came up from a split, everyone chorused, "Amen."

"Negro, preach!" someone shouted.

That outburst hyped the good reverend up even more.

"Not Ceely, but Big Momma. She was everybody's momma—yourn, yourn, and all of yourns," he sang, pointing to the congregation. "Whenever she saw somebody, ha." He coughed. "Whenever she seed somebody down, ha. I say whenever she saw that yous was hungry, ha. Do you hear me now, ha? I say whenever she seed you was feelin' bad . . . " He paused to moonwalk back to the middle of the pulpit. In a singsong voice he continued, "Yes, she was a good, haaaard working, loooooviiiiin' woman."

"The bitch was sho-nuff good, but cheap as Bazooka bubble gum. She still owe me two dollars for a TV I sold her for twenty."

The reverend turned beet red when everyone's gaze turned to Maddog.

After sufficiently making a fool of himself, in a drunken stupor, Maddog fell into the aisle, trying to snuggle up to someone's stockinged, kicking leg.

Still, this had to be the craziest funeral ever. Heck, I couldn't wait for somebody else to die. I was having a ball until Momma hit me in my mouth for snickering too loud.

Five days after Big Momma was in the ground, I said, "What up, home slice?" I stood in front of Li'l Man, who was still lying in his hideaway bed on a Monday morning. "Why you ain't ready? You know we got to help unload the truck at Akbar's."

"Man, I ain't with that working shit no mo'. Ain't you heard?"

"Heard what?"

"Slavery's over. With Big Momma gone, I gotta worry about how I'm gon' get paid."

"Come on, dog. Dude's all right. Man, we got busted. He coulda turned us in. We'd probably still be doin' time in a YDC juvenile. We owe 'im." I pleaded to blind eyes and deaf ears.

"Shit, I don't owe that nigga jack. I ain't ast him for a get out of jail free card. I'm trying to max and relax until I come up with a master plan."

"Do what you want, dog, but I'm out. I'm gon' pay mine." I walked out the door, leaving Li'l Man cocooned under his sheets.

After getting to work fifteen minutes late, I told Akbar Li'l Man couldn't make it because he was sick, but after a few days I knew Akbar knew what the deal was with Li'l Man.

Friday after I got paid, I used a handful of bill-sized newspaper clippings sandwiched between two twenties to make a false bankroll to impress the honeys. I hooked up with Li'l Man and we rode the train to downtown Five Points. We spent the afternoon trying to find something to get into. We was trippin' off this dude beating these white corporate-type cats out of their bread in three-card Monty when this brother, no older than eighteen, came out of some joint wearing more gold than Mr. T.

"Check playa out." I pointed in the direction of the gold.

"Dude's phonier than a three-dollar bill. Behind all that metal you'll probably find a Martian neck," Li'l Man laughed.

I looked up to see what store he had come out of when I saw the sign: ACE HARDWARE.

"Come on, I got an idea."

As soon as we walked into Ace, an anorexic, bifocal-wearing Richie Cunningham-looking white boy approached. "Can I help you?"

"Naw, doc. We just chillin'," I said.

"This is not a chill spot. If you don't have any money, I'll have to insist on you leaving."

He was much less convincing than he sounded. Li'l Man and I sensed this like a dog smells fear. I decided to run the mack game down on Richie Cunningham.

"Dog, you gave me what, twenty dollars last night, forty-five in the morning? Let's see." I put my left index finger to my temple as if I were in deep thought. Snapping my fingers I said, "Twenty-five dollars a couple hours ago, fifteen dollars ten minutes ago."

Li'l Man picked up my pause. "You forgot the twenty dollars we picked up around the corner."

Next I pulled out the impressive-looking roll of bills with a twenty on top, folded and wrapped with a rubber band. Richie Cunningham stood in awe, his mouth hung open truck-tunnel wide at two kids with more money than he made in a month.

"I'm sorry, I uh . . . "

"Go get me some heavy-duty cable cutters," I ordered the quarter-eyed, stammering salesclerk.

"Yes, sir. Yes, sir."

With his head bowed, he shuffled off to the tool section and brought back some red-and-gray cable cutters. He even carried them to the cash register where Li'l Man pulled out the roll I had given him. In front of the humbled salesclerk, Li'l Man peeled a twenty-dollar bill off the top and handed me back a roll of bill-sized newspaper clippings. I handed them to Mr. sales clerk and said, "Keep the tip."

We laughed all the way back to the train station.

After boarding the northbound I said, "Dog, we gotta step up our game. I don't know about you, but since Big Momma died, I been starvin' for some cheese."

"I feel ya."

"You 'member how easy Barney Fife cut that lock for Tarik?"

"Yeah."

"That's why I got these." I pointed to the cable cutters lying between us.

"Huh?"

"We go to Lennox and hit the bike rack. Shit, we get a couple Schwinns, ride 'em to the East Side, take 'em to Jack Leg Joe's and pawn 'em."

"I'm down, but you know that crab gon' try to get over."

"That don't make me no never mind. We gettin' 'em free."

We sold a few bikes here and there, but ridin' each bike five, ten, fifteen miles was too much like work. Then we had a storage problem. Momma would have knocked my brains clean out my head if I started bringing bicycles home. She didn't know what Li'l Man and I were doing, but she knew we were into something we shouldn't be. She was constantly putting the monkey foot jinx on us, talkin' 'bout us getting locked up.

"You'll reap what you sow, and nothing good comes from nothing bad," she would say.

Thanks to the gossipin' grapevine featuring blowhard bugga bear Bernice, Momma was always hearin' somethin' about me doin' somethin'. Momma and her friends had an intelligence network that could teach the CIA a thing or two. Even though we did our stealing and selling far from home, that didn't make us safe from the long arms of Momma and company. Of course, I denied all accusations.

Momma's favorite response was, "God don't like ugly, and what y'all doin' sure ain't pretty." The only reason she didn't peel my wig back was because her laws didn't include hearsay. If she wasn't sure I had done the deed, she waited until enough evidence was mounted to convict, then she'd peel my wig back.

After about six weeks of mall hopping and bike stealing, word spread that if you wanted a good bike cheap, a certain pair of 12-year-old kids were whom you needed to see. We even started to get orders for specific bicycles in specific colors. One particular order was for two red 26-inch Schwinn ten-speeds. One Saturday, late in the afternoon, Li'l Man and I had already been to South DeKalb and West End Mall trying to case the ten-speeds. We struck oil at the third mall.

We scoped out one red Schwinn and decided I would wait a couple blocks up the road at the Majik Market for Li'l Man to ride the bike there. Then we would hide the bike in the ditch behind the market and get a junkie to bring us back to get it.

I waited forty-five minutes before I figured something wasn't right. It never took more than twenty minutes for a lick to be put down. I walked back to the mall. When I got there, I saw Li'l Man standing at the bicycle rack next to the ten-speed with his back to me.

As I closed the distance I called out, "Dog, what up?"

When I came within twenty-five yards, Li'l Man screamed, "Run! It's a setup!"

Everything moved in slow motion. I ran, but before I could get out of the parking lot, five-O had me surrounded with their guns drawn. They acted like I was public enemy number one, and I wasn't even thirteen.

Mall security all over Atlanta had been on the lookout for us. Greenbriar Mall had gotten lucky and caught us on Candid Camera riding a stolen dirt bike and a women's ten-speed past Radio Shack, which happened to have been testing surveillance cameras. Next, security alerted Atlanta area malls about us. We were lucky to have eluded mall security this long.

"Boy, you going to the big house, you and your girlfriend." The cop pointed at Li'l Man handcuffed to the bike rack. He roughly twisted my arm and slapped the cuffs on my wrists. "You won't make it through the first night without being a bride in a jailhouse ceremony."

Seeing as though I didn't have a single ounce of respect for the police, I found it hard to be scared, although I was. My lack of respect didn't come from the way we had been treated, but from the countless acts of harassment and bullying I'd seen over the years in the hood. Five-O was just another gang to me.

Then I thought about Momma. She was worse than any gang. I was terrified.

Momma and Li'l man's sister, Bay-Bay, were in the station bailing us out a couple hours later. We were released after signing some papers. Li'l Man and I were being escorted out of the lockup area when Momma reached inside the door and slapped me upside my head. I ended up flat on my back.

"Get up, shut up, and don't say nothin'."

"But Momma—"

Pop! She slapped me again. Before I knew it, I was on the floor rubbing my face.

"Didn't I tell you to shut up?"

I nodded, too scared to speak.

Bay-Bay had Li'l Man in a chokehold, wrestling him out of the police station.

With a pained look on her face, Bay-Bay's only word to Li'l Man was "Why?"

This was the first time I'd ever seen Li'l Man cry. The disappointment on Bay-Bay's face made me temporarily forget about Momma.

I didn't have to worry about that for long. Momma played Ping-Pong with her hand on my head all the way home.

"Lord knows I try. I know you don't have no fancy bicycles and a lot of things the other kids have, but I try my hardest to make sure you always have clothes on your back, shoes on your feet, food in your stomach, and a roof over your head. But no, you ain't never satisfied. You don't appreciate nothing. I don't have no man to help me. Hell, I don't even have time for a social life. You, Marnease, and D'Andre are my life, but you won't be happy until you kill me from worry. Tell me, what you gonna do when I'm dead? You hear me talkin' to you?"

"Yeah, Momma, I'm sorry. I'll never do it again."

"I know you won't because I'm gon' beat the 'b' off your behind. You'll be too tired from standin' up the rest of your life." Momma's glare caused my stomach to do cartwheels.

When we got to our building, Momma Houdinied an extension cord from her purse. She caught me on my calf before I could Jesse Owens-hurdle over the trashcan in front of me.

Whap.

She dang near crippled me. Her Ray Charles aim punished my whole body.

Whap.

My best defense was to cover up while screamin'.

Whap. Whap.

Five-O was never around when you needed 'em.

I had welts on my arms, back, and legs by the time she got tired.

Believe it or not, the weeklong punishment that followed was worse than the whipping. The only place I could go to was work. On Monday morning I arrived at Akbar's, thankful to get bonded out the house.

While sweeping out the employee lounge, Akbar called me into his office. "Pull up a seat," he said as he sat in front of his desk with his arms crossed. "Some time around the early 1700s, a white man by the name of Willie Lynch came to America from the West Indies. Willie went around the South speaking to mass gatherings of white slave owners. I'll quote him: 'Your niggers are uppity and out of control. I am here to give you solutions that I'll guarantee will work anywhere from three hundred to a thousand years. First thing you do is cause strife and confusion to run rampant within your niggers. Turn the nigger boy against his woman; the old nigger against his younguns; light-skinned against dark; strong against weak; divide 'em and you'll control 'em.'"

Akbar stood and placed his hands on his desk and said, "I'm going to stop there. That's not the whole story, but that's the basics. You're probably wondering what this has to do with why I called you into my office."

Before I could respond, he yelled, "Everything!" He stared me down with infrared intensity.

"For hundreds of years, black people in America have been taught what and how to think. We've been trained to pull one another down, keeping us from rising from the crab barrel of ignorance. Why keep us ignorant and divided? Simple. To prevent us from ever rising to positions of power from which we could implement programs and curriculums geared to teach our story, heal our sick minds, and wake us from our two-thousand-year-long hibernation. If in fact we united through realization of the truth and through economic empowerment, we could demand the Man to adhere to our needs." Akbar became animated as he paced the floor.

He continued, "So, you see, little brother, when you steal from another, no matter if it's a brother or another, you are conforming to the ideology that Blacks are weak and inferior to Whites in that we have to rob someone because we are too dumb to go out and legally attain what we want. Your word and your self-pride are the most important things you have, something no man can take away." He shook his head. "You kept your word. You paid your debt to me. That in itself is a man's gesture, not a boy's.

"That's why I kept you on." He paused, and just as I started to feel a sense of pride he said, "Maybe I was wrong in my judgment of you."

I opened my mouth to protest, then decided against it.

"Over the short time I've known you, I have become very fond of you, but this latest stunt you pulled was plain dumb. I'm disappointed. The worst part is you've let yourself down. You have to start using your head. Think." He paused. I could hear the air breathing. The silence was torture. I didn't know what to say, what to do.

After a mini-minute millennium he said, "Now you may go back to work. Asalaam aleikum." He turned away from me, his hands clasped behind his back.

I was shaken up, especially since if I knew my father, I'd wished he was someone just like Akbar. The last thing I wanted was to disappoint the man I wanted to be like when I grew up.

Three months later, the juvenile court dropped my charges because it was a weak case without Li'l Man's testimony. Li'l Man was sentenced to two years probation and community service.

I continued to work for Akbar as a salaried employee; I even managed to save some money over the next few months.

In late October on a Friday, Li'l Man, Tarik, and I were hanging out at South DeKalb Mall taking inventory of the honeys. The mall was packed with Halloween costume shoppers.

"Man, look at that." Tarik pointed to a Hawaiian-looking number with an hourglass figure.

"Hey, slim. Yo, red," Tarik called out.

"Hay is for horses and I ain't red. I'm butter-brown," she said.

"Ah, don't be like that, shawty doo wop. I was just trying to get your attention," Tarik said with his bottom lip poked out. He looked at her with his puppy-dog brown eyes.

"You'll never get the attention of a decent young lady by addressing her as shorty or red."

He shrugged.

"Next time, try excuse me," she said. "So, now that you've managed to get my attention, what is it that you need?"

Tarik slid to her side and pointed to the ground. "You dropped something."

She looked down and turned around, her eyes retracing her steps.

"What was it?"

"Your smile?"

"Cute."

"A-ha, there it is." He winked a smile at her.

Shaking her head and smiling, she said, "I have to go."

"And leave me without a way to see your sunshine smile again?"

"You have something to write with?"

"Your voice is my pen, my mind is the paper."

"You need help." She laughed.

"Why do you think I'm crying out to you?"

"It's 981-4256. And it might help if you knew to ask for Meon."

"Meon. I was so caught up in the moment that I forgot myself," he said, extending his hand. "Tarik Jones. Glad to make your acquaintance."

I couldn't understand how he brought these lame-game, Buster Brown, dead-ass lines to life. He had her glossy-eyed and giddy galloping as she walked away.

We walked out of the mall around closing time. Tarik was hyped. He always bragged and talked trash after scoring. "The ladies love T.J. I'm their chocolate dream. I'm their ice cream. They dream to cream; chocolate Tarik will make 'em beam."

"Kill that noise," I said.

"What ho don't love puppy dogs?" Li'l Man asked.

"You punks just mad 'cause the only play y'all get is with Jackie Palm and the bottom of a bottle of lotion," Tarik replied.

We were headed to the bike rack when Tarik continued, "I got more flavor than Baskin Robbins, and everybody knows they got thirty-one. I got thirty-two. And got more game than Milton Bradley and Parker Brothers.

When we reached the rack, three cats about Tarik's age were standing around smoking Kools. A charcoal-colored troll built like a tree stump blew smoke in Tarik's face. "Nigga, what size them shoes is?" he asked, pointing to Tarik's red-and-white Dr. Js.

Tarik didn't say anything, so we didn't either. Next thing I knew, the troll and his boys were in front of us.

"Bitch, you hear me? Up ass my mu'fuckin' shoes, nigga." As the troll grabbed Tarik's arm, Tarik stole 'em in the mouth. The troll dipped to his left.

Pingpingpingping. Tarik put a Sugar Ray four piece on that ass.

Li'l Man and I were gravy on the other two. We held our own even though we were outweighed and outsized. "Ahhhh! Motha—oh shit!" Tarik screamed.

As I turned to look, a blow landed to my head. As I fell, I saw a lake of blood coming from Tarik as he lay on the concrete being kicked to sleep by the troll. Li'l Man turned in time to see a switchblade coming out of Tarik. The distraction was all Li'l Man's opponent needed. He grabbed Li'l Man's left arm and twisted until he heard cracking bone. Li'l Man's gut-wrenching screams of pure anguish got everyone's attention. The three dudes ran, but not before the troll took Tarik's new sneakers off his still body.

Security pulled up.

I was in a daze and no help. Tarik looked dead. His eyes were closed and his mouth was open. I glanced a few feet from Tarik, where my best friend was laid out on the ground, half his body lying in the street, the other half on the sidewalk. He was sweating and crying in pain.

After the longest fifteen minutes of my life, I finally heard the sirens.

A couple of hours later I sat in DeKalb General's sardine-packed waiting room with Momma, Bay-Bay, and Tarik's mom. Li'l Man's arm was set, and he was under heavy sedation in an emergency room cubicle. Tarik had lost a lot of blood. The blade had grazed his heart. He was in critical condition, and the doctors said it would be touch and go for the next twenty-four hours. With such a substantial loss of blood, they couldn't tell if Tarik had suffered brain damage.

Around two in the morning, five hours after being admitted, there was still no change in Tarik's comatose condition. Li'l Man was being released. Momma tried to send me home with him and Bay-Bay, but I couldn't leave my boy. Leaving would be like me givin' up on him. I wanted to be there when Tarik awoke. There was no doubt in my mind that he would wake up. He had to.

Me and my prayers kidnapped a corner of the wall, holding it hostage in return for Tarik. Even though Momma had never met Tarik's mom, she stayed to comfort and console her, one grief-stricken mother to another. That's how Momma was—a rock. That's probably why we stayed so broke. Any time someone needed, Momma gave freely.

"Girl, I really appreciate you staying," Mrs. Jones said. "Tarik is my baby, my only child. I just don't know what I would do if, if—"

"Girl, don't even think it. Everything will work out just fine."

"The last five years I've been raising Tarik alone. His father's in jail. I put in ten to twelve hours a day down at D.O.T. I'm not able to spend enough time with Tarik, but I don't have a choice. Oh God, why my baby?" she cried.

"Girl, Tarik needs your prayers, not your guilt. You have to be strong. He needs you. Give it to God. Put it in His hands, and He will take care of everything."

A nurse came into the waiting room at 8:30 the next morning and asked for Mrs. Sheila Jones. Tarik's mom jumped up teary eyed and ran to the nurse.

"My baby, my baby, is he—"

"Mrs. Jones, your son is awake and is asking for you. Follow me."

"Thank you, Jesus. Thank you, Lord," Mrs. Jones screamed, falling to her knees, arms flailing in the air.

Tarik was groggy, but otherwise fine. The hospital held him for another 48 hours for testing and observation. He made a full recovery, sidestepping any brain damage.

CHAPTER 7

A couple years had passed, same ol' same ol'. We were still getting our hustle on. Another school year, another economic opportunity, I thought as I began my eighth grade year at Southwest DeKalb High school. It was so much bigger than junior high. With so many kids, it was a hustler's paradise.

I just observed the first week. Tarik, now a sophomore, showed Li'l Man and me around, although he wasn't comfortable kicking it with a couple of eighth graders.

On Thursday of the first week, Li'l Man ran up to me Casper-faced. "How's it hangin', dog?" he asked as he slapped five with me.

"Ever so long and low, baby boy." I laughed, grabbing my crotch. "Where's the fire, trick baby?" I asked, rushing to keep up.

"I got something heavy to lay on you and Tarik, and I want to catch him before he finishes eating."

In school the upperclassmen ate first. When we walked in, Tarik was walking out with some of his friends.

"Babyboy, can we holler at you for a minute?" Li'l Man said, interrupting Tarik's conversation. Tarik and I followed Li'l Man to our conspiratorial, student bathroom/office.

"I saw the troll. His name is Steve. He's on the football team."

Tarik put out his hands, smiling. "Calm down, player. Take it slow."

"The troll, man. You know, the mall? The dude who tried to do you."

Tarik tensed up, his soft face rigor-mortised into evil. "I gotta jet," he said, scrambling. "Be back after school."

We went to the back looking for Tarik when school was over. School buses passed; cars maneuvered from the faculty and student parking lots. Band, cheerleading, and football practice were beginning in different areas of the school.

I thought of all the hustles I'd seen going down the first week as we waited for Tarik. At lunchtime, outside the gym downstairs, kids pitched pennies against a wall for dollars. That hustle was too slow; took too much coordination, dexterity, and practice. Another move I peeped was selling Now & Laters and Charms Pops. That was more my scene.

Tarik showed up just as the principal, Mr. Milton, was leaving the parking lot.

"Tarik! Over here!" I shouted.

He ignored me and tornadoed toward the football field. Li'l Man and I jogged to catch up, but Tarik ran faster.

When we got to the fence around the field where the team practiced, Tarik was already approaching the area where Coach Todd was lecturing his team. The players sat in a large circle on the grass in shorts and shoulder pads.

"This is a closed practice," Coach Todd shouted.

Tarik continued to choo-choo forward, deaf-earring the world.

"Boy, get the hell out of here!" the coach shouted.

Tarik braked, face-fronting the troll. "Bitch, where the blade at now?" he asked. "Remember me, punk ass nigga?"

"Yeah, ho," Steve replied, kissing the air in front of Tarik. "How could I forget a pretty bitch like you? I apologize. When I whipped your cotton candy ass I thought you were a man. I didn't know you were a bitch until I heard you scream. 'Ahhhhh, ouch!' " the troll mocked in a high voice.

The team erupted in laughter.

Pow. Pow. Pow.

The deafening series of blasts resounding from the nickel-plated, pearl-handled Smith & Wesson caused everybody on the field to scatter; everybody except the troll, who was lying on the ground covered in a sea of red. After hawking, Tarik spit on the troll, then turned and walked away.

Li'l Man and I stood owl-eyed at the fence. We still couldn't move when Tarik approached.

"Go home. No need for all us to go down," he said before running off.

I don't know how Li'l Man felt, but me and Tarik was down like four flat tires with a fat lady on top. I loved him like a brother by a different mother, but still, ain't no way I was going down with him on no murder beef. He didn't have to worry about me getting anywhere near his nuclear rattlesnake ass. I was too ambitious to rot in jail.

Tarik turned himself in that same night.

I told Momma what happened before she heard about it from her gossiping friends. As usual, Momma tripped, but this time not on me.

"Oh, baby, I'm so sorry. Are you all right?" Momma asked.

"Yeah, Momma, I'm fine. I just didn't have any idea he was gon' shoot that boy."

The next morning Momma called Tarik's mother. She told Momma that Tarik had taken her gun and that he had been charged with a multitude of charges, attempted murder being the most serious. She also praised God that the boy he shot was upgraded from critical to serious condition. He was in intensive care, but the bullets had passed right through him, and he was expected to make a full recovery.

Just before Christmas, Tarik pleaded guilty to the lesser charge of aggravated assault with a deadly weapon. He was sentenced to the Georgia Correctional

Center for Boys until his seventeenth birthday, a little over twenty-two months away. The judge was uncharacteristically lenient in Tarik's case. The two factors that contributed to this were the fact that Tarik was apparently not stable when the shooting occurred and the boy who had been shot, Steven Mayfield, had a long record of violence and theft.

I was back on my square, rolling in dough by Christmas. The candy business turned out to be swee-eet. No one could compete with my prices. Everything I stole, I sold—from one-pound Hershey bars to packs of tropical-flavored Bubble Yum bubble gum. Candy was easier to steal than steaks.

I traveled from store to store on the bus. Wintertime enabled me to steal much more than when it was warm outside. I wore a big, unzipped coat so it appeared I wasn't concealing anything. In the left and right linings of the coat I had made eight-inch incisions. I stuffed bags of candy inside the lining and a couple of bags of candy halfway inside my pants, letting my loose-fitting pullover shirt conceal them. Then I casually walked through the shortest checkout line and purchased one or two small items.

I didn't go out stealing every day. I usually went twice a week. I stole so much each time that I always had a surplus. I did this throughout my eighth grade year.

Akbar and I stayed close, even though I quit working at the store over a year earlier. Now I would go see him from time to time after closing hours and just rap with him about everything and anything.

Momma didn't give up scolding and fussing at me, but she had come to the realization that nothing she said would stop me from hustling. She didn't realize I was stealing all that candy, but she did know that selling candy was in violation of school policy. The couple of times I got busted didn't stop me. Detention nor suspension no longer fazed me. It just made me more cautious. I even hired flunkies to carry my candy bags to take the heat off. One of my mottos was "Just because a player gets popped don't mean the game gotta stop."

Rapping was the new craze, one I threw myself into mouth first. I was even pretty good. I evolved into deejaying, spinning records, and creating new sounds. By Christmas of my ninth grade year I had acquired two Technic 200-L turntables, an amplifier, speakers, a Radio Shack mixer, an omnidirectional microphone, and all the latest records. The stereo equipment was all courtesy of my expanding nefarious activities, made possible by the entrance of Yolanda in my life.

I was a freshman in high school when I walked up on her. She was an upperclassman, about five-five with a smooth, almond-brown complexion. She was big-boned with watermelon hips, cantaloupe titties, and a double-coconut ass. She was large but attractively proportioned—what you could call fat-fine. Best of all, she had a brain and a mouthpiece that could cut down the best shit talker. Her name was Yolanda.

"Big and beautiful, how about making a contribution to the charity of my choice?" I smiled and opened my bag, showing her my candy.

"Just because I'm big, you think I want to buy some candy? Every big person doesn't eat sweets." She stood at her locker, hands on her hips, tapping a foot on the floor. "I'm trying to watch my figure."

"Hell nah," I said.

"What?" she asked.

"I'm a figure watchologist. I don't needs no help. I'm watching enough for the both of us. From what I see, hmm . . . " I paused to take two steps around her. "It's all good. I guess we can add a couple peanut butter cups to feed your fineness."

We laughed loudly in spite of the stares from other students in the hall waiting for the morning bell to ring. I was a freshman, and Yolanda was a senior. I was big for my age, so it was a while before she found out that I was in the ninth grade. It must have been about ten minutes.

The love connection was cancelled when Li'l Man interrupted our chemistry with geometry.

"Yo, dog, you got that geometry homework we suppose to turn in today?" he asked.

That's when Yolanda knew that I was either slow for taking a ninth-grade math course or I was a ninth grader. That didn't stop us from starting a tight little hustlership, though.

I was Rico Suave for a minute. All my boys just knew I was hittin' it—all but Li'l Man.

Yolanda had too many syllables. She needed a hood name, so I christened her Yo-Yo. I got mad props from the fellas because shawty was fine as whipped butter- big, but fine, and she could dress her ass off, thanks to Neiman, BeBe and Macy's, her favorite stores to boost from. She stole only from the best.

"I been doin' this for two years, and ain't came close to bein' busted."

When she told me this, I knew I had to become her student. I did, and graduated Magna Cum Boost the Laude.

One day Yo-Yo and I were hanging out in the mall, checking out the home stereo and television section of Rich's department store.

"I'd sure like to get my hands on that amp," I said, pointing to a Pioneer high-fidelity 120-watt integrated stereo amplifier.

"Follow me." She didn't look back as she Queen Victoria-strode through the aisles.

We rode the escalator to the bargain basement where we walked to the audio and visual clearance section. On a shelf was a stack of amplifiers.

"Stand over there at the front. Act like you're interested in a VCR."

I looked at her crooked-necked.

"Stop lookin' like Igor."

"Huh?"

"Never mind. Just watch my back. If somethin' don't look right, signal."

She'd barely completed the sentence before she left carrying a Rich's shopping bag with my amplifier protruding from it and a receipt attached to the outside.

Wow. She had carried an already used, concealed, empty Rich's bag into the store with an old receipt stapled to it.

After leaving with the goods, we walked through the discount women's clothing and accessories department. She handed me the bag, picked up a pair of costume jewelry earrings and purchased them on the way out. I got the best deal in town: a $400 amplifier and some earrings for three dollars. Sweet.

Over the next couple of months I became your one-stop bootleg-backdoor audio shop. Li'l Man and I called my business Bitch's, the Black Rich's. When all was said and done, I had $5,000 worth of audio accessories, including a pre-amplifier, amplifier, three turntables, mixer, microphone, concert speakers, and all the latest vinyl. I had Momma thinking I got everything from selling candy, and from money I'd saved. She had no idea that my stereo equipment cost as much as it did.

I got pig greedy. I'd been hoggin' it up, being chauffeured around by Yellow Cab, stealing from every Rich's in the city. I was in stores more than the managers.

Three days before Christmas, Momma had to come bail me out again.

I got a pass, two years probation, thanks to all the brothers who got caught before me and to those violent offenders overcrowding the juveniles.

Momma did the best she could; it wasn't her fault. The streets were my heroin. And Akbar was my methadone. Akbar thought I possessed certain qualities that no one else noticed. He always tried to set me straight. He went out of his way to try to steer me onto a different path. He would even come to our apartment to check on me.

He always emphasized the importance of education, and I agreed. It was just that his definition was different than mine. I was obtaining a street education and getting different degrees on a constant.

Akbar asked about my plans after high school, which I thought was a dumb question.

"I don't know." I shrugged.

"I see a lot of me in you. You've got the drive, you just speed the wrong way on a one-way."

"I got a lot of time to find out what I wanna be. I'm only in the ninth grade."

"Time." He shook his head. "It goes on with or without you. You can chase it, but you'll never catch it."

"Huh?"

"You always chasin' a buck. You're always trying to find a back door or an alley. You want to get paid, right now."

Yep. He was right about the getting paid part, but the alley part might as well have been Chinese.

"If you really wanna get paid, you have to master the art of game."

Now he was talking my language.

"The long con is the best con, and the White man has been doing it for at least twenty centuries.

Akbar might as well have been speaking Chinese.

"Alexander the Great was schooled by priests at the ancient Egyptian mystery schools over two thousand years ago. Our people, ones who looked like me and you, the indigenous Africans, educated young Alexander for seven years. He took the knowledge back to Greece. Armed with the knowledge we gave him, he brought his now civilized troops back and raped Mother Egypt. After conquering her, the Greeks stole the Egyptians' land, their accomplishments and contributions to civilization, and worst, they stole their identity."

Crackers ain't shit, I thought.

"The White man understood that knowledge is power. The books he didn't steal from our great libraries, he burned; all part of the identity rape. We have never had counseling. We are still to this day sick, sick, sick." Akbar paused, taking a breath.

If church were like this, I'd be there every Sunday, I thought.

"They changed the truth in our storybooks into being his storybooks. This is how they keep the masses ignorant and divided. This is how they kept and continue to keep us subservient. You follow me?"

"I think so." I nodded.

"Once you know where to go, someone in the know has to show you the way."

Okay, he done went Chinese on me again, I thought.

"When I talk about the best con, the long con, I'm simply talking about an education. It is the key, with truth, knowledge, and overstanding, not understanding. Always go over, not under." Akbar made an arc with his arm. "You're on the same playing field as the man who conned you into selling your brothers into slavery, the man who is using your ignorance to control you.

Ain't nobody got no control over me. He got me twisted, I said to myself.

"You wanna really get paid?"

I nodded.

"Learn the why, and the how will follow."

I halfway understood his English, but this wasn't 1954; it was 1984, and he had already got his. Like Malcolm, by any means necessary, I had to get mine.

He didn't realize what was going on in my world. I knew all about oppression and how the White man kept his foot on our necks. That's why I had to keep running. Couldn't let the neck-pressin' foot catch up to me. Gettin' paid was the key, and I was finding new doors every day.

CHAPTER 8

It had been twenty-one months. In three weeks, Tarik would be released.

I was making chump change spinning records at school and doing parties, but I had never done a party the size of the one we were preparing for Tarik. His mom rented out the boys club gym. We passed out flyers announcing the "Bomb Jam," featuring the Gap Band on Saturday, August 29, 1985.

Tarik was my main man. Nothing was too good for him, so instead of charging five dollars to get in, I was only charging three. That was an awesome deal, considering everybody thought the Gap Band was gon' be there. What I actually meant by the flyers was that there would be a gap in the area where a band was supposed to perform.

On Friday, the twenty-eighth, Tarik came home. We didn't hook up until that night. He had to deal with baby momma drama. From what he had told me in his letters, Meon, the girl he met at the mall, and her family were creepy and cooky, mysterious and ooky. They were the black Addams family. Meon had been scared to death when she found out she was pregnant.

Her family was strict, Watchtower totin,' knock on your door, look in the window, hide in the bushes Jehovah's Witnesses. They had long ago forbid their daughter to see Tarik. Already under brain-pounding stress and stomach-churning fear, Tarik's arrest took her over the edge. After breaking down and telling her parents that she was pregnant, she sent a letter to Tarik in juvey telling him the same.

Although fornication was strictly forbidden, so was abortion. Meon's parents had no choice but to accept the fact that their baby was having a baby, but they placed all the blame on Tarik. He was lucky to have been in the security of juvenile detention. If Meon's ex-line backer, pro football-playing, six-foot, forever tall father would have gotten hold of him, it would be a lot of hymn singin' and flower bringin'. Meon was from a prosperous family that didn't hobnob with those who were darker than a grocery bag and were economically challenged. Tarik and Meon were doomed from the get go.

Tarik used to ride his bike at night way across town to the predominately White area of Buckhead to see Meon. He would remove the double screen and sneak into her unlocked bedroom window. His luck ran out one night when Meon's mother tipped out the house to sneak a smoke.

While sitting on the steps in her nightgown, trying to suck all the nicotine out the cigarette screwed into her lips, Meon's mom jumped at the rustling sound she heard over by the side of the house. She stumbled as she tried to catwalk toward her daughter's bedroom. She almost swallowed half of the burnt-out cigarette in her mouth as she tripped over the red ten-speed hiding in the grass.

As Tarik had one leg coming out the window of Meon's bedroom, her mother's night-frightening high-pitched screams went through the window, the doors, the roof, and to the next block. Tarik came through the window like he had a rocket in his butt. Still screaming loud enough to break glass, Meon's mom almost broke her ass as Tarik about bowled her over trying to get to his bike.

That night was the beginning of the end.

Even after Tarik was locked up, Meon continued to act up. One day, the football coach at Meon's school left his playbook in the locker room, so he jogged to get it. Once inside, he found Meon sandwiched between his quarterback and star receiver in the shower.

Meon's father blamed the school system for his daughter's behavior. Although they weren't together, her father knew Tarik loved his daughter from her dandruffed scalp to her baby toenails. He knew the news would crush Tarik, so he sent Tarik a copy of the school report along with Meon's expulsion order.

Tarik told me that once he read the letter from Meon's cheesy, jive-ass daddy, tears welled up in his eyes and his head was about to explode. He couldn't believe the funky-flipside bitch had played him and herself. Before he knew what he was doing he was banging his fist on the concrete wall of his cell. If it weren't for thoughts of his son, he would have easily broken his knuckles or worse. Thoughts of his son strangled any thoughts he had of killin' the bitch. The storm in his head had broken and the tears were raining down his face. He just wanted to hold his little one in his arms.

That's exactly what he did as soon as he was released; he went straight over to see his son. Tarik's son, Sean, was the only reason I didn't see him until later on during the night of his release, but when we caught up, it was as if we'd just kicked it the day before.

"What up, my nigga? Damn. Dog, you done got big as a mothafucka. Hercules on steroids and shit," Li'l Man joked, bear-huggin' Tarik.

"What happened to that little pygmy, squeeze-the-Charmin soft runt with the weak fight game?" Tarik asked.

"Oh, that nigga wit' dat man you call yo' momma," Li'l Man said.

"I heard them protein booty injections get you pumped like you on 'roids," I said.

"All bullshit aside, Linc, I got somethin' I gotta tell you," Tarik said.

My forehead creased into serious mode. "What's up?"

Tarik slumped over, dropped his shoulders, and shook his head.

"What's up, man? What happened?" I asked.

Tarik put one hand on my shoulder. "A long time ago, it was a windy day, the bush was blowing, and she only charged fifteen cents. I felt sorry for her. I had change for a quarter, and, well, let's just say you were conceived in the bushes. I'm your daddy," he said, nodding.

I hit him in the chest; Li'l Man went up under his legs. Before we knew it, we were on the ground wrestling.

"Say, big-ass nigga, all them muscles don't mean shit. I'll still whip that ass," Li'l Man joked from the bottom of the pile.

Each of us had grown and changed during the last two years. I had lost my baby fat, although I was still on the healthy side; Li'l Man had beanstalked, and Tarik looked like a black Hulk Hogan.

"So, what's been up wit' ya since lasterday?" Tarik asked with tears of joy in his eyes.

"Ah, same old, same old. Lincoln still hustlin' the stink out of shit. Me, man, I been busy beating the bitches off. What can I say? Hoes got style these days." Li'l Man massaged his mustache. "It ain't like the old beg-a-bitch days when you were king."

"Nigga, I should be getting royalties off every piece of pussy you get. I taught you the pimp game," Tarik said.

"Nigga, you taught me the simp game. 'Bay-bee, you got butterfly eyes and dill pickle toes.' You talkin' 'bout that lame-ass shit," Li'l Man said, imitating Tarik.

"On the fo' reala though, we've been through a lot together. We've been up, we've been down, but no matter what, we've stayed together. Y'all my niggas and I love you both. That's why we all 'bout to blow up like Hiroshima. Peep this."

Li'l Man and I were all ears as Tarik proceeded.

"When I went down, I shared a room with this cat named Bobby C. Although he had a murder beef, he was cotton candy. Others peeped his card as well. A coupla kids started pressin' him for commissary. Bobby always had money on his books, phat sneakers on his feet, and much groceries in his locker.

"At first I was like it ain't none o' my bi'ness, and I told myself that I wasn't getting involved. Hell, I had problems of my own. But early one morning, I was dreamin' 'bout goin' up in the Jet centerfold of the week. Man, I'm 'bout to bust when two tough-looking cats barge into my cell, giving my cellie a list of shit they wanted from commissary: Doritos, toothpaste, beef sausages, all types of shit. I didn't know if these dudes were retarded or just stupid, waking me up, disrespecting my space and shit. They jacked my whole nut off. Bobby told 'em he was short on money. One thug got all up in Bobby's face and bitch-slapped him.

"I guess that was even too much for lame-ass Bobby. He locked up with the dude and the other kid jumped in to help his partner, kidney punchin' Bobby. I jumped down from my bunk and said, 'Oh hell, naw. Ain't gonna be no gangin' up in here.'

"One of the cats said, 'Bobby, who's your new bitch? Maybe he ought to take care of this.' Then he balled up the commissary list and hit me in the nose with it.

"So I said, 'Let's step into the shower. Ain't no room in here and we don't wanna get caught.' Then side by side, me and Bobby walked down the corridor to the bathroom with our adversaries trailing. I made a big mistake, stepping into the shower with my back turned. Next thing I knew I was on a collision course with the moldy, discolored, doo-doo brown shower floor. I had been sucker-punched in the back of my head. I swiveled left just in time, dodging a kick to the head.

"When the guy with the bad kick misfired, it was over. I got up, smushed his face in the wall, and kicked the other punk to sleep. From then on, I looked out for Bobby. He was a'ight, just scared. Bobby threw me for a loop when he told me Blue was his brother."

"Blue?" I asked.

"Yeah. Big GripMoney Blue."

"Blue with the cream Bentley?" Li'l Man asked.

"Yep."

Blue was the man, one of the biggest dope boys in the ATL. A celebrity, he came up slingin' in the hood like most thoroughbreds.

"Word got out that I was looking out for his little brother," Tarik continued. "See, Bobby C was the only family Blue had. He even wrote thanking me. When I got out, he promised he'd put me on.

"Blue didn't waste time getting in contact with me. He's treating us to a night out tonight. Don't worry, I told him all about you lames," Tarik said.

Blue picked us up in a cocaine-white Sedan Deville limo. We pulled into an underground garage at the Palisades Condominiums off Fourteenth and Peachtree. He had a penthouse on the sixteenth floor. When we walked into the apartment, six half-booty-butt-naked, super-fine pinkies awaited us.

We started the evening sitting on two white polar bear rugs. Tarik, Blue, and the hoes snorted up Peru while Li'l Man and I smoked some killer herb. We partied like it was going out of style, two freaky white girls for each of us.

The next day, before Blue dropped us off, he gave Tarik a small black leather satchel. "Don't look inside. I set you up with three hundred-and-thirty-rock bombs. Bring me back a G." Blue spoke as if Li'l Man and I weren't in the limo.

"Man, this is the break we been lookin' for," Tarik said, staring at the black future in his hands.

"Prove it," Blue said.

"You ain't gotta worry 'bout that. I'm a real nigga."

"I know. That's why I'm holdin' you responsible if anything goes wrong."

I wanted to say something, but Tarik's eyes told me to keep my mouth closed.

Blue continued, "There's one code in this game: Silence. There's one rule: Honor."

This was some ol' black Scarface gangsta shit. I wasn't feelin' this scene. I'd seen too many movies. If something happened to the Man's money, the money handler would be found floatin' in a river. No, I was doing just fine being my own boss, doing small parties and selling candy. Li'l Man, on the other hand, saw this as his ticket to moving him and his sister out the projects. After seeing how Blue lived, my dogs were hooked.

CHAPTER 9

Li'l Man and I saw less and less of each other as time passed. We remained close, though. Tarik and Li'l Man were gettin' paid pimpin' crack while I was gettin' faded simpin' candy.

They moved to Lennox Villas in the high-rent, artsy-fartsy area of North Atlanta. Li'l Man was rollin' so hard he dropped out of school the beginning of our senior year. He went out and bought a tricked-out six series Beamer the day he got his license. At least he was smart enough to drive around with Tarik in a beat-up Oldsmobile so as not to attract attention from five-O while they worked.

I wasn't doing so well. I had been put out of school repeatedly for either selling something or fighting for something that was related to what I was selling. The coup de grace was when this nerdy-looking white kid parked his junkyard-reject, jaundice-yellow Honda behind the red Firebird I'd bought. It just so happened that I'd heard him before I saw him. He might as well have had a neon sign on his car that read: *My stereo system is worth more than my car. Steal me.* On top of that, this fool had plastic taped to a small, triangular, busted-out side window on the passenger's side.

Opportunity was knocking. I had to answer. As I watched this nerd, I was already making plans for my stereo system that was in his car. He had some nice three-way six-by-nine speakers that weren't even mounted. They sat in the back window just waiting for me to give them another home.

I cautiously approached the car after the owner was in class. I noticed a nice digital pullout Alpine that would complement my car. I changed my mind and decided to go to class. I had all day.

I had almost forgotten about the system when I saw the kid who drove the car at lunch. Afterward, I requested a restroom pass from my fifth-period math teacher. After being excused from class, I sneaked out of school and snatched everything. I wasn't in the car but two minutes.

I had just started my last class of the day and had less than forty-five minutes until the final bell when I was called to the vice-principal's office. The V.P., Mr. Ben, was notorious for being an asshole.

Why I hadn't just gotten in my car and left, I don't know. It didn't take a rocket scientist to figure out I'd been busted.

"What were you doing outside during fifth period?"

"I thought I left my lights on in my car."

"So why'd you get a restroom hall pass?"

"Because I had to pee first."

Mr. Ben pressed the intercom button, alerting his secretary. "Ms. Henry, would you please send Mr. Allen into my office?"

I never knew his name. All the kids called him Cottontop. He was a one-man security force. Around the time of Jesus's birth, he'd been a muscularly built man, but that had all turned to fat. Now he looked like Santa in a security suit. His body followed his stomach as he made his way into the office. He stood at attention in front of Mr. Ben's desk.

"Mr. Allen, tell me what you saw around 1:15 today."

"Well, I was making my rounds when I noticed someone in the math hallway. By the time I got to the end of the hall, he was gone. I turned to the window and saw this boy," he aimed a stubby fat finger at me, "gettin' out of a yeller Honda with somethin' in his hands. Next, he opened the trunk of a red Ponchac Fi'bird, and put whatever he stole inside. By then I was out the door and peeking at him from a good li'l distance behind some burshes. After the boy done come back inside the school, I realized that he'd broken into the yeller car and stole somebody's raytcho."

"He's a racist liar," I said.

"Who you think you talking to like that, boy?" Cottontop got all up in my face, huffin' and puffin', breath smelling like skunk death.

He was too close to my face and had called me one too many boys. I hauled off and hit his racist ass dead in his grill. After a stunned second, he covered his mouth with one paw and attempted to grab me with the other. I was too fast, but not fast enough to get out of the school ahead of the two cops running in, who grabbed, cuffed, and hauled me off to jail.

When we got down to the station, the police released me because the car's owner, Roger Smith, not only refused to press charges, but denied having anything stolen out of his car. Still, I was not only kicked out of Southwest DeKalb High School, but I was expelled from the entire DeKalb County school system.

Expulsion didn't stop me from coming back up to the school grounds the next day. I saw him headin' toward his ride after school.

"Yo, wait up partna," I hollered while jogging over.

"Yo, what up, playa?" Roger slurred like a brother.

"I got your system."

"Keep it."

"What? Why you didn't drop dime on me to the police?"

"Shit, I'd just stole the mothafucka last week from the faculty parkin' lot."

"Ah, man, that's wild." We both laughed, slapping five.

When Momma found out what happened, her reaction surprised me. Instead of fussing, throwing something, or putting me on restriction, she just cried.

Akbar was a whole different story. Momma called him. He was sitting in the dining room when I came home from seeing Roger.

"Why do you insist on constantly taking your mother through hell? I really wish you'd use your head for more than a hat rack sometimes. Can't you see it isn't meant for you to do wrong because every time, every damn time, you get caught? Son, Allah has a plan for you. I mean look at you. You're intelligent. You can be a force in the struggle. You're a born leader. At the rate you're going, you'll end up in jail or hell. Is that what you want?" Akbar's eyes were filled with tears.

"Man, I don't know." I shrugged. "Sometimes I don't even care what happens to me. I'm just trying to get ahead of the game."

"The game? The game? How many times do I have to tell you that without a good education your chances are slim to none at getting past Baltic, let alone Park Place, and slim just died. The only spot you'll get to in the game is to chance, and when you pull a card, it'll be a go to jail card, and there won't be any dice to roll to get out."

He was serious, but that was funny, and I couldn't help but smirk.

"Let me put it to you this way; you have to learn how to cohabit and work within the structure. In it, there are rules made by those who are in control. Now, if you, with no power, break the rules, then those with the power will bury you inside the structure. If you want some control and power then you have to work within it and absorb all the knowledge you can until you can build a strong foundation."

Although I had no idea what he was saying, I nodded anyway.

"When you get power, then you can buck the rules and implement change, reforming the structure. Lincoln, when will you see that you're part of the Black man's problem and part of the power structure's solution?" Akbar paused, shaking his head.

"I don't know."

"So, what do you plan to do about school?"

"What can I do?" I shrugged.

"If I can get you admitted to another school, would you be interested?"

"Yeah, man—I mean sir. I'd really appreciate that, and I promise you won't be sorry." I tried to put some enthusiasm into my voice after the heat Akbar just put on me.

"I have a friend who has connections with a company that runs four alternative schools for young adults such as yourself. Now, if I do this for you and you mess up, I'm through, so if you have any reservations about straightening up your act and going back to school, now is the time to let me know."

I knew Akbar cared about me, and I had no doubt that he meant every word. If I messed this up, even though Akbar loved me and all, he would surely cut me off.

I stood up. "I know what I'm gon' do, and I know what I have to do. You've got my word, I won't let you or Momma down."

With a pained look, Akbar said, "You still don't understand. You're not letting us down. You're letting yourself down."

CHAPTER 10

St. Luke's Area III Learning Center was on the top floor of a homeless shelter and soup kitchen turned into a makeshift high school for problem kids. If it weren't for the church next door that owned it, the nine-room upper level would have been condemned. St. Luke's Episcopal Church on Peachtree had donated the space. The school was overcrowded with a 150 to 175 students at any given time, ranging in age from fourteen to twenty.

One of the greatest men who ever lived was Dr. Albert Smith. Round and bald, he was minister, principal, counselor, and father to the students. Roughly six feet, three-fifty, and in his early fifties, he was lovingly known as Smitty. Akbar and Smitty had been friends for more than twenty years. They did time together for refusing to serve in Vietnam.

A prerequisite for attending any Fulton County School was to live in that county. I didn't, so Akbar toed the legal line and put my name on the lease of one of his rental properties in the area.

I was scared as a diamond-downed white woman in the projects on a Saturday night. I pulled into the gravel dirt lot behind the school. I figured I'd pull three to six years for second-degree manslaughter if I ran over the beehive of spray bottle sprayin', dirty rag, window wiping, Night of the Living Dead, shopping cart dragging zombies surrounding my Firebird.

"I ain't got no money, but I got three bullets in my nine," I bluffed, getting out the car with my hand in my book bag.

They scattered like roaches with the light turned on as soon as I got out the car. They would've gotten rich if they'd been selling incense, the way they had the area stinking. Damn, they had the whole area smelling like three-day-dead wolf ass.

The soup line was fenced around the building. I was nervous about leaving my car. I made the alarm sound twice so they'd all see I had one. Walking up metal stairs with my hand shielding my nose and mouth from the stench, I asked, "Where's Dr. Smith's office?"

"Smitty?" one of the three kids smoking cigarettes at the top of the stairs responded.

"I don't know, man. Yo, they just told me to go talk to Mr. Smith."

"You gon' be comin' here?" a tall, slim brotha with an eight-inch 'fro and a grill full of fool's gold asked.

"I don't know." I shrugged.

"Whatchu here fo' then?"

"You gon' tell me where I can find Dr. Smith or what?"

"Where you from?" Afro asked, jerking his neck.

"I'm from the Deck, dog."

"Nigga, what? So the fuck what you from Decatur. That supposed to make me scared or somethin'?"

"Man, you asked me. I don't want no drama. I'm just tryin' to get back in school."

"Nigga, I'm from the projects of Techwood, where real niggas reside. Why you tryin' to come to my school, anyway?" Afro asked, standing on the last step with one hand on the black rail and the other one on the door, blocking my way.

"You probably seened it on the news." I twitched my neck to the left and started wildly blinking. "I'm da one just got out, nigga".

Blink.

Twitch.

"Fo' killing my daddy with a rusty nail. Stabbin'-'im-stabbin'-'im-stabbin'-'im!"

Blink.

Twitch.

Blink.

Twitch.

"Thew da eyes." I smiled wide-eyed and gently rubbed my crossed arms, drooling onto my chin. "Thew da mu'fuckin' eyes, my nigga." Drool was dripping off my chin as I wildly smiled.

Afro almost got ran over by his co-conspirators as they rushed into the building. I Freddy Kruegered in right behind them, looking for the principal's office.

"Excuse me, Mr. Smith?" I asked after reading the brass nameplate on his cluttered, chipped desk. He reared back in a big green vinyl chair, sporting an unlit cigar in his mouth.

"My father was Mr. Smith. He's been worm food for over five years now. If you're addressing me, call me Smitty or Doc."

"Sorry, Smitty. I'm Lincoln Jackson. Akbar sent me."

"I know who you are, and I don't care if Ronald Reagan sent you. I'll ask you one time; why are you in my house?"

I stood in the doorway wondering what kind of trip this dude was on. My house? Hell, this was a school. This cat was playing games.

"I'm just trying to get back in school and make somethin' of myself."

"Why should I let you in? Why should I give you another chance?"

What did he want me to say?

"I have twenty too many make-somethin'-of-myself-give-me-one-mo'-chance knuckleheads already."

Why did Akbar even send me here? I wondered.

"What makes you so special?"

"I thought—" Before I could finish, Smitty stood, resting his humongous belly over his desk.

"Do you know who Lit was?" he asked.

"No, sir."

"Lit thought like you. He thought he pissed, but he shit."

I knew I was on my last leg, but I wasn't going to just sit back while this cat talked to me like some rooty-poot. Fuck this school. He wasn't 'bout to let me in no way.

"I messed up. I keep letting my folks down. Whether you let me in your school or not, I ain't gon' end up like them folks downstairs." I was set to jet when Smitty held out a leg-sized arm.

"As you young folks say, keep it real. That's all I ask. Do that, and we'll get along fine."

Dropping my Huey Newton posture, I asked, "So, I'm in?"

"Yes, but understand this."

There's always a "but," and if his "but" was a quarter of the size of the two dresses he'd attached together to make the pants he had on, I was in trouble.

"I'm the Big Kahuna. King Fish. HNIC. Captain Kirk. Get it?"

"Yes, sir," I said, with a smile.

Smitty returned to his seat before he continued.

"We are a close-knit family. I'm Daddy, and Momma don't live here. You have a hundred and seventy-three brothers and sisters, black, white, and yellow. I expect you to treat everyone with the same respect you treat me. Now, go around the corner down the hall, find Shirley's office, and tell her who you are. She knows you're coming. We've been expecting you."

"Thanks, Smitty." I waved.

I walked down a shabby hall with gray peeling walls and once-red carpet. I stopped and turned to an anorexic-looking white kid standing off to himself, looking as if he were lost in thought. He looked worse than the folks downstairs.

"What up? I'm Lincoln," I said, interrupting his world.

"Hey, man. Buddy." He grabbed my hand in his and tried to shake the skin off.

I pulled my hand back before he dislodged it from my arm.

"Where's Shirley's office?"

"Follow me, bud. I'll lead the way." He military marched down the hallway. Whatever he was on, it couldn't be legal.

Later on, I found out that at twenty, Buddy Graham was the oldest kid in school. He was a recovering heroin addict, and had been on the streets since he was fifteen. Smitty and the kids were his only family.

He led me to a closet with a desk and a couple of chairs inside.

"Toni, baby, sweetheart, love of my life, mother of all my unborn kids, how are you this fucked-up morning?" Buddy was a nut, but you couldn't help but like him.

"I see you're back to sniffing Elmer's finest," Toni teased.

Buddy introduced me to a vision of love.

"Hi. I'm Latonia Gresham. Don't pay him no mind," she said, swatting the air. "As a baby, the hospital performed drop tests on him."

I was gone. Her voice: sensuous Dandridge, deep Holiday, smooth Baker, street Hyman. Latonia Gresham and Sade could have been sisters. Toni had my hormones on spin dry.

"Huh? Excuse me? What did you say?" I stood there cave-mouthed, and marble eyed. I shook my head and closed my cave before she had me put in a backward jacket.

"I'm sorry. I was supposed to see Shirley."

"I'll get her." Toni grabbed her books and drifted out the office. She was so sexy she made my heart hurt.

"Go head and have a seat," she offered from the hall.

Ignoring her, I puppied behind her until we reached a sign that read WOMEN. After realizing the fool I was

84

making of myself, I slithered back to Shirley's office and took a seat.

After I met Shirley, filled out papers and took a placement test, Toni showed me around.

"What's up with this school?" I asked Toni.

"This is my second year here. It's the last stop. We got hookers, junkies, abused kids and juvenile delinquents here."

She showed me the classrooms and offices and even introduced me to a few people. I was so captivated by Toni that I walked right into Smitty.

"I see you've got good taste," Smitty said. "You all right with me if you all right with Toni. Between us, she don't like men too tough."

Toni hit Smitty in the arm. "Well, if I don't like men, I guess I'll have to stop going across the street to the hospital, getting you lunch every day."

He winked at me. "Okay. Dang. Girl, you know I'd roll over and die without you."

Ms. Heard the English teacher, Mr. Baker the math teacher, Mr. Terrell the history teacher, and Mr. Hill the everything else teacher gathered around me.

I haven't been here long enough to do anything, I thought as I watched the teachers watching me.

"It's a doggone shame that someone as smart as you has been wasting his time getting kicked out of school. You've scored in the genius category on this test," Mr. Baker announced.

I knew I wasn't dumb, but I wasn't a Benjamin Banneker either. School had never been difficult. I never had to study, and doing homework was against my religion. A genius? Nah, these folks had me mixed up.

The teachers were mad cool. They didn't put on airs. They cursed, they told yo' momma jokes and everything. The kids talked to them about anything. At St. Luke's the teachers really cared. They even took a special interest in me. They gave me props in front of the whole class when I made good grades. They made me feel so good that by my third month I changed my religion. I was studying and doing homework. By the third quarter I was making A's and B's in my college prep classes.

I became sort of like a big brother to most of the kids, even the older ones. Buddy rubbed off on me. I couldn't believe I'd become so tight with a white boy. We were different colors, but we came from the same crayon box. All of us did. We were all deemed as outcasts by society.

As good as my word to myself, Toni became my angel, my first love. We were a lot alike. Toni came from a broken home. She was homeless at thirteen, and a seasoned teenage prostitute by the age of fourteen. Her father was MIA, and her mother was somewhere strung out on any drug she could get. Toni robbed her tricks more often than she tricked off with them. She could game and hustle the best. One morning when she was fifteen, she woke up in a strange seedy motel with a black eye and a swollen lip. She had no idea what happened the night before. Then and there she decided to change her life before someone ended it. She remembered the name of a school that an old girlfriend who'd gotten out of the game told her about. A couple days later, she'd found the school, and here she was.

Toni was a year older and ten years more mature than me. She also saw something in me even I didn't recognize: she saw good.

I spent so much time with Toni that I hardly ever saw Li'l Man or Tarik. I quit selling candy because the school was too small and everybody was broke. So, out the candy business, I was in the hot car radios, rims, seats, and whatever business. I was doing all right, especially since Toni split the profits she didn't smoke up from her weed sales.

Early in the year, Toni wrote an essay on world peace for a national contest for high school students.

The ten winners would represent the United States in an international conference in Hong Kong. The purpose was to discuss the present state of affairs in each group's respective country and to find ways to a more peaceful co-existence.

Seven months passed, and Toni had forgotten all about the contest, but right after my seventeenth birthday, Smitty received a telegram from the United Nations Department of Special Affairs. To almost everyone's surprise, Toni was chosen as a U.S. representative to the World Peace Future Leaders Conference.

I wasn't surprised because I had read the essay, and that thing was the bomb. After all, she was my girl. On the real, though, Toni was unique in that she was a PYT and YGB—pretty, young thing and young, gifted, and black. She knew what she wanted and what it would take to get it.

Toni left for her ten-day journey to the Orient in mid-June. As soon as the plane departed from Hartsfield headed for La Guardia, I began to miss her. Ten days without my baby was going to be rough. We had been inseparable through the year.

Toni was gone and school was out. I decided to catch up with my boys. Some days I wondered where I would be if I had quit school and started rolling with Li'l Man and Tarik. I always came to the same conclusion: If I had dropped out I would never have met Toni, and no amount of money could make me as happy as I was when I was with her.

Li'l Man pulled up in an old, raggedy-looking, rust-colored Regal to the Dairy Queen on Wesley Chapel, where I hung out sometimes

"What up, my nigga?" he shouted over an Edward J tape blasting "Planet Rock."

"Where'd you get that big, ugly-ass hoopty? Never thought you'd find a ride that matched your face," I joked, climbing in.

"Dog, you know how it is. I can't be driving none of my cat traps during bi'ness hours. Besides, five-O ain't gon' sweat a nigga in this."

"I hear ya, dog."

"I can't wait to show you my new spot."

We rode out to his phat crib and pulled into a four-door garage as big as the apartment I grew up in. My boy was straight gettin' paid. He had two phat Beamers and a custom cocaine-white convertible doped-out Z.

Inside, the house looked like something straight out of Home and Garden. The kitchen boasted white Italian marble countertops, black oak cabinets, and a stainless-steel electric range along with a matching double-door extra-wide fridge.

The sunken living room had a rounded greystone fireplace and a cathedral ceiling. The three-bedroom house was nice-nasty and funkniciously furnished. I walked around, not believing my eyes. I knew my dog was getting money, but damn, I had no idea he had it going on like that.

As if reading my mind, Li'l Man explained that the house had belonged to Blue, and the tag on it was 250 Gs.

"Man, you got that kind of loot?" I asked, whistling.

"Not on me." He patted his pockets. "All I pay is twenty-one hun a month. Blue only charged me thirty grand to assume his loan."

Thirty grand.

"He turned me on to a tax lawyer who helped me and Bay-Bay get the crib the legal way. I put the house in her name."

"She's cool with you bein' in the game and shit? I asked.

"Not really. She worries and shit, but she likes the life I provide for us. Hell, we came a long way from living in the projects, cooking stolen hot dogs on candle fire and shit."

"Yeah, I remember those days." I nodded.

"If the folks come down on me they can't touch the house. The cars, I just left them under the previous owners' names. I never took the titles to DMV."

In ten days of running around with Li'l Man and Tarik, I learned more about business, finance, public relations, and customer service than school had ever taught me. We rode around exchanging Ziploc bags of rocks for brown paper sacks of money. We went from project to project. Wherever Li'l Man and Tarik's workers were, we ended up. Between stops we would sometimes have to go to one of the two houses they rented for cooking, cutting, and bagging dope.

Tarik was the chef. His ingredients were cocaine, baking soda, and water. He used glass cookware to turn cocaine into crack.

While Tarik cooked, Li'l Man oversaw the college girls who cut and bagged the chipped-tooth-looking crack rocks.

Li'l Man and Tarik had a great arrangement. The girls lived rent and bill free. It was a smooth system. Some days they didn't even make it home, staying out all night picking up, dropping off, and prepping blow. They got a lot of respect not only from their workers, but from everyone in the hood.

They didn't count money until the weekends. Sunday was Blue day. That was tally-up time, the day Blue was paid off. I had never in my life seen so much money the Sunday I helped. It took Bay-Bay, Li'l Man, Tarik and me over an hour to separate money into its respective denominations. It took another three to count it and rubber band it. The biggest problem was dollar bills. We counted more than six thousand singles. I think they made more than eighty-two grand that week.

The second weekend I was with them was Fourth of July weekend. Their workers ran us ragged. Li'l Man and Tarik's beepers were going off like police sirens. Every time we left one spot, another spot was beeping. They told me this was normal for the first of the month. Tarik called the first of every month Mother's Day because babies' mommas received their welfare checks and food stamps. Social Security checks arrived on the third of the month.

The poor stayed poor because they were the biggest spenders. Cocaine, weed, and alcohol were their ways to escape their own private hells. We were like doctors healing the sick.

"The projects are a dope man's paradise. Where else can a black man be king?" Tarik asked.

So that Tarik and Li'l Man wouldn't be forced to carry around trunkloads of cash, Bay-Bay met them in the streets to pick up money and take it to their stash spot.

Finally, that Monday night, we had a chance to take a break, or so I thought. We went to Li'l Man's house, where a carload of money awaited us. It was spread out all over Li'l Man's extra-large glass table. It made the prior week's take look like lunch money. I counted so much money that I lost track of time.

"Two hundred nineteen thousand, eight hundred and forty-seven dollars. Damn," I exclaimed to no one in particular.

A hundred and fifty thou went to Blue. Still, that left almost $70,000 for Li'l Man and Tarik. They were so happy about the week's outcome that they gave me $4,847. I was already spending it in my head.

"If this don't tempt my tummy, all this damn money," I said, fanning my face with a handful of bills.

"Nah, shawty, you doing the right thing. You got to get that degree, baby. Stay where you at," Tarik said, waving his index finger back and forth.

Tarik must've read my mind. I was tempted to never grace the doors of any school again, but if I did, I could never face Momma or Akbar. I could hear Akbar now; "A man's word is the only thing that no one can take, and keeping it is the sign of ultimate self-respect."

I made a promise to him, Momma, and to myself. Resisting temptation was hard as hell. Temptation was a motha for ya. Li'l Man didn't make it no easier, especially when he let me drive his snowflake-triple-white, chromed-out convertible down Fair Street, slow-rollin' by Spelman and Morehouse.

I felt like Superfly as the bass dropped from Keith Sweat's new jam, "Make It Last Forever." You could hear us two blocks away. I know the infirmary must've been overflowin' the next day with hoes sufferin' from chickenneckitis. Li'l Man was laid back, chillin' in the passenger seat, sportin' some dark-shaded Ray Bans. I was proposed to, kissed at, propositioned, and begged for a ride.

Once we left and I came down off my King Kong horse, I realized that it had been the car and what it represented—money—that attracted the women. But, at that particular time, I was seventeen, didn't have a cat trap, and was very much in love.

The attention I received from driving such a slammin' ride had me so messed up that I bought an Auto Trader car magazine and searched for a cat trap. Once I saw it, I had to have the 7-year-old RX7. It was white with a wide-body kit and a Porsche whaletail on the back. I didn't drive it two blocks before I parted with $4,500. The white honeycomb BBS rims were worth more than a G alone. The car even had butter bean beige Racaro racing seats.

I bought it the same day Toni was coming home. I met her just as she came out the gate. Even though she was no doubt dead tired, she still looked like honey.

"Baby, I missed you so much," I said, hugging her.

"I missed you too."

"I can't tell."

"Why you say that?"

"Baby, you s'posed to be pasted all over me. Instead, you got the ghost face."

"I'm sorry, Lincoln." She shook her head. "Long flight."

Once we left baggage claim and got to the parking lot, I said, "Baby, check our new ride out."

She smiled.

"Yeah, yeah, yeah. Tight, right?" I opened the passenger side door.

"It's nice."

Nice? Shoes are nice. An outfit is nice. My car ain't nice. It's the shit. And all she could say was "it's nice."

Minutes after leaving the airport, my prize, my Porsche-like Mazda coughed a couple times before going into screaming, vibrating convulsions. Within minutes my cat trap was dead.

I should have been the poster boy of the month for Charms lollipops.

I could hear Momma now; "Boy, that's why nothing goes right. You always trying to be like the Joneses." Now I was stuck with a lemon and sitting beside a sour grape.

Toni was always the one with an answer, always the one to add two dollars and two cents to any dilemma, but not that day. She offered nothing. It was as if she was just waiting for me to stop cursing myself out. After deliberating, I got out and had Toni steer while I pushed the car down the street.

I paged Li'l Man and Tarik from the mini-mart payphone. Tarik called right back, and thirty minutes later some booty-looking crackhead broad picked us up. We dropped Toni off and were on the way to have my Mazda towed when this broad told me that Tarik said to give her ten dollars. That was bullshit. Tarik would have already straightened the crackhead.

"You got me fucked up with one of your tricks. You can't run boo game on me, trick-ass ho."

She drove the rest of the way in steamy silence. When she dropped me off I gave her a ten spot anyway, only 'cause I felt bad for doggin' the ho. I knew she was just going to smoke the ten spot up along with whatever Tarik was gon' give her.

I ended up having my car towed to Joe's Auto Kare. I figured it was bad. I was stunned when the mechanic told me I needed an engine. He said a Frankenstein backyard mechanic had recently doctored the engine with sawdust and old parts to keep it running just long enough for a car-happy sucker like me.

I was stuck like chuck since I bought the car as-is. But if I ever ran into the cat who got me, he'd never eat solid food again.

At least I still had ol' Raggedy-Red, my Firebird. I almost considered selling it or just letting a junkyard have the Mazda, but I thought about them hoes and how they had hounded me when I was in Li'l Man's ride. Them hoes, I couldn't let them down. I had to sell Raggedy Red to help pay for a transmission and engine.

The phone rang as I was leaving the house to meet Li'l Man to borrow some money.

"Lincoln, Toni's on the phone!" Marnease shouted.

"Damn, girl, a nigga ain't deaf."

"I didn't have to call you. Hurry up, boy. I'm expecting an important call."

"Yeah, baby. Wha's up?" I said to Toni.

"Lincoln, I really did miss you."

"I missed you too, baby."

"I know you're busy, but when you get a chance, I need to see you. I don't care what time you come."

"What's up, baby? I mean, tell me what this is about. It might be a while before I can get there."

"Give me the phone. I told you I was expecting a call," Marnease said as she grabbed for the phone.

"Girl, don't make me bust you in the mouth. I'll be off in a second. Damn," I snapped. "Whatchu say now?" I asked after hogging the phone back to my ear.

"I'm not telling you anything over the phone. I'll tell you everything when you get here." The cracking in her voice told me not to press the issue.

I told Toni I'd be there as soon as possible. I dropped everything and rushed over there once I got off the phone. She sat outside on the steps of her sister's apartment building with her head down. After getting out the car and walking up the stairs, I reached out. She got up and walked into my arms.

"Baby, I'm here now. Come on and tell big daddy what's bothering you. I got my tools inside," I said, pointing to my heart. "So whatever it is, Dr. Love 'Em Long Time can fix it." I tried joking to lighten the mood. Her teary eyes told me that I'd failed.

Toni looked me in the eye, and I could see a sadness that penetrated to the core of her soul. She took a long, slow, deep breath and released everything in a sporadic rush. I can't remember word for word what she said because I shut down.

"In China, out of all the American students, there were only two Blacks, me and a guy named Gene from New York." Tears flowed freely as she spoke. "We spent a lot of time together, being that we were ostracized by the white American students. Well, one evening when everyone went to dinner, I stayed back at the hotel because I didn't feel well. I guess I was drained. I don't know," she said, shrugging.

"Gene realized that I wasn't on the bus to go eat, so he stayed behind. He came to my room to check on me. We talked, I cried, he held me. One thing led to another and, and it just happened."

Huh? What the—? What? I shook my head. What was she saying?

"I haven't slept since that horrible night. I haven't had an appetite or nothin'. I couldn't go on without telling you."

Oh my God. Oh-my-God-oh-my-God-oh-my-God.

"I'm sorry. You mean everything to me. Pleeeeaaaase forgive me, Lincoln. I love you more than I love life itself."

My knees gave out. I would have fallen flat on my face if it weren't for my quick reflexes. The stair railing reached out to me just in time. After regaining half my composure and balance, I seized a crying Toni by her shoulders. "Why? Why?" I let her go, turned around, and with tears streaming down my face, walked away.

I wanted to die. My suffering was beyond the realm of understanding for my seventeen years.

I started my car and raced backwards into a parked car. I jerked the gearshift into drive and flew over the speed bumps. I lost track of time as I drove aimlessly for hours.

I wouldn't take her phone calls. I refused to see her. I tried to shut her completely out of my life. The only way I felt I could stop the suffering was to eliminate the cause of the pain.

CHAPTER 11

A few days before school started, I was playing a little three-on-three in the park. I passed my defender by penetrating through a hole in the middle. I double pumped, went under the rim to lay the ball in, and came down, missing the backboard and net. Toni's best friend, Mia, broke my concentration.

"Lincoln. Liiiiincoln," she hollered.

"What?"

"C'mere."

"Damn, girl. You don't see me playin' a game?"

"Dog, what you gon' do?" my boy holdin' the ball asked.

"Y'all go 'head. I gotta handle this," I said, walking off the court.

This wasn't the first time Toni had enlisted help to try to contact me. I couldn't face her because I knew I'd break weak and take her back. My love for her consumed every second breath I took. Tarik explained to me that Toni, like most women, was a freak. His philosophy was "get the drawers before they break yo' balls."

He said that women used their bodies, makeup, hairdos and skimpy clothes as booty traps. Once they throw that thang at you, put the poo-tang beat-down on you, then they reel your wallet in.

"Some prime, USDA, Grade A poonanny will have a brotha payin' off like a slot machine. Ching, ching," he had said.

According to Tarik, it was all a game in which you scored or got scored on. That was the very reason I couldn't break weak. I'd already been faked out, played to the left and dunked on. Mia was wasting her time.

"What's up with you?" Mia asked with her arms thrust toward me. "It don't make no damn sense, you doing that girl the way you are. You damn well know she love yo' dirty drawers."

"I can't tell."

"So what, she fucked up. What woman you know gon' tell her man she screwed somebody? Men so damn dumb," she said, shaking her head.

"Calm yo' happy ass down," I joked, trying to play off the scene she was making in front of my dogs.

"How I'm s'posed to calm down when I see my girl drunk with pain because of you?"

"Because of me? Because of me? Hell, I ain't the one who went away for two weeks and got my freak on."

"She didn't have to tell you shit. Ain't like you got a crystal ball on yo' dick."

Somebody laughed behind me.

"She told you 'cause she love you." Then all of a sudden she broke down crying.

"Save that drama," I said.

"Toni's pregnant."

"Huh?"

"You heard me. Toni's pregnant."

It took everything I had not to run and scoop Toni up in my arms. I tried to hold back the tears. I inhaled, taking one long, eclipsing blink before manning up to ask, "Who the daddy?"

"Yo' momma. Who the fuck you think? You. You know she used a rubber."

"A'ight. I'm sorry. What she wanna do?"

"She ain't tryin' to raise no baby alone."

"What? She wanna have an abortion?"

"She says it's up to you. She wants you to call her at my house."

I shook my head. "Oh, hell nah. She can have the abortion. I ain't got nothin' to say to her."

"That's fucked up. You a li'l-ass boy playin' grown man games."

"Say what you want. Tell her to call the clinic and find out how much."

"I already know. I done had two senseless abortions, but this one she havin' makes all the sense in the world."

"What you mean by that?"

"You flush shit down the toilet, and anything that come from you ain't nothin' but shit." She paused with her fists on her hips. "She needs two hundred and sixty dollars."

"Fuck you, bitch."

"Nigga, fuck you," she said, jumping in my face.

"Bitch, you best get the fuck out my face. I ain't got no time fo' this shit. Gimme a few weeks."

"Toni ain't got a few weeks." She backed up. "She already three months."

"I'll have the money by Monday. I'll give it to you at school," I said before I raced away so nobody would see the tears running down my face.

I was mad. I was angry. I was scared. I was hurt.

I sold my Alpine and Rockford Fosgate $1500 car stereo at the crackhead price of $250. I had no choice. I had to handle my business and pay my Toni bill.

That same Monday, I was called into Smitty's office.

"Close the door, son," Smitty said as I entered.

It was trouble when he called me son. One thing about Smitty, you found out quick what was on his mind. He didn't beat around the bush; he tore it down.

"All right now, what's the problem with you and my girl?"

I shrugged ignorance.

"Come on, now. Ever since school started back she's been dragging her lip on the ground. I tried to talk to her, but you know how stubborn she can be."

I smiled, thinking back to the way she poked her lip out when she didn't get her way.

"She had the audacity to tell me that she was grown and would appreciate me staying out of her business."

That was her, all right.

"I don't mind telling you that I was hurt and a little upset. I can't jump on her, but I can knock you out." He balled one of his meat hooks up at me before continuing. "Remember our little talk about this being my ship when you first walked in here?"

I nodded.

"Well, now you're rocking my boat."

My emotions had built to the bursting point, and I had held them in long enough. Smitty had a way of pushing my buttons until it all came out in a diarrhea of the soul. I told Smitty everything except the part about Toni being pregnant. He nodded in understanding while I talked. Afterwards, I felt the elephant on my back turn into a butterfly.

Smitty seemed to be contemplating something as he leaned back in his worn vinyl chair. I had to ease forward, straining to hear his gentle whispers.

"Son, now I'm not here to tell you how to live your life, but I will tell you this: It is inhumane to treat anyone other than human. As humans, we err. When we do, we have to be man or woman enough to learn from our mistakes and move on." He paused, looking me up and down. "Ask yourself, are you happy without Toni?"

Of course I wasn't.

"Ask yourself, are you letting your pride get in the way when it comes to Toni?"

Of course I was, but what else could I do?

"Lincoln, you are my son, and Toni is my daughter. I want my children to be happy and productive. Right now, neither of you fall into either category. That pains me."

Me too. I've been having heart attacks from my nose to my toes since we broke up, I thought.

"Make this right. I know you can."

As I stood to leave, he hugged me. I was speechless. I knew he was right, but I couldn't trust her. Hell, I couldn't even trust my own thoughts. I didn't even know if Toni really had an abortion. Maybe she was never even pregnant. The hurt was too much to feel. I know what I told Smitty. Everything he said was right, but this was one time, I was going to make the decision to be wrong. I'd rather deal with Smitty's disappointment in me for not being able to forgive Toni than deal with the hurt in my twisted heart.

I don't even think it was the forgiving part. Shit, I knew Toni loved me. Hell, she wouldn't have told me about the buster she slept with if she didn't. It was the forgetting part. I could never trust her 'cause I could never forget the death I died every time I closed my eyes and saw another dude inside what I thought was my sacred paradise. It was time for me to move on without her. I couldn't keep dwelling on sad yesterdays; I had to search for happy tomorrows.

In spite of everything that happened with Toni, I maintained a 3.8 grade point average and a four point ho batting average. I tornadoed through most of the fine broads at St. Luke's then broadened my horizons and moved onto what I thought would be the more challenging community of the AU campus. The college hoes turned out to be as easy as the hood rats I was used to.

I had a couple of reasons for getting my freak on so hot and heavy. I called myself getting back at Toni for one, and two, I was a big freak. I had fully adopted Tarik's "ho get 'em" philosophy.

Even with all my extracurricular activities, I managed to graduate graduating from St. Luke's with honors. For once in my life I had done something to make Momma proud.

I penguin-strutted to the podium at the historic Hunter Street Baptist Church, where Dr. Martin Luther King's closest friend, Ralph David Abernathy, presided. Momma could have gotten a role in a Colgate commercial the way she beamed as she watched her oldest boy, who most thought would never live to this point, let alone graduate high school with honors. It felt damn good seeing her, Marnease, D'Andre, Tarik, and Li'l Man applauding, while Akbar kneeled near the stage with his eye to his camcorder. I was happy wearing my green robe, hat, and tassel.

Smitty spoke as I stood accepting my diploma. "I am proud to announce that Lincoln Jackson has been awarded a full-tuition scholarship to the prestigious Voorhees College. This was made possible by an organization that is responsible for sending thousands of underprivileged young adults to college. Let's give a hand to Black Men United," Smitty said.

Everyone in the church sprang to their feet and applauded. To my left I looked at my mother and sister who were shedding tears of joy. Akbar was whistling and leading the applause. Smitty smiled and held out his hand. I ignored it and hugged him.

A few minutes later, St. Luke's Class of '87 sang Jeffrey Osborne's hit "We're Going All The Way."

Li'l Man materialized as I left the stage. We hugged and he congratulated me. "You've got the green light. Run with it, babyboy," he whispered.

I had no idea what he meant, but I knew it was all good. I took off my class ring.

"I don't need this anymore, so I want you to have it. You pushed me to stay in school. It was hard watching my best friend flutter from being broke and in the gutter to be big ballin' and bankin' mad cheese and butter. I love you, man." We hugged again.

Momma pushed Li'l Man aside and smothered me with hugs and kisses.

After the ceremony, we all went to Akbar's two-acre ranch on the Westside. We had a mini family reunion. Chicken and turkey burgers were grillin' while we all sat at the pool chillin'.

The summer would have been uneventful if Tarik and Li'l Man would not have been avalanched.

CHAPTER 12

They never saw it coming. Tarik slammed on his brakes and Li'l Man jumped from the car with the dope and hauled ass through the projects. He might have gotten away if he hadn't tripped over a beer bottle and twisted his ankle.

They got busted by Atlanta's Red Dog Special Drug Task Force. Li'l Man and Tarik had been dropping off close to half a kilo in the Herndon Homes projects. The Red Dogs paraded in, surrounding them on four sides.

It took three days before their lawyer got them out on a $50,000 bond. After Bay-Bay paid it, business continued. It might not have been the smartest thing in the world, but they did take extra precautions. They knew five-O would be watching.

I made a lot of drop-offs and pickups the rest of the summer. Money was coming so fast I had a hard time going cold turkey when the time came for me to make the 3-hour drive down to Denmark, South Carolina to start school.

The town was so small that Hardees was the only fast food joint and Piggly Wiggly was the only grocery store. Denmark was clubless, movieless, malless, and would've been motionless if it weren't for the students living on the two college campuses across the street from each other. When I came, I brought the noise to the country-quiet town. Before anyone saw me, they heard me. Scott La Rock and KRS One's "Criminal Minded" blasted from my four earth-dancing, twelve-inch woofers. Everyone stopped and looked my way once I bent the corner and drove onto the yard. Some of the less modest girls waved or pointed.

I had three things going for me that couldn't miss when it came to getting the girls: My cat trap ride; my hazel brown, non-prescription contacts; and my black, knee-length riding boots. I wasted no time. The bait was sparkling; the sharks were circling. My pole was reeling-ready.

The sweetest babe on campus had to be Terrionne Snow. Her Betty Boop butt, her Porky Pig thighs, and her Bugs Bunny smile only accentuated her Hershey bar complexion. On top of being fine as all outdoors, she was president of the popular Alpha Kappa Alpha sorority chapter on campus. She got the nickname Champagne through pledging. She'd been ordered to take a few steps blindfolded while balancing a half-full champagne glass on her behind. She did it.

My eyes popped and my jaw dropped when she first jazzed by. No question, she was fine and good as mine. I was sure of myself. I just knew I was the best thing since Billy D and Teddy P.

A booty call too soon, I learned that a six-four, 240-pound walking, talking slab of muscle stood smack dab in the way of my destiny. This dude was Hercules on steroids. I discovered he was known as Truck and that he and Terrionne had been tight, on and off, for more than a year. He was a basketball star on the team across the street at Denmark Tech.

For better or worse, I didn't think, I just acted when it came to his girl.

I smooth talked Terrionne, and we started to kick it on the down low. On weekends I would take her to Orangeburg, the closest mini-metropolis, eighteen miles away. We went to the mall, out to eat, or just hung out on the campus of South Carolina State for three days straight.

It was a Tuesday when I brought Terrionne back to school from yet another one of our rendezvous. At the front of her dorm I was confronted by Truck and two of his pitbull-lookin' boys. I quickly ascertained my options, which were nil. I had maybe six feet of running room, which was not enough.

"Bitch, I oughta beat the hell out you."

Pop! Terrionne cartoon-flopped to the grass. Truck had slapped her so hard her dead ancestors must've felt it.

I flinched.

She was mute, but her face hollered.

"Nigga, I'mo fuck you up," Truck scream-breathed.

His boys lioned around me. All eyes were on me.

"Bruh? That's what's wrong with our people today. We warring—" Before I could finish my "I Have a Dream" speech, I was interrupted.

"Shut the fuck up," Truck said, barreling forward.

Ignoring him, I Martin Luther Kinged on, "Violence ain't the answer. What's jumpin' on me gon' prove?"

I felt Murphy's Law sucking my breath as I tried to think while the lions closed in. That was the last sound I heard before kissing the ground. They beat me down like a brother at a drunken backwoods skinhead rally. The physical pain was numbed only by the embarrassment of being beat down while half the women at Voorhees came to my and Terrionne's aid.

The next day my eyes were Delta red and Alpha black, and my nose ballooned from my pumpkin face. I couldn't hold my head up in class. I hid from all the sympathetic "What happened to you?" and "That's a shame what those guys did to you." I left before completing my classes.

Revenge consumed my Freudian thoughts as I NASCARed back to the ATL. I gave birth to a plan as I came up on my exit. A dance was scheduled in the Voorhees College gym that Friday night. I concluded this would be the best time to avenge my sorry whoopin'.

Whenever a social event was planned, Terrionne had to represent the chapter, as president of the AKAs. Most importantly, it meant that her watchdog boyfriend would be sniffing behind her.

I pulled off the exit and went to a payphone to call Li'l Man on his car phone.

"Yo, what up, dog?"

"Well damn, I thought you had forgotten all about us poor ol' dumb-ass half-educated Negroes. Ya know, with you being a college boy and all," Li'l Man said in his best Uncle Tom shuffling voice.

Just hearing his voice picked me up. I told him what had went down after we finished shucking and jiving, then I explained my plan.

"You know I'm always down for a beat down. Just tell me when's the party. Ain't danced on a fool's head in a while." Li'l Man was no longer anything like his name. He towered at six-three and weighed a good two and a quarter.

"Friday."

"Ah hell, I better have one of my hoes get me a fresh pair of steel-toe dancin' and head-prancin' boots."

"Man, you sure?"

"Nigga, dis me. Bitch-ass nigga fucks with you, he fucks with me."

"I'm sayin', you prob'ly done got a li'l soft since you been livin' big Willie, big ballin' and all."

"Nigga, you got me mixed up. Holmes and Ali togetha don't want none of me."

"Man, you stupid." I laughed. "Man, I'm gon' have ta hit you back. I gotta see what's up with Tarik."

"You know he'd be down. But somebody got to stay back. We got too much money in—"

We were disconnected. I fished another quarter from my pocket and called Li'l Man back from the Amoco gas station payphone.

"My bad. I paid thirteen hundred for this shit, and I keep losin' calls and shit. Anyway, I got everything covered. We'll bring Pork Chop and Li'l Bill. And I'll have them bring their boys Blackjack and Louisville."

"Louisville?"

"Slugger, fool. Louisville Slugger."

"Keep yo' day job."

"Shit, you think I wasn't? Nigga, I make more money than Bush, Jesse, and Operation PUSH."

"A good ol'-fashioned beatdown with no guns. Yeah, baby, it's on like beans and greens. We gon' beat all the country out them hillbillies," Li'l Man hyped. "That's exactly what I need to relieve some of this pressure I'm under."

"What pressure?" I asked.

"Five-O, sweatin' a nigga's ass, hot-ass snitches lurkin' behind ten-spots for rocks, and them stank ass pussy-for-pay hoes. Yeah, dog, it'll be like old times."

Friday afternoon we hit the highway with two of Li'l Man's boys tailing. We checked them into the closest motel, eight miles down the road in Bamburg, South Carolina. We didn't want to expose our hold card too early. They were just a little insurance in case Truck had a lot of boys down with him.

Late that afternoon, Li'l Man and I turned onto the school grounds riding in his fourteen karat gold-trimmed, midnight black special edition 636 CSI BMW. LL Cool J's "Rock the Bells" dropped mountain bass beats from the open sunroof.

After turtle-rollin' around the yard, getting the attention I wanted, I told Li'l Man to pull in front of the freshman girls' dorm, Battle Hall. I lowered the window and signaled to the small group of girls gawkin' and hawkin'. Naturally, they swayed over. I handed the one I knew best the bouquet of fresh flowers I'd picked up from some graveyard we passed between Augusta and Aiken.

"Janette."

She angled past a coupla girls. "Hey, Lincoln."

"I need you to give these to my baby and tell her I'll be at the dance."

"Okay," she chirped while ostrich-necking, trying to see who was driving.

Voorhees was a small school. With the girls hanging on every syllable, I knew word would wildfire that I was back and still trying to get with Truck's girl. Soon, Terrionne's trick-ass cartoon character boyfriend would get a play by play.

Li'l Man and I walked in the school gym around eleven. Our boys had showed up right before us. John Wayning in, we spotted Li'l Man's boys standing near the door.

Li'l Man and I wore baggy, dark Nike warm-ups—the better to conceal the mini Louisville Slugger bats strapped to our sides. After scoping the gym, I spotted Truck and his flunkies standing with their arms crossed near the deejay platform. We counted three guys with the unsuspecting Truck. Terrionne was nowhere around, which was good, considering. The party was bass-bumpin' and the students were rhythm-jumpin' in the oven-hot gym.

I signaled for Li'l Man's gun-toting thugs to discreetly follow.

"Just four of them." Li'l Man laughed. "This ain't even fair. A snowball got a better chance in hell."

Li'l Man eased his bat out and put it on a chair on the side of the dance floor. I almost dropped mine because I wanted this cat heads up. I looked at him and shook my head. The sucka hadn't fought me straight up, so why the heck should I? His size didn't faze me one bit; I knew he had a microscopic heart. He wasn't no man. A man don't put they hands on no woman. The more I thought about it, the more I wanted to break this mothafucka's back.

Truck didn't spot us until my bat crashed on his nose. Li'l Man blindsided one of Truck's boys with a

Bruce Leroy, steel-toe construction boot kick to the shoulder.

No one came to their aid while Li'l Man and I beat dat ass.

"Bitch nigga, I'm Lincoln mothafuckin' Jackson." I whaled away on his floor-moppin' ass. "You thought I was soft?" I kicked him in his butt. "Unball yo' bitch ass." I kicked him in the head.

He squealed like a pig as his blood fauceted on everything around us.

"Nigga, I'm nightmare's death." I kicked again and again.

Everybody stood around watching. Li'l Man had run Truck's boys off.

"Slap anotha woman, bitch." I bent down and slapped his head before Li'l Man grabbed me.

"Let's go."

In less than two minutes we were back in our cars. Two state police cars sped past us as we drove off. I drove back to Atlanta as fast as I could. I rushed Li'l Man to Grady Hospital. We later found out that he'd broken a thumb and cracked a couple of knuckles.

The next day I felt like Tony the Tiger. Li'l Man loaned me a .380 Beretta. I secured it under the Mazda's dashboard and headed back to Voorhees.

Once I got out the car, heading to the dorm, I noticed that girls who constantly fought for my attention didn't say a word to me. I walked into my dorm where guys gathered around the Ping-Pong table watching Eric and Travis slam the ball back and forth. I said what's up twice. Nothing. I was treated like a leper. My roommate was home for the weekend, so he couldn't shed any light on what was going on. I was starting to feel like I was in the Twilight Zone. Finally, I tracked down a kid I had gone to high school with.

"Man, what's up? Why is everybody treating me like a redhead stepchild?"

"Why you think?"

"I was just gettin' a little git-back."

"Man, you did a lot more than get a little git-back. You fucked Truck up for real. Two ambulances had to rush him to Orangeburg General."

Suddenly my elation turned to worry and fear. I wasn't worried about the trouble I was in. I was worried about Truck. I meant to do damage, but nothing too serious. I said a silent prayer.

"What have you heard? What's the damage?" I asked.

"Truck got cracked ribs, a broken nose, fluid in the knees, and a busted head that required twenty-seven stitches."

The next day I found out that no charges were going to be pressed.

I didn't have a chance to provide an explanation as I stood in front of the dean. Yeah, I was wrong and I knew it, but I never was one to lie down. I was expelled. Before I left campus I tried to see Terrionne, but she would have no part of me. I left school feeling worse than I had after snailing from the girls' dorm a few days earlier. The sad thing was that I was more depressed about what I had done to Truck than I was about my expulsion from school. I had no idea what I was going to do or how I was going to tell Momma and Akbar.

CHAPTER 13

A little over two years earlier, Momma had been encouraged by one of her girlfriends to apply for a job in reservations at Delta Airlines. Her strong, melodic voice and great enunciation skills helped her get the job. Momma would finally be getting paid for talking. Reservation Sales Agent of the Year was one of the many citations she received in her first year.

In that same pivotal year, Momma got off the state and bought a house in Decatur and a 2-year-old Chrysler. When the sun finally shone on Momma's life, I loomed as a cloud threatening to bring gloom.

Momma was upset, but she was also compassionate and understanding. Her intuition seemed to kick in, sensing the deep regret and sincere disappointment that I felt over the entire situation.

There was no way that I was gon' face Smitty or Akbar until I could figure out a way to make things right. I felt bad enough without having to explain myself to them. They both had done so much to prepare me for college, and I wasn't going to let them preach the same sermon that I preached to myself all the way home from school. I let myself down, so I had to lift myself up.

I remembered one of my boys tellin' me about how live Savannah State College was. He had also told me that it was pie getting in, so I got on the phone and called Savannah State's Office of Admissions. I spoke to a receptionist who sent me financial aid forms and applications.

In December of '87, a month before I was to register for school, Smitty died of a brain aneurysm. I never got the chance to show that the faith and effort he put toward me wasn't wasted.

I found out that I had been denied financial aid a week after the funeral. I didn't trip because I was still torn up over Smitty. Hell, by this time I was used to Murphy's Law kicking me in the ass.

The reason for denial was that Momma wasn't poor enough. The government claimed she made too much money. Ain't that a bitch. Moved out the projects and now we rich. Bullshit.

Momma had to wear high heels to see over her bills. We went from being on welfare, dead broke and disgusted, to off welfare, cracked and busted. Them fools in government must not have taken into account that Momma supported four people: me, my brother, my sister, and my sister's son. Momma had her car note, house note, insurance, and ten milliondee other notes. Considering all that, she was still supposed to be, as they put it, financially able to pay for my continuing education.

Knowing how badly I wanted to go to school, Momma stuck her neck out for me yet again. She took me to a bank to apply for a guaranteed student loan. We found out that there was no such thing as a "guaranteed" student loan; it was more of an "if we think you need" student loan. We were turned down again.

Thanks to Momma and the Delta Airline Credit Union, I enrolled at Savannah State College just three months after the Voorhees fiasco. I left for Savannah with more than $2,500 in my pocket; half of that was for tuition, room and board.

My car broke down in the hillbilly haven of Jim Crow Bibb County, right outside Macon, Georgia. Luckily, I was near a service station. Once I managed to get the car to the side of the road, I walked to the exit and into Mayberry.

I half expected to see Gomer Pyle when I got to the service station. Surprisingly, it turned out to be a Black-owned station, but with a black Gomer. Larry Joe got me running a few hours and a few hundred bucks later.

I knew I had to look for work as soon as I hit Chatham County. After I registered, I got my class schedule. Next I went job hunting. After striking out at three restaurants, I ended up at Bennigan's on Victory Drive.

I'd learned a valuable lesson at the Shoney's down the street. I went in, and while filling out an application, I saw this white boy go in and ask for the manager. Once the manager introduced himself, the white boy went on about how he'd been in the restaurant industry for five years and how he'd worked and ran these exclusive, high-falutin' sounding places. The manager fell all over the guy, offering him a couple of positions. This guy didn't fill out the first application.

So when I went into Bennigan's, I asked the hostess for the manager. After waiting fifteen minutes, a Dom De Luise-lookin' white guy came out of the back and said, "Hello, I'm Farley Jeffers. What can I do for you?"

After briskly shaking his hand I said, "Yes sir, I'm Lincoln Jackson. I believe you have my résumé." I lied. "As you already know, I'm looking at this restaurant as one I'd be interested in waiting tables at. As you know, I've waited at Chandeaux, Bellofante's, and Ingenues in Hollywood and Seattle." I paused and took two steps to look around the restaurant.

Continuing, I said, "Mr. Jeffers?"

"Yes, yes, Mr. Jackson."

I finger-chopped the air. "I don't expect to make the two and three hundred a night I'm used to." I traffic-guarded my arm out. "That's okay. I'm down here taking care of a sick relative, and I'm majoring in restaurant management at Savannah State College up the street."

"Mr. Jackson, I'd love to have a young man of your stature and experience on my staff."

"Thank you, Mr. Jeffers."

"Call me Farley, uh, Lincoln," he said, patting my back.

After we worked out my hours, the days I'd work, and when I'd start, I drove back to school to do a little ho huntin'. I had read some literature on the school and student enrollment, did some quick calculations, and found out that women outnumbered the men by almost ten to one. I was already contemplating hunting down my ten.

At first glance, the school seemed kind of lame, but I soon learned that half the students might have been from small Southern cities, but they sure knew how to party.

When I got there, I hooked up with Barado, a cat out of Atlanta. Every time someone asked about his name, he told them that he was French, Indian, and West African. Since Barado had attended Savannah State the previous quarter, he had the run of the place.

I was too pleased when he gave me the grand tour, starting with Lockett, the freshman girls' dorm. He was a real clown, but the girls liked him, so I wasn't mad one bit when I was introduced as his cousin. After the excitement of the first week of school, I settled down and got into the mundane routine of going to class and studying. Still, I managed to party four nights a week.

Neither the school's curfew nor the rule forbidding the opposite sex from going beyond the dorm's lobby prohibited Barado and me. We catted around in our black ninja suits after curfew, avoiding security. We spent many nights in Lockett and Bowen-Smith, the other girls' dorm.

Thanks to Li'l Man and Tarik, I kept some fire-ass weed. In no time, me and Barado had half the girls' dorm chimneyed up. It only took a rock thrown at one of the weed head girls' windows to get them to come down and open the doors. We went from room to room like we had a license. If we had been caught, we'd have been expelled.

Like anywhere else, you had to contend with the good Samaritan who went to a payphone and called security. Luckily for us we never were IDed, although many nights we had to hang-jump from the second-floor laundry room window and run through someone's yard, escaping the cartoon security cops.

Time seemed to fly as the days turned into weeks and the weeks into months.

Before I knew it, final exams crept up on me, almost catching me off guard, which wasn't hard considering my Dracula schedule—waiting tables, stealing tips, selling weed, and partying. Surprisingly, I did fairly well in school. Of course, I would have done better if I had kept my mind off girls and on my studies.

I still fooled plenty and many with my hundred-dollar fake eyes and my Hollywood game. Although I had my preference, I never discriminated. Fat, short, tall, slim—it was all good if the girl activated my middle-leg radar. My motto was "If they can bleed, they can breed."

One day, out of nowhere, she dropped from my dreams and into reality. She was nuclear. She was everything. Although she wore my eyes on her butt, she paid about as much attention to me as she did an ice cube.

Michelle Stanford was different. She wasn't no ho. She glowed with jazz, class, and style. A member of the girls' basketball team, she floated around carrying the light of an angel's halo. Not the loud or the gossipy type, she was poetry in motion, a beautiful sight to see. She was Carl Carlton's vision when he sang "She's a Bad Mamma Jamma."

She was a little snobby, but I could handle snobby. I tried and tried. I wined and dined, bought her trinkets, but still got no love. The more she resisted me, the more I respected her.

I gave up finally. I had established a reputation around campus, and I knew that was what killed my chances. Me being a ladies' man was something Michelle would not tolerate. Even when I told her I'd drop all of 'em, she wouldn't go for it.

During the last week of school, I was bogged down with finals. While in the library cramming for my last two exams, Barado rushed to my table where I had books and papers strewn everywhere. He told me that my mother had called the dorm and said it was urgent that I call her.

Momma never called. I did all the calling. An eerie feeling came over me as I jogged back to the dorm. I slowed down as I approached the payphone.

With more than 275 students in our dorm, it was odd that there was no one waiting to use the only phone. Everyone must have been getting some last minute studying in. With trembling fingers and clammy hands, I picked up the phone and dialed.

"Hey, Mom."

"When are you finished with your classes?"

"Tomorrow." I fidgeted as I spoke.

"As soon as you finish, come home, Lincoln."

"Why?"

"'Cause I said so."

I knew better than to pry, and when Momma issued an order you just obeyed.

"I'll be there around six."

I whizzed through my finals, wondering what had happened. I almost called Li'l Man, but I didn't want to worry him. He probably wouldn't know anyway.

I drove from Savannah to Atlanta, 250 miles in three hours and ten minutes. I pushed my little rotary Mazda engine as hard as I could. The speedometer never went under eighty-five.

"Momma, I'm home," I yelled as I entered the house and slammed the door.

Momma quietly descended the stairs to where I stood in the living room. Without saying a word she reached out, and I floated to her. Her protecting arms briefly shielded me from reality.

CHAPTER 14

I was at Caesar's Palace, cold chillin'. The chick that massaged my shoulders as I shook the dice had a body like Janet Jackson and a face like Toni Braxton. The broad on my left who held my chips was tight as my masseuse.

"Seven. Seven-eleven. Send the dice straight to heaven," I said as the dice flew out of my hand and landed on four and three, winning me mo' money, mo' money, mo' money.

I was on fire, having won over fifty thou. I turned to study myself in the mirrored wall. I smiled, showing all thirty-two. Everything was proper and in place as I stood, briefly admiring myself in my triple-black Hugo Boss suit, black paisley silk Visage shirt, Hermes white *L.A. Times* print tie, and black-and-gold Bally gators. I was the champ, and I looked and felt that way. My manager and promoter, Don, had earlier in the day given me a boxing ring-shaped, custom eighteen-karat gold and two-karat diamond ring. Engraved on the inside were the words The People's Champ. I wore it with pride.

I had treated tonight just like any other night. I was scheduled to fight some bum whose name I couldn't even remember. Two hours before the fight, I went back to my room to rest up. I laid down and closed my eyes while waiting for Don to call.

Suddenly, I found myself in the ring dancing, waiting for my opponent. The crowd was screaming and on their feet cheering, but the applause was not for me. As my unknown opponent slowly and methodically walked to the ring, the crowd went crazy. I strained to see his face, but his head was down and a shiny black hood covered his head. He ambled into the ring as if he were tired.

The bell sounded as soon as he stepped through the ropes. His back was to me. Confusion controlled me, and suddenly his robe dropped to the canvas. He turned to me.

His face was crimson. Blood seeped from every orifice of his anguished, death-drugged face. The metallic scent of blood made me gag. His body was riddled with bullet-burned holes. Before I could move, Li'l Man was on me, pounding me with astonishing speed. In slow motion I fell, but I never hit the canvas; I just kept falling.

I was crying. Li'l Man was crying. The crowd was crying.

"Where were you when I needed you? Where were you? Why did you let them kill me?" he asked.

Hysterical chants of "Why? Why?" resounded from the crowd.

"No, no!" I screamed as I watched the class ring I gave Li'l Man slide off his bloody finger. I knew that if the ring came off, I'd lose Li'l Man forever. "No. No. No."

"Lincoln. Lincoln, wake up. You're having a nightmare."

Li'l Man was shaking me awake. No. He was dead.

Momma hugged me, rocking back and forth. "Baby, it's just a dream. Just a dream."

"But Momma, it was so real. Li'l Man was there all bloody and screaming at me. Why, Momma? Why Li'l Man?"

"Shh, baby. Only Gods know why. There was nothing you or anyone else could do to change God's will. It is not meant for us to know why God does what He does. I know you loved Corey, and don't ever stop, but in his memory, let his lifestyle serve as a lesson for what you should not do. His death would be meaningless if you didn't learn from the mistakes he made. Just as you would want Corey to be happy and do well, he would want the same for you."

Corey "Li'l Man" Stevens had a small, closed casket funeral. Bay-Bay wanted everyone to remember her brother as he was, robust and full of life, not lying in some wooden box disfigured.

I watched the strands of the green and red carpet move as I staggered to the front of the church. It was as if I'd gone death. The church wasn't full. There were a lot of people there, yet I couldn't hear anything. And then I felt it. Eyes piercing my back, tunneling through to my soul. And then I heard it. Cries of love, cries of emptiness, coming closer. I turned and then I felt her. Her tears were waterfalls of pain gushing from a broken dam of hope lost. She was in my arms.

"Oh, Linc, they took my heart, them mothafuckas crushed my heart," Bay-Bay cried.

I nodded. "Babygirl, I'mo find 'em. Somebody gon' pay."

"They shot him right in Tarik's house. I'd just seen him and Tarik earlier that day. The police found cocaine residue in the kitchen, and that's all. No money nowhere," she cried.

And no Tarik or his crackhead bitch anywhere either, I thought.

"It was definitely a robbery, but what happened to Tarik? It just don't make sense," she cried.

Bay-Bay took Li'l Man's death very hard, which was expected on account of how close they were. I just thanked God that Bay-Bay's new man, who was a dentist, had been there for her.

I just couldn't quite accept that my dog was gone. I had never lost anyone close to me. Li'l Man was my best friend to the end, and the end had come. I kinda hoped I never learned who killed him. I didn't want to go down for murder, but no doubt I would if I knew. Shit just didn't make sense. Tarik had to have been there. Him and Li'l man were always together in the daytime. And I knew that crackhead ho Kama Sutra was laid all up at his crib like she was the queen of mu' fuckin' Sheba and shit. Naw, this mess was more confusing than Columbo and Kojak.

After the funeral I called down to DeKalb County Jail to find out when I could see Tarik, who I learned had turned himself in on a drug charge related to Li'l Man's death. "Hello, can you tell me when your visitation days and times are?"

"What's the name of the inmate you're inquiring about?"

"Jones. Tarik Jones."

"He was released yesterday."

What kind of shit was that? Tarik was out and he didn't even show up at the funeral? I was so mad that I had to dial Tarik's mom's number three or four times before I finally hit all the right digits.

"Ms. Jones, this is Lincoln. I just found out that Tarik was out, and I was wondering if you could tell me where I can find him."

"I-I don't know. I just don't know, Lincoln."

"You okay, Ms. Jones?"

"I'll—" She sucked her teeth. "I'll be okay. I went and got the boy out. He didn't say ten words. I thought he was torn up over Corey."

I nodded, holding the phone tightly.

"As soon as we got home, he got out the car and ran. I haven't seen him since."

"Don't worry, Ms. Jones. I'll find him," I said before hanging up.

Pissed beyond all pisstivity, I went straight for his weakness: pussy.

I tried his son's mother, but Meon hadn't heard from or seen him. I drove past his house, but it was still cordoned off with yellow crime scene tape. I even went to Magic City and hollered at his cokehead freak, Melanie

"Kama Sutra" Adams. She was no help. It was like he had dropped off the planet.

Well, fuck him. I was tired of playing Columbo. If he wanted to be found, he'd surface.

As I waited for word from Tarik, some of Li'l Man and Tarik's workers had started to sweat me about giving them some work. I had run into them in my search. They must have thought I was connected since I drove such a fly ride and I was so tight with Li'l Man and Tarik.

With Tarik's Houdini act and Li'l Man's death, I saw myself surrounded by omens. First, I was through with the school thing. Savannah State was fun, but I couldn't afford to continue. I wasn't going to let Momma go deeper into debt getting another loan. Now these workers were looking for me to get them some work. This was my opportunity to come up. Every time I tried to do the right thing, I got shitted on, but not anymore. Finally, I was gon' control my own destiny. I wasn't gon' wait on no handouts, and I wasn't gon' give them.

The difference between Tarik, Li'l Man and me was that I wasn't trying to get rich. I just wanted to make enough money to go legit and start my own business. I figured that after a year or two of grinding I could save a half-mil and quit slangin' dope. Why not? Tarik's and Li'l Man's crew was down to put me in the driver's seat. All I had to do was supply the product and they would move it.

From Li'l Man's wallet I got the pager number of their supplier, Blue. I beeped him, but he never returned my calls. That didn't stop me because I was determined to get some work.

With only $150, I hit the streets running. I got with this lame-ass chump I went to school with who was selling baby-weight. I bought an eight ball, which was three and a half grams of crack, from the cat. Next, I went to Third World Records and purchased 500 dime-sized Ziploc bags. Then I went to the East Lake Meadows projects and picked up Li'l Man's main cat, Chris, who slang for him. I told him that I was on, and I was putting him to work.

"Due to us losing so much money with the robbery and Tarik running off, we'll have to start from scratch," I explained.

Chris and I went to his mom's apartment in the East Lake Meadow projects and sacked up thirty-two fat dime rocks. That would turn into 320 bones off a buck-fifty investment.

After paying Chris $25 off every $100, which was $5 more than Tarik paid him, I came out with $245. From there it snowballed; money stormed in. I had 24 hours in every day, but I was so busy I could have used a few more. It seemed like as soon as I dropped off a package, Chris was paging me to re-up. I was calling my connection two or three times a day. It wouldn't be long before I would be able to put the whole crew back to work.

For a while I had to keep picking up the money and using it to buy more dope, leaving Chris high and dry with the crackheads fien'in'. The first week I went from being a one-fiftyaire to a fifteen-hundredaire. I could have made more if I could've kept enough blow and had more runners.

After my initial week, my connection decided to front me whatever I bought to keep down my traffic and also to make more off me. For every ounce I bought for a G, he'd front me one for which I had to bring him back twelve hun. I didn't mind the arrangement because I was making mad money, Monopoly fast. My main concern was keeping dope.

If I continued living at home I knew it would only be a matter of time before Momma got wind of what I was doing, so under the pretense of having a job at C&S Bank, I moved into my own apartment.

With Chris's help, I recruited all of Li'l Man's and most of Tarik's boys. I took all seven of my new crew to Shoney's for the Sunday morning breakfast buffet. After all the dope these cats sold for Tarik and Li'l Man, I was surprised that most of them didn't own cars. That would soon change, I thought.

Sitting at the head of the two tables we had put together, I laid the law down.

"All right, fellas, it's like this." I paused to make sure I had everyone's attention. "A lot of money and blow got fucked up when Tarik and Li'l Man got hit. I know they were paying you twenty off a hundred. I'm paying twenty-five."

"That'll work," Bam-Bam interrupted. He was a loyal soldier of Li'l Man and Tarik.

"I'm starting all of y'all off with sixty rock packages. Off $600, bring me back $475. And don't wait till you're out to re-up. Hit me as soon as you get my money so I can have you ready and you won't be left with your hands in your pockets.

"I'm gonna change things up a little. There's a lot of crackheads in Decatur and Lithonia. Most of them have to find transportation to get to the nearest dope spot, with the major ones as far as twenty minutes away. Therefore Bam-Bam and Pork Chop will be working out of Motel 6 and Bosa Nova Apartments on Wesley Chapel."

I knew what was coming, so I continued before either could object. "Give it a week. I'm telling you, when word gets out that there's some fire-ass dope around the corner, you'll be making Jordan money. Why? Because there will be no competition, at least for a while. And when some new jack comes in sellin' you'll have already established a strong customer base. I'll even pay for your room at Motel 6 for the first three days," I continued. "Lamont, Bull, and Rock, I'm leaving you three in the Meadows. "Chris and Dead-eye will start up another trap on Fulton Industrial. I've already scoped it out, and this spot is gonna be a gold mine. Peep this: They opened a Motel 6 behind the truck stop off Fulton Industrial. Now, you know what's up. Wherever there's a truck stop, there's crackhead hoes trickin' with them lonely, on the road all damn day and night truck drivers."

I felt good as I watched them nod.

"Another thing, whenever any of you save up a grand, I'll take you to Bishop Brothers Auction, and I'll match you dollar for dollar on a ride. It's time you stopped renting and giving geek monster crackheads a hit to use their rides."

"That's what I'm talkin' 'bout," Dead-eye interrupted.

"I don't care what time it is. If you got a problem, hit me up. You saw what happened to my boys. I be damned if a sucka comes and knocks me or any of you off your square. If a robbing crew rides down, we all gon' make sure they get their names in print in the obits."

CHAPTER 15

Q was my new woman. I used her Chevy Spectrum to carry my boys to their traps early Monday. Early for me was lunchtime.

The night before, Q and me had to bag dope for three and a half hours. It would have taken a lot longer if I hadn't taken an old antique mirror from Momma's and used a razor blade to cut up the three one-ounce crack cookies into dime rocks. After we finished, we had counted 542 dime bags, equaling $5,420.

Of course, I could have and should have made more money, but I decided to make the dimes pregnant so the crackheads would only buy from my boys, putting a hurting on the competition. The quicker the dope sold, the quicker I could get more out. In the long run, I'd still come out just as good or better than if I had made the dimes smaller.

Through one of my partners, I heard that Blue had caught a case and was locked up in New York. That didn't worry me. With me, my shit was correct. I wasn't about to see the inside of no jail. I was too smart for that. That's why I paid others to sell my dope, and whenever one of my boys met me to re-up, he met me far away. I had them meet me at a gas station or a grocery store where I could be inconspicuous. I never went down into a dope trap unless I was crystal clean because five-O knew these traps too. Crack was the bait, and once the fiend took a hit, he was trapped there.

Li'l Man and Tarik got busted down by a dope trap, and I knew if I kept going down into the trap, I'd be either pulled over or put under surveillance, sealing my fate. Even though I could most likely pay off five-O, there was no need to take chances.

I still planned to go back to school one day and get my degree, but at that moment the game was too sweet. If all these lame-ass busters I grew up around were out there getting paid slangin', I could too, and do it quicker 'cause I was smarter.

In the first three months, from time to time, my boys came up short. They'd find a way to lose dope. Either they had to leave it and run because five-O was bearing down or they got tricked.

I usually took the brunt of the loss, but I always gave them hell, if only to maintain an impression of strength and authority. After all, how upset could I get when I was making money hand over fist? Overall, things were smooth, until late one Friday night when I came home to find my door kicked in. At first I was scared to go inside, being gunless and all. I know it sounds stupid, but I never thought any fool would try and step to me. Shit, I was Lincoln Mothafuckin' Jackson. Why carry a gun when everybody thought I had one anyway?

After stethoscoping my ear to the door for close to ten minutes, I crept inside with a tire iron. My apartment looked like two tornadoes had a fight. I was glad the break-in had taken place late at night. I would have hated for my neighbors to hear or see the damage. Being the good citizens they were, they would've called 911. The police would have found dope residue, dope paraphernalia, or something that linked me to drugs.

The thieves found my stash. Over two and a half ounces of rock and $3,200 was gone. And I thought I had been careful.

I'd moved way out to Stone Mountain with the white folks to prevent shit like this. I was always careful to watch my back when I came home. Hardly anyone knew where I lived. Hardly anyone. That was it. Someone must have seen my girl Q with me. Q managed a convenience store. Someone probably followed her. That had to be it.

I went down to Tracy's Pawnstop the next morning after having my door fixed. I had Chris meet me with some cheese. I bought a Glock nine and a box of hollow-point shells. The proprietor gave me a quick lesson in cleaning and upkeep. He also informed me that Georgia was a plain view state, and that as long as I kept my gun on my seat or on top of my car's dash, it was legal for me to drive around with it.

I felt a surge of security and power as I walked out of the pawnshop with a gun in hand. My nine became like an extension of me. Just like the American Express card, I never left home without it. It was time to go see my contact, Sedric Coleman.

Sed was my age. He worked for his big-time brother, Stokely, for a while, but the two didn't get along too well. Sed made a couple of dollars, learned the ins and outs then struck out solo. By now I had dealt with Sed so frequently that he had become careless and had me come to his apartment for dope. In my eyes he wasn't all that bright. He was soft as baby fat and had the heart of a rabbit. You could hear it in his voice and see it in his walk. He put on airs like he was some bad mutha. In truth, he was just a lucky lame clockin' loot. Every time I came to his crib to re-up, he had a different broad at his apartment. That in itself was plain stupidity.

When I got to his place, I explained what happened out of earshot of the two broads in the next room. "All I got is twelve hun." I handed Sed a wad of bills. " I'll give you the rest in a coupla days. For now, I need you to front me a little somethin'."

"Man, what you think, I'm your personal bank?" he asked, raising his voice, using all kinds of exaggerated hand gestures. One of his carp-mouth skeezers came in the room, all catfish-eyed, tryin' to see what all the hoopla was.

Sed went on, "Boy, you bet' not be trying to pull that same ol' shit your boy Tarik pulled."

This nigga, really had me fucked up. I looked at him like he'd lost what little mind he had. I almost swung on his bitch-ass. I didn't go for no one, especially no soft-ass lame, dissing me in front of some bitch. The mention of Tarik's name caught me off guard. I didn't even know he knew Tarik.

"Why didn't you call me as soon as you got robbed?"

I looked him up and down one more time before I went off. "Nigga, you must think I'm one of your ho-ass bitches. Who you think you talkin' to?" I paused, pushing my finger in his face.

The wizard must have taken his heart back, the way Sed cowered.

"I told you that you'll get your seven funky-ass hundred dollars. If you don't want to help me get back on my feet, cool. But don't try to play me. I ain't a nigga to be fucked with."

Stevie Wonder nodding, he said, "Man, uh, you-you know how it is. A lotta cats be tryin' to run game."

"Game? Nigga, dis me." I patted my chest. "I done came correct for over three months."

"I know, but—"

"Hold on, Sed. Let me finish," I continued. "Furthermore, me and Tarik are two different people. I'd never go out like that." I had no idea what I wouldn't go out like, but I was fishing.

"Yeah, that's real fucked up how he jumped out the window and left your man there to die like that."

I was stiff as a corpse in concrete. My eyes were lead beach balls. One word kept going through my mind: why? "Where you get this from?" I asked.

"That freak, Melanie."

"Melanie?"

"Yeah, Melanie 'Kama Sutra', the strippin' crackhead freak your boy was all in love with," Sed said.

"You know her?" I asked.

"Who don't? Any nigga willin' to set out some lines of coke or some cheese know that pussy."

"So, what she tell you?" I asked through clenched teeth.

Sed must've sensed that his life depended on his next words 'cause he didn't take a breath.

"I was trickin' wit' the bitch on a regular 'cause she always brought me other bitches, and one night not too long after Li'l Man got smoked, I was havin' this little set with ol' girl and one of her friends. We was smoking some killa herb, and the bitches was doin' lines and shit."

"What the fuck she say, man? I ain't tryin'a hear all that," I said.

"Anyway, Melanie tells me how she lets some fool play her at the club for some info about Tarik. She says the nigga must've followed her to Tarik's pad. Anyway, he comes back, ties her up, makes her call Tarik with some lame story to come home 'cause the nigga can't find Tarik's stash. After your boys show up, the nigga and his boy throw down on your boys and Li'l Man pulls out on them dudes first. She said your boys had the upper hand, then Tarik went bitch and jumped out the window, and the rest is history. Word is that Tarik done even snitched on Blue and some other major players to get his case dropped."

Why? I couldn't understand it. As hard as it was for me to accept it, I knew Sed had to be telling the truth. It explained Tarik's disappearance. It explained a lot.

"Another thing—you know that nigga on that shit," Sed said, getting joy out of my pain.

"Huh?"

"Yeah, the bitch even told me that after her and Tarik fled the scene after Li'l Man got smoked, they was hittin' the pipe in the car. Between tokes the nigga even threatened her, tol' her if she went to five-O that he'd kill her and her momma."

I shook my head in disgust and rage. My boys had told me of their suspicions that Tarik had started dippin'. As bad as I didn't want to believe that he was smokin', it was the only thing that explained why he had disappeared.

Tarik playin' house with a crackhead should have red-lighted Li'l Man. Breach of security like a mutha. That shake-dancin' ho was probably the one who turned Tarik out.

"You said Tarik jumped out a window. What, you mean Tarik left Li'l Man to die?"

Sed knew of my rep. If he liked breathing unaided, he knew he had to keep talking.

"All I know was that Tarik jumped out a window and ran while Li'l Man was fightin'. That's all I know."

"Who did it?" I whispered.

"I-I don't know." He shrugged.

I cobra struck, grabbing his neck and screaming, "Who the fuck did it?"

"I'on't know. A couple of months ago, right before that truck driver shot her—"

"Shot who?"

"Melanie. Kama Sutra."

"She dead?"

"Deader than a doorknob."

"Damn."

"She was there. In the house. On the scene. She told me everything but who the two heads were that robbed and killed your boy."

I left Sed's crib in a semi-daze, vowing to never deal with his petty ass again. I knew too many cats I could cop from, and I didn't need this nut. My only problem was money. I ended up trading my Mazda for three ounces and a thousand dollars. I took a loss, but what else could I do? At least I was back on. I used the G to buy a clean white '78 Oldsmobile Cutlass. I typed up an insurance card for my ride, and I was rolling again. I saved a lot of money by typing up my own insurance cards. Why should I pay for car insurance when the only time I needed it was if I hit somebody?

I paid Sed off two weeks later and moved into a gated apartment complex with an alarm system on my unit. All the traps that the boys and I had set up at the Motel 6's and Travelodges were booming. I had helped all my boys buy cars. Even though four months had passed since we started, we still had breakfast together every Sunday at Shoney's. Still my treat, of course.

At the beginning of the fifth month, I planned to step up to buying powder, no more crack. I had bought crack that was too wet and dope too crumbly. It made it more difficult to sell. With coke, I could do like everybody else and put the whip on, taking a half or a kee of powder cocaine, baking soda, and water, and making it a kee and a half or sometimes even two. I figured that by the last week of July I'd have enough bread to buy a half a kee of powder and a cell phone.

When the first of the month arrived, I didn't want to mess with Sed ever again, but he was what the cats in the game called a chemist. He had mastered the whip. He charged me $750, but it was well worth it. I started with 500 grams, which was 18 ounces of powder. I walked out of Sed's crib with seven crack cookies and some crumbs weighing in at 790 grams, more than 10 ounces extra.

"Mother's Day" or "Welfare Check Day" fell on a Wednesday, and the third fell on a Friday. The third was Social Security and disability check day. My beeper never stopped buzzing. I was in my girl's car because I had to put my Cutlass in the hospital. It was sick with engine problems. I could tell Q's would be taking ill soon, too, the way I was pushing her slow-ass, four-cylinder Chevy Spectrum. I was trying to fill orders, buy dope, have it cooked, stop at payphones to call and curse my boys out for continuously worryin' the dog shit out of me after I'd told them I was workin' as fast as I could. I ran out of dope three times that Friday.

My other folks were holding me up. They were as busy or busier than I was. I couldn't afford to wait. Again I had to deal with petty-ass Sed. I knew I could go right to Sed's place, so I did.

I finally made it home around two in the morning, completely exhausted. As soon as I got in, I passed out on my bed, still fully dressed. My beeping pager woke me up seemingly as soon as I laid down.

"Damn," I grumbled. I rolled off my bed and reached for the phone.

It was one of the cats I went to high school with. From time to time he bought a couple hundred dollars of dope, usually around the first of the month. He was a customer I kept for myself.

My pager went off again before I could tell him that I was in for the night. I put him on hold and called the number displayed in my beeper.

"Linc, what's up? It's boomin' over here, man. I need another package bad, dog," Squirt pleaded. I had grown up with Squirt. He rapped at a lot of parties I used to do. After convincing me that he could move a lot of dope in the apartments he lived in, I put him on.

Greed overpowered all rational thought. My car was in the shop and Q had taken her car after dropping me off. I decided to give Squirt the directions to my place. I explained to him that he had to take me to serve one of my personal customers before I could give him another package. He happily agreed.

"Where'd you get the wheels?" I asked Squirt as we rode in a new red Ford Probe GT.

Squirt told me that his cousin was in town and had let him borrow his ride.

We took the dope to one of my customer's mother's pad. He was on the doorstep anxiously twitching. Afterward, Eric B. and Rakim blasted from the Probe's factory speakers as Squirt and I sped down South Hairston, heading back to my pad.

"I'm the black Mario Andretti."

"Slow the fuck down," I spat.

"Man, I race cars for a livin'." He hit the gas even harder.

"Oh shit!" I screamed as the curve came up.

I put my foot over the gearshift and tried to grab the wheel.

My world started spinning. Trees were running. The road was a blacktopped bucking horse.

Our screams fluctuated between earth and eternity.

I let go. Windows burst. I was flying.

CHAPTER 16

The last thing I remember before the accident was passing Treehill Apartments where my brother, D'Andre, and his girl, Trina, lived. Next thing I knew, *bam!* Groggy and half out of it, I opened my eyes to blinding light.

"Momma, Q, somebody," I said, struggling with words.

Then I was moving down a long, loud, bright hallway. Momma was crying. My face contorted as I experienced a never imagined degree of pain. The room started to spin. I couldn't speak. The lights were so bright—orange, red, green, yellow, then black.

My eyes fluttered again. What time was it? Where was I? I decided to get up and find out. Nothing moved. What was the problem? As I tried to move again, I felt an overbearing amount of pain. It felt like someone was nailing railroad spikes into my head.

Beyond the pain, it was fear and helplessness that brought tears streaming down my face. No matter how loud my brain screamed *Move!* neither my legs nor my arms would. I panicked when a young white lady appeared, obstructing the fluorescent-lit ceiling-sky. All this white was makin' my head spin.

"Mr. Jackson, I'm glad you decided to join us. You had us scared for a while. How are you feeling?" she asked.

I went through blinking spasms. I tried to focus or go back to black. Whichever happened first would be fine. My head was killing me.

"Water," I whispered.

I was lying in some bed, unable to move. Plastic snakes were eating from my arms, light was pounding my brain, muffled voices were stinging my ears, and some broad asked me how I was feeling. Give her the Nobel Prize for stupid.

She put a straw to my mouth. I gagged. The water hurt. Too heavy. Too hard. The colors came back, and my favorite was blinkin' in—black.

Again, I opened my eyes. What was going on? Where was I? This was a new light. It was dim. The room smelled different. Where was Momma? Where was Q? What was wrong with me? Was I dying? Where was the water lady?

"Mr. Jackson, are you awake?"

"Huh." I pushed out a grunt. What was wrong with my voice?

"I'm Dr. Bob. How are you feeling?"

That ignorant-ass question again.

"Hurt." I grunted.

"Mr. Jackson, I don't know how much you remember, but you and Robert Miner were in a car accident. You were thrown from the car. Both of you were lucky to have survived. When you see the car, you'll see what I'm talking about."

I breathed. My eyes fluttered. "How long will I be here?"

"I don't know. It's too early to say."

"What?"

"Mr. Jackson, your fifth and sixth cervical vertebrae have been fractured. In other words, you broke your neck. You're in Shepherd Spinal Center, where we specialize in treating spinal cord injury."

I heard him writing on something.

"What are you saying?"

Ignoring me, he said, "With your neck being in the condition it is, we decided to place you in traction. There is a metal ring around your head. Chains are suspended from this ring, with ten-pound sandbags at the other end, stabilizing your vertebrae."

"What? Wha-what does all this mean?"

The doc inhaled deeply. Exhaling, he said, "Your spinal cord has been damaged. It's too soon to say to what extent, but we seriously doubt if you will be able to walk again."

I heard my heart beat. It slowed. I tried to move. I couldn't. *Paralyzed.*

"You are a very lucky young man to be alive."

Lucky, hell. God, please take me. Why me? Why'd you let this happen? I ain't that bad. I ain't killed no one. I tried to do the right thing. It ain't my fault I couldn't get any financial aid to stay in school. I don't want to live. God, please let me sleep forever.

"Your friend is here, and he's had a successful vertebrae fusion operation. Your neck is too unstable to operate on just yet."

Pulling up a chair next to my bed, Doc sat down and proceeded. "Mr. Jackson, you have been tentatively diagnosed as being complete. What this means is that by fracturing the vertebrae in your cervical region, you also injured your spinal cord to the point where we strongly feel that you won't ever have use of your lower extremities, and your upper ones will be impaired. With all four limbs impaired, making you immobile, you are considered a quadriplegic."

Why me?

"During the last ten years, the medical profession has made leaps and bounds in the treatment of spinal cord injuries, but there is still a lot that we don't know or understand."

I closed my eyes and lay still. Waiting. No pain. No feeling. Waiting.

"Please understand, I gave you a tentative diagnosis. It's still possible that you may regain some feeling and motor functions in your legs, but as your doctor, it's my duty to tell the truth."

Paralyzed. God, please? I'm waiting.

"Over ninety-three percent of injuries at your level result in permanent paralysis."

How many times was he going to say that? I got the point. My life was over.

"Once we feel that your neck is stable, we will either perform surgery, fusing the bones in your neck, put you in another form of traction, or both. So at least you will be mobile and able to start your rehabilitation process. Do you have any questions?"

For maybe the first time in my life, I had no words. I tried to picture myself in a wheelchair. I couldn't. The only thing I could think of were my legs. God didn't seem to want to take me. It was insanity thinking He would listen. Hell, He let this happen.

My eyes wandered in a small circle. I couldn't see much. I couldn't move my head.

How could a human voice play God? Since God wasn't in no rush to let me sleep, I wouldn't accept paralysis. I couldn't. The doctor said ninety-somethin' percent didn't walk. That meant some did. I would. He was telling me that I was paralyzed for life. Suddenly my sadness blossomed into anger; my anger turned into determination.

"Dr. Bob," I said slowly, to enunciate my words, "I am going to walk out of this place. Do not consider me part of your ninety-three percentile. I am one of the seven percent who will walk."

No, I couldn't feel my legs. No, I couldn't move my arms. But I'm sorry, nobody, I mean no one short of God was going to determine my destiny.

All my life I had been told I couldn't do this or would not be able to do that. I didn't accept it then and I wouldn't accept it now. Suddenly, though still in pain, I felt good. I had a new resolve.

"Close your eyes and tell me if you feel anything," he said.

I almost passed out from the intense pain. It felt like pins and needles were being jabbed into my upper body. I couldn't scream because I didn't have the lung capacity, but oh boy, I tried.

"What did that feel like?"

"It hurt."

"Do you feel anything now?"

"No."

"You have no feeling in your feet, legs, or torso. Your arms are hypersensitive."

"What?"

"I tested you for feeling. Over the next few weeks you'll likely regain some feeling."

"I know. I'll be walkin'."

I could almost feel the wind from his doubtful shaking head.

The conversation and the probing pain left me winded. Next thing I knew, I opened my eyes to find the pain and the doctor gone. Thank God. I focused, and Momma, D'Andre, and Marnease came into view. I had lost all concept of time. I wondered how long they'd been there.

Momma was about to touch my arm when I stopped her. I spoke in the loudest whisper I could muster.

"No, Momma, don't. It hurts when anyone touches that arm."

"I'm sorry, baby. I'm so sorry," Momma whispered, crossing her arms.

"Hey, li'l brother. Me and Q stayin' at your apartment," Marnease said.

"Thanks."

"Q wanted to come see you but the doctors only allow immediate family in."

"That's cool."

"Please, everybody, come closer," I whispered.

For the first time I clearly saw D'Andre. His dark hands held the bed railing in a death grip as if he'd fall off the cliff of sanity if he let go. As I looked up, I saw big teardrops streaming down his face.

Holding back my own tears, I whispered, "I know that doctor probably told y'all that I'd be in a wheelchair. He was mistaken. I swear, I'll walk up outta here. Don't worry."

"I know you will," Momma said.

Marnease nodded and walked away. I could hear her crying. D' Andre was still speechless, but his grip relaxed.

The next day I became acquainted with my nurses and my physical therapist. My favorite was Nancy. She was a cute, bronze sister, probably in her late thirties with a full head of brownish-red weave cut into a long bob. She was one of my nurses on the day shift.

I had never feared another man until I came in contact with my weekend nurse on the graveyard shift. That creature scared the shit outta me. It was midnight-dark, had beady black eyes, and a drippety-drip, out of style, soul-glow, country-ass Rick James Jheri curl. It was hulking at six feet, and sweeter than a 5-pound bag of sugar. This cat's face looked like a bumpy dark road with a lot of little potholes. He spoke with a baritone lisp. I might have been paranoid, but every time he spoke to me I detected th'exual innuendo.

In my world, homosexuals were fags. Fags had that package, HIV, and I didn't want any part of it. There I was, lying helpless, unable to move or scream, while sugar bear put his hands on me every couple of hours, repositioning me so I wouldn't get bedsores. Curtains cordoned off my area, preventing anyone from seeing what sugar lumps was doing. If this dude touched me funny or let his big, clawlike paws linger too long where they shouldn't, I wouldn't feel it. I just prayed and kept my fears to myself.

I'd been doing a lot of praying since I was hospitalized. Even though I didn't go to church too tough, I was raised as a Baptist, and I believed in God. Now God and I had the chance to grow a lot closer. I always knew He was there; I just hadn't talked to Him much in the past. Now we kicked conversation on the regular. God was a good listener.

One day I met a slim, dark-skinned, middle-aged dapper brother. Melvin Davis told me that he'd been the one who called the ambulance when we wrecked.

"Thanks. I appreciate your help."

"No problem. I was on my way home from my lady's crib when I heard a loud thud. I came around a curve and saw a car wrapped around an uprooted tree. I slammed on my brakes, got out of my car, and ran back to the scene. I saw you lying in the grass on the other side of the street near a streetlight. I turned to the car and saw your buddy crushed against the wheel. I thought you both were dead. That's when I ran back to my car and called 911."

I lay with my eyes closed, trying to remember. Nothing.

"After seeing your buddy being cut out the car and you being lifted on a gurney with some contraption on your head, I had to come and see how you two were doing."

I opened my eyes. "Hey, what can I say? I'm breathin'."

After his initial visit, Melvin came to see me almost every day for two weeks.

After a week or so, I had regained feeling in both arms and a little in my right hand. I could even move my arms and fingers a little. Even though my arms were progressively getting more mobile, my lower extremities wouldn't receive the message that my brain kept sending—*Move*. I just wanted to get the plastic snake out of my dick, and not have nurses puttin' their thumbs up my butt to make me go. I wanted control. Once I met sugar dumplin' on the night shift, I immediately made sure he didn't ever perform the finger up the butt deal. I would never be accused of having the shit finger fucked outta me.

Once my arms started acting like they had some sense, I started running the nurses ragged. I know they grew tired of me. I was the little boy who cried wolf. I concentrated on moving my toes every waking moment, and at times I thought they were moving. Sometimes it was a spasm, other times it was my imagination. I pressed my call button every time I thought I was moving something. I had to show someone what I thought I could do.

The responding nurse would berate me for using my emergency call pad every time I cried wolf. No matter how much I paged the nurses, they always came running. I concentrated so hard I got headaches and broke out in a sweat.

At the end of one week, Squirt rolled into my room. "Hey, dog, I thought you weren't going to make it for a while," he said.

"C'mon, man. It ain't gon' be that easy to get rid of me. You still owe me close to a G."

"Have the cops talked to you?" he asked.

"For what?"

"I guess you ain't heard."

"If I had, I wouldn't be saying for what."

"Dog, how 'bout I'm fresh out of surgery with a clothes hanger holdin' my neck bones together when them fools send two detectives in? How 'bout them busters charged me with DUI? I'm tellin' ya, me and my cousin didn't have nothing but a few brews. You would've knowed if I was drunk."

I felt nauseated after Squirt's statement. "How the hell I'm gon' know if you drunk? I was tired, but nooo— you had to have some work. I ain't paid no attention to you until you started playin' racecar driver. You almost killed me. Now I'm laid up in this bitch with mothafuckas tellin' me I ain't gon' ever walk again."

"Come on, Linc. You know I wasn't drunk."

"How the fuck I'm gon' know that shit? Man, it was late as hell. All I know is that I'm lying here unable to feel my fucking legs. I can't pee or shit on my own. I got an anchor on my head and part of the beach holdin' me down. Swimmin' without no legs is a slow drownin'. You should've just killed me. Man, just roll the fuck out. I ain't trying to talk to you right now," I cried. "Damn. Damn. Damn."

"Man, you buggin'," he said as he slowly rolled out of my curtained area of intensive care.

While Squirt was rolling out, Melvin was strutting in with this big-boned, short-haired, fine-ass chick he introduced as Cindy. After a couple of minutes of shooting the breeze, he asked me if any lawyers had tried to see me.

"Naw. Why would a lawyer be trying to see me?" I asked. I couldn't think of anything I'd been doing where I'd need a lawyer.

Melvin interrupted me in mid-thought. "I call them ambulance chasers. Once the general population can come visit, lawyers who make a living off people like you will be blanketing you."

"I ain't got nothing for 'em."

"No, but your buddy's car insurance company does. See, they'll be especially interested in you because you have a million-dollar case. A good lawyer will at least get you that much."

A million dollars. Wow.

"The only way they get paid is when they win your case, and then they get forty percent of the settlement. For four hundred grand you will be bombarded with lawyers romancing your stone."

"Man, I'm more worried about my legs than anything else. What you saying sounds good and shit, but if I can't walk, that money won't even matter."

"Look here, little brother," Melvin said as he walked up to the bed, cracking his knuckles before he put his dark, manicured hands on my bedpost. "In just the last week, I've seen a lifetime full of shit that you've gone through mentally and physically. At twenty-one, hell, at any age, no one needs to go through what you have. One minute you're running wild, partying, full of hope, full of life, and the next you're flat on your back unable to move, damn near unable to breathe. For what?" He paused to catch his breath.

"I took it upon myself to obtain a copy of the accident report. That's when I saw that it was your buddy who was driving, and it was his alcohol level that was off the board. That makes him negligent. I can't stand to see one of my brothas go through all this for nothin'. It ain't right."

No shit.

"A close friend of mine specializes in personal injury cases, and he's a damn good lawyer. All I'm asking is that when you're up to it, you let me have him come and drop in on you."

I figured, what the heck? After all, Melvin had called the ambulance that most likely saved my life.

"All right, man. I'll talk to your man as soon as I get out of ICU."

Every weekday morning, a heavyset, middle-aged sister came and gave me a workout. She massaged my arms, legs, fingers, and toes. She did this for anywhere from fifteen to forty-five minutes. While working her magic with thick, soft hands all over me, she would tell stories of her adventures with her different "mens," as she liked to say. Tracy was a trip, and she was mad cool.

During one of her workouts, Dr. Bob interrupted my favorite time of day to check my vital signs. I could have told him my vitals were fine. They hadn't changed in the last four hours. That's how often they were checked, as if I were terminally ill.

Since the doc was here, I decided to get down to the bottom of this DUI thing.

"Doc, I heard that Robert Miner was drunk when we had the wreck."

"Mr. Jackson, Mr. Miner's blood alcohol level registered well over the legal limit. Cocaine was also found in his system."

I was speechless and remained that way until the doc was gone. All I could think of was how I could have missed the signs. I couldn't even tell Squirt had been drinking. I really was slipping. That fool was a crack head. And to think I had been worried about causing him legal problems. Not anymore. It was on now. I was going to sue the shit out of his ass.

Some time in my sixth week, Tracy came to perform my workout, and I pretended to be asleep. I liked her company, but I hated the pain she put me through when she did anything with my right arm. She said that my right side was hypersensitive, especially my arm. While my eyes were closed, Tracy started massaging my toes. As soon as she lifted my right leg off the bed, I screamed. She jumped, bumping into my peeing machine.

Recovering quickly, she asked me if I felt it when she had her hands on my legs.

"Hell yeah. That shit hurt."

"Look, fool, you've got feeling in your right leg."

The jolting pain was so intense I didn't even realize it meant I had feeling in my leg.

"Do it again. Do it again!" I exclaimed. I smiled for the first time in nearly two months.

She touched, I screamed. She touched, I screamed. Oh, I definitely had feeling.

"Okay, Lincoln. Concentrate. I want you to breathe in, breathe out. Now I want you to move your toes," she soothed.

I moved three toes on my right foot after several concentrated efforts. I did it over and over again.

With no word at all, she up and left. I didn't care; I was too happy. I played a drumbeat on my call pad. Once I got Nurse Nancy, I showed her my three-toe motion. I made her touch my leg. Of course, when she did, I screamed out in pain, but I had never been happier to be in pain. I wanted to keep feeling it.

By the time Tracy returned with Dr. Bob, I had nurses and an intern at my bed, showing off my gifts. "I told you I was a seven percenter," I said. "You can just go on and give my wheelchair away because I won't be needing it."

Everyone laughed.

"Well, I guess we'll just have to change your original diagnosis. Still, you mustn't get your hopes up. This could be the extent of your recovery. It's not unusual for a quadriplegic to regain feeling and even slight movement in his lower extremities. I'm going to have Dr. Strauss, our resident psychologist, come in to speak with you."

Doc was truly a hater. He tried to throw water on my fire, but the flame was too bright. I wasn't hearing any negativity. The last thing I said before Doc, the nurses, and Tracy left was, "Doc, I don't care what you've seen in the past, nor do I care how many degrees and plaques you've earned. God is a much higher power than you, and He has the last word on when and how soon I'll be walking."

About a half hour after Doc left, I heard the familiar whizzing sound of an electric wheelchair and the sound of my curtain being maneuvered. An unfamiliar voice greeted me.

"Mr. Jackson, I'm Dr. Strauss. How are we feeling today?"

"I don't know how we are feeling, but if I felt any better, I'd be ready to run the Boston Marathon." I could barely see the funny-looking man in the wheelchair out the corner of my eye.

"Mr. Jackson, I am a psychologist. Eighteen years ago, I was the sole survivor in a small engine plane crash that left three dead. My level of injury is the exact same as yours. Even though I have feeling in part of one leg and I can move a couple of my toes, I am still a quadriplegic and unable to walk, as I'm sure you've deducted. I'm here as a living testament, praise God, there is life after paralysis. I play basketball. I swim. I am very active.

"I'm not going to tell you that it's ever easy. What I am here to do is to tell you the truth. The sooner you accept your condition, the sooner you will be on the way to a productive life."

Was every doctor drunk on haterade?

"Remember this: there are clearer skies on the other side of the rainbow. You just have to persevere. At first, I was very much like you. Facing the reality of not ever being able to walk again was totally unacceptable. I was mad at the world. I questioned God. But in the long run, this has brought me closer to the Creator. Eventually, I came to accept and comfortably live without the use of my legs."

That's the difference between you and me. You accepted your condition, I thought.

"Now I dedicate a lot of time helping people such as yourself adjust to their new lives." He waved one of his arms in a comical motion with his fingers turned in, in a deformed-looking way.

Please leave. Please leave. Can't you see I don't subscribe to Haters R Us?

"You are surrounded by people who care and will help you to adjust before you go home to your new life. You will go through our program, which consists of a variety of classes here that will help prepare you for the world sitting down."

I tried to be patient and courteous, but he kept going on.

"Hold up, doc. You need to save your motivational, get-in-touch-with-reality speech for someone who it applies to. I don't need those classes. What part of 'I'm walking out of here' don't you understand?" I imagined the beet-red appearance that must have warmed the doc's face.

"Mr. Jackson," he said, exasperated, "I've been doing this for umpteen years, and I know what I'm talking about."

"Testy," I said, wanting to get my message across and teasing him at the same time.

Ignoring me, he continued. "You must face facts. Your chances of walking again are nil."

"Man, you ain't God. You don't know what I'll do again. You roll in, tryin' to destroy people's hopes and dreams. Just 'cause your ass can't walk don't mean I won't. Just because you gave up don't mean I will. Just get out my space. I need to conserve air, and you're breathing too much of mine up."

I was pissed and sick of people feeling sorry for me. I was sick of quackpot doctors trying to play God. I didn't know why, but the more they hated, the stronger my resolve became. There was no doubt in my mind that I would walk again.

A couple of weeks down the road I was out of the ICU unit and in a two-person room. I had a gadget on my head and shoulders to keep my neck from moving. It was an aluminum ring screwed into my head. Four aluminum half-inch rods went from the ring to my shoulders. The rods were screwed into something similar to football shoulder pads. The doctors called this contraption a halo.

The only thing I looked forward to as a resident of Shepherd Spinal Center was my daily physical therapy and massage sessions with Tracy. We now met in a small gym with all kinds of crazy-looking machines.

I had made exceptional progress in the nine weeks since the accident. I could feed myself with my right hand, and I could now pee on my own. While most people lost weight in hospitals, I gained. What I needed was a trough and some mud to waddle in. I went from a lean, mean 190 pounds, to a Pillsbury Dough Boy fat, soft 230 pounds. It wasn't pretty. Those mall cookies with the chocolate-and-vanilla icing became my drug of choice. They made me feel better than the Tylenol and the muscle relaxers I stayed on. I had the hookup on sweets. Momma was my sweet dealer. She kept me oinking.

There were three levels in Shepherd Spinal Center. Everyone under twenty-five was housed on the third floor. It saddened me to be hospitalized with so many kids who had been used to being able to run free and were now trying to adjust to life sitting down. Diving, motorcycle, car, and ladder accidents were the reasons for 95 percent of spinal cord injuries. Diving accident victims were more likely to have spinal cord injuries than anyone else. Surprisingly, the kids handled their situations better than the adults.

The exception to the children who were housed on the third floor was the living legend, Curtis Mayfield. On August 13, 1990, the famed writer, producer, and recording artist known to the younger generation for his Blaxploitation movie soundtrack to Superfly, was in a sound-stage lighting accident that left him paralyzed and unable to breathe on his own.

I learned to live in agony. My head was always in pain because of the contraption on it. It was especially painful when the nurse would clean the arch where the screws went into my head, or when the doctors tightened the screws with a crescent wrench. I had to be doped up just to sleep.

It was different during the day at my wheelchair adjustment and bowel and bladder classes. There, you could find me reclined in my Cadillac electric wheelchair—eyes closed, mouth gapped open, and a drool waterfall on the sides of my lips, chin, neck, and shirt. I got some of my best sleep in those classes, medication free. I didn't even attempt to stay awake. I attended them to take a nap.

Ten weeks after the accident, I regained control of my bowels and could even move both legs a little. Every day I got stronger and made more progress.

One morning after having spoken to Melvin about his lawyer friend, I met him. He was a tall, fifty-something, clean-shaven, Uncle Jesse-lookin' white dude. He sauntered into my hospital room carrying a tattered black case.

"Hey there, Lincoln. I'm Graydon Flowers. How's the air down there?" he asked, extending his hand.

I was resting from my earlier workout with Tracy. I looked at his Bugs Bunny smile before sayin', "I'm fine."

"I need your Lincoln Hancock on these." He put a couple of papers in my face. "Don't worry. They just say that you've retained me on a 60/40 contingency basis."

After signing them I asked, "Where's Melvin?"

"He's out chasin' down more clients for me. Don't know what I'd do without that ol' boy. Been workin' for me ten years."

I'd been played like a piano. I wasn't mad. I respected game. Melvin was good. I hoped I'd see him one more time to give him his props.

About a week after I'd signed papers agreeing to be represented by Mr. Flowers, he dropped a bomb on me over the phone. "Lincoln, we may have problems. In a follow-up report, Robert Miner told the investigating officers that he took Mr. Franklin's car without permission."

As I listened, Mr. Flowers said that this statement no longer made the insurance company, State Farm, liable.

Shaking my head, I said, "That's a damn lie. He ain't stole no car. That's his cousin. They tryin' to pull somethin'. Nah, man, I'm gon' straighten this out."

"Robert will have to change his statement," Mr. Flowers said.

"He will. This man done dang near killed me. He was drunk too. Ain't no way I'm going through this without getting paid."

Without even saying bye, I dropped the phone on the floor, spun around in my chair and road-raged my way toward Squirt's room.

I blew through Squirt's door, ignoring his father. "Man, what the fuck you trying to do? Look at me. I'm in this chair, unable to walk. I just started peeing on my own, and you tryin' to shit me out of any hope of getting any kind of insurance settlement."

"Man, I don't know what you talkin' 'bout."

"The statement you made to the police, where you said that you stole your cousin's car."

Brushing it off as if it was nothing, he said, "Aw, man, Al told me to say that so his insurance wouldn't be jacked up. I didn't know it would mess you up."

"Yo' bitch-ass cousin is worried about his mothafuckin' car insurance when me and you are tore up from the floor up and can't get up? I can't even get paid for you ruining my life because of some dumb shit your cousin coerced you to say."

"I didn't know."

"But you knew how to be a crack head. You knew how to drunk drive. You knew how to fuck me up on any ends I could have gotten for you messin' my life up."

"Man, I'm sorry. I didn't wreck that car on purpose."

"But you lied on purpose," I said.

For the first time since I began fussing like a madman, Squirt's father spoke. "Lincoln's right, son. You have to do what's right. You'll have to retract the statement you gave to the police."

"I know, Pop. I was just trying to help Al. I didn't know I was messing things up for my dog."

I was relieved, and I felt kind of bad for blowing up. He didn't know what he was doing. I was just glad that he was going to do the right thing. Mr. Miner told me to call my lawyer and explain the situation.

I did right then and there. I was surprised that Mr. Flowers didn't come down to the hospital and talk to Squirt and his family. Instead, he extracted a tape-recorded statement from Squirt over the phone. But he was the lawyer. I guess he knew what he was doing.

It was over three months before I was taking steps unaided. My equilibrium was off and my muscles were still very weak, but I was slowly starting to walk. The other kids at the clinic started calling me Robocop because I was so stiff and uncoordinated, walking with a cage on my head.

When asked about my miraculous recovery, my doctors couldn't explain it. Dr. Bob told me and my family that so little was known about spinal cord injuries that it was hard to pinpoint how I was able to regain muscle control.

"Mr. Jackson's excellent physical condition when he was initially brought in is one of the biggest determining factors for his recovery," he said.

Yeah, right. I wonder how the crow Doc had to eat tasted. It had been the will of God, and I knew it. I thanked God continuously.

"God had a plan for you, and being in a wheelchair the rest of your life isn't in His plans. Take heed, boy. You had a brush with what could've been death and powerlessness. Take this as a warning. Next time you might not be so fortunate. I hope you've learned that God don't like ugly. It always catches up to you," Momma lectured.

It was then that I was sure Momma knew that I had been selling dope, but that still wouldn't stop me. D'Andre got the word out to my boys that I was coming home. At one time or another all of them had popped in on me. According to the rumors in the streets, I was dead, I'd lost my legs or I was a crip, paralyzed and in a chair.

The latter was right, to a degree. I was still partially paralyzed. My whole left side was impaired; none of my muscles were fully operable. On my right side, I had no sensation. I couldn't tell sharp from dull, nor hot and cold. I experienced a dull sensation when my right side was touched. These symptoms led the doctors to re-assess their earlier diagnosis. Now they said I had Brown Secord Syndrome.

After four long, exhausting months I was given an early discharge. Actually, I was kicked out. I'd become too much of an insurance risk. Late at night, when I was supposed to be asleep, I'd get out of bed and into my chair. Then I would sneak to the elevator and go to the basement where the electric wheelchairs were kept. I'd steal one of the charged chairs and go either to the garden and smoke some herb that one of my boys had brought me, or I would go to the therapy gym and work out. My workout was sliding out of the chair and onto a mat, then trying to get back into the chair, which I never could. Even though I was able to take a few steps, I was still too weak to get up off the floor.

Other times, I would disappear next door into the bowels of Piedmont Hospital when I was supposed to be in one of my many "life after paralysis" classes.

I was a walking catastrophe waiting to happen. Humpty Dumpty ain't had nothing on me. Shepherd wasn't going to be held liable if I fell with that halo on, so the hospital was forced to give me my walking papers early. I had to go, halo and all. My therapists and the nurses gave me a pretty cool graduation party. I gave a short motivational speech to all of the kids.

"The only reason I'm standing here today is because I said I would. After all the doctors, psychologists, analysts, and specialists said I'd be in a wheelchair, I told them they were wrong. I knew they were wrong. They used statistics and other people's results to determine my fate. They were wrong. Don't let other people decide your outcome. You have to take control of your own fate. You have to take charge of your destiny. God is the most learned, most knowing specialist there is. Work with Him in faith, and you can do anything. If God can make a man walk on water, then surely He can make one walk on land."

CHAPTER 17

It was mid-December, 1990. Not a week out of the hospital, barely able to walk and with a cage on my head, I was back in business. D'Andre had looked out for me. It was times like these that made me sad I'd treated him the way I had when we were kids.

D'Andre Lamont Jackson, two years, two weeks and two days younger than me, was the only genius I had ever known. He could read any manual and immediately build and repair anything without having any prior experience. We couldn't have been more different. While I was always trying to find a side shortcut, D'Andre always took the long road.

I didn't treat him right. Growing up, he was my scapegoat. When something got broken, I was usually the culprit, but I blamed him. When something came up missing, yours truly was the cause of the disappearance, but guess who I blamed? When the Entenmanns pastry cake that Momma hid over the kitchen sink in the back of the cabinet vanished, the trail of crumbs led to my bed or to the locked bathroom where I would sneak away and eat away, but guess who I blamed?

I never knew how, but Sherlock D'Andre could always catch me in the act of wrongdoing.

"I'm gon' tell," he'd point at me and say.

By the time Momma got home I would already have a well-constructed lie. I'd meet Momma before she came in the house.

"Momma, D' Andre broke the window" or "Momma, D'Andre was standing on the cabinet trying to reach the Flintstone vitamins when he broke your casserole dish," I would lie.

If Momma saw through my lies or if D'Andre beat me to the telling, Momma tore my butt up. This would then facilitate me beating D'Andre's butt—the Jackson domino effect.

I remember one summer when I was ten and D'Andre was eight. It was a Saturday morning and Momma was at the laundromat. For two weeks, a lonely sealed can of Pillsbury's strawberry frosting sat in the cabinet messin' wit' me, callin' my name for no reason at all. Momma wasn't makin' my sufferin' no easier. She was takin' too long. She'd been promising to bake us a cake for forever, it seemed.

This particular morning, Marnease was MIA. D'Andre was awake, spread all over Momma's bed watching the Roadrunner and Wile E.Coyote.

"You want a Charms Pop?" I asked, waving one of my surplus suckers I sold at school in his face.

"Nope."

"How 'bout some Now n' Laters?"

"Nope."

"Momma said I could watch *Fat Albert*."

"Liar."

"Okay, you win." I shrugged. "I'll let you ride my bike all day if you let me have the TV."

"Blackjack, no trade back," he shouted, running out the room.

I locked the door and turned the TV to a *Schoolhouse Rock* commercial.

"Let me in. Let me in. I'mo tell Momma!" D'Andre screamed a few minutes later. I was so glad I never taught him how to use a butter knife to unlock the door.

He was probably upset because I hadn't bothered to mention that my bike was locked up to the water meter outside the back door with a broken chain and a flat tire. Yeah, I tricked him, but eventually he calmed down. He was used to it. I was bigger, older, and I could beat him up.

After *Fat Albert* and *The Green Hornet* went off, I gave him the TV back. I was starving anyway, so I went to the kitchen. I rinsed out a bowl, grabbed milk from the fridge, and took the Cocoa Pebbles from the cabinet. Then I poured eight little pebbles into that big bowl.

D'Andre had eaten the whole box. I screamed bloody murder while D'Andre laughed his head off. I ran to Momma's room. I tried to twist the knob. I don't know why he locked her door; he knew I could get in. If my hunger drums weren't beatin' so furious, my fists would have been playin' rump-a-pump-pump upside his head.

I stared into an empty refrigerator. We had bread, but no bologna. We had peanut butter, but no jelly. When I looked in the cabinet, that single can of strawberry frosting stared back at me.

Shoot, Momma probably wouldn't make that cake for another month. I could replace it before she ever noticed it missing.

After rationalizing for all of thirty seconds, I climbed onto the cabinet, stood up just enough to reach the can, dropped it onto the countertop, and jumped down, where I had the Wonder bread waiting.

I carefully and painstakingly cut a small incision into the aluminum foil seal. That way I could put the frosting back in the cabinet, just like new, if I didn't like it.

I toasted three slices of Wonder bread and spread a teensy-weensy, tiny-winy bit of frosting onto the bread. Now as I stared at the hot Wonder bread/strawberry cake, I thought about the whipping I would get if Momma found out. Was a whipping from Momma worth the luscious, heavenly, mouthwatering strawberry Wonder bread three-layer cake?

While contemplating, I accidentally took a bite and euphoria encompassed my fatness. I was high. It was exquisite. It was so good I threw all caution aside and toasted seven more slices of bread. I was making two and three-layer cakes when who showed up but tattletale, diarrhea mouth.

He jumped from the hallway, scaring me half to dang death. I almost dropped my triple-layer, extra-icing bread cake.

"Ooh. Ooh. I'mo tell. I'mo tell Momma, and you gon' get a whoopin', a-a-a-a whoopin'. You gon' get a whoopin' and it's gonna hurt," he sang.

I put my index fingers in my ears and shook my head. "Ahhhh," I yelled to tune him out. When that didn't work, I said, "Shut up. Shut up 'fo I kick yo' ass."

He pointed his 8-year-old finger in my face. "Ooh, you said a bad word. I'mo tell that too. I'mo, I'mo tell that too, " he sang.

"Ass ain't no bad word, fool," I shouted as I attacked. I hit him and wrestled him until he threw a crying fit, then I let him up because for some reason I always felt bad when I made him cry. It cost me my last quarter to make him stop. We struck a deal once he was standing and wiping his nose with his T-shirt.

"I'll tell you what. I'll fix my bike right now and let you ride it all day if you don't tell on me."

"All day?"

"Yeah, all day."

Three days later, I walked into the house and smelled the unmistakable aroma of flour and sugar baking. Momma was baking a cake. I almost soiled my pants right in the middle of the living room. I watched Momma reach for the almost empty can of Pillsbury strawberry frosting.

Momma had herself a champion hissy fit.

"Who in the hell ate up all this frosting?" she screamed at the three of us.

The Fifth Amendment went into effect immediately. We all stood in front of Momma looking real crazy.

"All right, since don't nobody know nothing, everybody go to bed. I'll be in with my belt and then we'll see if you can talk. Go," she ordered.

"Saturday morning I caught Lincoln eating frosting on toast and he, he beat me up and told me not to tell," D'Andre said.

"Momma, he's lying," I cried, tears flowing. "D'Andre ate it, and he's trying to blame it on me. I always get blamed for everything."

"That's okay, I'll find out," she said. "Uh-huh, I'll find out the truth in the morning, and when I do, I'm going to get the extension cord out and whip the guilty party until they can't sit down for a week," she said, frowning. "You gon' wish you had told me the truth. Just wait. I'm going downtown to the police station and find out whose fingerprints are all over this." She held up the frosting with two fingers so as not to disturb the prints. "Now go to bed, all of you."

Restlessly, I lay in bed. I tossed and turned. I couldn't sleep for thinking about that long, brown snake that would be wrapped around Momma's hand, coming down on my legs and behind as I struggled to get away. It was a waking nightmare.

Around midnight, I'd say, I couldn't stand it any longer. I snail-crept into Momma's room. The closer I got to her side of the bed, the faster the tears ran.

She continued reading her book as if I weren't even there. I knew she'd seen me, though. I sniffled as I spoke. "Momma, D'Andre ate up all the Cocoa Pebbles, and I was starving."

At ten years old, I was not five feet tall, but I tipped the scales at 120 pounds, so it would take some doing before I starved. "Momma, there was nothing to eat. I-I-I-I ate the frosting," I stuttered and stammered, crying crocodile tears, almost tripping over my two feet as I shuffled back and forth.

Now as I reflect back on the scene, the only reason Momma didn't light into me was because of the anguished look on my face, my bloodshot eyes, and the unending tears. She figured I had suffered enough. Telling on myself was one of the hardest things I had to do as a child.

As the years passed, D' Andre would continue to be my punching bag or my co-conspirator whenever I paid for his silence. The more I settled into a role of nonconformity, the more D'Andre conformed.

D'Andre made all A's and B's through school. He was studious without ever having to be pushed. He overachieved in everything. He grew into a gifted artist as well as a high school football star, playing both ends of the ball and lettering as early as the ninth grade. Shy and quiet, he was the opposite of my loud, always-wanting-to-be-seen self.

In seventh grade, D'Andre shot up like a tree, tall and wide. By eighth grade he had me by an inch and twenty pounds. While he grew, I shrunk, shedding a stomach and half an ass. As time passed, D'Andre got wider and wider. Mind you, he wasn't fat-fat, he was just big, stocky, and He Man strong. But no matter how strong or wide, he still was no match for me. I was the only one who could play the big bullying brother role.

D'Andre had zero hustle in him. He wouldn't even take an extra newspaper out of the machine. During his first week in high school, a fat-ass cow started picking on him. Clark Jordan was trailer park trash. The boy was a fat, pink zit with a rep as a bully. Clark was also a professional student—eighteen and still in the tenth grade. Rumor had it that the only reason he had made it out of ninth grade was because his teachers were sick and tired of his musty-dusty ass stinking up their classrooms for two years.

One day this Clark cow tripped my eighth-grade brother, sending books and papers flying down the already crowded hallway. Clark and his entourage laughed and kept walking while D'Andre struggled to pick up his scattered papers, books, pens, and pencils. After getting up and gathering his things, he rushed to class, trying to ignore Sasquatch and his crew of misfits.

Clark picked on my brother for three days before word got to me. Clark was in my fourth-period gym class when I overheard him laughing about how he was going to beat up my little brother after school. The fool had to be sniffin' Elmer's. I was hotter than hell in July.

When the sixth-period bell rang, I sprinted out of class to D'Andre's locker. I wanted to make sure he was in my sight at all times. While at our bus stop waiting for the big yellow ride home, I smelled Clark before I saw him. Soon he and two others surrounded D'Andre. A crowd gathered.

"A fight, a fight, a nigga and a White," some of the other students sang off key.

Before a hand was laid on my brother, I ran up to the towering Clark. I drew my fist back to Mississippi, swooped through Tennessee, and made my way down to Georgia before I touched down on his jaw. I sent that dinosaur crashing to the ground. I wore his butt out and eclipsed the whipping by having D'Andre grab a handful of grass and stuff it in Clark's big fat mouth. His boys just stood there offering no help. Clark dropped out of school the following week.

By the time D'Andre was a senior in high school, college football scouts and coaches from around the country salivated at the idea of him playing for them. Scholarships were extended to him like handshakes. You would think anyone with an iota of sense would have jumped on such opportunities, but not D'Andre. Something drastic happened to my naïve younger brother his junior year—a female. Trina René McClemore was a skinny, shorthaired redbone shaped like a wall. She put the bumpkin in country, and if she was a couple of shades lighter she could have passed for a Clampett.

She wasn't the sharpest knife in the rack, either. I despised the little loud-mouthed, no-lip child. D'Andre worked with Trina at Wendy's. I knew he could do better; he had too much on the ball to be falling for this girl.

Whenever Trina called the house and I answered the phone, she had nothing coming. When she asked for Dre, as she called him, I always claimed to be on the other line or said that he wasn't home.

One day the little chicken-head girl stood up to me. I did my usual, telling her that D'Andre wasn't home.

"You know what? You's an ass."

"And you need one."

"I know Dre's home. I just got off the phone with him."

"Oh, really."

"But that's okay, baby balls."

"Yo' momma."

"Fuck you, you black, fat bastard."

"Yo' grandmomma."

"You should be the poster boy for pro-choice." Click.

The crack-baby hung up on me. I didn't believe that shit.

"D'Andre," I yelled, "you tell your anorexic-ass, retarded, crack head girlfriend to quit calling here playing on this damn phone 'fore she get her head split."

I wasn't really mad, at least not because of her antics. I was angry with my genius brother because he had decided to forego college and turn down all that free money for school. Especially after all that trouble I had getting into school.

He claimed that he was tired of going to school and that he just needed a year or so to rest. It didn't take a rocket scientist to see what was holding him back like

162

metal on a magnet—Trina. She had his nose open wide enough to park an eighteen-wheeler in it.

After graduation, he and Trina got an apartment together. She got a job working for AT&T and he got a good job installing car audio equipment and car alarms.

After my apartment was broken into, I often had D'Andre hold money for me. If there was anyone I could trust, it was him. After his graduation, and as I got more involved in the dope game, D'Andre and I grew closer. And what surprised me even more was that I started liking Trina. I found out that she wasn't such an airhead. While D'Andre kept my money, Trina separated and counted it. She even shopped for me when I needed her to.

After I realized she wasn't so bad, I had to accept the fact that it wasn't her fault D'Andre had passed up his chance to go to school. After all, she never put a gun to his head. She even surprised me by decorating my new ground-level apartment that she and D'Andre had prepared for me after I was released from the hospital.

I hadn't moved in good before I was back in business, barely walkin'. I couldn't miss out on the New Year's Eve money. Folks liked to bring in New Year's with a bang, many times telling themselves it was their last time getting high. I had D'Andre's friend Mike drive me around while I was in traction.

Mike was family. He and D'Andre had been inseparable growing up. They even began to look alike, but that's where the likeness ended. Mike was a high school drop out, a hustler, and often looked to me for guidance. I was the big brother he never had, and I was an equal opportunity older brother.

I went upside Mike's head and tricked him as much as I did D'Andre. I gave him the name Red Mike. He was vanilla-brown and when he got mad, he turned hotsauce red. But this wasn't the reason I called him this. It was because he didn't like it.

While at Shepherd, Mike kept me abreast of all the happenings in the streets. He had been dibbling and dabbling in the dope game, and I had never tried to help him because he was hardheaded and hung out with shady characters who were into everything from carjacking to armed robbery. But while in the hospital, I made him a promise. I told him I'd make him my number two man. He'd be responsible for overseeing my boys in the projects and the motel lodges. The only stipulation was he had to let go of all the fools he hung with and do what I told him. I even moved him in with me until we got him his own place.

The halo was removed a couple of months after leaving Shepherd. I was still partially paralyzed, my left side was considerably weaker than my right, and I strained the scales at a smothering two-sixty, but the money was once again rolling in. By my twenty-second birthday in April '91 I started to relax and appreciate the flow of money. Dope was plentiful, and so were the hoes.

In '91, old cars became trendy. They were referred to as hoopties. If you were getting money, you had to have one. All the dope boys were driving around in drop-top '64 Impalas, early '70s Oldsmobiles, Delta '88s, '70s Deuce and a Quarters, and '60s Mustangs. If you really had it going on, you had a *vert*—a convertible. These cars looked like something out of a car show after they had been painted, with the interior plushed out, blasting a boomin' stereo system that anyone could hear from a block away. These big-ass tanks had hydraulics that could raise the cars two and three feet off the ground while cruisin'. And you just had to have the thirty-spoke rims and the vogue tires to complete the package.

I wanted to be like the Joneses, so I decided to get a vert. I didn't want to buy one from another hustler. That would be inheriting his or her heat with five-O or with any robbing crew that had them under the scope. So I turned to Willie.

Willie was a geek monster and a damned good mechanic who lived down the street from Momma. He worked on my cars all through high school. I saved a lot of money because I paid him with dope. Willie had been smoking crack since before it was called crack.

Anyway, Willie had this old, ugly, grass green, drop-top '69 Ford Cougar in his backyard. For fifteen years he let himself and all of his possessions go. This ride was no different. The top was black, dry rotted, and sported several holes. If it hadn't been for a car cover, the elements would have destroyed any hope of restoration. So much was wrong with it, Willie never bothered to repair it. It was scrap metal to somebody without vision, but I visualized new life for this car.

After a little finagling, I gave Willie fifty dime rocks that were worth less than $200 and $250 in cash. Within a week, he ended up smoking up the two-fifty along with the dope I gave him.

The Cougar had a strong 351 Windsor engine that Willie rebuilt along with the whole front end and the transmission. I had to replace the battery, alternator, radiator and belts, and I added a Holley four-barrel. A half-ounce of rock and three weeks later, Willie had my baby purring like a kitten and running like a cheetah. But it still looked like rolling shit.

I took the Cougar to Mike's pop. Mr. J had been a surrogate father to me. I had him put some thirty-spokes and vogues on my car's feet. A car wasn't nothin' without clean shoes. Next, he took the car and had it stripped down to the metal. He had all of the original chrome dipped. He replaced the battered top with a new white-piped black ragtop. He redid the seats in white Naugahyde with black piping. The dash was dyed white, the carpet was lights-out black, and to top it off, the car was painted pearl white with a rose tint.

While all this was going on, I had D'Andre install a ten-speaker, 250-watt, two-channel bridged Alpine stereo system. Ninety days and nine Gs later, my original vision became a reality.

I drove in concert, breakin' necks, leaving sweating eyes on sidewalks in my wake. Top dropped, with J.P. Gaultiers covering my eyes and a serious gangsta lean, I basked in the limelight as I stopped traffic. The first day I drove my ho panty-wetter was my lucky one, for more reasons than you can imagine.

I pulled into a car wash to get my baby detailed, blaring Randy Crawford's classic hit "Street Life" when I met Woody. He was sporting an ash-gray Hugo and a pair of matching Mauris. This old cat was sharper than Rambo's knife. While he was having his blue Impulse cleaned, we got to rappin' about my ride. He told me that he owned a bronze '68 Cougar. We got the conversation over to sports and soon discovered we were both avid boxing fans. We stood out in the Georgia spring sunshine, deep in conversation as traffic whizzed by. I don't know how, but the conversation took a heavy turn.

"What messed it up for everybody was the coke price dive and young kids being introduced to the game. Now look what's happening." Woody threw his arms in the air.

What the hell was he ravin' about?

"Kids who couldn't even pee straight were out on the corner playin' grown folks' games, sellin' girl."

I wondered where this was goin'.

"They drivin' around in flashy cars worth more than the cops make in a year. They already can't stand to see a black man with anything. You don't think they know what's going on? Driving around in these fancy cars, blasting stereos, wearing mountains of gold."

Hmmm.

"These kids might as well drive around with a personalized license tag surrounded by neon green and orange lights reading I'm the dope man."

I ain't never looked at it that way.

"Eight or nine years ago B.C.—before crack—a kilo cost fifty Gs, and only a select few were allowed to buy in. It was a gentleman's game. Today, anybody with eighteen to twenty-five Gs can pick up a kilo. No one carried guns. But now cocaine is plentiful and cheap. Anyone can get high. What happens?" He paused to take an overdue breath.

"You have fiends puttin' pistols to heads, out there hustlin'. You have these half-baked robbing crews jackin' and smokin' cats like it's legal. So the dealers not only have to carry guns, they have to be prepared to use 'em."

I nodded. I had never looked at it that way.

"Back ten years ago, you couldn't buy ya-yo in the projects. Cocaine wasn't sold on every street corner. It was respectably sold out of houses and in high-rises. And anybody couldn't come up and knock on the door. You knew your customers. Now the game is a friggin' free-for-all. It's gone from a gentleman's game to a scavenger hunt."

The whole time Woody spoke, I knew he was referring to me as part of generation crack. That was the beginning of a whole new consciousness.

All that noise, and he still became my supplier and teacher in the world of high finance hustling.

Even though I was raking the money in and living like Solomon with a harem of hoes, I still wasn't satisfied. Even that was starting to get old. I was tired of screwin' through the white pages. It was getting expensive.

My boy from college, Borado, and I were still close even though he was 250 miles away at Savannah State. On some weekends and holidays, he came home and we hung strong. Around Thanksgiving 1991, Borado and I were chillin' at my crib kicking the bobo, smoking some killer herb. We were waiting on some freaks from Savannah State.

They popped up after about two blunts, and we all played spades and smoked more herb. I don't know why, but I asked one of the girls who I knew to be a close friend of Michelle's about her. She was still on my mind after three years. Michelle was like the North Star. She shone bright. You could stare at her light, but never really get near her. I begged Candy, Michelle's friend and soror, to make sure that Michelle called me collect.

A few days later, I was on I-85 on my way to look at a 911 Porsche Carera I had seen for sale in Buckhead, when Michelle called me on my cell. Just hearing her songbird voice turned me on.

I pulled over to the side of the highway. We talked and talked. Eventually, I invited her up for the weekend. She turned me down, saying she couldn't afford to come.

I called her dorm the next day and left an urgent message for her to go to Western Union. Awaiting her was $500 and another invite. She came, and we were down like two flat tires after that.

Her simplicity made her so cool. She didn't care about my money. She tried to stop me from buying her stuff. She hated the way I spent money. She was there for all my big purchases, like the 3600 square-foot tri-level suburban home I bought for my brother and his girl in an upscale community. In two months I had it completely redone, adding wall-to-wall carpeting, track lighting, and ceiling fans. I had a 200-gallon fish tank mounted in the living room wall.

I bought cars ranging from a Limited Edition sixteen-valve custom Benz, to a plain '78 Oldsmobile Cutlass Supreme. The whole United States became my playground. My favorite spot to play in, besides Michelle, was Vegas. Vegas was exhilarating, a playground for big ballers and the rich. It was where you could go all out: clothes, money, and jewelry, without five-O jockin'.

It was the lights, the high rollers, and the various stars that drew me there. It was the Holyfield-Holmes fight that really turned me out. I was in the Mirage shooting craps when Naomi Campbell almost bumped into me. I saw Magic Johnson to my left checking out the scene. All I could think about was that I had arrived. I was ballin', and back home I was straight shot callin'. If you had enough loot, you could get in anywhere. I got buck wild partying with the stars.

I was on top of the world when the drought at the end of '91 hit. As part of the so-called War on Drugs campaign during the Reagan/Bush administration, the U.S. Border Patrol and the DEA beefed up their forces. Over eighty-five percent of the world's cocaine supply came out of Colombia. With the use of informants and tracking devices, several cargoes were seized coming into U.S. coastal waters. The largest seizure was in October '91.

The DEA got a big break when an informant who worked with the Medellin cartel supplied information on how a lot of dope got past U.S. Customs. In the same month, U.S. Customs and the DEA seized more than thirty thousand pounds of cocaine. In a span of ten days, three cargo ships carried 5,500 kilos of cocaine in a hull built under the ships. These freighters came from Portugal by way of South America. The Medellin and Cali cartels, the world's two largest cocaine distributors, were shipping the drugs to Europe, trying to bypass stricter surveillance. Upon those ships docking off the coast of Maine, U.S. Customs and the DEA sent a 160-man task force to seize the shipments.

These busts and several others were the catalyst that led to the drought from December '91 to June '92. The dealers started to feel the crunch two months after the stream of busts began. The panic was on. Street prices shot up from eighteen to thirty Gs a kilo in a month. The drought didn't affect me until the beginning of March '92. In the three months from December '91 to March '92, I made more money than I had in all of '91. No matter how high I jacked up the prices, I still couldn't meet the demand.

The reason Woody still had dope when hardly no one else did was because he only had me and one other cat who bought blow from him. Woody would buy two to three hundred kilos at a time. He never rushed to sell one gram. The man's patience and caution were probably the main reason he had never been popped. He slowly jacked his prices up, but so did I. But, like all good things, this came to an end. Before I knew it, Woody went dry.

In March, I was running around frantically trying to find blow. I had decided in December of '91 that I would sell all the blow, make all the money I could, and by spring of '92 get out the game. I was hot. It was just a matter of time before five-O closed in.

I figured I'd open a business and get my groove on legitimately. If I could find some dope during the dry spell, I could get out by my birthday in April.

Mike paged me in mid-March.

"Linc, I'm at Derrick's mom's house shooting pool. He just slipped up and told me that his uncle was on."

"Straight up?"

"Hold on. I'll let you holler at him."

"You know how I feel about Ma Bell and five-O."

"Oh yeah, my bad."

"Naw, that's okay. I'm driving down Glenwood. I'll be there in ten."

After I dropped this little freak off at OV's to get her weave done, I raced to Derrick's.

Derrick was a short, bigheaded, stuttering, loud-mouthed, lying soldier-behind-a-gun who Mike sold

170

dope to from time to time. When I pulled up into his mom's driveway, Mike and Derrick were waiting for me.

"Playa, playa, tell me something good."

"Shit, you got it," Derrick said as we ghetto-hugged.

"I'm trying to cop. Mike tells me your folks is holding," I said.

"My uncle's folks are some kingpin Cubans who have a few kilos."

"Bet. What's the ticket on each bird?" I asked.

"I already set up a deal for Eddie."

Eddie Doverton was a lame that I went to high school with. He'd been in the game a couple of years longer than me. I didn't mess with him 'cause when I first started off after Li'l Man got smoked and Tarik got ghost, cashflow on *E*, this busta kept givin' me the run-around. Nigga treated me like Billy Bologna. I would have respected Eddie if he would have kept it real and just told me he wasn't gon' fuck with me.

"Man, why you messing with that lame?"

He shrugged.

"How much blow he gettin'?"

"Four birds."

"How much is Eddie paying?" I asked Derrick.

"Twenty-two a bird."

I could hardly believe my ears. That nigga hit the crack jackpot.

"Put me down with the lick. I'll put an extra six Gs in your pocket."

Two days later, at 7:00 in the morning, I met Mike at my downtown third-floor condo. I gave him a black plastic oblong box packed with sixty-six Gs, and I carried another twenty-two in a muddy-brown cassette carrying case.

"Bro, I need you to take I-20 to Thornton Road. Turn right off the highway and follow the road to Shoney's. It'll be on the left side. Grab you some breakfast, stay there until I hit you up on the cell," I directed.

"I don't know about this shit, man."

"Baby boy, that's why you holdin' most the cash," I said reassuringly.

"What if them niggas rob you?"

"That's why I got this." I pulled my Glock out my pants pocket.

"You know how that nigga Derrick lie," Mike said.

"He'll end up being fertilizer if he pull some dumb shit. You know he scary as hell."

"Yeah, you right."

"I'm always right, li'l nigga. Let's make this shit happen."

We walked out the crib and took the elevator down to the parking garage.

I picked Derrick up and drove to a convenience store on Thornton Road. We pulled up to a triple-black SS Monte Carlo with tinted windows. A Latin-looking guy wearing dark glasses got out. Something didn't seem right. I guessed I was being paranoid. Derrick got out of my '78 crayon-white Cutlass. He and the Latin-looking guy shook hands, then another guy got out of the passenger side of the SS, a white guy. I dang near shitted. I had a no-cracka-action-transaction policy.

I was under the impression that we were going to follow these dudes to a house or some secluded area, but Derrick got into the SS with the Latin dude. Greed was the only thing that stopped me from leaving Derrick's ass. What was he doing? This fool should've known that you don't do a deal like this in public. A minute later, Derrick got out the car and came up to my window.

"Dog, you got a bag?"

"A bag?"

"Maybe you can cover up the blow in your jacket?" He pointed at the matching green Cross Colours ensemble I was wearing.

Now frustrated and nervous, I was ready to do anything to get this over. I got out the car while Derrick got in and retrieved the cassette case with the twenty-two Gs.

When I got inside the SS, the Latin driver greeted me and reached into the backseat. He retrieved a gray duct-taped, football-shaped package. Just looking at it, I could tell it wasn't cocaine. The package was too light and too soft.

As I opened my mouth to protest, the driver shouted, "It's Miller time!"

Both doors of the SS were thrown open. I was roughly pulled out the car and shoved onto the asphalt. I was surrounded by shotgun-wielding white men in task force uniforms.

CHAPTER 18

Down at the Powder Springs Police Department, Derrick and I were being interviewed by the arresting detectives. I sat quietly fuming while loosely handcuffed to a metal floor-mounted table. Anger took over the fear I had been feeling. Motor mouth Derrick was on autopilot as he tearfully included me in his attempt to make a deal with the devil.

"So, whatever happened to Eddie?" Sergeant Freck, head of the sting operation, asked.

"He's the one you want. He's big time. He's moving a lot of weight."

Freck listened while typewriter keys buzzed in the background.

"We just doing this for Eddie. We-we-we don't even sell drugs."

"Hmm, I don't know about that." Sergeant Freck paused, one hand braced his leg and the other combed his black goatee. "Your compadre here, Lincoln, has a thousand-dollar cellular phone, a digital pager, and we got eight hundred and thirty-two dollars off him aside from the twenty-two thousand." Sergeant Freck shot an arrowing look at me. "Can you explain that?"

Like a dummy, I went right for the bait.

"Look, man, Derrick gave me a thousand dollars to drive. I had no idea what I was getting into. I just wanted to make what I figured was some easy money. As for the phone, I work construction, and I need it since I'm always out on different job sites."

"Linc, what's Eddie's beeper number? Ain't no use in us going down for somebody else. He wouldn't go down for us."

I shot Derrick a murderous look. If he could've read my mind, he would've seen that I thought he was losing his. I glared at him, all sweaty in an air-conditioned, morgue-like room.

"I don't know what you talkin' 'bout."

Sergeant Freck held his hands in prayer mode under his chin. "Look, fellas, I'm going to explain the facts of life. This is no game. You're in serious trouble. We got you on an 841, attempting to buy and traffic multiple kilos of cocaine. We also got you on 924C, firearm charges. With what we got, you're facing twenty to life. Now, if you gave us your full cooperation, maybe we could reduce your charges."

Derrick looked like he would've given up his own momma. "Stop playing around, Linc. Give me Eddie's number. I'll set him up by myself. You ain't got to do nothing," Derrick pleaded.

"I don't know no Eddie."

"All right then, give me Mike's number."

If looks could kill, he'd be rotting somewhere. This fool was trying to blackmail me by bringing up Mike's name. He knew Mike's number and he should've had Eddie's too.

I knew how desperately scared he was when he brought Mike's name into it. He knew Mike would've killed him, sure as shit stinks. I decided to flip the script.

"I'm tired of this shit, man. Stop lying. Everybody know you the man. Hell, you probably makin' up some character named Eddie. I ain't never heard of no Eddie. You might as well just go on and tell the truth."

"Nigga, why you mothafuckin' playin' games? You the one crossed Eddie out in the first place."

I was still fucked up from the car accident, but I still would've been heavily favored if we went to blows. The police separated us, locking me up in a holding cell. They realized I wasn't going to be any help.

I was asleep when the Cobb County Sheriff's Department came and got us. They took us to the Cobb

County Detention Center where we were ordered to strip. While we were in line with three other new arrivals, standing butt-ass naked on a cold, dirty concrete floor, with me holding my balls, an officer barked, "Palms out. Arms up. Mouth open. Lift up your nuts. Turn around. Feet up. Bend over. Spread 'em. Cough." After being thoroughly humiliated, we were thrown some skid-marked used boxers; dingy, too-small T-shirts; loud orange Cobb County jumpsuits; and a bedroll that consisted of a gray wool itch-looking blanket, two sheets, a pillowcase, towel, washcloth, and a generic hygiene kit.

"Open cell block H," the guard called over his radio.

Derrick and I walked into a large open area that looked like a dorm with metal doors. Everything was steel and concrete. The cellblock was so packed that we had to sleep outside the cells in the common area on the cold concrete floor. I wanted to call my connect and friend, Woody, but I called D'Andre and told him to call Woody. I spoke so fast I didn't give him time to ask questions, nor time for the shock of me being locked up to register in his mind. Next, I told D'Andre that under no circumstances was he to tell Momma.

The next morning I was up early after sleeping about fifteen minutes. The floor had my back so stiff I couldn't bend down to eat breakfast. I waited in line for a phone. When my turn came, I called Woody collect.

"I messed up."

"I'm already on the case."

"So, what I need to do now?"

"Sit tight. I've talked to my lawyer, Monroe Searcy. He beat two cases for me. Just have your brother bring me ten thousand, and we can get you outta there. You know I got to look out for my number one nephew."

Tarik had used this lawyer, Monroe Searcy, before, so I knew a little about him. He came from poor white farmers and vowed to do whatever it took not to live and die like his parents, who had been sharecroppers in Macon, Georgia. Thanks to financial aid and a will to persevere, he graduated at the top of his class from the University of Georgia's Law School.

Monroe had been in private practice for five extremely profitable years. Before he went solo, he'd been a U.S. Attorney for the Northern District of Georgia. After twelve years as a head honcho federal prosecutor with a ninety-eight percent conviction rate, he grew bored.

Even though he was one of the highest paid lawyers in the state, it wasn't money that motivated him. It was power and control—controlling people's futures. Winning was all that counted, no matter who had to be hurt. He had been an underhanded, dirty, low-down dog U.S. attorney who was now a scummy, gutter-rat defense lawyer. He collected and documented others' dirty laundry from petty criminals to high-ranking government officials. When a case was on the line, other people's dirt (specifically a judge, a prosecutor, or even a witness) could be used to throw a monkey wrench in whatever blocked Monroe from winning. He was a helluva lawyer, and right now, that's what I needed.

I told Mike to take Woody ten grand. Later that day, Monroe Searcy sent a paralegal to the jail to interview me. A gangly, bookish, clean-cut white dude not too much older than me introduced himself, and after shaking hands we got down to business. He took out a tape recorder, pad, and pen.

"Mr. Jackson, tell me everything you did from the time you woke up the morning of your arrest."

I told all I could remember. Afterwards, I asked, "When am I gonna get a bond?"

"I don't know. You'll have to ask Mr. Searcy about that."

I made the call as soon as I got back in lock-up. "Sir, this is Lincoln Jackson."

"Hello, Lincoln. I'm sorry I wasn't able to personally come and see you, but I had to get your police report so we could find out what our men in blue have on you."

"I understand. I appreciate you taking my case. How long do you think it'll be before I get a bond?"

"I know how bad you want to get out, but bond usually isn't granted in gun and drug cases, so for now I'm focusing on the procedures the arresting officers followed. Now, I'm not saying you won't get bond, but I can't guarantee it. However, I promise I'll do everything I can. Just keep your head up.

"One more thing—under no circumstance are you to discuss your case with anyone in prison or anyone over the phone. There's a lot of informants in there, and the phones are monitored. If you think you have something relevant to your case, call me and I'll send someone out there to get a statement."

I was ready to cry when I hung up. I turned around to see if anyone was waiting to use the phone. There were three Whites and a Black in line.

"Fuck that," I said to no one in particular. I wasn't getting back at the end of the phone line. I turned around and called Mike. If the dudes waiting wanted some drama, we could get down.

I was relieved when no one made any move. I almost forgot I was in no condition for a fight. I was, after all, just barely walking.

First thing Mike did when I called was to tell me all about some super-duper lawyer/judge named Brad Blackman.

"Lincoln, Blackman is the lawyer who got Cecil and Li'l Dre off on that case where they got caught red-handed selling dope at the car wash on Candler Road, and guess what else?"

"What?"

"He got Big Kicker twelve months county time on all them armed robberies. I got his number right here."

"Call him on the other line."

"Hold on."

I crossed my fingers and said a silent prayer while I waited.

"Blackman, Horowitz, and Associates. May I help you?" a woman's chipper soprano voice came over the phone.

"May I speak to Mr. Blackman, please?" I asked. After going through the routine questioning and holding for another five minutes, Mr. Blackman came on the line.

"Brad Blackman, can I help you?"

I introduced myself and explained my dilemma. Then I asked him if he could get me a bond.

"It shouldn't be a problem, but before I can do anything I'll need ten thousand dollars as a retainer.

"I just hired a lawyer. I gave him ten thousand dollars a coupla days ago."

"If you want to retain me, when we hang up you need to call him and write him a letter explaining that you don't need his services. He should give you your retainer back since he just took your case. Now, the ten thousand will be applied to my twenty-five thousand-dollar fee. That includes your trial, appeals, hearings, everything."

The assurance in his voice convinced me that he was the lawyer for me. After hanging up, I had Mike call Mr. Searcy. I fired him and sent Mike to get my money.

Mr. Blackman came to see me later that day. He was a tall, fiftyish, gray-haired, pasty-faced white gentleman. He looked like he might have played football in his younger days. The interview went well.

Back at the cellblock, I called Mike again.

"He only gave me twenty-five hundred back."

"Say what?"

"He said he'd already put in a lot of work and time."

"That's bullshit."

"He told me he didn't have to return none of it."

"Man, fuck that. I'm gon' get my money."

A week passed, in which time I played cards, dominoes, and talked shit all day. I was in a block of mostly Blacks who were in for anything from petty theft to murder. Every day somebody had to be taken out of our block to see a doctor because of an inmate-inflicted injury. Cobb County Jail was a gladiator school. I was all right because a few cats in the Chain Gang knew me. This was a gang of cats who allegedly robbed a string of liquor stores where, in one instance, a salesclerk was beaten to death with chains.

Derrick, being the coward that he was, was in a state of constant fear until we made the front page of the Cobb County newspaper a few days after we were locked up. After Derrick got wind of the article that depicted us as leaders of a multi-million-dollar drug operation, he developed a following of young small-time drug dealers locked up in our block. Being a compulsive liar, he started lying about his riches, including a half-million-dollar house he was having built, and the various exotic cars he collected. He especially loved to tell stories of all the dope he moved and how and who he sold it to.

I didn't rain on his fantasy, but after four days of covering up lies with more lies, his little crew grew skeptical and suspicious. I wasn't in the cell when things went down, but from what I heard, it was no joke.

A country, buck-toothed, charcoal-dark kid no more than nineteen got fed up. Billy was around six feet tall, nail thin but tack sharp. Five cats were in Billy's cell when Derrick had the floor. Billy snapped his fingers and pointed, saying, "I remember where I seen you. A few months back, I was outside the Phoenix Dance Club when you drove up in a big daddy, money-green Acura Legend with some chromed-out three-piece BBS rims."

"Oh yeah, man. That was me. See, I had to do a repo job on this fool who owed me fifty grand," Derrick said.

"A nigga like me don't play the piano. I took that nigga car."

Billy patted Derrick on his back. "You the man, dog. Them gold-plated rims really set that Ac' off."

"A real playa got to do what he got to do. You see, it's all about dead presidents," Derrick bragged.

"Are you gonna keep the Ac' diggy in your four-car garage at the house you're having built?" Billy asked.

Derrick rested one leg on top of the stainless steel seatless toilet in the cell, seemingly deep in thought. "I don't know. Right now I can't say. I might end up keeping it in one of my hoes' garages."

The others in the cell quietly listened to the exchange without a clue to what was going on.

Derrick was so caught up that he didn't pay attention to what came out of his mouth. Billy got in Derrick's face, looked him straight in the eye, and lashed out.

"You's a wannabe, lyin'-ass bitch. I just made up the Acura story. I know yo' broke, soft ass ain't got no Acura. An Acura Legend is a front wheel drive, and you can't put no deep-dish three-piece BBs on no front wheel drive. I done went from chrome to gold in two minutes and yo' bitch-ass fed right into it."

Derrick stood slumping on the wall as if the weight was getting too heavy for him.

Billy continued, "Two days ago when you described the house you was having built, you said it had a six-car garage. Bitch, I just asked you about a four-car garage."

The four others in the cell had left Derrick's side and were now sitting on the bed close to where Billy was standing.

"I made a few phone calls yesterday. I got a cousin in Decatur who knows you. He say you ain't got no heart unless you got a gun. He say you live with your fat-ass mammy. He said you ain't shit and ain't never gon' be shit."

Sweat beaded up on Derrick's brow.

"Now, that's where my cousin was wrong. I'm gon' make somethin' outta you. I'm gonna make you my bitch."

"Daaaaaamn," the others chorused while Derrick silently frowned.

"When we turn in our commissary lists, get me three bags of Doritos, three packs of Snickers, two pairs of large drawers, and a double-X T-shirt. Oh yeah, and get me four packs of Newports."

Without a word, Derrick got up and left the cell. Billy and the others followed him downstairs to the first tier where I was playing spades, and Billy told me everything.

I cried laughing.

"Why you didn't tell me how full of shit your boy was?" he asked.

"He ain't my boy, and I knew that his mouth would eventually overload his ass."

"You mind if I break my foot off in his ass if he don't get my shit off commissary?"

"Break one off for me. That lying ass Negro is the reason that I'm here."

That evening, everybody was eating snacks from the prison commissary. Everyone but Derrick. He sat next to me with a long face. After spending his money on Billy, he didn't have jack.

I told Derrick I'd give him fifty Gs if he would corroborate my story, telling the police and my lawyer that I didn't know anything about a drug buy, that I just drove for what I thought was easy cash.

"After all, you lied to me. You said you knew your uncle's people. I should've known you was fulla shit. In a drought, ain't no way dope was going for regular street prices." I tried my best to convince Derrick to try to clear me, but he didn't see it as I did.

"Naw, man. We in this together. I ain't 'bout to lie and get in more trouble."

"What you mean lie? Man, you been lying since we got busted."

"Ah, Linc, you know what I mean."

"Hell, nah. I don't know what the fuck you mean. All I know is that you trying to take me down wit' yo' silly, dumb ass."

"Ain't nobody force you."

"Shut the hell up."

After being locked up for fifteen days, my attorney came through. I got a $25,000 bond.

Before I called anyone to post it, I got on the phone and called John Baker, my probation officer.

"John Baker, probation."

"John, this is Linc. Wha's up?"

"It's about time you called."

"Man, I've been under hella stress."

"I can imagine."

"So you know."

"Since the day of."

"I'll explain the deal to you when I get out, but right now I need you to make sure."

"I already took care of it. We won't put a hold on you."

"Man, I 'preciate it." I sighed.

"It wasn't easy. Two drug charges in less than twelve months."

"You know the other charge was bullshit."

"No drug charge is ever bullshit."

"Yeah, you right. That was some stupid shit I did."

"Look, as soon as you hit the street, come and see me. I've got some papers for you to sign. You'll be on intensive probation until this mess is over."

I hung up, shaking my head. I'd almost forgotten about the little run-in with the Black Cats in May 1991, a few months after I got out of Shepherd Spinal Center.

I had dropped my Cougar off at the auto repair shop for a front-end alignment and some other minor work. I had Mike come and get me due to the too-long wait. On the way back to his apartment, the Black Cat special drug task force got behind us.

"Mike, I know you ain't dirty."

"Shit. I got two eight balls in that bag." He pointed to a small, white plastic Russell Stover's candy sack sticking out from under the cream-colored armrest of his tree-bark brown '72 Impala.

"Man, they about to pull us over." I tried not to panic as I assessed our options. I removed two small powdery rocks wrapped in Saran Wrap from the bag.

How could Mike be so careless? He knew he was on fire. When the Black Cats pulled him over a few weeks ago, one of his boys jumped out the car and hauled ass with the dope. Since Mike didn't give up his partner, five-O retaliated by impounding his car. The following day, Mike's pops had to go and have the car released.

"Man, I can't believe you holdin' in this hot-ass car," was all I said before another police car got behind us and turned on its siren. "We ain't got no time. Swallow this. You can throw it up later." I scrambled to give him one of the small packages while I half chewed, half swallowed the other.

"Okay. Okay." Mike nodded while pitching the package in his mouth.

"When they let us go, we'll go buy some milk and throw the dope back up."

I couldn't get mine down. I chewed. I swallowed. By the time Mike pulled over, I had powdery residue around my mouth. When one of the officers asked me about it, I said it was toothpaste. One of the other cops took out some kind of plastic file and scraped it across my lips. Next, he dipped the file in a blue liquid.

We were in trouble now.

After sitting in a police car for over an hour, we were finally taken to DeKalb County Jail.

I was delirious. I started foaming at the mouth. My heart fluttered. Mike got real scared for me. The paramedics checked me out, but apparently they figured I'd live. Once we were locked up and processed, Mike called his pops.

About the time Mr. J showed, Mike started fading in and out of consciousness. I was about to call for help when Mike grabbed hold of my hand.

"No."

I would have gone against his wishes if a guard hadn't come and let us out of the holding tank right then. They processed us in a hurry; we were given signature bonds. I explained to Mr. J what we did and he went slam off.

"That's the stupidest shit I ever heard. You'll both be lucky if your hearts don't explode," he carried on as he rushed us to DeKalb General.

I checked out okay, but Mike was in bad shape. All the color was drained from his face. His lips were dry and his eyes were glassy. He was hooked up to a blood-filtering machine and a heart monitor, and they force-fed him liquid charcoal.

"Sir, we've done all we can. It'll be touch and go throughout the night, but if he makes it through, he'll be all right."

"Thank you, doctor," Mr. J said.

I couldn't belive how stupid I'd been. Somebody had almost killed me in a car the year before, and now I'd almost killed someone in a car. Oh, God.

"Mr. J," I shook my head, "I'm sorry."

He nodded.

"God, please let Mike live. I promise I'll straighten up. Please let Mike live," I whispered.

I'd seen plenty of geek monsters smoke way more than what we swallowed. Hell, my mechanic, Willie, could smoke an eight ball in a couple of hours.

I was thinking about my life and how jacked up it had been when the doctor somberly came toward us. Mike's pops jumped up.

I shook my head and sighed.

"Sir, your son is fine. We'll keep him a couple more hours then we'll release him to your care."

Thank you, God, I said to myself.

"Thank you. Can I go see him?" Mr. J asked.

"It's better you don't. He's resting."

Eventually, Mike's case was dismissed, and I pled guilty to simple possession of a controlled substance, for which I received two years first offender's probation. The probation was still in effect when I got arrested with Derrick.

When I got bond, Derrick got one too. The date was April 3, my girl, Michelle's birthday. I hurried to call her at school.

"Baby, Big Daddy's comin' home."

She screamed in my ear.

"Can you come to Atlanta after school?" I asked.

"Yes."

"We'll do something real special for you birthday."

"You holding me is all I want."

"Stop playin', girl. You know you want Big-Daddy-Jook-'Em-Good to take you out."

"No, seriously. This will be the best birthday ever if we just stay at your place and you hold me all night long."

"A'ight, baby. I am your humble slave for life."

"I can be in Atlanta by 4:30."

"I'll see you at the condo downtown."

Not long after I hung up, Woody posted my $25,000 bond.

I was outside the prison waiting on D'Andre to come and get me when a deputy sheriff stepped outside. "Mr. Jackson, can you please step back inside?"

"Huh?"

"Step inside."

When I did, I was rearrested. A teletype had just come through informing the deputy that I'd been violated. I could hardly believe what was happening. I wanted to crawl in a corner and cry. My probation officer assured me that he wouldn't violate me. Back in lockup, I called my P.O.

"Mr. Baker, please."

"John Baker here," boomed a baritone voice.

"Mr. Baker, this is Lincoln Jackson."

"I'm really sorry. My supervisor violated you. Ms. White fears for the safety of her son. She came down here and made a big fuss. She convinced my supervisor that you had threatened Derrick's life and that you posed a threat to him and the community."

"What I'm s'pose to do now? Fuck."

"I really tried. I told my boss how you have been an exemplary probationer with not so much as a traffic ticket."

I knew John did his best. He had no choice, considering all the shit I had on him. I wondered where he was getting his weed from since I'd been locked up.

"How long do I have to stay in here this time?" I asked.

"I can't even tell you. Your best bet is to get your lawyer on the case ASAP."

Later that day, I was transferred to the much worse DeKalb County Jail. Michelle and I communicated frequently by phone and mail, during which time we forged a very strong bond.

At the time of my initial arrest on March 19, 1992, I hovered at around 260 pounds. By mid-May I weighed in at 220 pounds. It wasn't a planned weight loss. I had been forced to lose it. I called it the sure-shot prison diet. The food wasn't fit for human consumption. For breakfast, we were marched to a cold cafeteria where we ate two supposedly hot meals. We were given literally three minutes to scarf down our food before we were herded back to our cell dorms. Breakfast consisted of a child's portion of cold powdered eggs, sand grits, and some kind of fatty, greenish-brown pork or bologna. If you got lucky, none of the food moved. It wasn't unusual for a little extra protein to be crawling around on your plate. The roaches and weevils were probably the healthiest part of the meal.

The first time I found a roach sunbathing in my grits was the last time I went to the cafeteria. Lunch was usually the only meal I ate. Sack lunches with dry, off-green, pink-brown bologna sandwiches on white bread, a jellyless peanut butter and jelly sandwich, an apple that sometimes was hardly rotten at all, and a small lukewarm container of milk were brought to the dorms. We didn't have a chemist on hand to break down the components and filter out all the excess grease, so we just called what they served us at dinner mystery meat. Dinner also included a small, tasteless serving of cooked vegetables and watery mashed potatoes. Some days I didn't eat at all.

A fire that I didn't know I had inside me burned furiously. I was in prison, powerless to do anything about what was going on around the country. I watched television as rioters tore up cities across the U.S. when an all-White jury found the pigs who beat Rodney King to sleep, not guilty. I wanted so bad to be a part of the protest. I wanted to be down with my people punishing white folk, but I was helpless in jail, mad and hungry. It just went to show that a black man over a hundred years removed from slavery still couldn't get justice in their "just us" system.

I could hear Akbar now. He would no doubt be dropping mad science on our peeps in the hood. Man, did I miss Akbar.

The week prior to Memorial Day, my lawyer came to see me.

"Son, it looks as if the feds are going to take over your case. I'm trying my darndest to keep it in the state," he said. "Right now, I need your help. Sergeant Freck with Powder Springs Police is outside. He wants to speak to you."

"About what?" I leaned forward on the scratched wooden table in the cell-sized lawyer-client conference room.

"He's agreed to help me get you out," he said. "That is, if you cooperate."

"I don't understand."

Mr. Blackman crossed his legs. "We can probably get your charges dropped or lessened dramatically, and we can definitely get your probation expunged."

My home. A bath. My bed. My woman.

"Freck wants you to give up some information about others who are involved in drug activity. I tried to tell Freck that you weren't involved with drugs. 'My boy just got tricked by a shady character,' I told him. 'He was just an innocent victim caught in a crossfire.' Sergeant Freck was unmoved. He insisted on your cooperation or no deal."

"So you telling me if I set somebody up, I won't do no time?" I asked. I already knew the answer; I was just stalling for time to put some believable lies together.

I needed to formulate a plan to convince Sergeant Freck to have me released. I wasn't stupid. Blackman had wasted his breath with that long, drawn-out sob story of how he tried to convince the cops that I was an innocent, naïve young black man. If he didn't think I would capitulate, he wouldn't have brought the police to interview me. "It's very likely that you'll serve little to no time. Depends on the extent of your cooperation."

"Okay, bring him in," I said.

Sergeant Freck strolled in casually with his arm extended to shake my hand as if I were a friend. He wore faded, butt-stranglin' Wrangler jeans, a stomach-huggin' Fruit of the Loom T-shirt, and some black-and-gold vinyl Payless cowboy boots. A fire-redhead Elvis throwback was the best way to describe him.

"Mr. Jackson." He nodded before taking a seat behind a brown client/attorney visitor's desk. "You seem like an intelligent young man who just got a little greedy. I'm going to give you a chance to walk away from this whole ordeal smelling like roses, but I need your help."

Oh, the magic word—*but*. There was always a *but*.

"What can you tell me about illegal drugs being sold in your community?"

Country, fake, wannabe John Wayne-Roy Rogers racist cracker. I wanted to scream, "Don't you mean the nigger community?"

Sergeant Freck had pen and pad in hand. I was ready for him.

I made up two stories about two guys who sold dope. I named real hangout spots that my fictitious characters frequented, such as the Blue Flame and Magic City strip clubs. I had Sergeant Freck engrossed as I creatively wove my tales.

He ate it up. The weasel wrote furiously as I spoke.

"We need you to stage a buy—a big buy with these guys."

"No problem, but I need to be on the streets to do it."

CHAPTER 19

Two days later, on the Friday before Memorial Day weekend, I was released from DeKalb County Jail. This time I didn't wait for anyone to come for me. As soon as I left the jail, I limp-jogged-crooked-leg ran. I looked like the next star of either the Special Olympics or Saturday Night Live. I got two blocks before I was bent over on heart attack alert outside the Waffle House on Memorial Drive. There I begged up on fifty cents from an old, white, pancake-piggy-looking grandma leaving with her load of waffles.

I paged D'Andre and Mike from a pay phone. Ten minutes later it rang.

"Mike?"

"Who dis?"

"How many cats use the code 750, nigga?"

"Lincoln. You out, my nigga?"

"Nah, fool, I'm just pagin' you from prison. What you think, crack baby?"

"Where you at?"

"The Waffle House up from the prison."

"I'm there in fifteen."

I was happy as a hungry fat kid in Willie Wonka's chocolate factory when I saw Mike pull up in his custom metallic purple Mustang.

"Daaaaamn, you done lost weight. Look like you been on a crack diet. For real, though, you look good, dog," Mike said.

"You'd look like you'd been on crack, too, if you were locked up in that hell hole," I said pointing in the direction of the prison. "Man, I wouldn't feed massa's dog that shit they serve. I damn near lived on stale potato chips and half-rotten apples."

We drove downtown to my condo. While I showered and changed into some too-large Guess acid-washed jeans and a Neiman Marcus dark silk shirt and matching loafers, Mike got me caught up on the haps.

"Man, I don't know what to say about your boy Sonny."

"Whatchu mean?"

"Well, I know you told me to pay Blackman with the twenty Gs Sonny owed. I didn't want to tell you over the phone, but that fool had me waiting at the Blockbuster on Redan Road for an hour. He never showed. I been beeping him ever since. He's been straight dodging me. I know he got your money, 'cause ol' boy Devo, you know dude who got that body shop on the West Side and sell dope outta it, told me he came to him twice, and each time he bought a half a bird."

"Devo tell you how much he was spendin'?"

"Sixteen-five each time."

"Okay. The little pie-face Puerto Rican tryin'a play me."

"Linc, if I catch him, it's over. The chump's even got somebody else answering his beeper."

"Don't worry, I'll find his punk ass," I said.

Later that day I met my man, Woody, at Houston's by Lennox Mall. As usual, he was tailored from head to toe. We sat and ordered seltzers. I told him everything about my ordeal with Sergeant Freck and the game I ran to get out of jail.

"Watch your back. You dealin' with a whole new element now. The cops are the best and most organized crime organization there is. They play for keeps," Woody explained.

"Man, I got this," I said. "Trust me."

"I've had to deal with them on three occasions. Back in the seventies, I hijacked trucks. I got busted unloading five hundred cartons of Camels. Since I was black and criming in the all-White community of

Dunwoody, the cops tried to pin a murder rap on me, along with hijacking. Allegedly, I fit the description of the perpetrator who raped and killed a white woman in her Dunwoody home.

"The rape/murder took place two hours earlier on the same night as the hijacking and about twenty minutes away from the victim's residence. If it wasn't for Searcy getting me off on a technicality, I'd more than likely be sitting on death row or rotting away in some joint with a cellmate named Bubba," Woody explained.

"The second downfall was in May of '82. The cops got a tip from an old nosy cracker living across the street from my stash house. He told five-O that I was involved in illegal activity because he saw me hauling full garbage bags into my house late at night. Well, the cops staked out my crib from the all-too-happy-to-oblige nosy cracker's house. When they saw me moving the bags into my house, they busted me with 300 pounds of Kentucky skunk, some of the best herb around. No search warrant. No nothing. Searcy got me off again.

"The cop who blew the weed case was down-sized from detective to street patrolman. He busted me for speeding a year after I beat the weed case. After writing the ticket and searching my car, I was arrested for possession with the intent to distribute two kilos of cocaine. I served eleven months in prison before Searcy proved the cop planted the two kilos in the car."

Woody was starting to make me nervous. He finally switched gears. He told me he was back in business. He eased his briefcase toward me. "Now you're back in business too."

"What's the deal?"

"There's two kees in the case. Bring me back sixty."

"Gotcha."

As he got up and walked away, I couldn't help but think that I'd been tested and that Woody knew I'd already struck a deal with the devil before I told him how I got out.

Mike waited for me in the mall. After I was back in the car, his beeper went off while we were on our way to Shelly's apartment. Shelly was an old girlfriend who I paid to hold dope for me.

He returned the page. A few seconds later he handed me the cell.

"Yeah?"

"This is Michelle."

"Hey, baby. Where you been? I've been calling you all day."

"I'm at South DeKalb Mall. When did you get out?"

"This morning. I'll meet you at Camelot Records in thirty minutes."

I could hardly wait to see those wide mocha-brown eyes and caress her soft, sexy, tanned banana-brown body. I could finally live out the dreams that I'd been having since being incarcerated.

It took us an hour to wrap up our business and get to South DeKalb Mall. Once we got there, as we were walking toward the main entrance, Michelle and a girlfriend were coming out and heading our way. When our eyes met, time stood still. The world ceased to exist. It was just her and me. The wind treadmilled our legs in motion. Face to face, lips to lips and soul to soul, we were one, in each other's arms as the world watched. Rain-teardrops streamed from our eyes. I felt her warm tears cascading onto my mustache as we kissed.

I gave Michelle the key to my condo and we agreed to meet up in an hour. I still had to holler at my boys and get in touch with lame-ass Sed. I needed him to cook up my blow. Mike was doing a pretty decent job of handling things, so I let him continue. On the way to Sed's house I paged trick-ass Sonny. I still couldn't believe this fool ran off with my money after all I did for his punk ass.

A few minutes later one of his flunkies hit me back. "Yeah?"

"Let me holler at Sonny."

"Who dis?"

"Linc."

"What's up?"

"I'm short on time, hustler. Just let me holler at Sonny."

"He out of town takin' care of bi'ness. I'm handling thangs while he gone, so what can I do you fo', shawty?"

"When you speak to him, tell him to beep my brother. Tell him I'm back."

"A'ight."

After hanging up, I told Mike, "I raised that sucka from the cradle. Now I'm gon' take him to the grave."

"I'll do 'em. Just say the word."

"When I met him, he didn't have a place to lay his head. I took a chance, startin' him out with a quarter ounce. I even loaned him five grand to move his fat-ass sister here from Puerto Rico."

"Just gimme the word," Mike shot back.

"Chill. I got him. I'll handle this my damn self."

After meeting Shelly and getting one of the two kilos we gave her to hold, I got in the car with her while Mike took the dope to Sed. Shelly was a doll-faced, Dolly Parton-breasted, almond sister with shoulder-length burnt-brown hair. I paid her a grand a week to hold dope and make runs. She was toe-suckin' nuts about me. A straight nympho—anywhere, anytime, anyplace— she was down to get her freak on, and I wasn't one to disappoint. I tried to oblige her any and every time I could.

I had her drop me off at my condo. Before she began to make plans in her freaky little mind, I explained that Michelle was waiting for me. Of course, she didn't like it, but she knew Michelle was numero uno. Before I got out of Shelly's red Paseo, she unzipped my pants in one move, snaked her hand down my drawers and started giving me a Swedish ball massage. "Tell Momma you miss her."

"Girl, quit playin'. I gotta go."

"Don't make me marinate it," she said, provocatively licking her teeth.

"We in pu-pu-public. C-c-c'mon now."

"I'm goin' down." She started her dive.

"Okay. Okay. I miss Momma," I said, lookin' around while pushing her hungry head back up to the starting position.

"When you gon' make Momma cream and scream?"

"Tonight. Here's my parking garage opener." I gave her the little black box. "Meet me down here in five hours."

"Three in the morning?" she asked.

"Yep."

"You gon' let Momma make that thang throw up?"

"Hell yeah," I said, massaging my rocket.

"You gon' let Momma lip wrap it, slam suck it, and mouth fuck it?" she asked, squirming, her hand up her skirt.

Beep. Beep. A horn blew behind us.

I jumped out the car and ran to the lobby. I adjusted my pants while getting on the elevator with two old, staring white women.

I lightly knocked on the door. "Good googly goop. Mmm-mmm-mmm. Damn, baby. Look at you," I wailed. "Look at this."

I was astounded. Michelle had cleaned the condo. If not for the sweet-smelling candles the place would have been pitch dark. Jodeci's "Forever My Lady" softly floated through the air from my Carver surround-sound stereo.

Michelle wore a lacy purple silk two-piece thing about the width of a shoestring. I was salivating and ready to attack, but this was her show, so I let her lead me to the bedroom where she kissed me lightly, starting at my forehead and slowly working her way down to my toes. The whole time, she methodically undressed me. Her smell, her body, her aura had me so overheated that beads of sweat formed on my forehead. I thought I was going to explode.

We made love, hot and heavy, on the bed, the floor, the bathroom countertop, and in the shower. After an exhausting 3-hour marathon, Michelle fell asleep. I was field-slave tired, but I had to stay awake.

At a few minutes 'til three I slipped out of bed on rubbery legs. Luckily, I had showered after the last round. I had to meet Shelly. If I stood her up, her dumb ass might show up at door. I bumped into the wall next to the kitchen door. I shook myself awake and prayed that Michelle hadn't heard the thud.

When I made it to the fenced metal cage with individual storage units inside, I walked in my four-by-six bin to find Shelly oiled down, butt-ass naked in pink high heels that matched her marble-hard nipples.

"C'mere. You gon' be my bitch tonight," she said.

I held my hands up, shaking my head. "I'm sorry. Ain't no way I can do it. Oh, shit."

She dropped to her knees, snatched my shorts down, and mouth-raped my johnson. She started humming her own remix of Rick James and Teena Marie's "Fire and Desire" on my balls while she violined her fingers on my chest.

"Shit. Mothafuck. Damn. Shit. Oh fuck. Shit. Mmm, yeah, mothafucka. Hot damn." I developed an instant case of Tourette's Syndrome.

"Hmmmm. Hu-hu-hmmmmm. Hmmm-Hmm-Hmm."

"Oh God. Oh God."

She started humming the new Tupac jam "Trapped," as I said, "Turn around and bend over. I'm gon' make that pussy OD from this dick."

"Fuck this pussy, Daddy. Ooh, yeah."

"Bitch, who pussy this is?" I asked, rocking the cages.

I had her bent over, her hands shaking the fence as I commenced my back-archin', pile-drivin', waist-grippin', shoulder-bitin' Godzilla fuck.

When I made it back upstairs, I showered and slipped quietly under the covers, exhausted. The waking sun began to seep through the curtains when Michelle started rubbing me all over with oily hands. Before I knew it, she straddled me. I don't know how—I was numb, I was raw, I was tired, I was dead—but I managed to stand up one more time.

Our whole weekend was spent mostly in the confines of my 900 square foot, one-bedroom, third floor love nest. The only reason we left was for food and to rent movies from Blockbuster. Tuesday, the day after Memorial Day, I decided to pay a surprise visit to Maria, but it was me who was surprised when I got to a vacant apartment that used to be occupied by Sonny's sister and her kids. The more he eluded me, the angrier I got. I had a rule I always followed: Fuck me, I'll fuck you harder.

The next day while I was in a blue funk over Sonny, Mr. Blackman paged me.

"Lincoln, how was your weekend?"

"Fantastic."

"Glad to hear it. The state has dropped your drug and gun charge."

"Yeah!" I screamed.

"The bad part is, the feds picked them up, and they've indicted you."

"Ah, damn."

"You'll need to surrender at the Richard Russell Federal Building downtown on MLK Drive at nine on Thursday morning. This will be looked at favorably at your bond hearing."

"I just paid twenty-five hundred on a twenty-five G bond."

"What can I say?"

"Somethin'. You my lawyer."

"Don't worry. I'll be there, and you'll most likely end up having to post a property bond. If you know anyone who owns property who is willing to help you, have them at the Russell Building at eleven with their deeds. In my experience with the feds, most bonding companies won't take cash in drug cases. It's too risky. Property is usually the only way out."

My heart rested in the pit of my stomach. My head pounded. This shit was crazy. I couldn't win. Fuck.

The only person I was willing to turn to was Mr. J, Mike's pops. He was in debt to his eyelids, but I knew he had a lot of equity in his home. He knew I loved him and wouldn't do anything to hurt him. I knew he loved me like a son. When I went to him, he immediately agreed to put up his house.

I was processed and locked in a holding cell after surrendering the next morning. At ten, two Brooks Brothers suit-wearing, clean-shaven, collegian-looking white dudes unlocked my cell, handcuffed me, and instructed me to follow them.

"I thought the bond hearing was at 11:00."

"It is," one of the guys responded.

They led me through a maze of small offices. Once we entered a conference room-like office, they took the cuffs off and told me to be seated. They introduced themselves as ATF Agent Gene McCoy and DEA Agent Mark Murphy.

McCoy informed me that I was facing up to forty years in the penitentiary. On top of that, he explained that I would do an additional five years for having a gun. The whole time he read from the federal guideline book, which he explained was what the judge would have to go by.

"At the least, you'll do about fifteen years. There's no parole in the federal system. All inmates do eighty-five percent of their sentences. Now of course, you'll probably get more than fifteen years due to the severity of your offenses."

Agent Murphy sat on a corner of the table and looked at me while McCoy paced the office, explaining my fate. "I've read your case, and I think that you got a bum deal. You just made a dumb move. You're pretty smart. You're young—what, twenty-one, twenty-two?"

"I just turned twenty-three in April."

"So, that'll make you, let's see, around thirty-seven when you get out. That's if you get the minimum. It's up to you whether you serve two-plus decades in the pen. Play ball or spend the better part of your life in the dugout. It ain't no sweat off our backs if you don't cooperate. The next man will. Remember, this is the only way the judge can throw a curve ball." McCoy paused to let the gist of my situation set in. "Give us some dealers. You know, make a buy, set up a sell. Comprende, amigo?"

They were fucked up if they thought I was gon' be a snitch. But I had to play ball. My main focus was getting back on the streets. I'd worry about doing time later. I agreed to cooperate. By the time they escorted me to my hearing, we had exchanged pager and phone numbers.

By 5 o'clock that afternoon, I was back on the streets thanks to Mike's pops posting a $100,000 property bond. After being released, I went to Blackman's office. He told me basically the same thing the DEA and ATF agents had. Even my own lawyer was pushing me to cooperate, but snitching was the furthest thing from my mind. I left Blackman's office depressed, thinking about my future. Things looked bleak. I was coming to the stark realization that I was going to do some serious time.

Once I got home, I called my accident lawyer whom I hadn't heard anything from in more than six months.

"Mr. Flowers, this is Lincoln Jackson. I'm calling to see what's going on with the case."

"Lincoln, can you hold a second?"

I heard papers shuffling and muffled conversation in the background.

"Hey, uh, Lincoln, how ya doin'?"

"Not too well."

"Oh, I'm sorry to hear it."

"My case, Mr. Flowers. You haven't called me."

"I haven't called because I don't have much. Like I told you, Mr. Miner's statement put a damper on things."

"But you got the statement retracting the one he gave to police."

"I know, but State Farm's legal counsel is refuting the second statement."

"How can they do that?"

"They're saying it may have been coerced."

"Man, that's bull. When were you going to tell me?"

"I've been swamped with work. You know you're not my only client."

I could have jumped through the phone. I wanted to scream. I closed my eyes, took a deep breath and said, "But I'm a client."

"Don't worry. It's not over yet.

Don't worry. Fool, I'm lookin' at hella time. Don't worry? I thought.

"We still have a chance."

What in hell?

"These things take time."

Time, I don't have. Can you spell prison?

"As soon as I get a court date, I'll let you know."

After slamming the phone against the wall, I screamed, "I'll send you my forwarding address, fuckhead!"

I was glad I didn't tell him about my current dilemma. It would have just given him another excuse why I wasn't gettin' any money. I was glad he didn't bring up the suit we had against Squirt. I would've lost it. Hell, Squirt was in a wheelchair. He didn't have any money. I wasn't going to ask for part of his disability. He got me into this, but he was much worse off than me. He'd have to live the rest of his life in a sitting position.

I had to do what I had to do. Ain't no way I was gon' do time and get out butt-naked broke. I decided to sell a farmload of dope and stack my paper, then I'd liquidate my assets and use my bank to open a stereo installation and sales shop for D'Andre. When I got out of prison, I'd be set.

D'Andre had been working as the number one installer in a car audio shop for a coupla years without a salary. He was paid forty-five percent of the installation fee. J.R. Audio was pimpin' him. D'Andre was pulling in over seven, eight hun a week. I couldn't imagine how much the shop was pulling in with three installers and equipment sales.

Two days later, I had D'Andre take off work. I had him and Mike meet me at my condo. There, we counted a little over eighty thou. Mike had a half kee in the streets; he owed me sixteen. I had eight out, so I was lookin' at somethin' like a hundred-four, a hundred-five.

I explained the plan. "D'Andre, you find out everything you can about running the business."

"I have a couple business cards from some distributors the manager at JR's buys from," D'Andre said.

"Good. Make as many contacts as you can. We need prices. We need to know how much inventory to keep of each product. We need to know what sells the most."

"I already know that. It's Alpine, Sony, and Kenwood in radios; MTX, Kicker and Orion in woofers; and Boss,

Sherwood, Fosgate and Sony in amps. I'll have the rest in a couple of weeks," D'Andre said.

"Mike, you gotta step up. I'm gon' do a big deal, and I'm givin' you two kees. I'm going to turn over Chattanooga and Greenville to you. We'll have Shelly follow you with the dope. I'll explain the details later."

"Bet," Mike said, smiling.

"Mike, I need you to put word out that I'm selling my ninja ZX-7, Cougar, Vette, the new Benz and the Cutlass."

"You gon' keep the old Benz?"

"Yeah. That's my baby."

I had D'Andre's woman, Trina, talk to a real estate broker about putting my condo on the market. I decided to buy D'Andre and Trina a house of their choice and pay for whatever renovations they wanted. I'd furnish it with my furniture, high-tech stereo, and big-screen television. In turn, they would be responsible for the upkeep, mortgage, and other bills until I got out of prison.

I accepted that I would do some time. I didn't know how much, so I was just setting myself up for life after prison. I had no doubt D'Andre would take care of business. I looked at prison like going into the military on an extended overseas tour. When I came home, I'd still be relatively young. With a house and business, I figured I'd be set when I finished my tour.

As for the shop, all I wanted was for D'Andre to put a little money aside from time to time, if business allowed. But most importantly, I told him to make the shop a success.

"How long do you think you'll have to do?" D'Andre asked.

"Probably about five years," I lied.

Once I said this, D'Andre's whole demeanor changed. He looked like a sick puppy. I was sure glad I hadn't told him the truth.

The following weekend I drove my Vette down to Savannah. I wanted to surprise Michelle. I pulled up to her dorm around 8:00 on a clear, microwave-humid night.

This was the first time I had been back to Savannah since my accident two years earlier. I had the whole student body gawking at my ice-crystal, diamond-white Vette with the top dropped and Earth, Wind and Fire's "Reasons" resonating in the air. Everyone seemed to be hanging out in the yard adjacent to the upper class girls' dorm. I left the Vette running and jamming, illegally parked in front of Bowen Smith Hall.

By the time I walked into the lobby, Michelle was downstairs. In front of everyone, I gave her a diamond-studded fourteen-karat gold ring that read I love you in diamonds. Her nosy girlfriends screamed and gathered around a completely overwhelmed Michelle. I left her standing there, walked out of the dorm, got in my Vette, and drove almost four hours back to Atlanta. Personally, I thought that was some cool Rico Suave type shit.

The next week, Michelle graduated with a BA in business, left Savannah, and moved in with me in Atlanta. She disliked and even complained about the way I made a living, but she sure didn't have any problems with the comfort my lifestyle provided.

That same week, D'Andre reported to me, telling me that the average markup for retail audio equipment was from twenty to thirty percent. "The real money is in installations," he said.

I'd already figured that out. He was on the ball, getting business cards from three different major distributors who represented Atlanta—Bob Jones of Alpine, Kim Lan of Kenwood/Sony, and Lynn Carter of Orion. I arranged meetings with the three, and after each meeting I left disappointed. None of them could do business with me. They had agreements they had to honor. One stated that he couldn't sell to anyone who

ran a business within a five-mile radius of a retailer he
sold to. The only way I could deal with the company was
to open a store way out in Buck Tussel, Nowhere,
Georgia. I was about to give up hope until I ran into a
hippie-looking dude D'Andre and I had bought and
traded car stereo equipment with since we were kids.

Rick Fare managed Stereo Unlimited, a new and
used car and home audio store in Decatur. Rick gave me
some literature about a consumer electronics show that
took place every year in Vegas. It was the largest show of
its kind in the world. On display and for sale to retailers
and distributors were all kinds of new, updated,
futuristic electronic equipment. People from all over the
globe attended the four-day exhibition.

"If you've got the money, you can stock a hundred
stores," Rick said. "You'll meet distributors and product
reps from all over the world. I guarantee you'll be able to
stock your store with whatever you want. Here, take
this." Rick gave me two phone numbers to call for buyer
passes so I could attend.

I was so engrossed in learning the ins and outs of
the retail sales business that I forgot about my
upcoming court date. Throughout that summer, the ATF
and DEA agents badgered me. I continuously gave them
false leads while dodgin' 'em as I managed to sell a
warehouse of dope. I knew the feds weren't stupid. I had
to make a move before they pulled me in. It was just a
matter of time. I had to do them or they'd do me. I had
to plan an escape.

CHAPTER 20

In late June I was in Vegas having fun. Me, Woody, Derrick and another partner of Woody's stayed at the Mirage. Every time we stepped out of our hotel rooms, we were modeling some Italian's clothes. Mr. Armani and I had become very close, mainly because Armani was one of the only top-notch designers I knew of who made big boy suits. Unfortunately, I was putting back on the weight I had lost in world-record time.

Woody was quite influential as far as my appearance was concerned. Clothes really did make the man. The women I attracted proved that to be true.

On our way to Harrah's buffet, I nearly stumbled over the all-elusive Sonny.

"Bitch, I ought to kill your mu'fuckin' ass," I said as I stood over him, reaching into my inside jacket pocket.

"Don't shoot. Man, I got yo' money. Please don't kill me," Sonny cried like the little bitch he was, from the ground, covering his head.

"What? Fool, get yo' ass up."

"No. No. Don't do it."

This fool thought I was pulling a gun on his bitch-made ass. We were in the bathroom. It was just him and me. "You didn't know I had somebody followin' you, did ya?" I said.

"No."

"Shut up!" I shouted. "You wanna live?"

"Yeah-yeah."

"I done told you shut the—" I slapped him upside his head. "Where my money? Bitch, you hear me talkin' to you?"

"You said—"

"Shut up. I mean, where my damn money?"

"Is this restroom closed?" a fat Hawaiian shirt-wearin' cracka came in, interrupting.

"No. My friend has hepatitis." I coughed. "He's recovering from a recent attack. He's fine. Come on in. Join us."

That fat bastard almost ran through the door gettin' outta there.

"Nigga, get up."

"Uh, uh, Li-Linc, m-my man, I, uh . . . Look, man, I-I fucked up. But I was gon' call you. See, I got your money. I uh, uh, see, I, uh, got robbed and, um, uh—"

"Save the drama for yo' high-yella momma. You just get my money or you stop breathin'. Whichever." I shrugged. "Don't make no difference to me."

"I'm going back home tomorrow. As soon as I touch down, I'll hit you."

"Don't beep me. I'll page you tomorrow night. Make sure you call me back and not one of your flunkies."

"Okay. Don't worry. I'll hit you right back. Just put in 750 after the number so I'll know it's you."

"I always put in 750. I ain't playin'. I want my money tomorrow."

"Oh-oh, I gotcha." He nodded.

"To dodge me is a good way to bring ya family together for some hymn singin' and flower bringin'."

"No sweat, 'migo. Are, uh, you back on yet?"

"Yeah. Matter of fact, come on in with my cheese and I might front you something," I lied.

"Bet that up. Don't worry. I won't keep you waiting."

I figured if I added a little icing on the cake I'd stand a better chance of getting my money from his trick ass.

As soon as I got back to GA, I beeped Sonny five times. I developed a migraine waiting and seething. Why did I let him get away when I had him in my grasp? I was more upset with myself than with him. Sonny was doing what coward-ass weasels did best: hide.

Street Life

I made my decision. I didn't feel bad at all for what I was going to do.

CHAPTER 21

Twenty-seven days after seeing Sonny, I was in court. I pled guilty. I was caught dead to wrong, and Derrick had already snitched on drug dealers he did and didn't know, including yours truly. Derrick lied on anyone and said anything to get his sentence reduced.

Even though I signed a plea agreement to ten years, the judge sentenced me to eleven. Six years for my drug offenses, and five for the gun I told them like a dumb ass I had under my seat at the time of the arrest.

When the judge passed sentence, he sure seemed happy at seeing the despair on my face. I wanted to cry. I wanted to scream. I was too smart to be in this trick bag. But what could I do now? I made my bed, but I wasn't tryin' to sleep in it. Ten years of my life were being raped away unless I pulled a Houdini.

"No, unh-uh," I said to no one in particular. I enjoyed my freedom too much to give up ten years of it. I knew what I was facing, but like my car accident, I didn't believe it. I really had to implement my plan, and now was the time.

After court, I was permitted back on the streets. The feds knew what they were doin', givin' a young nigga a gang of time then letting the dominoes fall. I left the courtroom on a mission.

I was on my way home to the tri-level, $90,000 house that D'Andre and Trina had picked out in Stone Mountain and I assumed the loan on. I had sold my condo, which I had in my brother's name, making a lazy-low $1,500 profit. I took a beating on my Vette. I would have been better off insuring it and having it torched. By my court date, I'd just about liquidated everything.

After leaving court, on my way home, I stopped at Radio Shack and bought an answering machine that recorded phone conversations. After arriving home, I paged Sonny eight times back to back. Instead of my code, I put in 911 after the number. Everybody and their great-grandmomma's code was 911. Everyone thought they had an emergency. I'd been pacing for fifteen minutes, devising a script in my head of what to say, when the phone rang.

"Who dis is?"

"Where Sonny?"

"He outta town."

"When he coming back?"

"Hell if I know. Who dis be?"

"This Linc. I'm trying to handle some bi'ness."

"Oh, playa. Holla at me."

"Partna, I don't know you. You might be the po-po," I said.

"Naw, pimpin'. I ain't on that type of time. I'm 'bout that paper."

"What you holdin'?"

"Whatcha need?" he shot back.

"A bird."

"Man, I don't know if I can do a kee, but let me make a call. You gon' be at this number for a minute?"

"Yeah, but I ain't tryin' to pay out the ass."

"I got you, big dog. I'ma hit you right back."

"Bet that up," I said as I hung up.

I played back the conversation. It was clear as a bell. Shit, I had to stop using so much slang. I had to use real words.

A few minutes later the phone rang.

"Yeah."

"This me again. I just talked to my folks, and we can serve you up a half. It's ready, ready, though."

"A half a kilo, hard, already cooked up crack," I repeated.

"Yeah, man. What else?"

"So, what's the ticket, uh, I mean, the price?"

"Thirteen-five."

"Damn, dog. You could at least kiss me before you fuck me."

"Playa, you know it's hard times out here. Shit, that's damn near what I pay for it."

"Bruh, work wit' me," I said.

"Look, it is what it is. You want it or not?"

"Thirteen-five?"

"Nigga, this ain't no whip or no flex. My nigga, dis crystal hard—no flake, no water."

"I gotta run pick up some cheese."

"Nigga, I thought you was 'bout bi'ness," Sonny's flunky said.

"You betta ask somebody 'bout me, playa. I ain't Memorex. I'm a real nigga. I just don't keep that type of cheese in my back pocket."

"So, when you tryin'a do this?"

"In the morning."

"What about ten?" Sonny's flunky asked.

"Thata work."

After hanging up, I called Mark Murphy at DEA and explained what I had. He asked me to come to the federal building's sixteenth floor immediately. When I got there, he and two other agents reviewed the tapes and put together an undercover squad to assist in the deal. I told them they needed a black guy for this to work.

"Ain't no brotha gon' deal with no white dude," I explained.

That's when they brought in Mallory Gray. He was a tall, slim, Ivy League white dude with a brown face. We made plans for me to introduce Agent Gray to Sonny's flunky the next morning.

I was in the elevator, leaving the federal building about 9 o'clock at night. I thought, *Hell, this cat probably spendin' the money Sonny shitted me out of.* He and Sonny were probably laughing at the irony of me comin' to him for dope. *Eleven years in jail. Fuck that. A nigga gotta do what he gotta do.*

The following morning, I paged Sonny's beeper from a special phone in the DEA's office.

The phone rang.

Agent Murphy gave the signal.

"Yeah."

"Somebody beeped me?"

"This Linc."

"Linc?"

"Yesterday, the half."

"Oh yeah."

Agent Gray whispered, "Get a name."

"You ready?" I asked.

"Always," he responded.

"What name you go by?"

"Kyle. Why?"

"Because I gotta have you meet my man. Sonny-a tell ya I don't do no hand-to-hand."

"Whatever."

"He'll be driving an old, plain-Jane gray 560 SL."

"Where he at now?" Kyle asked.

"Near downtown."

"I'm gon' hit you right back. Gotta call my folks and set up a time and place."

"When you call back, Zeke will pick up."

"He your boy?"

"Yeah."

"He got the cheese?"

"Of course."

"He gon' be at this number?"

"Yeah."

"Hit ya right back." Kyle hung up.

I'd done my part, so I left for home feelin' lower than crab shit. I was tired. I just wanted to sleep. Sonny had to be behind this deal. I needed to get my time reduced because my baby, Michelle, was taking it hard, and she didn't even know how much time I was looking at. I had told her what I told everyone else—five years.

I woke up with the TV on. The 6 o'clock news was on as a special report came across the tube.

"This is Amanda Mason. I'm coming to you live from the Blockbuster Video Plaza in Stone Mountain, at the intersection of South Hairston and Redan Road."

Damn, that was right up the street.

"Four young black males were arrested today, trying to sell five hundred grams of crack cocaine, street value one hundred thousand dollars, to an undercover agent."

A hundred thousand. What planet were they talkin' 'bout?

"It is alleged that these black males have been under investigation for months. Also, several guns were seized."

You couldn't milk thirty thousand out of half a kee, I thought.

I called my lawyer after the report. He assured me that I had just knocked off at least half my sentence. "One more sting like that and you won't do any time."

He was crazy if he thought I was gonna sell out anyone else. There was no way I was messin' up somebody else's life. Sonny wasn't even one of the four strangers on the news.

After the bust, I quit rolling altogether. I concentrated on the stereo business. I'd made more than enough cheese to hook the shop up. Dope sold like toilet paper over the six months I slung while on bond. I had made a few hundred thousand right under the DEA's nose. I decided to shut down and tie up all the loose ends in my life before I went in. Besides, there was no telling how much time I had left.

It was a sunny 65 degrees on Christmas Eve 1992. Michelle and I sat outside on the balcony of our suite at the Ritz, listening to the Isley Brothers crooning "Drifting on a memory."

"Baby." I got on my knees and placed her hand on top of mine. "I would die a thousand painful deaths and come back to you." I kissed a lonely finger to her lips. I reached into my pocket and emerged with a minute forever. Her eyes sparkled. I opened the beige door and held a new diamond sun out to her. The wind smiled as she gasped. I continued, "Finish me. Complete my puzzled heart with your soul. Make me whole. Be my wife." I shook her soul through her hands. "Be my life." I placed the diamond sun on her finger.

"Yes. Yes. Yes. Oh, Lincoln, I love you," she cried.

I pulled her to the balcony floor. We kissed, we hugged, we loved while the Isley Brothers were talking about livin' for the love of you.

CHAPTER 22

Michelle and I planned to marry on New Year's Day, but my sister threw a sledgehammer into my whole program.

"Don't make that girl wait for you. She might think she wanna marry you now, but you can't predict what she'll think tomorrow, next month, or next year."

I nodded, shocked at the way Marnease was speaking.

"Give her the option to change her mind. If it's meant to be, marry her when you get out. I gotta go pick up your hardheaded nephew from school. Talk to you later." She hung up.

She was right, I kept thinking thirty minutes later as I drove down Candler Road in Decatur. I whipped my SL into the Flea Market Plaza. I had an idea. This was one of the hottest shopping spots in Decatur. The parking lot was jammed.

The Korean-run flea market was housed in an old Zayre department store building. It was home to more than sixty-five booths that sold everything from African art to authentic fourteen-karat gold-plated jewelry, to Guess What and Tommy Go Figure jeans.

What got my attention was the closed-off section of the building that used to be the auto repair department of the old store. Right there, I had a vision. That would be the perfect spot for my stereo sales and installation shop. I just knew it. I dialed the number on the Flea Market Plaza billboard from my car.

"Yes. I'd like to speak to someone about leasing."

"Oh, you want rent space?"

"Yes, ma'am."

"Hold, minute."

A few moments later, someone picked up.

"Charlie Kwan."

"Yes, sir. My name is Lincoln Jackson, and I'd like to discuss leasing the unused side of your building to open up a car audio sales and installation business."

"This even, six-clock, you come in flea market. Office in back, left corner."

"That'll be fine, sir. Thank you." I hung up, doing the robot in my seat.

That evening, Mr. Kwan showed Mr. J and me the building. It needed some work, but it was ideal. It was 2,800 square feet and had five garages.

"You take, you pay fifteen hundred month for five year. First, last month up front."

I looked at Mike's pops. He nodded.

"Deal." I shook Mr. Kwan's hand and followed him back to his office where I counted out $3,000.

After signing the lease and leaving the building, Mr. J said, "Anywhere else you woulda paid three times what you're payin' now."

That next day, I paid Mr. J to drop what he was doing and begin work on the shop, bringing it up to code. It took a little over a month of around-the-clock work to get the shop ready. Mr. J, D'Andre and I worked fast and hard, especially after I received my notice to turn myself in at the Manchester Federal Correctional Institution in Manchester, Kentucky (wherever that was), on February 3, 1993, to start serving my 132-month sentence. I was down after receiving the notice, but I was too busy to dwell on it. After all, my lawyer assured me that at least half my time would be knocked off.

We installed a drop ceiling, a sprinkler system, electrical outlets, two walls with safety glass, new carpet and display cases. The storefront we built was complete with large bay windows and glass double doors. Although only three were operable, all five garage doors still closed. After being turned down for shop insurance because of no alarm system, I immediately had Wells Fargo install one.

My next obstacle was Worker's Comp Insurance. This was crazy expensive, but there was a loophole. If I didn't have more than three employees outside my immediate family, I wouldn't need it. Needless to say, my family would soon grow. D'Andre opened up a DBA account and got a business license for C & C Cartunes.

That name just popped into my head one day while I watched Mr. J supervise the shop's renovations. C & C was short for Custom and Competition. Thirty thousand dollars and forty-two days after signing the lease, I was ready for business—almost.

D'Andre and I flew out to Vegas a few days after Mr. J finished the shop. The largest electronic trade show in the world took place in Vegas every year in January. D'Andre and I were astounded once we entered the Vegas Hilton to attend the Consumer Electronic Trade Show. At each exhibit, company sales reps assisted buyers. With a checkbook filled with starter checks, D'Andre and I dove into the world of wholesale quantity buying.

We bought amplifiers, car stereos, speakers, alarms, pre-amps, wiring, and other car audio accessories. We bought everything from Orion, Hifonic and Alpine to Boss and Pyramid. We stocked the shop with high-line, mid-line, and low-line car audio equipment. We made sure we had a little something for everyone—the players and the paupers. We spent more than sixty thousand in two days.

I hated paying cash, but I had no choice. D'Andre couldn't get credit or any kind of start-up loan. The banks told him that he had to be a proven business, whatever that was. I never expected the banks to help finance the shop anyway.

All the distributors I dealt with in Vegas were out of California and Texas, except Hifonic, which was based in Atlanta, and Orion in Jacksonville. I became a direct dealer for both companies. For paying cash we received a ten- percent discount, which worked out well. The discount paid for our shipping costs.

Our grand opening was held on January 16, 1993. It turned into an all-out parking lot/in-store block party. D'Andre had a Benz, a '64 droptop, his Jimmy, a Porsche and a Volkswagen bug, all with freaked-out custom systems he'd installed. We showed off his skills in hopes of attracting all the dope boys and whoever else's business we could. The people he did the work for were glad to loan us their rides.

The shop was a huge success. We stayed busy. In the first couple of weeks, things were so hectic we hired two installers and a salesperson. Of course, for insurance reasons, the new hires were my long lost but now found brothers.

I had Michelle and Trina go to ten different stores that sold car audio equipment and accessories. At each one they wrote down the prices. Then, we compared prices. Next, I marked my stuff five to ten percent lower than the average price of all the stores. I wanted to advertise our store as having the lowest prices around.

I hired a guy who I went to Savannah State with to handle our taxes and other financial shop-related business. Since he was an accountant, I figured he'd know everything.

I gave D'Andre almost every nickel I had. It was just enough to pay the shop and house expenses for six months. I could tell he was leery about being handed the responsibility of running the shop, but I was confident he could handle it.

That dreaded day was finally upon me. No more anticipating. I toughened up, trying my hardest not to seem down when I said my good-byes.

D'Andre and I had grown very close. I'd always loved my little brother, who now outsized me by over thirty pounds and a couple inches. He would always be my little brother. I told him this as we hugged and said good-bye. At first we shook hands, then suddenly he dropped our lifeline and hugged me.

Mike was so torn he couldn't face me. These were my brothers, my family.

As Michelle drove me to the Richard Russell Federal Building to turn myself in, I couldn't help but to feel like a sucker. I was thinkin' the feds were givin' me a chance to run, but instead I was checkin' my own self into jail. At least I was going to make them get me to Kentucky. I damn sure wasn't going to have my girl drive me all the way there just to go to jail.

I turned to glance at Michelle out the corner of my eye. She was holdin' up like a true soldier. That shit had to be hard. I knew she was frontin', but I was glad she was. I couldn't do tears now. I had to be hard. I had to handle mine like I'd handled all the other mess in my life. Hell, I was Lincoln Mothafuckin' Jackson.

As I was about to get out the car, I went into my pocket and pulled out a wad. "Baby, this is three grand. Having the Benz and stayin' with Trina and D' Andre, you should be okay."

"Yeah, especially with teaching school."

We kissed. I got out. I felt her eyes on my back, slowing me down as I made my way into the building.

Once I got to the lockup on the seventh floor, a deputy marshal made a phone call and told me I was supposed to report to the Federal Correction Institution in Manchester, better known as FCI Manchester in Kentucky. I lied to him, saying that I was dead broke and didn't have transportation and didn't even know where this Manchester was. That sufficed. They put me in a holding cell.

Street Life

Late that afternoon, two marshals awakened me as I lay on a metal bench inside the cell. I was taken with others to Bartow County Jail. If the Atlanta Federal Penitentiary wasn't so overcrowded, I was told, I would've been taken there.

CHAPTER 23

"Lights out," a drill sergeant-like voice boomed over the intercom shortly before the cellblock's electronic steel doors closed. Out of the thirty-eight inmates in my block, only three of us were black. The other thirty-five looked like a bunch of Hell's Angels Klansmen in orange.

First thing I thought when those steel doors had electronically opened was that there must have been a mistake. I glanced at the guard's tower-like station overhead. I got no reaction. So, clad in my orange Bartow County jumpsuit and carrying a bedroll, I held my head high and pimp-strutted in like I ruled the world. Hell, I ain't never been intimidated by no crackers, and I wasn't about to be now. They may have cracked the whip during slavery, but no cracker was going to crack nothing over this boy.

Fortunately, the inmates ignored me as I walked throughout the block searching for a cell. Deep down I was glad I'd been ignored. I could tell myself whatever made me feel like Dolomite, but the reality was that if them white boys felt froggy, I might as well have put my head between my legs and kissed my black butt good-bye.

I was a 269-pound chocolate Jell-O Pudding Pop. The muscle function on my left side was impaired and I had no sensation on my right, stemming from my car accident. As my pimp strut turned into a limp strut, a light-skinned, bald, massive-looking brother greeted me.

"Islam, black man. I'm James Smithbay. Call me Smithbay."

Islam?

"Come on. You can room with me if you don't mind a top bunk."

Silently, I let out a sigh of relief. "I'm Lincoln Jackson. Everybody calls me Linc. I can do a top bunk, no problem. I just need somewhere to lay my head."

I made my bunk, took a shower and ate dinner—an apple and half a bag of sour cream and onion chips—compliments of my gracious cellie. By lights out, I was mentally and physically drained.

It took a few strained efforts before I managed to get my bulk onto my springless steel slab of metal. My back hurt just thinking about sleeping on the one-inch blanket they called a mattress. In bed, developing back problems, contemplating sleep, I played the what-if game. What if I had taken off, leaving lying ass Derrick at the gas station the day we were arrested? What if I had sent Mike? What if I had left my gun at home? My mind wandered from one what-if to another. I must have lay there feeling sorry for myself for an hour before Smithbay came in.

"I wanted to give you time to settle in and get yourself together before I came in, black man."

"Good lookin' out, dog. I'm just reminiscin' about the streets, my bitches, them hoes, you know—shit a nigga don't think about 'til too late."

"Ho-hold on, li'l brother," he said, waving. "Ninety-nine percent of our brothers, including yours truly, came into the system with the same contagious disease you have."

"Bro, I'm clean as the Board of Health. I wraps my jimmy up like a mummy."

"Nah, brutha. You don't overstand." He smiled, shaking his head.

"You mean understand."

"No, I mean overstand."

"Huh?" I replied.

"Our problem is that we are so busy trying to understand we never get it. We have to stop going under, taking shortcuts. We have to go over the stand to understand."

"Ooooo-kay," I said, thinking this cat had gone coo-coo for Cocoa Puffs.

"I, too, came to the prison-plantation behind, with little hope of ever catching up."

"Catch up? Catch up to what?" I asked.

"You see, Brother Jackson, for over four hundred years we've been plagued with the gravest sickness ever known to man. The European injected a virus in us that passes down through generations, and it's responsible for the condition that we find ourselves in today."

Oh lord, one of them Malcolm X-Farrakhan cats. They say everybody comes to prison and get muslimfied and shit, I thought.

"The worst part is the European has the cure, but instead of healing us, he sets up institutes, schools and universities designed to spread the virus."

"What virus?" I asked.

"Perpetual ignorance, or better yet, mentacide. We have been misguided, misinformed, and miseducated. We've been missed all around the board. The only thing we didn't miss were the boats that brought us to the Americas."

I sat up with my back to the wall and my ear to the air.

"I mean, just look at us. We walk around in circles demoralizing one another."

"Man, on the streets I stayed to myself. I ain't demoralize nobody."

"Just listen," he said. "We playfully address one another not as gods, which is our true selves, but as the exact opposite."

Gods? Oh Lord, now the brotha thinks he's God. What next?

"We walk around talkin' 'bout 'What up, dog.' 'You my dog.' 'Cat-daddy.' 'My cat.' 'That's a cool cat.' Even worse, we call our sistahs bitches and foxes." He paused to ponder.

"All of these, animals. We've been so far removed from reality we don't even know that we don't know who we are. Since we've been told for so long that we're not human, we unconsciously and subconsciously believe it, so we identify with the animal kingdom."

Deep.

"And that word nigga. We call each other nigga in casual conversation so much, the White man no longer needs to."

"Yep." I nodded.

"Carter G. Woodson said it best some fifty years ago. 'We've been going to the back door for so long, no longer do we have to be told. We automatically go, and if there is no back door, we will carve one out.'"

"Man, that's heavy."

"We have been dehumanized and demoralized for so long, called nigga, and our women called whores, that is what and who we subconsciously think we are today. The seeds were planted, and they have grown and spread like weeds. We dehumanize our mothers, sisters and wives, calling them bitches."

I nodded.

"What is a bitch but a female dog in heat? If our women are bitches and whores, what does that make her children? Dog. Big dog. My dog.

"You see, Brother Jackson, the White man has implanted this virus in us to keep the Black race subservient to him and to keep us from ever rising black, not back, but black to our original state. We are the first, the original, no special recipe. No extra crunchy."

Sounds like KFC.

"We've had everything stolen from us. We don't know the truth, our history, our religion—hell, we don't even know our names. Take for instance, your name."

"My name?"

"Yes, Lincoln Jackson, your slave name. That is what it is. You're named after the same white man who tricked us into believing he freed the slaves. Abraham Lincoln said if there was any other way to preserve the Union, he would have never freed the slaves. He called us inferior, but your parents gave you that name to wear as a badge of honor." He got up to take a leak.

This was a lot to comprehend. The White man was much worse than I ever thought. I ain't never liked no cracka, but now I understood why the Muslims hated the White man so much.

He continued, "Yeah, you and all Mr. Jack's slaves were called Jack's boys or Jack's sons. So at the time we were freed, your forefathers kept the slave name alive by calling themselves Jackson, identifying themselves with the plantation they came from.

"Everything I'm saying is written in books, but you know the saying, the best way to keep a secret from a black man is to put it in a book."

"Huh?"

"We don't read. At least we don't read it if massa ain't gave it to us in a schoolbook or advertised it in the media or told us about it. In slavery, we weren't permitted to read, and still today we have mental barriers that stop us from picking up a book. For so long we've been forced to do and think a certain way that now it has became engraved in our subconsciousness to do these things, believe in these ways. We're trained to loathe one another as well, until whatever semblance of self-esteem and unity we possessed is no longer existent.

"You have to excuse me, little brother I don't mean to be going this deep on your first night in the belly of the beast, but I just can't remain passive while I see and hear the self-hate manifest in one of my own."

I was awestruck. What was this brother doing in prison? This cat—I mean this brother had a mean game. Reverend Ike couldn't shine this brother's shoes. If I had game like that, ain't no way I'd be in no prison. I ain't never heard anyone break it down like that. Even though I didn't quite understand all he was laying down, I still felt a surge of pride and hope unlike anything I'd felt before.

"Mr. Smithbay? That was, that was heavy, man. I mean, I felt that right here." I touched my chest.

Speaking to him made me think of Akbar. If I'd listened to Akbar, I just wonder where I'd be now. That night we stayed up talking. I found out that he was Muslim. He called himself a Moor, and he told me that Islam was the word used for greeting others. It simply meant peace.

James Smithbay was serving a 47-year sentence for conspiracy to traffic two kilos of crack cocaine. Unlike my case, no physical evidence was found. His conviction was solely a result of testimony given by two convicted drug dealers already doing time. They told the DEA and the grand jury that some five years back they both purchased large quantities of crack cocaine from then James Smith, who, at the time those statements were being made, was a successful stockbroker, real estate investor, husband, and father of two.

Despite his excellent standing in the community and lack of physical evidence, James Smith was indicted under a law called conspiracy, where physical evidence wasn't needed to convict. The only thing the courts needed was testimony from two or more people alleging a past or continuing criminal activity. Anyone could ruin the lives of someone else just by testifying to their criminal involvement.

The DEA, FBI, and ATF had no qualms about accepting coerced or false testimony. So long as two people conspired to ruin one man, it was fine in the government's eyes. After all, the government, whenever drug cases were concerned, seized the convicted one's assets. They were ruining not only that person, but that person's whole family structure.

After that first night, I wrote to Akbar, apologizing for not keeping in touch with him when I was in the free world. I told him all about Smithbay and our conversation. I explained how I wanted to learn everything I could about the plight of black people.

I had to get a rap down like Smithbay's. That shit was so heavy it was hypnotizing. I ain't never read, nor ever wanted to read a book. If it wasn't comin' on TV or to a theater, it would remain a mystery to me. I surprised myself. I had a new hunger for knowledge that had to be fed.

I started reading *Visions for Black Men* by Na'im Akbar. I couldn't get into it. Next, I grabbed another one of Smithbay's books, *Christopher Columbus and the Afrikan Holocaust* by John Henrik Clarke. Didn't feel that one either.

"Black man, check this out." Smithbay handed me another book.

"Man, I don't know. This reading stuff ain't me."

"Here. Just try this one," he prodded.

Pimp, Story of My Life. Iceberg Slim.

I sat down on his bunk, and I didn't get off until count time. Before I knew it, I was twenty pages from the end.

"Yo, dog, this book is the bomb. Iceberg was a mothafucka for ya. This nigga was pimpin' to the highest of pimptivity," I told Smithbay.

The pimptation to read gangsta pimp shit was staggering. Next, I went through the Donald Goines series in less than two weeks. I loved reading. I loved this gangsta shit. This was my world. This was my reality. I went into the common area where Smithbay was playin' chess with one of the Klansmen.

"Black man, glad to see you came out for air," Smithbay joked.

"What's next? I'm finished."

"Excuse me, Jim," he said, getting up from the table. I followed him back to the room where he gave me the book *Visions for Black Men*.

"Man, I done already tried this. It wasn't me. Where's that gangsta shit?"

"Black man, this is as gangsta as it gets. This book is so gangsta, it's real. This is the book they, the ones who are in power, hide from you. They don't want you to wake up. They fear that if you do, you may wake up everybody and free the slaves."

"Free the slaves?" I questioned.

"Yes. We are still in bondage. As long as we let the powers that be, who happen to be Whites, control what we learn and read, we are still slaves. When interviewed, Harriet Tubman, the mother of the Underground Railroad said it best when she explained, 'If I could have convinced more slaves that they were slaves, I would have freed thousands more.' "

After he walked out, I gave it another try. I finished it in a day. It was the deepest revelation I've ever read. Na'im Akbar was serious. From there I devoured the few books about the African and African-American experience that Smithbay had. The more I read, the more I realized that black folks were sick and in trouble.

A month in, I called Momma. She was blown away. My zest for reading shocked her, and that wasn't easy to do. She had always been an avid reader. I think she would have sent me anything to read that I requested. She was just as excited as I was that I had found so much joy in books. I asked her to buy me four while I was in Bartow County Jail. Next, I called Akbar. He was just as shocked, and told me that he would start sending me books as well.

Smithbay had told me that any day I would be leaving to go to Manchester, Kentucky. I would have no advance warning, and I wouldn't have time to send anything home, nor could I take anything with me.

Within weeks, I became a staunch, radical revolutionary. I started questioning everything white people did. Like why did white always move first in chess? Why was white associated with good and clean, and black with evil and filth? Why did the white ball knock all the other balls in, and saved the black ball for last? Why were the other balls numbered and the white ball was not?

Unfortunately, my comprehension of the books that I read provided me with a limited view of reality. Nonetheless, I became bigheaded, adamant and stubborn. To me, you were a mule, a sell-out Uncle Tom or just plain brainwashed if you didn't have the same conviction or feel the same way about white folk as I did. Huey Newton had me ready to die for the people. W.E.B. Dubois had me ready to join forces with other brothers to build an economic stronghold. Che Guerva and Malcolm X had me ready to kill all the white folks who held us back, by any means necessary.

Now, when I sat in the television area and watched *Soul Train*, I no longer saw fine-ass bitches dancing. I saw Nubian queens. I saw the milk and honey of the earth, and when I focused on a white broad, I saw a tired, made-up, implanted, wannabe sistah whore.

My boys were no longer dogs or cool cats. They were my brothers, African, African-American, black men. They were little-g gods.

Just like Smithbay foretold, after six weeks in Bartow County, I was awakened in the middle of the night and escorted out. I did manage to leave Smithbay my mom's address so he could write me. I was handcuffed and shackled. Along with several other holdover inmates, I was taken to the big house.

The pen. For over four hours, twenty-seven men were crammed in a six-man, cold concrete-slabbed holding cell. It was barely big enough for six, let alone twenty-seven musty, foul-breathed, farting inmates. It was rainy and below freezing outside. The only heat we had was from one another, and with a room full of hard-up men, no one was trying to get any closer than we were forced to be.

We were served the normal meal inmates in transit received: a stale peanut butter sandwich; a dry, hard, often stale bologna sandwich; a piece of fruit; and a small carton of warm milk. With meals like this, I had no problem sticking to the diet I'd started in the county. It was a simple plan consisting of foods that were not going bad or had gone bad, food that didn't move around or run off my plate, and of course I had to be able to identify the food I ate.

After jumping on the scale while talking to a physician's assistant about my medical condition, I was given two shots that I tried to avoid. As the needle went in, I thought about Tuskegee. I had read the story back at county. I prayed I wasn't being experimented on.

During the screening process I asked the counselor in charge why I was not on my way to Manchester.

"You're here until the bus going to your designated institution arrives."

"When is that?" I asked.

"Can't tell you that. Violation of security. You might have the bus ambushed for all I know." He laughed. Next he asked me if I had ever assisted any law enforcement agency in any way.

"No."

Reading from some papers I couldn't quite make out, he proceeded. "It says here that you assisted the government in a sting operation setting up a drug buy, and four people were arrested as a result."

"Oh yeah, I—"

"One of these four is being held in open population, right here." He emphasized every single word, making it sound like I was a dirt-dog snitch. I felt like one too. Since one of the brothas in the sting operation was being housed at the pen, I had to be placed in administrative segregation—the hole.

The counselor said I couldn't be in population for security reasons.

I was held on the fifth of six tiers. The hole looked like a scene out of an Alcatraz movie. It was dark and rat-puke filthy, and there was no heat. Some too stupid to be ignorant-ass inmates had busted out every window in the hole years ago, and they had never been repaired. The hacks gave out wool blankets, but the cold wind monsooned right through.

I shared a cell with an older, sick cougher. I wished he would just die so I could've gotten some semblance of sleep. He coughed, hacked and spit all night. If it hadn't been so damned cold, I would have given him one of my blankets. At night, several inmates on the lower tiers slid their mattresses through the bars and set them on fire, causing them and everyone else to form a coughing choir concert trying to breathe.

The place wasn't fit for a rat, although the rats had free reign of the place. The Atlanta pen was the best place to be to get over a fear of rodents. Before I got out of bed, I had to throw a shoe to scatter any loitering rats. One morning one stood up on its hind legs in a boxer's stance like it wanted to try me. My fear of rabies saved his life. He might have been big as a small cat, but I would've taken his ass. I wondered why the Board of Health hadn't had this part of the prison condemned, but it didn't take me long to figure it out. The same people ran both businesses.

We were only allowed to make one 15-minute phone call every other day and a shower only on Mondays, Wednesdays, and sometimes Fridays. The shower looked like it hadn't been cleaned since the prison opened a hundred years ago. There was a garden of nasty-looking bacteria growing on the discolored, cracked tile walls.

Day and night, inmates screamed and hollered at each other from tier to tier, cell to cell. Between the freezing cold, the noise, and my trying-to-die coughing cellie, sleep was a mirage. Every time I thought it was coming, a cough, a fire or screams stopped me.

The food was cold and horrible. The healthiest and safest part of the meals was the crawling protein that I sometimes found bathing in the food. Once again, I survived off a high-cholesterol diet of potato chips and candy I purchased from the prison commissary, thanks to Momma and Akbar sending money to put on my books.

Never in a million years would I have imagined being so happy to go to prison, but when it came time to leave for Manchester, I jumped out my bunk, gave out a scream, got on my knees and thanked God.

CHAPTER 24

I was handcuffed and shackled for all seven hours of the bus ride. When we arrived, I saw that things were really looking up. From the outside of the triple-metal electrical razor-wire fence that surrounded the prison compound, this place didn't look like any prison I had ever seen on television. It looked more like a college campus. This was a pleasant change compared to the rat and roach dungeon I'd just left. I was even given a choice of whether to live in a smoking or non-smoking unit. I lucked up on my room assignment. I ended up sharing a two-man room with another socially conscious brother.

Dawoo Ali Muhammad was in his mid-thirties. He had four years in on a 300-month sentence. Up until 1989, Dawoo owned and ran a prosperous fresh fish market on the east side of Detroit.

Mario Lot was Dawoo's sole deliveryman. Unbeknownst to Dawoo, Mario also had a lucrative side job. Acting on a tip, Detroit's finest obtained a search warrant, and while Mario was at work, they thoroughly went through his upscale apartment. There, they uncovered a triple-beam scale and crack shavings.

Next, the police got a search warrant for Dawoo's fresh fish market, and they found a little more than a half-kilo of crack cocaine in Ziploc baggies wrapped up inside a homemade coat on a rack in the back of the market. They also found Dawoo's Smith & Wesson .357 behind the meat counter where he'd always kept it.

Dawoo was arrested along with his three employees.

Mario confessed to the detectives that it was his dope and neither Dawoo nor any of the other employees even knew he sold. After forty-eight hours of good cop/bad cop "holler and we'll let you go" games, Dawoo and his employees were released.

Feeling a need to help, Dawoo hired a lawyer for Mario, who was seventeen, a high school dropout, and had been working for Dawoo for two months as a delivery boy. His mother was a crack head who ran out on her son four years earlier. His grandmother had been his guardian until she passed away a year before. He'd never known his father. Mario was a ghetto child running wild, doin' whatever to survive.

Mario had been lured into the dope game, and after his arrest he was pressured to produce some hard evidence, so he assisted in a sting operation, resulting in one of his contact's lieutenants being busted. One week later, Mario was gunned down as he was leaving his apartment. The feds took Mario's murder as a personal affront. They cracked down on the investigation.

Not a month after Mario's death, the feds indicted Dawoo. Even though the state had Mario's sworn testimony that Dawoo didn't know anything about his drug involvement, the government still managed to railroad an innocent man. Coerced false testimony from informants who did not even know Dawoo helped convict him. He was found guilty on one count of conspiracy to distribute crack cocaine, aiding and abetting, and carrying a firearm in the commission of a crime, even though his .357 was licensed.

"Man, I don't see how you stay up, especially the way you been played," I said to him one night.

"Played?" Dawoo frowned.

"Yeah, played. You and a lot of other brothers in here done been stolen from your families by an ice-cold system that boasts justice when it's about just them. They brainwash society into believin' you innocent until proven guilty, when for a black man, as soon as you're born you spend your life stamped with guilt until you prove you're innocent and able to assimilate with European ideology."

Dawoo put his arms behind his head and leaned back on his bunk. "I have two choices: either I do this time or it does me. So what, I was blindsided. I got hit way below the belt. That's what happens in war. This is war,' my brother," he emphasized. "A war against evil. Against injustice. Frederick Douglass said it best. 'Without struggle, there's no progress.' It's a constant tug-of-war. I just lost one of many battles. I am but a part of a whole—a linebacker on the Black team."

"So, you just walk around smilin' after massa done broke his foot off in your behind?"

"Little brother," he said, "my plight is minuscule compared to the plight of right over wrong. The plight of the mentally oppressed. Our people are being slaughtered in droves. It isn't a 'me' thing, it's an 'us' thing. Brother, I'm doing well. I'm alive and healthy, fighting this tyrannical terrorist mirage of a justice system.

"Too many of us are weakened by ignorance, therefore we conform and accept our condition, even if they are conditions that contradict those of Allah. As long as I strive to stay on the Siralt'l Mustaqeem, the path of righteousness. I'll be victorious, and I'll stand behind truth, not color. Whatever color you jump out the crayon box wearing, if you're about truth, change, and my people, I'll go through a wall with you."

"Man, I feel you, but I can't be down with no white man. The Bible even say the devil gon' come at you from the left, right, back, and front. He knows the truth better than we do, same as John Q. Cracker." I paused, collecting my thoughts. "It's them racist crackers who came to us in truth as friends, tricked us into selling each other out four hundred years ago, and they're still doing it today with this snitch system. They've oppressed or have tried to oppress every people they've come in contact with."

"Open up your eyes, Lincoln. Look out the window." Dawoo got up and pointed out the window facing the rec yard. "See those hillbillies over there and old Bob over there feeding the chipmunks?"

"Yeah."

"Those white men couldn't be racist if they wanted to. How could they possibly oppress us? You see," Dawoo paused, sitting back on his bottom bunk before continuing, "to be a racist, one has to be in a position to put the wheels in motion to oppress a group of people."

"You're right, but white folk have had their feet on our necks far too long."

"These are the minority. Only five to seven percent of white folk are responsible for the mindset of society. It's not the physical state of a man that makes him racist, it's the socioconscious collective thought, fueled by racist dogma, that makes a man hate."

I nodded.

"Hate ain't nothin' but fear. You combat fear by controlling it. You divide your fears. You confuse that which you fear. You enslave the fear. The way you do all that is to know the origin of what you fear."

"I don't know if I follow you," I said, shaking my head.

"Example: The wealthiest Europeans lived seven, eight hundred years ago. They lived in a state of fear, always scared the poor were going to learn what they knew. If the poor learned the truth, then they would have what the rich had—freedom. With true freedom, there can be no class divide. There can be no rich."

"Okay, I'm feelin' you."

"The rich spent their lives harboring knowledge and coming up with ways to divide the people, keeping them in a state of unknown. Couldn't do it with color, so they did it with class." He smiled. "You had kings, Pharisees, noblemen, aristocrats, serfs and slaves, all in a class struggle to rise to the next level. Less than one percent made the decisions. Less than five percent ruled the kingdoms."

"So, you sayin' the concept of racism was created to divide different shades of people so that the minority can continue to rule through mass confusion?" I asked.

"Exactly." He nodded. "Willie Lynch just picked up a book and got the divide and conquer scheme from his ancestors. We give him too much credit. He ain't invented no parts of the wheel."

"You've given me a lot to think about. I guess I have to keep reading."

"Always."

"One last thought. You've got the finished product, now you have to know how it's built to destroy it."

"Huh?"

"To be an oppressor, to be a hater is a learned behavior. When a baby is born into the world, it is born in God's image, free of all 'isms'—haterism, sexism, colorism, and racism. A person is taught all of these 'isms.' Maybe a better example is yourself. Lincoln, look at you. Your emotions, the way you act and feel are based on what influences and experiences you've had and what someone has told you."

"Wow, man—I mean brother. I never thought of it like that."

Dawoo went to his locker and pulled out some books.

"It's no coincidence you're in this cell with me. Wherever you travel on your life's journey, you will gravitate toward brothers like yourself. They will help you grow stronger and fight harder. I'll be free when you become free. I'll live, breathe, and fight through you when you get out. You have been called. It's up to you to answer," he said.

"I don't know about being called. I'm just trying to break the chains."

"I wish more young brothers read our story instead of his story. Check these out." He gave me books by Cheikh Anta Diop, George James, Dr. Yosef Ben-Jochannan, Comrade George Jackson, Na'im Akbar, Rudolph Windsor, Assata Shakur, Frances Cress Welling, John Henrik Clarke, the Honorable Minister Louis Farrakhan, Michael Bradley, William Cooper, Ralph Epperson, Malcolm X, Frantz Fanon, Ishakamusa Barashango, Gerald Massey, Ivan Van Sertima, Dr. Maulana Karenga, and Carter G. Woodson.

I snatched them up and was ready to start reading and studying when Dawoo invited me to Muslim services, Jumah Prayer. It would interfere with my walking program, but after being shown so much love, I couldn't decline. I was curious anyway to see how a Muslim service was conducted.

I walked in the prison chapel at 1:45. I felt a lot of energy, a vibration from the brothers, who were in several stages of prayer. A few minutes after I sat on a chair in the rear, a brotha got up and centered himself in the front of the room. Next, he put his hands to his ears as if imitating reindeer horns, then he started some musical chant. Afterward, everyone sat in lines, and a minister gave a 30-minute speech on life, religion, and spirituality.

He talked about religion being man-made. He spoke of spirituality. He often referred to a prophet named Muhammad. He spoke of duality in thought. The biggest surprise came when he read from the Qur'an and said something about the believer had to believe in all God's messengers and works.

The believer had to believe in the Torah, Bible, and the Qur'an. The last part of the service was a long prayer where everyone stood shoulder-to-shoulder and toe-to-toe and followed the minister in prayer. Everyone kept bending over, getting on the ground and getting up. It looked like they were exercising in slow motion. After the service, on the way back to my dorm, I took in my surroundings, looked around, and I just shook my head.

There were twelve hundred inmates housed in five buildings at FCI Manchester. There were more brothers in the FCI than in the whole city of Manchester. The majority Black and Hispanic population changed the name FCI Manchester to FCI Klanchester, due to the hillbilly, pre-Civil War Southern mentality of the staff. I would've been surprised if they weren't all card-carrying Klan members with Confederate flags in the rear windows of their pickups.

In prison, everyone was assigned and forced to work a full-time job such as landscaping, food service, being an orderly, or UNICOR, which was prison industries, where inmates made everything from mattresses to helicopter harnesses. Only medical restrictions allowed you to be excluded from work.

I purposely sabotaged my medical screening and physical. After all, I was partially paralyzed, overweight and out of shape. I overexaggerated my paralysis so well, I would have been a shoe-in for an Academy Award. My game plan for doing time had nothing to do with me working for the modern-day slave system. I was a revolutionary. I had to prepare my mind and body. I had to get into the best mental and physical shape I could. A lot of work had to be done on my body, but my mind needed a foundation to get me started.

Once I'd bought some sweats and sneakers from commissary, I tried my hand at weightlifting. I got on the bench, lifted the 45-pound bar in the air, brought it down slowly, and it got stuck on my flabby chest. I squirmed and I prayed. I still couldn't get that damn bar off my chest. I was embarrassed when a Happy-Meal-sized brotha came and did a one-handed yank, snatching the bar from my chest and putting it back into the rack.

I decided to build my strength and endurance by walking the quarter-mile track and doing whatever calisthenics I could. I vowed to get back to the weights before long. I didn't want anyone trying to take my worm-weakness for Charmin-softness. I couldn't have anyone trying to press me for money, commissary, or anything else. My fight game may have been at ground zero, but my heart registered high heaven. I didn't worry about fighting, but I was cautious. Every day someone got his head split, and most fights and stabbings were over the television or the phone.

One day, three brothas and I were watching *MTV Jams* when this Arnold Schwarzenigga nut-case we called Psycho roughed off the TV, changing the channel like it was his.

Tidbit was a little wiry Jamaican kid, maybe five-seven and a buck twenty-five soaking wet. "Turn de box back," Tidbit stood and shouted to the massive six-foot-and-change nutcase.

"Uh-oh," I said under my breath. Tidbit must've had a death wish. Too bad. I liked the little dude. The last thing I wanted to see was Psycho mopping the floor with Tidbit's face.

Before anyone could intervene, Psycho was choke-close to Tidbit's neck, flexing his massive eighteen-inch biceps.

"Midget test-tube sissy, you turn it back," Psycho raged.

My cellie, Dawoo, was mopping the hall when Psycho's big mouth attracted his attention. He and another brother came into the TV room and tried to squash the situation.

"Come on, Psycho. Calm down. You can't get no points taking out this kid. Let it go," Dawoo pleaded.

"I guess you right, cuz." Psycho pointed at Tidbit. "You lucky this time, you little rusty blood clot."

With lightning speed and bulls-eye accuracy, Tidbit hit Psycho dead in the mouth, busting his lip. Dawoo and his friend knew they were helpless to stop the forthcoming massacre.

A mad scramble took place as everyone grabbed a chair, moving them against the wall, so there would be room to fight without attracting the guards. Tidbit dodged and weaved Psycho's charges. Tidbit dodged right, faded to the left, and hit Psycho with a three piece, cutting his face above his left eye.

Psycho, a little more cautious this time, charged once more. Tidbit punished him, unleashing a flurry of rights and lefts while expertly dodging Psycho's wild haymakers. Beaten and bloody, Psycho managed to grab one of Tidbit's arms. Big mistake. Tidbit used his free arm to land a bone-crushing blow that broke Psycho's nose.

Dawoo, two others, and I broke up the fight before Tidbit could do anymore damage.

Psycho was pumpkin-faced when the blood was washed away. Ten minutes later after going to his cell, Psycho charged from his room, running past the officers' station and out the front door. He was carrying a sharp-looking shiny piece of metal.

Tidbit was chillin' with a couple of gumps, the prison name for feminine homosexuals, smoking a Newport when he saw Psycho coming. Tidbit dropped his Newport and took off. Psycho chased him, finally tripping on his own feet.

When Tidbit saw this, he turned, ran toward Psycho and tried to kick him to sleep. Before Tidbit could accomplish this task, several guards were Rodney Kinging both of them while Tidbit's jailhouse wife screamed.

Gumps were not only accepted, they were popular by demand behind prison walls. Gumps decorated themselves to look like women. Everyone from the power weightlifters to the Bible-toting hellfire and brimstone preaching Christians paid well to be sexually serviced by the gumps.

It was interesting to me that inmates who were sucked off didn't consider themselves gumps. It wasn't an unusual sight to see a stud all hugged up with a gump on the weekdays, and on the weekends that same stud would be playing with his kids and visiting with his wife. Usually, whenever some stud tried to claim some gump as his private property, this meant trouble.

Michael Adams, a.k.a. Zsa-Zsa, was the queen of Klanchester. He was also one of the most dangerous and deadly inmates. He was serving a 60-year sentence for armed robbery and murder.

Zsa-Zsa had shoulder-length, blue-black, wavy permed hair and stood five-nine. Thanks to hormone shots he smuggled in and aerobic conditioning during the ten years he'd already done, he looked just like a woman, from his Adam's apple to his fingertips. He sported a slim, half-hourglass figure with little bitty titties.

He walked around the rec yard, leading his small band of gumpettes. Zsa-Zsa got a kick out of taunting and teasing inmates as they worked out. He always wore a knotted up T-shirt and altered extra-short, hip-hugging shorts. During basketball games, Zsa-Zsa and his crew cheered from the sidelines. They usually cheered for Homicide's team, performing routines they had made up and using shredded newspaper glued together for pompoms.

Shawn Jones, a.k.a. Homicide Jones, was the six-foot-four Michael Jordan of Klanchester. The kid had unbelievable moves and handles. He could have easily been the next NBA superstar.

Homicide never made it past the ninth grade. He was just another kid ensnared into street life. He was raised in a single-parent home with eight siblings and a mother who, despite loving her children, hadn't a clue on moral values.

His mother was a baby when she started having babies, and her mother was also a teenage mother. The men in their lives passed through like traveling salesmen, dropping off seeds before they moved on. The real fathers were the city or county, makin' an appearance on the first and third of every month. For these young mothers, it was too overwhelming to raise children. The kids were left to be raised by the cold, hard, heartless streets, as was Shawn Jones.

Shawn smoked weed at the age of twelve then graduated to geek joints (weed laced with crack), and by the age of seventeen he was a crack addict. To support his habit, he did just about anything. Stealing cars became his forte. On his eighteenth birthday, Shawn was found sleeping in an illegally parked Z-28. The police found a little over three ounces of crack cocaine under the spare tire. Shawn had no idea drugs were in the car he'd stolen only four hours earlier. The owner never reported the car stolen and denied the drugs were even his.

At nineteen, Shawn Jones was sentenced to ten years in federal prison.

Three hardcore gambling DC boys tried to press Shawn into throwing a prison basketball game one day. Shawn had only been down for five months at the time. He reluctantly agreed to throw the game, but when the game began, Shawn was in another zone. Needless to say, his team ended up punishing the other team.

The DC boys caught him alone in his room, resting on his bunk. No one knew that Shawn slept with a corkscrew-like, concrete-sharpened, half-straightened bedspring and a razor blade melted into a toothbrush handle strategically placed under his pillow. As they rushed in, Shawn pulled his survival tools from under his pillow and sliced and cut like a butcher in a slaughterhouse.

One of the dudes got away, screaming and carrying part of his intestines. By the time the dorm officer rushed to see what the screaming was about, Shawn was ankle deep in blood and guts. The officer ran away, throwing up his lunch.

This act of self-defense earned Shawn the name Homicide, and forty years to run concurrent with his 10-year sentence.

Like a meat-eating beast in the wild, Zsa-Zsa preyed on weakness. He loved to toy with Homicide. Zsa-Zsa enjoyed exploiting the young kid's ignorance. Homicide was ribbed up by some of his friends to put Zsa-Zsa in check.

"Yo, dog, if that was my bitch, she wouldn't be trickin' with no other stud," one dude said.

"Come on, 'Cide, you got to show yo' ho who's boss," said another.

"Yeah, check that bitch. Nigga, you Tarzan. The bitch bow down to you," the first one shot back.

Zsa-Zsa sashayed up to Homicide about the time his cronies were laying down game on him.

Homicide hauled off and slapped Zsa-Zsa so hard that he left a handprint on Zsa-Zsa's reddened face. Zsa-Zsa was more embarrassed than hurt.

Two days later, Zsa-Zsa sneaked up on Homicide while he was catnapping before the 4 o'clock standup count. Zsa-Zsa worked his shank like a surgeon. Homicide woke up in the city hospital. He had to have extensive surgery. For six months, Homicide relieved himself through a surgically attached plastic bag.

During all the drama that went on, I kept my eyes and ears open, but I continued to engross myself in books and journals in hopes of elevating and freeing my mind. The more I learned, the more I wanted to learn.

I began to see things more clearly. I became frustrated whenever I saw us in prison, on television, and in the print media doing things that I thought were counterproductive to us as a people.

For example, the *Jerry Springer* show exploited the poor and the ignorant. And we were making those kinds of shows more popular by supporting them. The television room was always crowded when Jerry came on. This may have frustrated me, but it fueled the fire burning inside me to change the world.

After attending two Muslim services, I made my claim of *Shahada*, proclaiming myself as a Muslim by saying, "La-I-la-ha-Ill-Allah Ash-Adu-Anna-Muhammad-dan-Wa-Rasullalah." Those words meant that I bear witness that there is no God but Allah, and Muhammad is his last prophet and messenger.

Through reading books explaining how religion, Islam and Christianity, have been used to enslave the masses, I came to the realization that our oppressors never meant for us to be free. The Bible was what we were given to find peace in during slavery; the Qur'an was forced on us twelve hundred years ago in Northern and Eastern Africa by the Hyksos kings. These books were all we were allowed to read, for those who were allowed. And often times, an agent of the oppressor attended services to make sure we did not stray from the Word.

Through my page-turning travels, I found that Islam was the path that I could identify with better than the other monotheistic paths. It is the only untainted bible written in its original language. If I were asked what my religion was, though, I'd scream Christian, holler Islam, and shout Jewish. But more importantly, I was a God-fearing black man enslaved in a country run by men who never meant for me to be free.

Oftentimes, inmates latched onto the Muslim community for protection against the many threats that awaited the weak. The Muslim community was respected because of its discipline and uncompromising values. Everyone knew a Muslim without having to be told. Minister Farrakhan dropped the seeds best when he said, "When you have a clean glass and a dirty glass side by side, no one has to point out the clean glass."

The first few months of my incarceration I shared everything I was learning with my girl, Michelle. We talked on the phone at least twice a day. Every time she answered the phone, I was excited just to hear her voice. Prison was turning out to be my university, but Michelle could have cared less. She was caught up in herself. The transformation I was undergoing was trivial to her. All she talked about was her friends and how lonely she was. She had a way of bringing me down. She acted like she was the one in jail. I don't know what got me down the most, her attitude or the prison snitches.

Everybody despised snitches, but every joint had more than its fair share. There were snitches who continuously went back to court on writs to give information or to testify on someone else. Who better to catch a criminal than a criminal? Five-O's job was made easy. It was modern-day slave trading, akin to the way we went into the jungles while the slave traders waited on the sandy shores for our return, with our own people to sell.

Over ninety percent of the inmates in federal prison were there because somebody dropped dime on them. The lowest, most despised inmates in prison were the dry snitches. These were inmates who informed on other inmates, keeping the prison COs (compound officers) current on what was happening in the joint.

At Klanchester, we had our own special inmate snitch patrol. The Itty Bitty Snitch Committee was a handful of guys who acted when someone was labeled a snitch. The committee usually gave a blanket party to the snitch. The committee would put bars of prison-issue soap into tube socks and meet up with the blanket general, who was always the snitch identifier.

While the snitch was asleep, the committee would throw the blanket over his head, concealing the identity of the committee members, then they would commence to wailing on the snitch with their socked soap.

Usually, the inmate under the blanket would check in after receiving medical treatment. Checking in meant telling the officers you feared for your life and needed protection. In turn, you were thrown in the hole until they decided what to do with you.

After being in Klanchester for four months, I was called out on a court writ. Before I left, I told some brothers about a fictitious state charge I had to go back and face. I knew everyone would be thinking I was hot. It was the normal prison paranoia. I had just gotten there and already I was going back to court.

I got back to a scorching Atlanta June. Back in the hot hole at the Atlanta pen, I thought I was going to die. It must have been a hundred degrees in the shaded sun and a hundred and ten inside the dungeon hell. It was so hot, we all slept on the cold metal floors of our cells with the creepy crawlers. The only air conditioning we had was a large fan on the tier at the end of each corridor that circulated dust and hot air.

Inmates and guards had heat strokes and suffered from other heat-related ailments. Early every morning, a quack doctor's assistant quietly raced past every cell when most inmates were sleeping. You had to really be on your toes to catch him as he ran his rounds. That little beady-eyed, gray-haired, middle-aged West Indian black man earned the title Dr. Dolittle, which was exactly what he did—very little. He gave aspirin for everything that ailed. If you told him you were severely constipated, he'd give you aspirin. If you complained of chest pains, aspirin. You had to be damn near dead before he'd prescribe anything.

Due to the inhumane conditions, the inmates grew very hostile. We would keep small cartons of warm milk we received with our breakfast for three, four, five days at a time. After the milk was rotten-rank, we'd bomb the small cartons out our cells and over the tier, hoping to hit one of the COs in the head. Some inmates were creative, mixing milk and piss together. Even though we were firing blind, we'd know by the cursing and screaming when we scored a direct hit. The whole unit would get ecstatic, and the CO rarely caught the perpetrator because he never saw it coming.

At night, three to four hundred inmates in the hole would chant. "Black officer, why you wanna put us in a coffin, sir?"

One scorching day while lying drenched in sweat, I came up with a sweet plan. Every day we got one hour of rec outside in a concrete and metal birdcage. One day, on the way out to rec, handcuffed and all, I fell on my face. I quietly lay there while the officer in charge radioed for a stretcher. Soon, I was on my way to the hospital unit. There I complained of shortness of breath and chest pains. I stayed in the hospital for six euphoric, air-conditioned days.

After my vacation was up, I was escorted back to hell. Finally, my lawyer had me moved to snitch central, Paulding County Jail. I would say 99.9 percent of the federal inmates held there were hot as fire. It was nothing to see and hear a group of inmates talking about who they were testifying on and who else they could tell on. You had dudes who didn't even know the person they were testifying against, but that didn't stop them from getting on the witness stand and telling lies.

The sad fact was that I knew a lot of these cheese eaters. I'd come into contact with them on the streets. If I didn't know the rat, I knew who they were plotting on.

What hurt most was that I couldn't do anything about it. If I tried, I'd get charged with obstruction. Finally, after a month and a half, I went to face the music.

I was taken to the Richard Russell Federal Building, which unfortunately I'd become familiar with. I was escorted to a mini law library-looking room. I was too nervous to accept the soft drink I was offered. Minutes later, a gray-haired, Barnaby Jones-lookin' white man walked in and introduced himself.

"Bob Martin." He nodded. "I'm the D.A. in charge of prosecuting the case you helped make against Phillip Turner, Leon Glover, Trent Best, and Kyle Dawson. Mr. Best has already plead guilty and turned on our side." He smiled. "Now we need your testimony. Remember this—the better you make us look, the happier we'll be and the better you'll be treated when it comes time for your sentence reduction."

"Yes, sir." *You just don't know how much I do understand,* I thought while smiling.

"Now, I'm going to pose several questions to you. Just answer in the affirmative," he coached. After a brief pause, letting what he said sink in, he continued. "Their lawyers will ask trick questions. Stick to one-word answers. If you need time to ponder a question, ask the lawyer to please repeat it. Stay relaxed out there, okay?" He massaged my shoulders.

I nodded.

"You ready, buddy?"

"As ready as I'll ever be."

Even though I sold my soul, I still had an ounce of dignity left.

Once I was on the stand, I became the witness from hell for the prosecution. At times, I thought Barnaby "Bob Martin" Jones was going to be hospitalized. He kept stuttering until he lost his voice altogether.

A week after the trial began, Leon Glover and Phillip Turner were acquitted, and Kyle Dawson was sentenced to 138 months. He was dead in the water from the start because he was the one who set up the deal. It was hard to believe that his shade-tree lawyer let him go to trial. It was hard to tell the good guys from the bad nowadays.

A couple of weeks later, I was back in Klanchester. The negative was always the first assumption when anyone went out on a writ. The only thing I could do about the innuendo that surrounded me was to ignore it. I fell back into my routine of walking the track, reading, and participating in the Muslim community, although they treated me differently once I got back.

Not even a month later, I was cuffed and shackled, on my way back to Atlanta on another writ. It did not take a brain surgeon to see what Uncle Sam and his boys were trying to do. This time, the excuse I used was that I was going to the hospital to have surgery on my neck. I didn't know what else to say.

When I went to court, it was really for my sentence modification hearing.

My prosecutor, who was black, only recommended a 2-year reduction. I couldn't believe it. No, I could. He was just another sick brother miseducated by White America's mis-educational school system. He had hobnobbed with the other man so long that he tried to think and be like the other man. This sell-out Uncle Tom had told my lawyer a year ago that he'd recommend a fifty-percent reduction of my sentence.

The judge looked old enough to have owned slaves, but he showed me more love than the Oreo prosecutor. Still, I was hit. The judge settled on a forty-four month reduction, leaving me to cope with an eighty-eight month sentence.

I was all torn up. It was my fault. I set the game up, the home team was a shoe-in to win, and in the ninth inning I tried to throw the whole thing. It was only natural for the team owners to retaliate.

It was a week before Christmas 1993.

Back in the county jail, I computed my new release date—April 13, 1999. Well, at least I would still have a successful business whenever I did get out, I thought.

For the last few months, I'd been hearing wild stories from Mike about D'Andre throwing away money on strip joints, girls, and cars. This was hard to believe because that had never been my brother's style, but Mike had no reason to lie to me. Trina's brother, who worked at the shop, told me that D'Andre had been opening up at different times each day and some days he'd be there just to open, then that was the last anyone would see of him until closing.

I started getting nervous. To me, it sounded like too much money was going out and not enough was coming in. The next time I spoke to D'Andre, I nonchalantly inquired about the allegations. He staunchly denied any wrongdoing, for which I was relieved.

A week after I came from court, on Christmas Eve, Mike dropped a bombshell on me.

"Your brother ain't right. Closing the shop was some dirty-ass shit."

"What?" I screamed.

"You didn't know?"

"Hell no."

"He wouldn't renew the lease. He just closed down. I told you he was jackin' off all your money. You would have been better off leaving some money with me to flip and putting the rest in a safe deposit box."

I couldn't believe it. I knew things weren't going smoothly, but I couldn't believe my little brother could be so damn irresponsible.

"You know he sold the house, right?"

"What house?"

"The one you bought."

"Oh, hell no. Why you just tellin' me?"

"Hell, he just sold it after Thanksgivin'."

251

"I'm gon' fuck his fat ass up." I slammed the phone against the wall.

The fat fucka probably hid it from Michelle since she had moved in with Momma a couple of months ago. I took a deep breath and dialed.

"Let me speak to D'Andre."

"He's in the tub," Trina hesitantly responded.

"I'll wait." A minute passed, then two.

"Uh, hello."

"What the fuck you done did?"

"Don't talk to me like that," D'Andre shouted.

"Like what? Mothafucka you done fucked me outta everything I worked for. I trusted you."

The next thing I knew, I was shouting to a dial tone. Immediately, I tried to call back. No answer. Hysterical, I called my mother. After I explained what D'Andre had done, she said, "It goes to show you. I've always said that nothing good can come from anything bad."

"But Mom, I sold everything. I had nearly a quarter million invested in D'Andre and the shop."

"Whatchu want me to do, Lincoln? Huh?" She paused. "I wish you wouldn't put me in the middle of this shit. Instead of screaming at me, you need to worry about yourself, not what's happening out here that you have no control over."

"Mom," I shouted, "you don't have a clue." I hung up hurt, mad, and in tears. That was the last day that I talked to my brother while I was in prison.

When I got back to Klanchester, I was a leper.

I was at an all-time low. I'd sold my soul for freedom-dreams promised by the same folks who set me up and locked away my mind. My own family sold me out. I'd read so much and run so far on a treadmill in reverse. I had no one to talk to, no one to share my pain.

Back in my cell, I decided to try to transfer my frustration from my brain to paper. I picked up a pen and started writing. So much had happened in my life. I was a pressure keg on the verge of bursting. I don't know what made me start, but once I put that pen on notebook paper, my fingers developed a mind of their own. I just wrote.

I wrote about prison, about life, about the struggle. I wrote about the brainwashing that Blacks were subjected to from the time they started watching Big Bird on *Sesame Street*. I wrote about anything and everything I was against and the things I was for and loved.

I used my writing as an outlet to vent my hostilities, my pain, and my frustrations. When I sat down to write, I entered a trance-like state. My body was projected outside of the prison walls and directly into the scene I was depicting with my words. I'd be gone for hours sometimes.

Writing helped me pass the time, relieve tension, and get through the loneliness that threatened to consume me. I felt like it was me against the world, and no one could see what I thought to be so obvious. The authors I read and the inmates I vibed with had opened my eyes. I had to share what I learned with my best friend, my pen and pad.

I began to let others read some of my writings. I wanted people to see what I saw, feel what I felt. I wanted to take away the pain, the loneliness of not knowing. I wanted to let black men know they were not alone. Through my writing, I wanted to change the mindset of the people. Just a year earlier I wanted to kill all white people. That was my limited view. Now I wanted to change the world.

I was a desperate dreamer, searching for an ear that could hear me roar. I hardly talked to Michelle anymore, even though I still felt something for her. When my lonely Jones came down, I called her, trying to rekindle sparks where there had once been fire.

Street Life

I was transferred to a minimum-security prison camp in Atlanta, eighteen months after turning myself in. Maurice Grant was almost ten years my senior. He was very intelligent, a good listener, and a lover of practical jokes. He became the big brother I never had. He was my too-harsh critic and sometimes editor. He seemed to enjoy my writings, and even though he didn't always agree with my philosophies, he always remained open-minded. He was my second set of ears, even when I wished he wasn't.

The others in our dorm called us Fred and Barney because we argued about everything. Sometimes I started arguments just to play devil's advocate. I liked to test Maurice.

Maurice's new bunkmate, Donald Southern, arrived with an 8-month sentence. This dude cried and carried on like he had life. I thought he was gon' have to be put on suicide watch.

One day, Maurice walked into the counselor's office, and while the counselor was occupied with another inmate, he stole some government stationery. Then, he went into the law library and typed up a professional-looking document that in essence read that Donald Southern #43054-060's sentence had been overturned; therefore, the above named person was hereby granted immediate release. The Honorable Judge Hunter Dickey was forged on the bottom of the form.

Maurice took the envelope and typed his bunkie's name and inmate number on it.

That afternoon, Maurice and his bunkie were walking the track when the mail was delivered. I put the official-looking letter along with Donald's other mail on his bed. The whole camp heard a feminine scream when Donald read the letter. Before count was over, he shot out of his bed and ran to the officer's station.

After reviewing the letter, the officer stated, "There's nothing anyone can do until Monday when your case manager comes in."

Donald didn't care. He called his wife, other family members and friends. He even called old employees, telling them the news. He boasted to everyone at the camp how he never deserved to be in prison and how he was going to sue the government for wrongful imprisonment.

By Monday morning, Donald had cleared out his locker, packed, and took his bedclothes to the laundry. When he went to his case manager, she was appalled.

"When did you get this?"

"Friday. I came in from the track after mail call and it was on my bed."

"Mr. Southern, I'm sorry, but you've been the victim of a cruel practical joke."

I don't know for sure, but it was rumored that Donald was seen leaving her office in tears. Once Donald found out Maurice was behind the joke, he didn't say another word to him for the next five months.

CHAPTER 25

Before prison, Maurice was a square living with his wife and daughter in San Francisco. He worked as an executive for a small advertising company. Having a good heart, Maurice took in an old army buddy he hadn't seen in years. His buddy claimed he'd fallen on some hard times and needed a place to crash for a few days.

On his way to work, Maurice dropped his buddy off at some rundown house in a crime-ridden area of town. On the third day, five-O rolled down on Maurice as he parked to let his buddy out. After a half-ass search of Maurice's Hyundai, the cops uncovered a small bag of crack cocaine under the armrest between the passenger's and driver's seat. Maurice was so green he didn't know what the police had in their hands.

Maurice's buddy turned out to be a full-time addict and part-time dealer hiding out from some dudes he owed money to. To save his ass, Maurice's ex-army buddy took the stand and told the jury that not only was the crack Maurice's, but he had witnessed Maurice put the crack under the armrest. Even though Maurice's lawyer proved the witness was a crack addict and liar, Maurice was still convicted and sentenced to ninety months.

Maurice's wife of nine years left him shortly after he was sentenced. Like me, he'd lost everything, but he handled his loss better than I handled mine. His inner strength, determination, and will to bounce back gave me strength. He was a motivating force for me to put the past behind me, look to tomorrow, and prepare for my future.

At the Atlanta prison camp, most inmates had no problem admitting they would do whatever it took to get home. We had a saying at the camp. There were three types of inmates: those who told, those who wished they'd told, and those who didn't have anyone to tell on.

By 1997, I felt good and looked good. My body was toning and tightening up. I'd lost more than sixty-five pounds, bringing my weight down to 205. Instead of walking, I was running five miles a day.

While running, I often found myself speeding up and going longer as I wondered what the doctors at Shepherd Spinal Center would have to say about the black kid they said would never walk again. "How ya like me now?" I'd like to ask them.

As time passed, my essays became popular around the camp. I was thrown in the hole on occasion, charged with attempting to incite a riot and attempting to run an inmate organization without a charter. I wrote about life, spirituality, and culture in a gangsta Goines-Iceberg-Browder-Akbar style.

I was surprised when I was asked to speak at the camp's Black History Month program.

Maurice thought I was crazy. He said, "You know they settin' you up. All they gon' do is fabricate a charge, jack your level up, take your good time, and ship you back to the pen."

"If I don't step up to the plate, then every essay I've written, everything I've said is for naught. How can I lead if the enemy leads me? I gotta stand up."

"Go 'head, Malcolm Garvey Martin Luther Farrakhan," Maurice said. "Represent, baby. Black power," Maurice shouted, shooting his fist in the air.

We laughed all the way to the visiting room.

It was a Sunday evening. Visitation was over. A vast majority of the African-American inmates were playin' cards and shootin' the breeze.

As Maurice and I entered, I could feel tension. Eyes burned my back as I walked toward the front. Some thought I was a radical because I was so outspoken.

Others thought I was a hypocrite because I sat in church on Sunday and attended Jumah on Friday, but everyone was interested in what I was going to say at this, the camp's first Black history program.

I started out with, "A few short years ago, I was part of the problem. Now I'm part of the solution. I went through different stages to get to where I am now."

"Yeah, we all did," someone in the crowd shouted.

"Let the man speak," another hollered.

"I've always been a nonconformist, but for the wrong reasons. Now I'm a nonconformist with a cause," I said and paused. "My cause is to contribute to the uplifting and education of my people. If I can reach one, teach one through my writing, I'll be happy. If I can stop one brotha from killing himself, I'll be content. If I can inspire one sistah to read Assata, I'll be happy. If I can reach one who's in the know to begin to show, then we can begin to grow. Grow from our infantile state of reacting to the adult state of acting. Grow from being perpetrating killers to pro-active healers. If I can do this, then we as a people can start our ascension into rising black to the pinnacle of success. Not the success popularized by Western society, but the success of peace of mind, cohabitation, freedom, justice, and equality for all people."

"Speak, black man," someone interrupted.

"I know I'm reaching, but we have to make a difference. We've got to stop kids from going through what we and so many brothers and sisters go through: growing up in an oppressive environment that purposefully prepares our children to move through the revolving doors of America's prisons, rather than the doors of America's higher learning institutions.

"When you're mentally imprisoned, the physical manifestation looms as the next phase in the cycle."

"You got that shit right," someone stood and said.

"We have to overstand the evolutionary process we've faced since being stolen from our homeland. Chattel slavery was just the first stage of our dehumanization process. Stage two was reconstruction—reconstruction of our minds through school, society, and the media. Now we've arrived at the finished product, stage three. That is self-imposed slavery. Mentacide."

"Make it plain, black man," a voice bellowed from the crowd.

"I think Carter G. Woodson summed it up best when he said, 'You have to be first willing to unlearn what you've learned, to break the chains of ignorance.' "

"Allah Hu Akbar," another shouted.

"We have to ask ourselves, why have the hate groups like the Klan become inactive? It's because we've been taught to hate ourselves more than any hate group ever could. What you hate, you try to destroy. We are Willie-Lynching ourselves way more than massa, Jim Crow, or Vietnam ever did."

"Nah, they don't hear ya."

"If it weren't for brothas like all of you caged behind these prison walls waking me up, I'd still be at war with myself and my people. Brothers with twenty, thirty years and life sentences led me toward truth. Now I have a chance to go back and give my life to the cause. I owe it to those same brothas to make a difference. I owe it to myself. I owe it to the people I poisoned with dope to come back and bring them hope."

"Praise Jesus."

"Harold Melvin and the Blue Notes sang the song that I'm dancing to now—'Wake Up Everybody'."

CHAPTER 26

The Atlanta prison camp was tolerable and very laid back, until Warden Willie Scotch arrived. Willie Scotch was a grizzly, towering, six feet six inches of evil manifested. He was coal black and ten times as oppressive and sadistic as any of the card-carrying Klan member officers in Klanchester, Kentucky. Clarence Thomas was Huey Newton compared to Willie Scotch.

I expected to be sledgehammered by white officers, but from another black man, never.

His reign of terror started shortly after the Million Man March, when the crack law was upheld. Not too much shocked me anymore, but this man was Hitler reincarnated.

In 1986, what was called the "new law" was passed in the federal system. These laws eliminated parole and introduced the mandatory minimum sentencing guidelines. These laws made it mandatory for all federal inmates to serve eighty-five percent of their sentences.

The infamous crack law was a major part of this. Crack offenders' sentences were a hundredfold more severe than comparable cocaine offenses. For two ounces of crack cocaine, the minimum sentence was ten years. For the same amount of powder cocaine, the sentence was probation.

This law was designed to enslave young black men, forcing them to sweat in the dungeon factories of America's prisons. Crack and cocaine are the exact same, with the exception of baking soda, water, and a little heat. The major difference between the two was that crack was a cheaper form of cocaine sold and used predominantly by Blacks, Hispanics, and poor Whites. Powder cocaine was a recreational drug circulated in the mid- to upper class White social circles. Institutional racism and slavery at its finest.

Once enslaved, all inmates were forced to work for $5 to $40 a month. Federal prison factories such as UNICOR were modern-day plantations. Talk about slave wages. This was the highest paying job inside the prisons. As an incentive, the salaries ranged from $.40 to $1.15 per hour. Inmates manufactured whatever products the prisons were contracted to make. We made products like shoes, clothes, mattresses, helicopter harnesses, bulletproof vests, office furniture, and much more. These products were mass-produced and sold to the U.S. Department of Justice and the federal government, causing small businesses to fold because they couldn't compete with prison slave labor.

We continued to work for UNICOR out of ignorance of our collective selves. We were taught to be limited in our thinking, so all we saw was the me, my, mine, minuscule self-perceived monetary gratification.

We lived in a controlled environment that preached to the people about rehabilitation. That was a lie. How could one be rehabilitated when he had never been habilitated? How can you educate when all the programs for education have been cut? That's why I couldn't understand why another black man, Warden Willie Scotch, could play the overseer for massa.

Ever since this new law came into effect, the crack law was fiercely debated in the House and Senate. Once the Reagan/Bush era came to an end and Clinton took office, we stayed glued to C-Span and CNN. We knew these immoral laws would be changed, especially the blatantly racist crack law. When Clinton appointed a female district attorney from America's drug capital, Miami, to the position of attorney general, inmates were recomputing their sentences, making plans to go home. After all, Janet Reno was a liberal who believed in education and rehabilitation.

In November 1995, the crack law was up for a vote before the House. Democrats and Republicans voted overwhelmingly in favor of keeping the crack law in place. A sprinkling of Blacks in the Senate and the House spoke out against the racial disparity and injustices of the crack law. Their pleas were drowned by tyranny.

The outcome of the hearing and vote spurred prison uprisings around the nation. Inmates rioted and vandalized the prisons. The entire prison system was put on lockdown after the guards regained control.

With the lockdown in effect, inmates at camps around the system were forced to work twelve- and sixteen-hour shifts at the penitentiary to keep it running. Inmates on lockdown screamed all kinds of derogatory things at the campers as they cleaned the prisons and fed the inmates.

"Hey. Hey, all y'all sellout-ass hot mothafuckas. Next thing you know, you'll be wearing badges and radios."

"Nah, doc, they'll be wearing horsewhips to use on us unruly nigras," another voice shouted from behind a cell.

"The people don't know about these caveman laws," another voice boomed. "Can't you see? We rioted to get the public's attention."

Another shouted from the end of the corridor, "We're just sayin', you give us justice or we'll tear this mother up. We keep the prisons running, not the guards."

A soft voice broke in. "Just like in slavery, the slaves kept the plantations running, not master."

Another picked up the ball. "The man ain't gon' do it. We gotta force change."

I'd suffered a case of I-can't-work-I'm-paralyzeditis the first week of the new, work-around-the-clock slavery. After a week, the camp inmates organized a mass meeting in the camp's visiting room.

One hundred and fifty inmates, Blacks and Whites, turned out. During the meeting I stood.

"This is not a White or Black thing. This is a 'just us against justice thing.' Dr. Martin Luther King, Jr. said, 'A threat to justice anywhere is an injustice everywhere.'"

I held the inmate audience's attention as I turned the floor over to Mr. Winters, an older white man who was an instrumental leader in the Civil Rights movement. "We need to move, now. If we don't stand for something, we'll die for anything," he said, coughing.

"If our brothers being held captive behind the prison walls want to be heard, then we'll scream to the top of our lungs."

Shouts of "Yeah!" followed fists in the air and domino-applause.

"We'll make a joyful scream on the softball field during the most important inmate count around the system—the four o'clock count, this Sunday."

I was hyped as a bunch of excited inmates headed for the exit.

As we filtered out of the visiting room, smoke rose from the recreation area. A few steps later, Maurice ran up the visiting room stairs to tell me that some clown had set fire to the camp library. Other inmates extinguished it before it could cause any major damage, but as a result, the entire camp was placed on lockdown.

At the camp we slept in open dorms, in two-man cubicles, with thirty-two cubicles in a dorm. Around 8:30 p.m., an officer came to each of the eight dorms. He ordered everyone to remove our shirts and lay flat on our beds on our stomachs.

Shortly afterward, several men clad in military gear went from dorm to dorm, stomping and mercilessly beating us with clubs, booted feet and fists. This group of sadistic goons was known as the SORT team, made up of volunteering officers trained for riot control. There was no riot, no reason for SORT to be called. There was no discrimination as to who got beat. They beat old and young, big and small. They even beat the camp's elderly blind inmate. It was a scene from a Third Reich movie. The Fuhrer, Herr Scotch, even showed up to witness the beatings.

More than seventy inmates were removed from the camp. Those who were beaten were taken to three different hospitals so the prison wouldn't attract too much attention. After the hospitalized inmates were released, they were sent to the hole.

The next day we walked around in a daze, feeling violated and defenseless. The phones stayed off until the Prison Legal Department came up with a plan.

I was so mad I couldn't think straight. I prayed for the death of every officer on the SORT team. Even some of the staff was outraged when they found out what happened. A couple were so fed up they quit. Rumors began circulating that an inmate died; a couple had suffered from disabling injuries.

After a few days, news of the beatings got out to the public. Ex-congressman/ex-inmate, Pat Swindall, got word out via his radio program about the injustices that we suffered that night.

The Bureau of Prisons was prepared when the news media got the story. A prison spokesperson adamantly denied the beatings. So much noise was made that the FBI held a news conference. They agreed to have the Amnesty Council investigate the allegations of inmate beatings at the camp. A big joke. The Amnesty Council investigating federal prison was like the hens investigating the henhouse.

After spending forty-eight days with no hot water and two showers a week in a frostbite-freezing, three-cold-sandwiches-a-day, arctic air-conditioned hole, all the inmates were offered a plea bargain on Christmas

Eve. The physically and mentally beaten prisoners were given two choices: either sign a statement exonerating the prison or spend the holidays and a few more months in the North Pole hole, get charged with inciting a riot, lose good time, and be transferred to a penitentiary.

All but three signed.

Seven years had passed since my car accident. I hoped for good news as I ripped the letter open. It was from my accident lawyer, butt-face Flowers.

State Farm Insurance and the car's owner, Mr. Franklin, had filed for a dismissal on the grounds of inactivity. The motion was granted. As I sat on my bunk, mouth agape, I pondered what I had just read. I wasn't surprised, just shocked. After all, Murphy's Law and I were old friends.

By this time, Michelle and I were barely friends. We had long ago broken off our engagement. She now roomed with a girlfriend in an upscale apartment complex. We'd really grown in different directions. I'd grown into a socially and politically conscious "Save the Black Race" revo while she seemed more like Madonna. Not "Like a Virgin" Madonna, but like a "material girl stuck in a material world." She had a good heart, though, and I'd be lying if I said I didn't still care. There would always be a place in my heart for her. She would always be a queen.

After the beatings, I applied for an educational transfer. I didn't care where. My case manager was happy to grant my wish. I was thought to have too much influence over the inmates. I was lucky and surprised that I was passed over on the beat downs, but I knew it was just a matter of time before Warden Sellout got to me. One way or another I knew I had to leave the Atlanta Federal Prison Camp. I was really glad on that day in June 1997 when I transferred to Terre Haute Federal Prison Camp. Not only was I happy to put a few hundred miles between Michelle and me, but I was glad to be out of the Nazi concentration camp I had been at for three years.

Terre Haute Federal Prison Camp, in Indiana, was home of the Hoosiers and heart of the Klan. As soon as I got off the bus, them hillbillies let me know where I was.

"Boy, you get yo' black ass in gear and strip," a tobacco-chewin' redneck CO ordered. The staff at Terre Haute didn't even try to hide their feelings about non-Whites. Regardless of the blatant racism shown there, it was still a utopia compared to the tyrannical Atlanta camp.

After six months, I landed a job working in the camp's electronic shop. It was there that I learned to troubleshoot and repair the prison's TVs, VCRs, and typewriters. It was there that I managed to start my own inmate radio, headphone, fan, and book light repair business. I made around $200 a month in commissary.

Once I got down to a year, I started writing a book based on my life. A year prior to this, I read Nathan McCall's *Makes Me Wanna Holler*. Ultimately, it was his story that made me want to tell mine.

So many authors had been so prolific and instrumental in changing my life; I wanted to have that power, that same influence on tomorrow's leaders. I owed it to Assata Shakur, Ra Un Nefer Amen, Amir Bakhari, Rudolph Windsor, Claude Anderson, and countless others. I hoped my journey would help deter young men from falling into some of the same sinkholes I had.

There were only two brothers I let myself get close to while at Terre Haute.

Brotha Salladeen had the biggest heart in the world. He would do anything for anybody. This brother had the discipline of Ghandi and the intelligence of Garvey. He was the 24-year-old Muslim leader at the camp. He had been in prison for five years, and he had a truckload to go. He studied the Qur'an like no one I'd ever seen. Very staunch in the faith, he refused to study anything other than Islamic material. He and I stayed at odds. I took him *The Aquarian Gospel of Jesus Christ.*

"Shakran, broth," he thanked me with a smile. "I don't need to read that."

I took him *Yurugu.*

"Shakran," he said, holding up the Qur'an. "In this lies all answers."

"I agree, but it's books like these that help you understand who you are. In understanding self, you can understand how to make others' stories relative to you and your people."

"My people are Muslims, and this is our story." He pushed the Qur'an toward me.

Stanley Heart was my ex-drug-dealing cellie, the complete opposite of Salladeen.

By watching his actions, you'd never know we shared many of the same views. My first impression, and that of most Blacks in Terre Haute, was that he was a white boy wannabe. Stan spent most of his time runnin' with Whites.

He was a firm believer in the saying "Keep your friends close and your enemies closer." Stan was the Sojourner Truth of Terre Haute. He befriended the Man to find out what he was up to; he used this info to come up, then bring his people up. Stan referred to what he did as the art of politicking.

Stan worked in the prison kitchen. He stole everything edible that wasn't locked up, and when something was locked up, Stan did his sucking-up politicking routine with the kitchen hacks to get what food he wanted.

I would often take a laundry bag to the back door of the prison kitchen. Stan would give me a box of raw chicken breasts which I would conceal with dirty clothes so the guards wouldn't see what I had. From then it was nuke, sell, and get my eat on. Over the years, I'd learned how to cook anything in a microwave. The way Stan and I got our grub on, it was a wonder we both didn't end up looking like sumo wrestlers.

Stan was of the belief that the government owed him, so he didn't view what he was doing as stealing. The difference between the before-prison Stan and the almost post-prison Stan of the present was that he consciously played the Man's game of "divide, conquer, control, and destroy." Stan played the Man and not his game. The King Makers Policy was how Stan referred to the Man's mind-control, economic-empowerment Monopoly game. He felt you had to master the master's game to have a voice in Caesar's modern-day Rome.

"That's the only way we can ever really seriously bring the noise," Stan would often say.

Stan and I didn't always sing the same song, but we always danced to the same beat.

Yesterday—seven years, twenty-five days, six hours ago, I entered the prison gates. Back then, I lived in Never-Never Land. I was a dysfunctional, obese, lost, confused, mad child running wild. Now I was sprintin' to the Promised Land.

At 190 pounds, I was the Beast Master, AK-47ed with knowledge that I'd acquired over the past seven years. I'd mastered the beast within, so now the beasts that vultured around me were no longer a threat. I was no longer the hunted; I was the hunter. We had a saying in the joint: Help the bear. If anyone saw a bear chasing me, they'd better help the bear 'cause I was running him right into a fur factory.

"Inmate 43018-019," a hack called out as he entered my room.

"Yep."

"Pack it up."

CHAPTER 27

It was a breezy, unseasonably cool mid-summer day in Atlanta as I walked to work from the Buckhead train station. I couldn't help but think that at this same time a year earlier, I was burning up in an air-conditionless prison, dreaming about being free. It was ironic that I was once in a wheelchair, and ten years later I was the top membership sales person in the Sportslife health club's almost twenty-year history.

On this day, I was in my own world, minding my own, walking from the train station to Sportslife when a toxic-noxious odor assaulted my nostrils, giving me an instant migraine.

"Damn," I said, breathing from my mouth. I knew I should have run until I could safely breathe again, but no, I had to play Columbo.

I turned to see if I could find the culprit responsible for raping the air. A man of indeterminate age moved toward me looking like *Night of the Living Dead*, and he smelled bad enough to make a vulture fly backward.

"Uh, bruh, I'm a little down on my luck. I ain't had nothing to eat in two days. Could ya loan a good brotha a dollar?" Mr. Stinky asked, his crusty hands outstretched, showing all three of the rotten teeth he had left.

There was something about Stinky. Where did I know him from? I couldn't think straight. I felt like I was gon' throw up. His stench declared war on my immune system.

I was doing good. I was getting paid selling gym memberships and personal training. The least I could do was to help a brotha out, even though he was probably an equal opportunity drug addict—if it got him high, he'd smoke it, drink it, or inhale it.

I went into my pocket, and in slow motion he reached out to me. I saw it. I froze.

My past flashed before my eyes. A few seconds took me back to a yesterday of forevers. I could not believe what I was seeing.

Momma's words drummed in my head. "Boy, you'll reap what you sow."

My ring. My high school class ring that I'd given to Li'l Man on my graduation day over thirteen years ago. It all came back. Everything.

The fight. Us. The stabbing. Tarik. The hospital. Tarik. The shooting. The troll. The game. Tarik. The game. Li'l Man. The robbery. Who? The betrayal. Tarik. Death. Li'l Man. The ring. Li'l Man. The robbery. Who? My ring. Li'l Man. The robbery. You!

I buried my fingers in death's arms.

"Let me go, nigga. Is you crazy?" He jerked and twisted, trying to break the lifeline.

Years of pain, anger, and hate were balled up in that grip.

Oblivious to his stench, oblivious to the traffic, oblivious to the passersby, I breathed, "Li'l Man was my best friend. That ring. My ring. Li'l Man's ring." I tried to pull his emaciated arm from his body. You stabbed Tarik, and you killed Li'l Man."

"I killed that nigga, got away scot clean, ain't never been sorry. Wish I'da killed the other one too. Hell, he the one shot me when I was in high school, on the football field." He spat. "Bitch-nigga," he said.

I let one arm go, twisted his ring arm behind his back, and squeezed my class ring off his finger.

"What you gon' do? You gon' kill me now, bitch? Aughhh!" He screamed as I twisted his arm like a wet rag.

"No. I can't do anything worse than what you've done to yourself. You've suffered a dozen lifetimes more than Li'l Man ever did."

"Fuck you, nigga. If I ever catch you around here again, I'm gon' kill yo' punk-ass too," he hollered as I walked off, shaking my head in disgust.

I was too emotionally disturbed to go to work that day, so I turned and walked back to the Marta train station. The troll had pushed me over the edge. I'd wanted to change my name as soon as I got out. Working twelve to fifteen hours a day, saving money to publish my book had deterred me, but seeing the troll, cracked out, confused, with no identity of self, catapulted me into action.

A poem I wrote back in prison came to mind, its words perfect to express the feelings I was having after running into the troll.

I was that nigga
I was that nigga, nigga
I was that li'l nigga, that big nigga, what-up nigga
Or just plain old nigga
I was a straight
Representation-duplication-manifestation
Of a
Sleeping nation
No
Forty acres and a mule
No
Reparations
But, yet and still
They allowed me to be
That
Subconscious unseen drowning morbid deadly
Reality
I was
Native Son's *Bigga*
Yes, suh
No, suh
Too confused to figga

Just one of millions
Of niggas
Guns to the dome
Enslaved in Caesar's modern-day Rome
Pulling triggas on niggas
pullin' triggas on
What
My niggas
The power exerted over me
Was bigga
Bigga-bigga than a word
But a
Social-concious-pre-defined-redesigned-viral-
mentacidal-recreation
Of the entity
That Chris planned on the Mayflower
Way back
For me to be
Covering my
Third eye
Losing sight of
My story
Making it
A mystery
Indoctrinating me
In his-story
Nothing about
Isis, Set, Horus, and Osiris
The aftermath of
Willie Lynch's
What?
Mentacidal nigga virus
So much focus
On the chains
And bars
That we can see
But not nearly enough about

The chains on our minds
The reality of why
We've never been free
So caught up
In these
So-called
Traditions
But have you ever asked yourself
Who authored the first edition
Of your tradition?
Could tradition be the reason
For the Black man's plight?
Our residual, horrendous condition?
I know so
Why?
'Cause I was that nigga
That nigga-nigga
That bigga-nigga-my-nigga-kool-nigga
That hard-ass, real, mu'fuckin nigga
That nigga
Given only one way to believe
Only one book to read
When and while they raped, murdered, and stole my
seed
Taught me to have faith, pray, and just hope
While my brothas and sistahs
Were being hooked in droves on
Government-experimental-laboratory-shipped-in
What?
Dope
Ask yourself
Would the deceiver give the deceived
Would the tricker give the tricked
Would the enslaver give the enslaved
A key to freedom?
And end over two thousand years of rule
 over God's vast, glorious kingdom?

Street Life

I think not
I'm not saying
That book you read
Every Sunday
Isn't valid or right
But to begin to understand
You have to first realize
The how and the why
It is you
Black man
Who is the essence
And filament
Of the light
First, we have to
 Break the chains
 Be willing to unlearn
 Everything we've been taught
Treat everything as if a trap
In which we've been
Ensnared or caught
As your career
Is a reflection of what you do
Your name should tell the story
Of you, you, and all the yous
How you live
Your ancestry
Your plight
Casting the rays
Shining from your individualistic, melanated light
You see
I was that nigga, that nigga, nigga,
At times I even thought my name was Nigga.
But now
I know who I am
I am Jihad
Striving. Struggling. Revolution. War
I am Shaheed

Witness to the truth. Seer of the light
I am Uhuru
I am freedom
I am the sun
I am the essence of life
Where all men come from
I am da-da, ba-ba
I am me
I am you
I am
Jihad Shaheed Uhuru.

I went downtown to the courthouse.

Momma didn't agree, but she didn't argue about my name change. She was just glad I was trying to do something positive with my life.

A couple of months after running into the troll, I drove until I ended up in front of 1402 King Street. I took a moment to reminisce about all the good times I had on this street as a kid. I knocked on the door.

"Who is it?" a child asked.

"It's Jihad—uh, Lincoln Jackson," I shouted through the thick oak door.

"Grandma, it's Jihad-uh-Lincoln."

Before I could correct him, the door swung open and in front of me stood a wide-eyed, miniature Tarik.

"Hey, Little Man, what's happening?" I stuck out my fist, waiting for the little brother to give me some dap. He just looked at me.

"That's what my daddy calls me. You know my daddy?"

"Yeah, I know your daddy." I kneeled so we could be eye to eye. I couldn't get over how much this kid resembled his father.

"I ain't never seed you."

Tarik's mother bounced into the living room, saving me from the miniature inquisitor.

"Boy, stop asking Lincoln all them crazy questions. Go somewhere and play while Grandma talks to Lincoln."

"Aw, Grandma, I wasn't doing nuttin' wrong."

"Boy, go on, now." She raised her hand.

He was out of there like oiled lightning.

"Lincoln Jackson. Look at you. Come here, boy." I walked into Ms. Jones's open arms.

"Boy, you look like collared greens and sweet potato pie on a hungry day. How long you been out?"

"Going on two years."

"How's yo' momma?"

"She's fine."

"Still workin' at Delta?"

"Yes, ma'am. I paused and took a deep breath. "I figured it was past due for Tarik and I to clear the air. Is he around?"

"You didn't know?"

"Ma'am?"

"It'll be a long time before you see Tarik. He's back in jail." An aura of gloom encompassed the room.

"What happened?" I asked.

"It's a long story, but I'll tell you the short version. After Tarik got out the first time, he got with some exotic dancer. Anyway, she got pregnant. I was scared to death because she was smoking that crack. Thank God Corey turned out normal.

"Tarik kept losing job after job, and things around here kept coming up missing. That's when I figured out that he was on that stuff too. Next thing I know he in jail for bank robbery. He right up the street at the Atlanta Penitentiary doing thirty years."

First her husband, now her son. My heart went out to her.

"I tried to help Corey's mother after Tarik left. I checked her into rehab, but she left after the first day. She started avoiding me. Whenever I saw Corey, he was dirty-dog filthy and straggly lookin'. I heard she'd been leaving him with strangers while she went off to turn tricks. I'd had it when she tried to pawn my grandbaby."

"Are you serious?"

"Yeah." She nodded. "Luckily, the dope dealer was one of Tarik's friends. He came to me with Corey and told me she'd left him until she came back with money for the dope that she smoked up.

"That was it. I had her declared an unfit mother and I adopted my grandson."

I felt really sorry for her, her son, and her grandson.

"What happened to Meon and Tarik's older son?"

"That girl got married and up and left."

"Where'd she go?"

"Don't know." She shrugged. "Last time I talked to her was in, hmm . . . '94. Corey was just born."

"She just up and left with Tarik's son, without no forwarding address?"

"Uh-huh." She nodded. "Can't blame her. She told me what she was plannin'. I told her go on 'head."

I shook my head.

"No child need to be around that madness. Wished Corey could've went with them."

"So he ain't gon' never know his brother."

"Who knows?"

"So, Corey's what, six, seven?"

She brightened. "Seven going on twenty-three. That boy got too much of his daddy in him. Fight all the time." She shook. "He come home beat up or he's beat up some other kid. He's already been to two schools. Don't get me wrong, the boy is smart as a whip. He makes good grades, but he's obsessed with violence."

As she went on, a storm brewed in my brain. Before I knew it, the storm broke and words flooded from my mouth.

"Ms. Jones, I've got a good job and I wrote a book that I'm in the process of publishing."

"What about?"

"It's about all the stuff me, Tarik and Li'l Man been through and what happens to ballas, playas, pimps and hustlas. I'm tryin' to get folks to see reality and not the fantasies we hear in rap music and see on TV."

"I'm so proud of you." She smiled. "Back when you and yo' momma sat with me in the hospital, I knew you was gon' be somethin'."

"Thank you, Ms. Jones."

"Pshhh."

"If it's okay with you and Corey, I'd like to come get him from time to time and just, you know, be like an uncle to him."

She looked at me with smiling eyes. "That's an honorable gesture, and God knows the boy needs a man's guidance." She paused, as if seeing me for the first time. "You've grown into a fine young man. I'm sure Tarik would appreciate that."

Corey had to be about to fall through the door eavesdropping, because after my proposal, he burst into the living room.

"What do you think?" I asked. "You wanna hang out with me sometimes, Corey?"

"Li'l Man."

"Huh?" I questioned.

"Daddy said he named me after a great man. Corey, C-O-R-E-Y." He turned his finger in my chest. "But he call me Li'l Man. L-I-man."

I was speechless. So Tarik did have a heart. I felt tears welling up.

"You gon' take me to Chuck E. Cheese and Six Flags?" He was ready to bargain.

"If you stop all that fighting and mind your grandma."

"It's all good, dog," was all he said before running upstairs.

I felt I owed it to every confused kid in the streets. I had a role model growing up, but I didn't listen. If Tarik or Li'l Man had been exposed to a Jawanzaa Kunjufu or an Andre Frazier at an early age, they might be here today.

I had to do this. I had no choice. Someone had to set a precedent. Someone saved me; I had to pay it forward. On my way to my town house, Corey had me thinking about fences—fences that needed mending. I picked up my cell.

"What up, shawty? Dis Mr. Good, that is Big Daddy Jook 'Em Good."

"Whatchu want, boy?"

"I want my momma. Are you my momma? I mean, I ain't heard from her in a week. I'm just callin' to see if she still live there."

"No, she no live here no more. She leave note. She say her son need to check messages."

"Momma, stop playin', girl. You ain't called me."

"Check your messages."

"Momma."

"Jihad."

"I need you to call D'Andre and get him over there tonight."

"Why?"

"It's time we started acting like brothers."

"You just don't know how happy that makes me to hear you say that." She paused. "He'll be here."

A few hours later, after seven years of no communication, we stood face to face in Momma's basement.

"D'Andre, I ain't here to argue. I'm here to put yesterday behind us."

"Okay."

"I'm sorry for the way I talked to you. I was upset and confused. I felt betrayed."

"I was young. I started runnin' the streets. I hung out with drug dealers. Women were comin' at me. I don't know, I lost it."

"What were you thinking?"

"I wasn't."

I shrugged.

"I'm sorry. You know I didn't mean to blow everything."

I nodded.

"By the time the IRS came at me, it was over."

"The IRS?"

"Yeah, they audited me three months before I closed the shop. I had to sell the house and everything in the shop to pay off the forty thousand-dollar fine they imposed."

"Why didn't you tell me?"

"You wouldn't let me."

"I'm sorry."

"They told me that if I didn't come up with the money in ninety days, they'd indict me."

"Damn, bruh. I'm sorry." I shook my head. "Whatchu doin' now?"

"I'm back working for J.R. Audio."

"Damn, you know you too good to be workin' for someone else."

He shrugged.

"How's Trina?"

"She's fine. Still crazy. Still workin' for AT&T."

It was a shame for someone that book smart not to have an iota of mother wits. But he was and always would be my brother, and I still loved him. I couldn't fool myself. I'd always look out for him.

******

A year later I received a letter from Tarik.

Dear Lincoln,

I hope this letter finds you in the best of health and spirits. First and foremost, I want you to know that I had nothing but love for Li'l Man. When the shit hit the fan and all hell broke loose, I broke weak, plain and simple. You and Li'l Man didn't know, but I was getting fucked up then, and I was high when it all went down. I know that ain't no excuse for my bitchness, and I don't want to make it seem like I'm making excuses, 'cause I'm not. And right now to this very day, I still haven't been able to come to grips with the way I left Li'l Man. As a result of my addiction to that "white girl" cocaine and her sister, crack, my life is ruined. I was weak and as time passed, I got weaker, but my love for both my sons never faltered.

I see so much of me in Corey, and that's what scares me. Him and my older boy are the only positive things that came out of my negative existence. Man, that boy is innocent just like we used to be. He don't deserve to go through the shit we did. Look at him, Lincoln. Look closely, then you'll see why I'm scared. That boy is me. And look how I turned out. I followed in my father's footsteps to the letter—A for armed robbery. I often wonder if my son is next. But now I feel like I have a string of hope. You, Linc.

Momma told me all about how you've changed and what you requested. I know I'm asking a lot, but what choice do I have? Lincoln, you're five times the man I will ever be. My son needs a real man. I am not him. I'm an animal, a product of my environment. I'd given up long ago. I just didn't know it. I really appreciate you being the role model that my son so desperately needs.

Oh yeah, Momma told me about your book. You always was the smart one. I guess that's why Li'l Man and I never pressured you about getting into the game. Dog, I'm proud of you. Before I let the pen drop, I just want to reiterate, I ain't got no one else to turn to. You

Street Life

know how it is in here. Please, bro? Don't let my child end up like me. Love you, dog.

Peace and Love,
Tarik Jones

CHAPTER 28

I grew attached to Corey over the next couple years. We had a great time. We went to movies, played ball, and just rapped. As I was driving Corey back home one day, he threw me for a loop.

"Uncle J, can I ask you anything?"

"You know you can, Li'l Man."

"Anything in the whole world?"

"Of course, shawty."

"When is my dad coming home?"

I pulled into a Winn Dixie parking lot just as it was getting dark.

"Corey, I've always been straight with you, right?"

"Yeah, I guess so."

"There's no need for me to start lying to you now." I paused. "Your daddy is in prison because he broke the law, which is a bad thing. That doesn't mean he's a bad person. You'll be all big and grown up before he gets out."

Corey tried to remain passive. He did all he could to keep a straight face. "Uncle J?"

"Yeah, Corey."

"Promise me you won't ever do no really bad things."

"I promise, " I said. "I've been where your daddy is. I ain't never going back. Besides, if I go to jail, I won't be able to beat you down in Monopoly and Scrabble." I slapped his head.

"Tomorrow is a teacher's workday."

In grown folks' English, that meant no school. I wondered what a teacher's workday was. What was it the teachers did the rest of the school year?

The next day I scooped Corey up early in the morning. I decided to take him to a gym and enroll him in a boxing clinic. I figured this would provide a more constructive outlet to expend some of his inexhaustible energy. It would also teach him some self-discipline.

After leaving the gym, we went to my crib, showered, and changed, and went to Jumah Prayer at the mosque. I'd been slowly teaching him the magnificence of Islam and Christianity. The knowledge I was dropping on Corey was much too advanced for an ordinary 10-year-old, but Corey was extraordinary. The more I told him, the more he wanted to know.

A few months later, I was at the gym watching him in his first fight. The boy was good—I mean real good. By his third fight, he upset last year's boys club champ.

"Muhammad Ali Uhuru," he shouted after the bout, jumping around, gloved hands championed in the air.

"Okay, Ali, let's go." I laughed.

"No, unc, I'm serious. Muhammad Ali Uhuru. That's who I am now." All I could do was smile as my eyes began to water.

"You've chosen an excellent attribute for a name. Give me some dap, Ali." I stuck out my fist. He was Ali, and I was Broke-lee.

I'd been selling books for eighteen months like Muslims on street corners selling *Final Call* newspapers. I was on the corners, in grocery stores, at Black bookstores, jazz clubs, everywhere. The best part was speaking at boys clubs, churches, and juvenile detention centers. Unfortunately, I didn't sell enough books to pay my bills.

I was thirty thousand in debt to Visa and Master Card before Urban Books publishing house picked me up. Thanks to a book deal and a nice advance, I could finally exhale.

CHAPTER 29

Street Life went all the way to number two on the *New York Times* bestsellers list. That was dead awesome for a black author. Heck, that was amazing for any author, especially since I was turned down by over one hundred agents and publishing companies. Most of them said the same thing: black men don't read, and this book is written with black men in mind. Many of the rejection letters I received also said that women wouldn't be interested in this type of book. Well, I guess they were wrong. I'm just glad that my publisher, Carl Weber, didn't share the same sentiments as the other publishers.

I was paid to speak all around the country. I even hit the talk show circuit. The one that gave me the most gratification was at a high school graduation. I was asked to be the keynote speaker at St. Luke's Area III Learning Center class of 2004 graduation ceremonies. This particular invitation was so special because this was the school from which I had graduated.

A couple of days before I was to speak, I dropped in on Akbar. He looked as fit and young as he did when I was a snotty-nosed kid stealing from his store. I took Corey, now known as Muhammad, to meet Akbar.

"Well, hello Muhammad. How are you?" Akbar bent over and asked.

"Asalaam aleikum," Muhammad said.

"Waleikum asalaam," Akbar replied. "I hear you're the next champ."

"Well, you know." He did a double shrug, smiling.

Akbar and I were closer than ever. We'd lost touch for a while, but while I was in prison he sent me a planeload of books.

"Son, I'm getting old. Before I get too old, I'd like to do some traveling. The first places I want to visit are Mecca and Medina. I need to make the Hajj pilgrimage. While I'm gone, I need somebody to run my businesses."

I nodded.

"I always looked upon you as my own son. You see all of this." He waved his arm in a wide arc. "You're looking at thirty-two years of blood, sweat, and tears."

"I still can't believe what you've done with the plaza. You turned this place into a ghetto paradise."

While I had been running around trying to be Nino-Brown-Scarface-Nicky-Barnes, Akbar was building businesses. He bought an undeveloped area of land and built the Peaceful and Plentiful shopping complex. The project was completed while I was in prison.

Akbar's Health and Grocery Super Store was the first of several businesses in the mini-mall. It now looked like an elegant Kroger Superstore with plants everywhere and soft jazz piped in over the P.A. system. He even had a large, staffed romper room for children. When customers entered the store, they were greeted by a Black-owned minibank (of which Akbar was the majority stockholder) equipped with five teller stations.

Akbar later opened a beauty salon; laundromat; check-cashing store; Barnes and Noble-like bookstore; movie, video, and music store; and children's clothing store. He left two spacious buildings in the plaza unoccupied only because he hadn't decided what to do with the space.

"All praises to Allah. But now, it's time for me to hand over the torch to a soldier I can trust to keep the fire burning for freedom, justice, equality, and the mental emancipation of our people.

"It took a long time, but my voice can be heard now. Through empowering yourself economically, you can be heard too. And then you can force change."

Akbar stood before the window of his office, which overlooked the grocery store, with his hands in the pockets of his slacks.

I sat down while Muhammad stood at the window. I felt something coming.

"Jihad, have you ever considered running your own business again?"

"I already have. My book. Remember how that turned out?"

"I mean the plaza."

"I wouldn't be able to find the time with my writing."

Akbar turned in my direction. "Time? The business runs itself. You hire and train a general manager, come in from time to time, sign store reports and see how things are going." He snapped his fingers. "I'll tell you what, you come work for me, and in one year you'll know all there is to know."

My own business.

"I don't know. Can you give me a week?"

"No problem."

Muhammad and I went back to my place in silence.

CHAPTER 30

"This year's 2007 Reginald Lewis Humanitarian and Outstanding Achievement Award goes to a student who is an exemplary model for a greater tomorrow that old and young can follow. Accompanying this award is a four-year full tuition scholarship to any of a number of historically African-American colleges. Without further ado, I'd like to announce this year's recipient, Muhammad Ali Uhuru."

Was my mind playing tricks on me or did my Muhammad win? Must have. He started walking toward the front of the stage proudly wearing his green cap and gown, tassel swinging.

"That's my boy up there," I shouted.

I was a proud father to another man's son. As the dean was putting his hand out for Muhammad to shake, I sprang to the stage, grabbed my boy and hugged him. I didn't mean to embarrass him, but I knew I had by the way he said, "Aw, man."

"Your father would have been proud of you. I sure am," I said, holding him. I was oblivious to the audience and the standing ovation he received. As I left the stage, I couldn't help but wonder if Tarik was really watching.

His death had come as a complete shock—more like an explosion in all of our hearts. No one on the outside ever knew the true cause of death.

About seven months before the end, Tarik told us he'd been in a fight and had lost his visitation rights. For six months, I didn't give it a second thought. A red flag should have gone up when one month after he told Muhammad and me about the loss of his visitation rights, he was transferred to Springfield. He said it was a disciplinary transfer.

From my time in prison, I knew it took at least six months to forever for a disciplinary transfer. And Springfield was a prison hospital. If it hadn't been for the prison doctor notifying Ms. Jones with only days left, we would have never seen him alive again. As soon as we got the news, Ms. Jones, Muhammad and I flew up to Springfield, Missouri. Honoring Tarik's request, I was the first one to see him.

As soon as I entered the Lysol-scented white room, I smelled the faint odor of mothballs and death. I gasped at the shrunken old man staring at me with tired eyes, sinking in a quicksand of white sheets. He was so small I could see the veins pumping in his forehead. A tube ran up his nose, two were in his ash-coal arms, and another was in his deflated chest. He also had a catheter. It took every ounce of strength I had not to break.

"Babyboy, I really fucked up this time," he said, coughing.

"Man, why? Why didn't you tell us?"

"For what? So you and everybody else would feel sorry for poor Tarik? I don't want sympathy. Sympathy didn't make me sick, and it sure won't make me well.

"But—"

"But what?"

I shook my head. "I don't know, bruh."

"I was the one going up in them crackheads and anything else with a hole between her legs without no jimmy on. Not you. Not my boy. Me," he said, coughing.

I grabbed the cup of water on the side of his bed and put it to his mouth.

He gripped my wrist. "Thanks to you, my boy is a man."

"Thanks to him, I am too," I said.

A tear trickled down his cheek.

"But you still could've told me."

"I didn't want to do anything to distract Muhammad from keeping his eye on the prize. There was nothing anyone could do." He patted himself on his chest, coughing.

"But Tarik—"

"Let me talk, Jihad," he said with quiet calm. "My life was over long ago. I was just taking up space and breathing up oxygen. I told you my sons were all I had. I haven't seen Sean since I don't know when. But Muhammad," he beamed, shaking his head, "even in death, I'll live through him."

My head lay on my chest. I just couldn't bear to look at him. It strained his lungs and vocal cords just to talk.

Bummed out and drained, I said, "Tarik, I love you, man. You didn't deserve this hell."

He cut me off with his razor-sharp tongue. "No, I had my chance. The system ensnared me like it does so many. I may have awakened too late to save myself, but not too late to stop Muhammad from ending up like his father and his grandfather. The chain has to be broken. Thanks to you, I think it has been," he said in between coughs. "Thank you for being the father that I didn't know how to be. Thank you for being the friend I was too weak to be."

I waved my hand and shook my head. "Hold on, bruh. Don't thank me. I should be thanking you. Muhammad has helped me grow more than you will ever know. He's taught me to care for someone other than myself. Books taught me the significance of accepting responsibility, but Muhammad taught me how to be responsible. Him looking up to me and depending on me to always come through gave me one more reason to succeed. He's been a godsend. It's you I have to thank for trusting me to help in the nurturing of a strong black man.

My voice broke into a thousand syllables, and my eyes became sparkling glass. As I paused, the volcano erupted and clear lava zigzagged down my face.

"Man, I hope you're not shedding tears over me. I'm tired. I'm ready to go." He closed his eyes. "If God takes mercy on my soul, I'll hope to see and hear Tupac and Biggie jazzin' together while four little girls from Alabama are dancin' with Emmett 'til chocolate dawn, while me, Malcolm, Martin, and Marcus eat strawberry peace pie."

I sat on a corner of his island.

"If anything, those tears should be tears of joy for me finally being liberated. For so many black men in America, death is freedom."

I reached over my brother's bed and carefully hugged him. I knew his last words to me were so right.

As I left the hospital room, I turned as I placed my hand on the door handle and said, "The Lord is my shepherd."

"Jihad, Jihad." Muhammad shook me.

"Huh? Yeah." I jerked my head from side to side, trying to clear my mind.

"You all right?"

I rubbed my hand over my eyes before I responded. "Yeah, I was just daydreaming. I'm cool. I'm just so proud. You've come so far."

"Not far enough," he whispered.

Two years had passed since Tarik's death.

It took me six years to own forty acres of land. Instead of a mule, I had six flourishing businesses and two not so good ones in the shopping plaza I took over from Akbar. My mother and I lived in two of the twelve four-thousand-plus square foot luxury homes I built in a two-street, private subdivision.

After he graduated from truck driving school, I helped Mike start his own commercial dump truck business. He had since married and had five kids who looked just like him.

His pops retired and was having the time of his life with Mrs. J. After working for over thirty-five years, Mr. J was finally able to relax and enjoy himself. Money, which always seemed to be a problem for him, was no more. I'd given him a small percentage of my holdings, which provided him with a decent living and a chance to enjoy his golden years.

My sister, Marnease, was on her fourth marriage. She just couldn't get the marriage thing right, but she was the excellent queen mother of five beautiful girls and a handsome son. She owned a daycare. She'd always been my heart, which was why I always sheltered her from my madness back in the day.

D'Andre managed a car, home audio, and home security business in the plaza. Out of my eight stores, the one he ran was by far the most profitable.

Momma took early retirement from Delta to go back to school. She was getting her degree in child psychology. She wanted to start a private school focusing on Afrocentricity. She said that seeing what learning our story did for me inspired her to want to taught our heritage to others.

Akbar moved to Ghana, West Africa, where he and his wife teach African-American history at a local college.

Me, well, I'm just a black man working for the collective body of third world people everywhere. I'm always looking for a way to get stronger and make more noise. In the play of life, I'm trying to enact my part to the fullest. I like to think of myself as one trying to prepare the people for the Revolution for Inclusion.

Che Guerva once said, "One doesn't wait for the right conditions for revolution. The forces of revolution itself will make the conditions right."

CHAPTER 31
Today

Laying out my heart and soul in an attempt to wake up these three knuckleheads to reality had me burnt out. Surprisingly enough, they stayed real attentive and seemingly engrossed in the 3-hour recap of my life. I didn't have the heart to keep them hog-tied to my 200-pound work-and-tool station like they were animals, so I had untied them a couple of hours earlier. I wasn't worried about them getting froggy. The threat of my stun guns took all the buck out of them. To think these young brothas followed me home and put a gun to my head a few hours ago. Of all people, these kids tried to rob me. If nothing else, they learned a lesson.

"Mr. Jihad, man, so you know what time it is? You see how helpless we feel. At least how helpless I feel," the tall leader, Mario, said.

I was listening to what I was hearing, but my mind was on the craziness of what happened. I mean, I come to the door and *bam!* Out of the bushes at the side of my front door, this wannabe black Jesse James kid pops me upside my head with a .44. That woke me up enough to insert the black security card into the panel on the cobblestone wall where a buzzing accompanied the electronic sliding Plexiglas door panel.

The four of us stepped inside, and I introduced them to my world. Thank God for small favors. It would have been the least of their problems if my housekeeper, Marva, had been there to see us walking on Herman, my 5-inch thick, ivory white Turkish carpet.

"Man, this is off the greasy-heazy, fo' mu'fuckin' fo' sheazy, my neazy," Baby Fudd exclaimed.

English obviously wasn't his forte.

"Yeah, dog. Pops got it going on, on the fo' realla, Magilla," the leader, Mario said.

"Pops, tell me something. How you livin' Big Dilly Willy?" the short, stocky, charcoal black, soft-spoken driver asked.

At which point Mario chimed in, "Use yo' head, dummy. Pops got to be movin' some serious X or Paradise."

"You know if a black man ain't playing sports, he got to be rollin' some heavy shit to live like this," the driver said.

"Yeah, Pops, you ain't foolin' me, Jack. That check-cashing joint you run on Thirty-third at the plaza ain't nothin' but a front. Mr. Charlie ain't gonna give a brotha nuttin' but a hard way to go and a long time to get there, unless you slangin' Para, X, or that ya-yo."

"This shit is all good and gravy, but we got bi'ness to handle. Let's get to it, Pops," Mario said, waving his gun.

I led them through the sitting room on the way to my office. On one wall I had six built-in hundred-gallon exotic salt and freshwater fish tanks.

"Dee-amn, check this out." The driver pointed.

On the wall adjacent to the tanks was a mural accented by remote-controlled skylights, depicting elders teaching the children to fish in an African village.

"Wow." The Baby Huey, Elmer Fudd-looking fool bounced his wide-body butt on my eclectic King Djoser quadrangle back, goose down sofa.

"Yo, dog, peep this James Bond system," the driver said as he gawked at my stereo.

I had a sixteen-chip, surround sound, voice-imaging remote Carver stereo with Bose chips attached to the thirty-foot shadow box ceiling.

Finally, we reached my office. My library covered the entire left wall and was filled to capacity with assorted works from a variety of authors. In front of us was a 6-

foot long Menelik II desk with four wide-back Ethiopian hand-carved chairs.

The beginning of a smile creased my lips as the boys roamed through the room. My office was the trap, and the safe beside my desk was the cheese.

"Damn, I can't take you fools nowhere." Mario paused, looking at his stargazing partners. "Open the damn safe, Pops."

While I was spinning the wheel, Mario continued, "Get ready to take us on a tour through your bedroom afterwards. I'm sure you got some phat jewelry and shit."

This tall, ill-formed kid, green as grime, was trying to put the press game down on my five-eleven, 200 pounds of muscle. The boy was starting to make the veins in my neck breathe.

On the floor. Click.

"Oh, shit."

I rolled to my left, firing like some futuristic Jesse James.

"Watch out!" one of the kids yelled.

I sent enough electricity through Mario and the fat kid to incapacitate them for a good hour. The driver ducked down between the door and the bookshelf. He must have realized my stun guns were out of juice as he barreled from behind the door.

I jumped on the desk, bad knee first. I tried to swan dive over to where I had another stun gun hidden on the bookshelf. This kid was either Superman or adrenaline-juiced. He caught me in mid-dive. I elbowed him in the mouth and caught him in a full nelson. He bucked like a Brahma bull. I rolled him to the floor. He gave up just when I was about to lose my grip. He went limp and dropped to the floor.

I scattered books across the floor as I held onto the shelf, trying to pull myself up. By the way I looked, you wouldn't know whether I or the bear won. I reached onto the bookshelf, removing an empty book with only a cover and a binder. From behind it I pulled out another stun gun and blasted a charge into the slovenly bear. The hardest part of it all was carrying those fools down to the basement. I had to try to wake them up as I had been so long ago. I just hoped it worked.

"Pops—I mean Jihad. Jihad! You okay, man?" the driver asked.

"I'm sorry. I'm cool," I said, shaking my head.

"So, what's up now? What's our next move s'pose to be? I ain't tryin' to go to jail, but I gots to do what I gots to do. If I go to prison in the meantime, hell, it can't be too much worse than the way I'm livin' now," he said.

As I listened, I thought of how I must have been out of my mind for trying to save these kids from their own reality. But then again, the more I thought about it, the more I knew I had taken a step in reversing the cycle of recidivism. I decided to tell them about my guy George Jackson who died like they would if something wasn't done immediately to break the chains.

"A revolutionary, powerful, militant brother by the name of George Jackson, killed by the system in the early seventies, once said, 'Black men born in the U.S. and fortunate enough to live past the age of eighteen are systematically conditioned to accept the inevitability of prison. For most of us, it simply looms as the next phase in a sequence of humiliation. Being born in a captive society and never experiencing any objective basis for expectation has the effects of preparing me for the progressively traumatic misfortunes that lead so many black men to the prison gate. I was prepared for prison. It required only minor psychic adjustment.' "

"Sounds good, but how is this gon' help us?" Mario asked.

"Can't you see? What you're goin' through ain't new. Brothers been feelin' hopeless since John Hawkins brought the first slaves to this country. By readin' to understand your story, you can read about how others who look like you have overcome that systematic feelin' of hopelessness. If you read about Reginald Lewis, Malcolm X, Geronimo Pratt, Johnnie Cochran, Vernon Jordan and Thurgood Marshall, you'll see how these brothas defied the odds. You can use their game plan as a blueprint for the one you three will have to map out. These brothas came from hoods not too much different than yours."

"That's some powerful game, Pops. Just jokin', Jihad," Hector, the driver said.

The chubby one they called Junebug jumped in. "Okay, you made it. That's all good, but just look around the hood. Look at how many of us are stuck in the gutter. I even know some old head in the hood who went away to college. He workin' at the 7-Eleven baggin' groceries."

"Yeah, and my uncle John got his business degree, and the only business he's doing is behind a cash register at Rich's," Hector said.

"Calm down," I said, gesturing with outstretched arms. "Everything you said is real. Black folk gon' stay on the low end of the totem pole if we don't start studying the mistakes we made yesterday. These colleges ain't teachin' us about Paul Cuffe, Dr.Charles Drew, or Dr.Ben Carson. They teachin' us about Lewis and Clark, the Roosevelts, and Columbus. This is all foreign to us. This just confuses us even more. We can compete playin' on the football fields and the basketball courts, but we can't compete in the Supreme Courts because we're not taught to play there."

"I feel you," Mario said.

"We're taught to go to school to get a job instead of going to school to make and provide a job like we've done for thousands of years. Do you three overstand where I'm coming from?"

*Yeah*s and nods dominoed around.

"What I'm saying is some of the most oppressed and poorest Blacks are college trained. I use the word trained because they go through all this schooling to be indoctrinated in the ways of the oppressive forces who only make up a little less than five percent of the population but control the vices from which we derive our beliefs. Now think about it. The men who profit from the poor, why would they teach you how to come out of your condition of being poor when that would only cut into their profits? So a lot of times we go to the secondary educational institutions called colleges and are taught or rather trained more so in the arts—the arts of self-hate. When we come out of this training, oftentimes we alienate ourselves to the problems we face as a people by trying to assimilate with the man who we went to school for twelve, fifteen, twenty years to learn about. That's how we end up at the local 7-Elevens."

"Yep," Junebug said.

"That's why it is a must that we educate ourselves and that we have to spread the love to our downtrodden brothers and sisters. That's the whole reason I risked my life trying to save you brothers. If any of you had killed me, then so be it. I've never been passive. I've never been one to sit around and let others take anything from me without a fight. I can't let the system take you youngbloods without a fight. When I see you, I see myself as I once was. I was lifted out of the grave. Now I'm offering you three a chance."

"What's that?" Mario broke in.

"I'm offering you a job where you'll be trained, and if you assert yourselves, you'll be promoted. I'll pay for any schooling you want. If by chance any of you chooses to attend college and earn a four-year degree, I'll buy you a new car. No matter what you decide, what happened today will be forgotten."

"How much?" Hector asked.

"No questions." I put my hand out. "I want you all to think about today. I don't want anyone to make a decision now. If you're interested, you'll be at this office Monday morning at nine." I reached in my pocket and pulled out some business cards, then I handed one to each of them. "Not 9:15 or 9:30, nine sharp."

They studied the cards. Mario nodded.

"Let's head on up, fellas," I said.

We walked up the stairs in silence. When I opened the door, they rushed to the car. Not even five minutes after I closed the door, the doorbell chimed.

"You forgot the money." Hector smiled like a loyal puppy, handing me the bag of money from their jackleg, half-robbery of my check-cashing store.

"Thanks."

Before I got a chance to close the door all the way, Hector stuck his foot in it.

"Ain't you gon' check it?"

"Why? It ain't like y'all gon' rob me." I stuck my hand out to get some dap.

"By the way, my whole name is Hector Gonzales." We shook hands before he left.

While Hector walked back to the car, I pulled out my cell chip, the latest in microchip-sized cell phone technology.

"Mike."

"Yeah?"

"Call your folks off."

"Everything cool?"

"Like whip, baby."

"You gon' fill me into why you had me send some boys to wait three hours at the corner of your street?"

"Yeah. It's kinda funny. I'll tell you all about it tomorrow."

"All right. Later."

"Peace in the Middle East." I hung up.

Street Life

I looked down at my cell chip. I was surprised it picked up so clear in my basement. It hadn't before. I wonder what I would've done if I had to run upstairs to get a phone while the fellas were taking an electricity nap.

CHAPTER 32
Tomorrow

Monday morning, Hector Gonzales, Mario Jones, and Shamar "Junebug" Miller began training as landscapers on my new landscaping detail. It took three weeks before I lost one of them. I had a feeling I was going to lose Junebug. I checked on the boys' progress every day. I was told that Junebug was coming to work high. Soon as the second payday rolled around, the brother never came back.

Eight months later Junebug called me from the DeKalb County Jail. He'd been arrested for selling Paradise, the new drug of choice, to an undercover. As bad as I wanted to help him, I could not and did not. He had to attend my school. I just prayed the brothas did for him what they had done for me.

On the day of Junebug's arrest, Mario registered for his GED at Huey Newton. When he first started school, he told me he'd have his GED by year's end. From reviewing his atrocious pre-GED test scores, I thought there was no way.

"If I get my GED before the New Year comes in, you loan me the money to buy a used car with no interest, and I get a ten percent raise to cover my loan payments. If I don't get my GED, I'll paint the outside of the plaza in my spare time, for free."

"Deal," I said. That was four months ago. I found out that he studied in the hot sun during his lunch hour. This made me curious enough to stop in and have a chat with his teachers. All of them told me that he was one of the most studious students they'd ever taught. He was also their most improved. It looked like I was going to have to buy another car, but a car and a little money

301

are tangible items worth far less to me than the intangible, the infinite knowledge that Mario was receiving.

It was hard to tell by listening to him, but Hector was very intelligent and a quick study. Now and then he needed a jumpstart before you could get him going, but once he did, he'd put in a hundred and ten percent. And he did everything well. Slow, but well.

Hector and Mario were both coming along much better than I'd anticipated. I felt good about their progress, but I was no fool. I knew it would be very easy for them to fall back into the bottom of the barrel of crabs. Hopefully, one day we would burn an empty barrel, for all the crabs would have helped one another other climb from the barrel walls of oppression and emerge to bask and prosper in the rays of freedom.

Only one fourth of the sorrow in each man's life is caused by outside uncontrollable elements. The rest is self-imposed, caused by failing to analyze and act with calmness.
  -George Jackson

The following is the first chapter from Jihad's eagerly anticipated upcoming novel

RIDING RHYTHM

This book will be available in stores in October 2005

ENJOY!

ACT 1
Growing Up Black
MOSES

I grew up in a home where every sentence had Jesus's name in it. My older brother Solomon broke the news to me when I was four. I still remember Solomon and I were watching Roadrunner blowing up Wile E. Coyote for the hundred millionth time on a Saturday morning. Momma went to callin' Jesus's name like he was in the room with us. I jumped up and started towards the kitchen when Solomon asked me where I was going.

"Momma callin' me."

"How you know?"

"She done said Jesus Lord four times now," I said with four fingers in the air.

He fell off the bed laughing his behind off.

I looked at my 9-year-old brother. What was he laughing at? I looked at the TV; a commercial was on. I didn't see what was so funny, but I started laughing anyway.

"You must think your name is Jesus Lord?" Solomon asked.

"No, dummy. I'm Moses Jesus Lord King," I said.

"No, your name is Moses Toussant King. There is no Jesus Lord in that."

Oh, that's why Solomon and my dad sometimes answered to Momma's *Jesus Lord*s. When I asked Solomon why Momma called us Jesus instead of by our names, he told me I was too young to understand.

My brother was my hero. He was always showing and teaching me stuff. I later learned that whenever he told me I was too young to understand something, it meant he didn't know either.

I was always asking questions. I wanted to know everything and I still do. I loved learning new things. I wasn't like most kids. My favorite subject in school was school. As long as I could get closer to knowing everything, I was happy. A discovery in fourth grade changed my life forever.

It was burning up in the fourth grade school trailer when I first heard him speak. I'll never forget it. It wasn't even Black History Week. School had just started. It was August 28, 1963. I was nine years old when my class squinted to see the little black and white television that was stacked on top of books on Ms. Tyson's desk.

This black man was out front. The world seemed to listen as he spoke. The cameras started showing more black folks than I thought even existed out in the streets of Washington DC. He even had white folks standing in the streets. I'd never even imagined there was a man that looked like me that could keep so many folks' attention. He had to be the smartest man in the world, I thought. I moved my desk closer to the TV as I listened to Dr. Martin Luther King for the first time.

"The average Negro is born into want and deprivation. His struggle to escape his circumstances is hindered by color discrimination. He is deprived of normal education. When he seeks opportunity, he is told in effect to lift himself by his own bootstraps, advice which does not take into account the fact that he is barefoot."

"Wow," was all I could say. I ain't never heard no black man speak so hard and so doggone proud.

It didn't matter that I didn't all the way understand what he was saying. It was how he said it. Dr. King talked hard. He wasn't 'fraid of no white man. From that moment, I knew I was gon' be a hard talking, proud, fearless, suit-wearing black man. I was gon' stand up when everybody else was sittin' down. I was going to be the voice for black people everywhere. People was gon' listen to me. I started telling folks that Dr. Martin Luther King was my uncle since we had the same last name and all. It wasn't long after I heard him for the first time when I started to listen to others who were down with the Black thing.

I heard a brother on the radio named Malcolm X, who knocked me off my chair. He made the reporter and the questioners sound real stupid. His words had power like I had never imagined. The hardest words I heard Malcolm X say were, "If you are not ready to die for it, then put the word freedom out of your vocabulary."

Heck, I was free and everyone I knew was free, so I didn't understand that statement until I watched the news one day while I was twelve. I could hardly believe what I was seeing. Police were sicking dogs on black kids somewhere in Alabama while they played around a spurting fire hydrant. A few days later I wanted to cry because I was defenseless to do anything about Cornbread Jones.

Me, my boy T-Hunt, and a few others were in front of J.J.'s pool hall when the cops rolled down on Cornbread. They were four deep in two cars. Next thing I knew they had the neighborhood winos and a few poor hustlers spread-eagled on the wall outside of J.J.'s.

While this was going on, Cornbread was standing at his fruit cart a few feet away from all the action.

"Get on over here, boy. That fruit ain't goin' nowhere," one of the officers said.

Cornbread went on spraying down fruit with a water bottle.

"Nigga, you hear me talkin' to you, boy?" the cop said as he approached Cornbread's makeshift, broken-down fruit cart.

"Name Cornbread, sir."

"Boy, you best get over on this wall with the rest of 'em now."

"Name Cornbread, sir," Cornbread said louder while he continued spraying water on his apples and oranges.

"We got ourselves an uppity nigga here, boys."

"No, sir. Name Cornbread, sir."

Before I could blink, a nightstick was upside Cornbread's head. As he was falling, he grabbed at the officer. Next thing anybody knew, all four cops were beating Cornbread while the winos and hustlers hemmed up on the wall ran away.

No one stood up. No one came to help. Everyone knew Cornbread was slow in the head, yet no one said anything. I stared at Miss Georgia Smith's Help Center down the street as I silently apologized to Cornbread and promised that I'd never stand by and watch something like this happen to anyone again.

*****

Four years floated by. My pops passed a year earlier from diabetes, my older brother Solomon was off in the DMZ trying to spread the word of God while fighting the Viet Cong, my mom was cleaning homes on the Northside, and I was policing my hood on the Southside with my crew.

I was always teased about my name being Moses and all, so me and my small group of friends started calling ourselves the Disciples. As we grew, we started calling ourselves the Disciple Nation. We began having meetings to discuss how we were going to make money and protect our folks from the sporadic beatings and cross burnings that the Klan and the dirty cops inflicted.

Soon, word got around that a group of young boys wearing black ski masks was robbing and beating up white folks who ventured into our hoods at night. Before

I knew it, it seemed like every kid wanted to be a Disciple. Half the stories that floated around about us were just that—stories. We walked around booted and suited, lookin' like soldiers on business. Black or blue suits with black combat boots were the uniforms of the Disciples.

I came up with the idea of suits from Malcolm and Martin. Every time I saw them on the TV, they were wearing suits. But they weren't ready for war, so I figured my army would look good and be ready for war at the same time. At first we started hijacking trucks to finance our efforts. I figured since neither I nor any of my people got forty acres, a mule, or were paid for slavery, we'd take what was coming to us. I was the black Robin Hood of the Southside of Chicago, and the Disciples were the forty thieves in multiples. We fed the hungry, orchestrated book drives, sent kids to summer camps, and other things that we deemed constructive to the community.

Pretty soon, it became evident that we had traitors among us. The pigs knew too much, too quick. I decided to split the disciples into twelve groups with twelve leaders. None of the twelve knew my true motivations. This way we could narrow the traitors down, find them, and destroy them; at the same time, we could expand more efficiently. I got this idea from Sun Tzu's book *The Art of War.*

I even had a special set of qualities that every disciple had to exhibit. I called them the LIGHT: Loyalty, Integrity, God, Honor and Trust. Once someone earned his LIGHT, he was initiated as a Disciple for life. Until then, he was a Scribe.

Scribes wore boots but not suits. Scribes had to exhibit each commandment until one of the Twelve Kings brought the Scribe before the council of kings and initiated him in as a disciple, then gave him his suit.

The Twelve Kings were the strongest brothers that I hand picked to oversee their own set in the nation. If anyone violated any of the five bulbs in the LIGHT, that person had to pay a fine. If a violation occurred three times in one year that person had the choice of expulsion or walking the white line.

The white line was a 50-foot line of white tape stuck to a dark street. The offender was to walk this line slowly and quietly while being beaten mercilessly with fifty belts from fifty disciples.

Education was the platform on which the Disciples stood. Every week we read books and gave speeches on what we read. Our discussions were mostly held in abandoned apartments we broke into. The police harassment, and being a gang leader slowly became too much. I started to feel that what I was doing wasn't enough. I had to do more, but as the leader of a large gang I was sending the wrong kind of message, even though we were doing the right kind of things.

Although I pledged allegiance for life to the Disciple Nation, I resigned a couple years after I started the gang. The Kings understood my reasoning. I just felt that I could do more out in the open where I could speak to anyone about anything without being harassed or looked down on. I'd always be a Disciple; I would just be inactive.

Three years later, I was twenty years old and two years out of high school. I was helping to run the Ida B. Wells Youth Help Center on the Southside. As a youth coordinator across the street from the oldest and largest project housing development in the country, I was finally seeing the difference I was trying to make.

I was at the center early one morning cleaning up after the previous night's birthday party we had given one of Miss Claudette's welfare kids when Billy walked in.

"Boy, why aren't you in school?"

He shrugged his shoulders.

"What are you?"

"A proud black man."

"Who are you?"

"One of God's finest."

"Well, hold your head up high, look me in the eye and speak to me instead of shrugging your shoulders."

"I'm sorry, Moses. I just want to hang out with you all day. You know, help you out," he said.

"Come here, little man. Cop a squat," I said as I sat down in a yellow chair.

He came to my side and sat next to me.

"I know it's hard out there, but hard is either going to break you or make you strong and stand out from the crowd," I said.

"Moses, you don't understand. In school, I'm the fat-ass welfare kid with no real parents, and at home I'm just a paycheck for Ms. Claudette. The Help Center is the only place I feel good. Moses, you make me feel like, you know," he shook his head before continuing, "like I'm somebody."

"Remember when we read the *Autobiography of Malcolm X*?" I asked.

"Yeah."

"Everyone thought Malcolm was the coolest, hippest dude ever, right?"

"Yeah."

"Malcolm became a welfare child, remember?"

"Yeah."

"Remember the book we read a few months ago?"

"Which one?"

"The one about Marcus Garvey and the U.N.I.A."

"Yeah, Marcus Garvey was true to his."

"So, you thought Marcus was hip too, right?"

"Oh yeah, no question," Billy said.

"Marcus Garvey was a chubby kid and a chunky adult, but he was still a bad dude that got much respect."

He nodded.

"So, what am I trying to tell you?"

"Uh, that I shouldn't let others make me feel bad," he said.

"No," I put my finger in his chest before continuing, "I'm telling you that you shouldn't give anyone's words that type of power. It is your words and your actions that should have power over you and others if you are to be a leader. Before you can become a Malcolm, Martin, or Marcus, you have to become Billy Johnson. You have to get a good education and continue reading if you want to be the coolest and hippest dude around."

"You forgot one," he said.

"Huh?" I asked.

"You forgot Moses. That's who I wanna be like when I grow up."

"You still wanna hang out with me the rest of the day?" I asked.

"Can't do it. I gotta get to school," Billy said, running out the door.

"Take it easy, little man," I shouted at his back.

"Thanks for last night. I'll never forget my thirteenth birthday."

A year before, I would have been pouring with sweat while cleaning up this place. I couldn't understand how the city could fund a program for kids and would not provide air conditioning.

I'd been volunteering at Ida B. Wells Youth Help Center since Cornbread got beat down by the police. For six years, all the kids from the projects across the street and I had been burning up in the summers. One day, I asked Miss Smith how she survived on the budget she was given. All she said was "God and my two good feet." We could barely keep the doors open with the shoestring budget we were on. The city wouldn't even allot money for renovations. This was the reason I chose the kids over college. When I left the Disciples, I used the thirty grand I'd saved for college and began renovating. The Ida B. kids like Billy Johnson made my investment worth more than what any college could ever give me. I remember as if last year was yesterday.

I gathered up about twenty older kids from the center.

"Ladies and fellas, this is our home. I don't like our home, so I am going to fix it up. Now, I need a show of hands for everyone who wants to get paid three dollars an hour for a lot of hard work and a great learning experience."

As I figured, everyone raised his or her hand. After about two months, one of my kids' family members came by the center asking questions.

"Excuse me, ma'am. May I help you?" I asked.

"It's hard to believe what you all are doing with this old building," she said, looking around at the colorfully painted walls in the game room.

"Thank you, Miss . . . "

"Gina Garan. I'm sorry. My nephew Sean Carter can't quit talking about what you all are doing here. My nephew seems to be under the impression that one of your staff members is footing the bill for all of this."

I nodded as she continued

"Is Moses King around? He's the savior my nephew speaks so highly of," she joked.

I extended my hand to her. "Hi, I'm Moses, and it's nice to meet you too, Miss Garan."

"Oh my God. Can you help me remove my foot from my mouth please, Mr. King?"

"No need. The look on your face says enough. So, what can I do for you Miss Garan?"

"I'd like to do a story on you and the center. A little publicity may help to bring more money in to help you with the renovations," she said.

The story went well. Money started pouring in from all over the state. At twenty, I was speaking at high schools and colleges all over Illinois. My motto was "Come into unity to make a positive community." I even had my best friend T-Hunt, now head of the Disciples, speaking with me on occasion. Everything was mashed potatoes and gravy until I started receiving too much press and my gang ties caught up with me.